INFINITY UNIVERSE

DOWNFALL

MARK BARBER

ZMOK BOOKS

Downfall by Mark Barber
Cover courtesy of Corvus Belli SL
Line drawings by Tommaso Dall'Osto
for more on Tommaso see TommasoDall'Osto@tdosto

This edition published in 2022

Downfall is published under license with Corvus Belli SL

Winged Hussar is an imprint of

Winged Hussar Publishing, LLC
1525 Hulse Rd, Unit 1
Point Pleasant, NJ 08742

Copyright © Corvus Belli SL
ISBN 978-1-950423-54-5 PB
ISBN 978-1-950423-91-0 Ebk
LCN 2022932124

Bibliographical References and Index
1. Science Fiction. 2. Infinity. 3. Space Opera

Winged Hussar Publishing, LLC All rights reserved
For more information
visit us at www.wingedhussarpublishing.com

Twitter: WingHusPubLLC
Facebook: Winged Hussar Publishing LLC

For SB, KG and DG, thanks for helping me at the beginning of the writing journey.

Downfall

NORSTRALIA CONTINENT

SEPTENTRIA CONTINENT

PARADISO

SYLDAVIA

QUBILAH

YINGXIAN

KOKOYO-3

GHAZIRAH

GAYATRI

DAHENG

ASYUT

LEMURIAN OCEAN

BARRIER SEA

XIAJUXU OCEAN

INVERNACULUM I.

ZENDA I.

FREE ISLAND OF SALVORA

YINFENG ARCHIPELAGO

FUKAITANI

MOLOKAI I.

FLAMIA I.

PanOceanian Fusilier Platoon Structure

PanOceanian Fusilier Platoon Structure

HQ Team (5 Soldiers)

- [ ] Second Lieutenant or Lieutenant (Combi Rifle) Communication Callsign 'Zero'
- [ ] Sergeant (Combi Rifle, Forward Observer) 'Zero-One'
- [ ] Fusilier (Combi Rifle, MediKit) 'Zero-Two'
- [ ] Fusilier (Combi Rifle, Hacking Device) 'Zero-Three'
- [ ] Fusilier (Multi Sniper Rifle) 'Zero-Four'

Number One Section (10 Soldiers)

Rifle Team

- [ ] Corporal (Combi Rifle, Forward Observer) 'One-One'
- [ ] Fusilier (Combi Rifle + Light Grenade Launcher) 'One-Two'
- [ ] Fusilier (Combi Rifle, Hacking Device) 'One-Three'
- [ ] Fusilier (Combi Rifle, MediKit) 'One-Four'
- [ ] Fusilier (Combi Rifle) 'One-Five'

Support Team

- [ ] Lance Corporal (Combi Rifle) 'One-Six'
- [ ] Fusilier (Heavy Machine Gun) 'One-Seven'
- [ ] Fusilier (Missile Launcher) 'One-Eight'
- [ ] Fusilier (Combi Rifle) 'One-Nine'
- [ ] Fusilier (Combi Rifle) 'One-Ten'

Number Two Section (10 Soldiers)

Rifle Team

- [ ] Corporal (Combi Rifle, Forward Observer) 'Two-One'
- [ ] Fusilier (Combi Rifle + Light Grenade Launcher) 'Two-Two'
- [ ] Fusilier (Combi Rifle, Hacking Device) 'Two-Three'
- [ ] Fusilier (Combi Rifle, MediKit) 'Two-Four'
- [ ] Fusilier (Combi Rifle) 'Two-Five'

Support Team

- ☐ Lance Corporal (Combi Rifle) 'Two-Six'
- ☐ Fusilier (Heavy Machine Gun) 'Two-Seven'
- ☐ Fusilier (Missile Launcher) 'Two-Eight'
- ☐ Fusilier (Combi Rifle) 'Two-Nine'
- ☐ Fusilier (Combi Rifle) 'Two-Ten'

Number Three Section (10 Soldiers)

Rifle Team

- ☐ Corporal (Combi Rifle, Forward Observer) 'Three-One'
- ☐ Fusilier (Combi Rifle + Light Grenade Launcher) 'Three-Two'
- ☐ Fusilier (Combi Rifle, Hacking Device) 'Three-Three'
- ☐ Fusilier (Combi Rifle, MediKit) 'Three-Four'
- ☐ Fusilier (Combi Rifle) 'Three-Five'

Support Team

- ☐ Lance Corporal (Combi Rifle) 'Three-Six'
- ☐ Fusilier (Heavy Machine Gun) 'Three-Seven'
- ☐ Fusilier (Missile Launcher) 'Three-Eight'
- ☐ Fusilier (Combi Rifle) 'Three-Nine'
- ☐ Fusilier (Combi Rifle) 'Three-Ten'

Chapter One

Chapter One

It was the quieter, more persistent sounds that seemed to characterize the vast, sprawling jungle; the rattling of insect wings that merged into a monotonous hiss when swarms of the thumb-sized creatures clumped together to perch atop giant, rubbery leaves of vibrant greens and yellows. As the blue-violet sky above darkened with the setting of the sun, the melodious chirps of colorful jungle birds faded away, soon to be replaced with the deeper, more threatening rasps of the nocturnal lizards that prowled the dry earth between the thick foliage. As evening fell to envelop the encampment in the jungle clearing, the temperature too fell with it, providing some respite from the relentless, humid heat of the cloudless day.

A cheer erupted from the soldiers gathered in the small clearing in the center of the encampment, signifying another fallen wicket in their game. Brother-Sub Officer Kyle Hawkins stopped and looked over his shoulder at the eight Fusiliers of Number Two Section as they gathered in the middle of the improvised cricket wicket, drawing up the stumps from the dusty earth as the falling light levels made continued play impossible. The Fusiliers wore an odd concoction of clothing, mixing sportswear with camouflaged trousers and shorts, most of the men topless in the stifling heat. Two or three of the Fusiliers eyed Hawkins silently as he passed, the smiles from their game fading as they did so. He continued to follow Fusilier Natalie Southee toward the eastern perimeter, his helmet held in one hand and his MULTI Rifle in the other as he paced after her.

Hawkins hoped silently that it was *what* he was rather than *who* he was that drew the ceaseless ill atmosphere from the soldiers of Number Three Platoon, A Company of Number One Battalion of the 12th Fusilier Regiment. It was only his third day embedded within the men and women of the platoon, but it was the first time he was openly displaying his own organization's colors rather than his normal daily wear of combat fatigues not dissimilar to their own. Motors whirred away silently within the joints of Hawkins' heavily armored suit as his feet thudded against the ground with each step. He had only qualified to wear the coveted red surcoat of the Holy Order of the Knights of Saint John of Skovorodino mere days ago, and it had been a long and grueling journey to achieve such an accolade. Yet, now eyed with wariness by the very men and women that the church had ordered him to serve alongside, he mentally chastised himself for feeling self-conscious and awkward for the white cross emblazoned on his red surcoat.

Whilst the sight of a Holy Order knight in full armor was something Hawkins was now well-accustomed to after four years of harsh training at the fortress-monastery of Skovorodino, he appreciated that it was a rare sight to the rank and file light infantry of PanOceania's army. As a knight of the Order, Hawkins found himself as a rather odd blend of history and cutting edge technology. He wore an all-encasing suit of heavy combat armor, consisting of thick, angular plates of dulled, blue-silver alloy. He carried a CineticS Radjun 4.5mm MULTI Rifle, capable of nearly instantly switching between a variety of ammunition to combat any threat. Yet, atop this garb of the most modern armor available to the most technologically advanced of all humanity's many splintered factions, he wore that same red cloth surcoat and white cross of Christianity that his Order's forefathers had worn in the darkest, most violent ages on Earth; although the modern smart-fabric would at least subdue the color tones when standing out was no longer desirable. On his left shoulder was painted a white Maltese cross on black; the Order of Saint John's icon that dated back to the 12th century. The symbol Hawkins' spiritual forefathers had fought and died for throughout the bitter, bloody crusades on Earth a thousand years before.

"You sure you're okay with this, sir?" Fusilier Southee asked, dropping back to walk alongside Hawkins as the two made their way past the picturesque, gently flowing stream cutting through the middle of the site toward the camp perimeter. Their path took them through the crude accommodation blocks, storage areas, and the platoon's HQ block, all converted out of air-lifted, rectangular cargo containers that had been dumped in the clearing when the research facility was first set up.

"Oh, yes," Hawkins nodded enthusiastically, "yes, quite sure."

"It's just… officers don't normally stand guard duty. Especially not… officers from outside our own ranks. Sir."

Hawkins looked across at the young soldier. Of average height and slim build, Southee's recently somewhat sun-burnt face was crowned by straight, auburn hair that fell down to the nape of her neck. Her light blue beret stood out in stark contrast to her light body armor, which had been hastily sprayed in hues of green, brown, and tan to match the pattern of her combat trousers and shirt. Her accent, like many of the platoon's soldiers, had that distinct non-rhotic twang that marked her out as having descended from an Australasian lineage.

"You don't have to call me 'sir,'" Hawkins offered what he hoped was a friendly smile. "I'm not part of your chain of command, really."

"S'alright, sir," Southee returned the smile. "Lieutenant Shankar explained that all to us just before you arrived, but she said we should treat you like a Fusilier officer with how we talk to you, an' salutes an' all? She was… pretty insistent."

Hawkins followed Southee to the lip of the shallow plateau that formed Alpha Four-Four: the research site and its meager military defenses.

Below them, the dense, green jungle stretched out in every direction across the undulating terrain, eventually leading to the Fairbanks Sea to the north and to the city of Valkenswijk to the southwest. The jungles of Paradiso were notorious for their deadly vegetation as well as a horrific range of dangerous animals, but Hawkins had been assured that Alpha Four-Four sat in a region well away from the worst of them. Karava vine-traps and bloodbriars were certainly visible amidst the ubiquitous, drooping palm trees but not as widespread as the deadly jungles to the north. However, the average temperature in the region was notably hotter.

A handful of dull metal sensor posts dotted the site's perimeter, but these had already proven to be all but useless. In a jungle absolutely teeming with life, sensors designed to detect nothing more than signs of life and movement provided no viable warning of intruders. From what Hawkins had been briefed by Lieutenant Shankar, this was of little concern. The research site built around the Cosmolite had attracted nothing more interesting than the occasional rogue lizard in the six weeks that A Company had been charged with ensuring the safety of the scientific research staff of the MagnaObra company.

"The eastern perimeter spans this section here, sir," Southee pointed to the two ends of the plateau. "It's two hours on, two hour off for our eight-hour shift 'til Number Three Section take the duty again, so only two stints. Just check in with Corporal Lanne every five minutes."

"Understood," Hawkins replied.

"Corporal Lanne is in the Platoon HQ block, running the PSC – the Perimeter Security Control," Southee continued. "He is monitoring the perimeter sensors and the two security drones above us, as well as getting direct visuals from our tactical lenses. He can see everything we can see, as well as the other sensor feeds and IFF. The five soldiers from the off duty team are in the HQ block with him, ready to respond. Although obviously, that never happens."

"Right." Hawkins nodded earnestly.

"That's... sort of it, really, sir. Just pace up and down here and try not to fall asleep. Nothing happens. But being here makes the civvies feel safe, I guess? It looks better for them to have Fusiliers on the perimeter instead of just drones and sensors."

Hawkins looked down at the endless canopy of green stretching out ahead of him, marveling at the sight as the shrill call of a hidden creature perhaps a quarter of a mile away caused a flock of colorful birds to flutter up into the clear sky above the trees. Southee waved across at Fusilier Marinho at the far end of the perimeter, signifying that he was relieved of sentry duty for the next two hours.

"Right," Hawkins smiled, "well, thank you. For letting me have your duty. It is... nice to be permitted to do something useful."

"No probs, sir!" Southee grinned with a wink. "Nearly saluted you there, but that could'a killed you! Need to be careful I don't identify you as an officer in front of all those Shasvastii snipers in the trees behind you!"

Hawkins turned and looked out, his eyes wide.

"Wh...oh! Good one! For a second, I thought you were serious!"

Southee let out a brief laugh as she backed away from Hawkins.

"Thanks again, sir. Give me a call if you need anything, I'll be on comms. I'll figure out how to repay the favor, I'm sure."

"You're too kind! I hope you manage some rest."

Hawkins issued a smile and a wave and then turned to look out at the jungle ahead, glad that at least one of the Fusiliers had decided to show some consideration toward him. He took in a deep breath. This was it. Finally, after weeks of an intense and demanding selection process followed by four years of what was widely regarded to be one of the most physically and mentally demanding training processes – within or outside of the PanOceanian Military Complex – he was on duty on the front line. Weapon in hand, live ammunition loaded. He had arrived.

It only took perhaps an hour for Southee's words to sink in and the reality of the situation to become apparent. Hawkins was not so much on duty on the front line as merely walking up and down a grassy verge in a clearing hundreds of miles from civilization, surrounded by nothing more than strange and alien sounds of indigenous wildlife as the jungle's nocturnal inhabitants arose from their slumber. This was a backwater research facility whose location close to the border of Yingxian might fool an outsider into thinking that it was a dynamic environment; a powder keg ready to explode at any moment. In reality, it was a sleepy assignment that had immediately and utterly failed to deliver Hawkins the war stories he had wanted to take home when he enthusiastically volunteered for the task.

Still, Hawkins had stepped up to do a job, and he intended to do it well. Pulling his helmet on, he connected his armor's own sensors to the perimeter sensor posts to augment their range and fidelity. Dialing through a variety of visual outputs, ranging from night vision through thermal to motion detection, Hawkins saw nothing more than a swarming mass of creatures of every size. His cruciform-shaped visor flickering through a dozen visual spectrums revealed only a range of animals from the tiniest insects to slothful, almost comedically slow lizards the size of large dogs dragging themselves through the dark night amidst the endless trees.

"All positions, this is One-One, check in," Corporal Lanne's voice chimed in Hawkins' ears, as clear as if the lanky NCO was stood right next to him.

"North, clear."

"West, clear."

"South, nothing going."

"East perimeter," Hawkins replied, "all clear."

Hawkins glanced down at his MULTI Rifle and raised his brow. He remembered the hive of activity at the fortress-monastery when word reached them about the alien Evolved Intelligence's Combined Army landings at Concilium Prima. He remembered wave after wave of knights leaving the fortress to deploy to the region. Most of all, he remembered volunteering time and time again to go with them in any capacity. His entire course of knight-aspirants felt the same way. But the answer was always the same – complete your training. Yes, the Order did cut a few minor corners in the training program, but it only succeeded in shaving days off the long wait to qualify; not weeks. And despite the battles that raged in space over Helheim, even upon finally being commissioned into the ranks of the Order, that answer barely changed.

There were other commitments; other areas that required an Order presence. When a chance to volunteer to deploy to Paradiso in support of a detachment of Fusiliers engaged in security duties became available, Hawkins was the first to ensure his name was on the list. Whilst it already seemed that the events on Paradiso were already yesterday's news, given the Combined Army's latest focus, it still seemed closer to the proverbial coal-face than Skovorodino.

At least up until this moment. Hawkins sighed. Three days of being flat ignored until he managed to persuade the platoon commander to allow him to stand guard duty, and now only a single hour into that and he found himself realizing the gaping chasm between his expectations of Paradiso and the reality of his situation.

Hawkins' attention was brought back to the present when a thin line of interference suddenly ran across his visor. Then a second. Within moments, half of his field of view was disturbed by white lines dancing in front of his eyes. He quickly cycled through his visor's other modes of vision but found the interference was common in all settings. Grimacing, he took off his helmet and winced as the closeness of the still, dense evening air hit his face. Whilst he would be the first to admit that he was the furthest that one could be from a veteran operator of ORC heavy infantry armor, he had certainly never experienced a failure of all modes of vision simultaneously.

"East Perimeter," Lanne's voice chimed in his earpiece, "this is One-One. Check in."

"East Perimeter," Hawkins replied with some confusion, aware that only two minutes had passed since the last five minute check in.

"You all good?" Lanne asked. "It looks like both east perimeter sensors have just failed."

"Yes, all good here," Hawkins replied, switching his helmet's power source off and then on again to attempt a reboot and initiate its built-in test

7

function. "Nothing to report."

"North Perimeter," Lanne continued, his tone wary, "check in."

"North, clear."

"West Perimeter..."

Hawkins froze in place. Down at the bottom of the plateau, just on the other side of the bend in the stream, he saw a shape in the shadows. Constrained to relying on nothing more than the Mark One human eyeball and the partial augmentation provided by his tactical contact lens, with darkness rapidly falling, the observation was a one in a million. The shape was man-sized, near stationary, crouched over behind the bushes at the edge of the tree line. There was a form to the shape, with straight lines forming the edges of the silhouette that simply could not be formed by nature. Hawkins swallowed. His heart thumped in his chest. He knew the platoon's authorized Rules of Engagement – he was mandated to shout a verbal challenge to any potentially hostile presence encountered whilst on sentry duty. He opened his mouth, but the words froze in his dry throat. The shape moved. Hawkins pulled his MULTI Rifle up to his shoulder as he dropped to one knee, and he opened fire.

***

Sergeant Jim Cochrane scratched his bearded chin as he leant back in the flimsy, fold out canvas chair, his thick fingers rapidly shuffling the deck of cards. The makeshift recreation room's air filtration unit buzzed above him at irregular intervals as indisputable proof that the repair work carried out on it was to a poor standard, if indeed the work had been done at all. Sat around the similarly flimsy, fold out rectangular table with him was Corporal Angelo Garcia, the leader of Number Two Section, and Fusilier Lucas King, one of the platoon's more recent additions.

The recreation room itself was fashioned out of two cargo containers, welded together with the inter-joining walls removed to create one larger, open space. A drinks cooler, a Maya terminal for connecting with the sprawling, mesh network of the same name, and some simple furniture was all that populated the spartan, off-white interior. The persistently promised gaming suite was yet to arrive.

"Alright, Luc," Cochrane grinned as he tossed the cards into three piles across the table, "this one is five card draw. If you can play Texas hold 'em, I'm sure you can get your head around five card draw."

"Yeah, Sarn't, I know how to play. Read up on it last night." The thin, blond-haired soldier nodded enthusiastically.

Cochrane flashed a grin to Garcia. The muscular corporal folded his broad, tattooed arms and issued a barely detectable smile in return. Cochrane inspected his cards, shaking his head in derision as he saw King commit the amateur mistake of arranging his own hand in order of value. Glancing down at his own cards, Cochrane observed a pair of jacks. Not a bad start.

"Ten," Garcia commenced the bet, pushing a simple plastic chip across the table, beads of sweat already forming on his bald head.

"One thing I forgot," Cochrane remarked dryly, "if you win, Luc, I'll take you off sentry duty for two days. If you lose, you're doubling up in platoon HQ and running the PSC terminal, watch on stop on, and the corporal here gets the downtime. Got it?"

King looked up at Cochrane.

"Wh…what if you lose, Sarn't?"

Cochrane smiled broadly.

"Me! First off, I never lose. Second off, I write the sentry roster, so I've already won. Privilege of bloody rank, mate. Now, what's your plan?"

King looked apprehensively down at his cards.

"Raise ten."

Cochrane exhaled. That was confident. Too confident for this stage of the game.

"Haven't seen you much today, Jim," Garcia grunted. "You still trying the moves on that researcher girl?"

Cochrane glanced across at the shorter NCO. In part, he did not appreciate that line of questioning in front of a very junior soldier, but mainly because Marcia Gamble from the site's research team had already politely, but unequivocally, rejected his advances.

"Slow burner, that one, Ang." Cochrane winked. "Marathon, not a sprint."

"Not like Natalie Southee, then." Garcia grinned slyly.

King's eyes widened.

"You've nailed Nat?" he exclaimed.

Cochrane slowly placed his cards down on the table. He glanced across at Garcia. The squat, burly corporal continued smiling. As a professional soldier with nine years' experience, Cochrane was well aware that physical relations with a subordinate were a high road to disaster, let alone a disciplinary offence. But that sentiment of dedicated professionalism was almost immediately deposed by that seemingly ceaseless, primitive need he so often found in himself to prove he was the alpha male.

"Twice," he smirked across the table at the young Fusilier. "Girl liked what she got. Raise five."

Cochrane immediately regretted his words. Garcia let out a snorting laugh and shook his head.

"Bloody hell, Jim, you can talk some shit. First off, you think she came back because she can't resist you? Use your head, mate! *She* played *you!* Second off, might be worth watching how you talk about shit like this. You could get into a lot of trouble."

Cochrane glowered down at the shorter NCO. A warning shot across his bows like that from an old friend was fine, but as soon as a young Fusilier was within earshot, that conversation instantly became a jumped up, insubordinate corporal talking out of turn to a sergeant. Cochrane opened his mouth to speak, but the words were cut off as a burst of gunfire erupted from outside the recreation block. Cochrane and Garcia both jumped to their feet and dashed over to the room's entrance to haul on their body armor. King rose warily to his feet.

"What's going on?"

"Get your bloody armor on, digger, and grab a weapon!" Cochrane yelled, shoving his comms link into one ear and snatching his Combi Rifle from the weapon stowage by the door. He opened the door warily, heard a long burst of gunfire, and saw a trio of Fusiliers running off toward the east. Having ascertained it was safe to do so, Cochrane quickly and carefully exited the block. He recognized the three soldiers as Southee, May, and Dubois from Number One Section.

"You three! On me!" he shouted and then picked up his pace as he jogged toward the sound of gunfire before connecting to the platoon's communications link via his wrist-mounted comlog.

His ear was instantly bombarded with a confused cacophony of raised voices.

"Where's the firing coming from?"

"Dubs! Get your lot on the south edge of the ridge! I'll set up north!"

"Who's shooting?"

"Erm…One Section…I'm here…I'm engaging…"

"Who's got east sentry?"

"Jonny! I'm on the ridge! There's nobody fucking here!"

Cochrane shook his head and cursed at the litany of panicked shouts over the platoon communication net as he ran past the site's main research hub toward the eastern end of the encampment.

"Zero-One on comms! I now have tactical control! All of you, shut the fuck up!" Cochrane yelled as he drew closer to the sporadic gunfire, the three Fusiliers from Number One Section still in tow. "One-One – set up your Fireteam on the south side of the ridge! One-Five – set up the missile launcher and HMG on the north end, how copied?"

"One-One, acknowledged, I'm on the way over from HQ," Corporal Lanne replied, signifying he understood his orders to set up his five-man Fireteam – half of the section – to the southeast of the encampment.

"One-Five, copied," Lance Corporal Dubois responded – one of the runners behind Cochrane who was now tasked with ensuring the second Fireteam, equipped with a missile launcher and machine gun in addition to their three Combi Rifles, would take position to the northeast.

Cochrane reached the end of the research facility building and sprinted along the edge of the stream leading to the open ground forming the eastern edge of the site. He quickly brought up his left arm and glanced down at his comlog. Rapidly cycling through the controls on his forearm, he brought up a local area map, projected from his linked contact lens directly into his retina. He noted that each of the Fusiliers was rapidly activating their own IFF – Identification Friend or Foe – emitters so as to appear as blue dots on friendly comlog displays and highlighted in blue on tactical contact lens. He saw the evening sky lit up ahead by flashes, his experienced ears recognizing the familiar sound of short, sharp bursts of automatic fire from Dayak Combi Rifles.

"Zero-One, this is Three-One, on comms," Cochrane heard Corporal Rossi check in, signifying that she had mobilized the ten Fusiliers of Number Three Section to join the defense.

"Zero-One, copies," Cochrane replied, "set up your rifle team on the north perimeter and your support team on the south."

"Three-One, understood."

Cochrane exhaled briefly in relief; with one of his sections positioning along the axis of threat to the east and a second section splitting to move across to cover the north and south in case of a flanking move, he now had a viable C-shaped defensive position – even if it was thinly spread. He checked the comlog's tactical map again, the top-down view of the immediate area projected directly onto his retina and appeared in the upper left corner of his field of vision. A defensive perimeter of sorts was now established. He noted with more than mild concern that whoever was on sentry duty and fired the first shot was not displaying on IFF.

"Jim!" Garcia called from behind him. "D'you want me here or shall I fall back and get my section in order?"

Cochrane looked over his shoulder.

"Get back, mate! Get to HQ, man the PSC, and then get your lot together! Check in on comms as soon as you're good to get in position! We'll have a better idea of what we're dealing with by then!"

The stocky corporal nodded, tapped Fusilier King on the shoulder, and then headed back toward the center of the encampment. Cochrane reached the eastern end of the site where a single Fusilier lay prone at the edge of the gentle plateau, reloading a fresh magazine in front of the pistol grip of his Combi Rifle. The air stank of burnt propellant. Cochrane dove to the ground a few meters behind him and rapidly crawled up to the lip of the ridge, Southee following him.

"What's going on, digger?" he demanded. "What are you shooting at?"

In the darkness to his left, another Fusilier arrived, dropped to the ground, and then the entire ridge exploded in a blinding, continuous flashing of yellow light as his heavy machine gun opened fire. The weapon sprayed a ceaseless stream of bullets down into the jungle below, carving up vegetation and sending leaves and branches twirling up into the air in a swath of green destruction.

"Cease fire!" Cochrane boomed. "Cease fire, you fucking prick! That goes for everybody! None of you fire a shot until you've identified a clear target! Missile launchers, that especially goes for you!"

He turned back to the pale-faced soldier who lay next to him.

"Fischer," he glowered, "what the bloody hell were you shooting at?"

"Something down there, Sarn't!" the young trooper replied breathlessly. "I saw movement and gunfire! Human shapes through my scope! There was no IFF, so I fired!"

A sickening nausea clawed at Cochrane's gut as the slow realization of what the situation might actually be began to kick in.

"Zero-One to all teams!" Cochrane called over the comm net. "Cease fire! Nobody fire another shot unless you have visually ID'ed and confirmed your target is hostile!"

Corporal Lanne crawled over from the darkness to Cochrane's right, his blue IFF silhouette displaying clearly on Cochrane's lens well before his eyes actually made him out.

"Jim, are we shooting at ourselves here?"

Cochrane exhaled and shook his head. Silence descended back on the jungle. The ceaseless rattle of insects broke the silence. A few jungle birds and lizards cawed and hissed from the dark trees ahead. A new voice joined the platoon's tactical communication network.

"Zero, on comms."

Cochrane swore under his breath.

"Zero, this is Zero-One," he reported. "I currently have tactical control of the platoon. One Section is deployed on the eastern ridge in two teams. Two Section is split north and south. Three Section is still mobilizing."

"Yes, I can see that," Lieutenant Shankar replied. "I have tactical control. I'm moving to Platoon HQ to coordinate from there."

Cochrane glanced back across to face Lanne. The tall, red-haired soldier was dimly visible next to him as the light continued to fade.

"Who was on sentry duty here, Jonny?"

"Sub Officer Hawkins," Lanne replied.

Cochrane's eyes widened.

"The Hospitaller?! Who the hell authorized that?"

"I did," Shankar spoke calmly over the tactical net. "PSC now back online, I have you all on display."

12

Cochrane grunted under his breath and peered down into the dark tree line ahead. The jungle remained silent. A small surveillance drone, barely larger than a gull, whined invisibly overhead.

"One-One from Zero," Shankar transmitted from the HQ, "bring your rifle scope two points left. I think there's somebody down in the trees."

Cochrane looked through his own riflescope, rapidly changing and filtering the display to optimize the light levels. He saw a figure crouched low by one of the trees ahead. The figure was still and did not display on the map as a friendly blue dot. Cochrane reactivated his comlog and created a waypoint on the platoon's shared map display.

"Zero-One to all positions, I am visual with a possible friendly at Marker Alpha, not emitting IFF. Check your IFF and call in if you're not transmitting."

After a brief silence, a voice crackled onto the comm net.

"Zero-One, this is Eastern Sentry," Hawkins said. "I…I think you are looking at me. I'm a few meters beyond the tree line. My visual display, map, and IFF aren't working."

"Eastern Sentry, this is Zero," Shankar said slowly, her voice wary. "I have your visual display. It shows you are in position on the ridge, right next to Zero-One."

Cochrane swore again. Either the Hospitaller's visual feed to the PSC was frozen and caught in a loop, or something more sinister entirely had happened.

"Zero, this is Zero-One," Cochrane said. "He's not here with us. I can see him below at Marker Alpha."

"Sentry, chop channel two," the lieutenant commanded.

Eager to remain in the picture as to what was occurring around him, Cochrane also activated the comlog second channel to listen in to the conversation.

"Kyle, it's Priya," Shankar said. "We've got eyes on you. Are you hit?"

"I'm… not sure. My helmet visuals all failed so I'm working without. I'm not hurt. Not sure if I was hit, though. There was a lot of incoming fire."

Cochrane stared across angrily at Fischer.

"You've just been shooting at one of God's warriors, you dumb shit!" he growled. "If God existed, you'd be buggered, mate!"

"All positions, this is Zero," Shankar called back on channel one of the comms network. "We have a friendly trooper not transmitting on IFF at Marker Alpha. He's moving to Marker Bravo. Hold fire. Hold fire."

Cochrane stared down into the tree line below. Nothing else moved.

"Kyle," Shankar spoke again on channel two, "we're not visual with any enemy force. You're clear to come back up to us on the eastern ridge."

"I saw something," Hawkins said, "I'm sure I saw something."

Cochrane shook his head in despair. The entire engagement was a complete farce of wasted firepower. Every shot fired was in error. The administrative work and follow up investigation would be a nightmare. All of the training in the world and all of the money spent on cutting edge armor and weapons in the Military Orders was no substitute for experience. And the Hospitaller had none of that.

"Move back to the ridge," Shankar insisted, "we've got you covered."

Cochrane watched as the armored bulk of the Holy Order knight stood and carefully moved back up the shallow slope to drop to one knee next to the Fusiliers. He pointed back to the tree line below.

"There were a couple of figures down there," he gasped, "maybe even three. I fired and they moved off. I advanced on them but didn't see anything again. My... visuals all failed."

Cochrane's brow furrowed. Just as quickly as the sickening feeling arrived over the thought of a friendly fire incident, it quickly reversed to create a similar level of unease in the opposite direction.

"Sir," Cochrane looked up at the young Hospitaller, "just confirm to me that you simultaneously lost all of your visuals, your map, and your IFF?"

"That's right," the dark-haired knight nodded.

Cochrane brought up his comlog and checked the eastern perimeter sensors. Both had failed.

"Zero, from Zero-One," Cochrane transmitted to Shankar. "The eastern sensors are both offline."

"That's right," Lanne chirped in, "they both failed just before this all kicked off."

"I don't think this is a blue-on-blue," Cochrane declared. "Sir says he saw something. Just before that, two independently powered sensors and multiple systems on sir's armor all failed. We've been hacked. There's some bastard out there."

The tactical communication network fell silent for a few moments. Shankar hailed Cochrane on a new channel.

"Jim, you used to do this sort of stuff in Indigo," she said. "If you were probing an enemy site, what would you do if they opened fire?"

Cochrane paused for a moment's thought before responding.

"Depends," he replied, "depends on what the team was cleared to do. If it was a recce and we were busted, we'd do the Harry and bugger off. If we had less restricted RoE, I'd double my team around and have another go from the west."

Another few moments of silence on the communication network, buzzing insects and whining drones in the darkness above passed by.

"All teams, listen in," Shankar called on the comm net. "We may have

14

a hostile force probing from the east. Two Section, hold position. Three Section, take up a defensive position on the western perimeter. One Section, advance to Marker Alpha and commence a sweep of the area."

Cochrane winced at the commands, agreeing with most of his platoon commander's thought process but certainly not all. And whilst she held the rank and the authority, he certainly possessed the lion's share of the experience. He hailed Shankar on their private channel again.

"Priya," he began in a hushed voice, "I agree with your plan to form a defensive perimeter, but I don't think we should be sending guys and girls out into that jungle. If I was falling back with a recce team, we'd be planting explosives all over the place. We don't know what we're facing."

"Okay," Shankar replied, "understood. But we need to at least investigate that tree line. See if there's any evidence of intruders."

"Yeah, fair enough," Cochrane said. "I'll take them down and have a look."

"No, you get back to Platoon HQ and coordinate this with me. We need to control this centrally, not from the front."

"Priya!" Cochrane urged, struggling to keep the volume of his voice down. "Half of this lot have never even been shot at! If there's some SF team out there, you need me down there with them!"

Cochrane heard Shankar sigh in frustration.

"Jim, I need your ideas, not your trigger finger. I need you here with me to coordinate this mess. Corporal Lanne can lead a section in a brief search. I need you up here with me."

Cochrane placed his Combi Rifle over his shoulder to magnetically clamp to the back of his body armor. The smallest hint of a cool, refreshing breeze momentarily wafted across the clearing atop the plateau. He looked up at the twin moons above in the clear, dark violet sky.

"Sure thing, Boss," he replied, before turning to Hawkins. "Sir, you'd best come with me."

Cochrane tapped Lanne on the shoulder and warily retreated back toward the center of the site, away from the ridge line. He brought up the map display on his tactical lens and watched as the three sections of the platoon moved into their positions. Lanne led his ten Fusiliers down to the tree line to scout through the swath of destruction wreaked by the HMG only minutes before. It was not long before an excited voice blasted out over the comm.

"Jonny!" Fusilier May called out. "I've got something!"

"Comm discipline, dick heads!" Cochrane snapped.

"Err… One-One, this is One-Six. I have something."

"One-Six, this is Zero-One," Cochrane cut in, "get a picture and send it to me."

Cochrane cycled through his comlog and brought the image up on the right hand side of his visual display. A darkened patch of grass with the unmistakable, rectangular prism shape of a single round of unfired caseless ammunition.

"Get me a picture of the back of that," Cochrane ordered.

The picture came through moments later. Cochrane swore. He reconnected to the channel with Shankar.

"Nine point five mil," he confirmed. "We only use those in sub machine guns, and we haven't got any sub machine guns with us. One of them must have had a stoppage and ejected an unfired round to clear his weapon. That's it, then, Priya. Somebody's been here and had a pop at us. I think we need to pass that up the chain to Company Command."

"Already on it," Shankar replied.

Chapter Two

Alpha Four-Four's Platoon Headquarters block was, like nearly every other military building on the site, a simple conversion of a large storage container brought in by air or by truck. Three terminals dominated one of the dull, white walls; the Perimeter Security Control, the Platoon Briefing Facility, and a dedicated long-range communication terminal. Four of the five soldiers inside the block sat on the ubiquitous, fold out chairs that regularly punctuated the encampment; the final soldier leaned back against the long wall opposite the terminals, the chairs being unable to support the weight of his armor.

Lieutenant Priya Shankar looked across at her four colleagues. Sergeant Jim Cochrane was, in many ways, everything that most of the platoon's soldiers aspired to be. Thirty years old and standing as a wall of muscle, the tallest in the room by some margin, the indigo-colored beret he was still permitted to wear with his Fusilier uniform marked him out as a veteran of Spec-Ops. A thick, brown beard covered a broad, almost crude face that was not without some charm. That charm, coupled with a dark but endearing sense of humor was, in the year he had been Shankar's platoon sergeant, an attribute that she had witnessed him exploit far too often.

Stood behind him was a man who was, in many ways, Cochrane's polar opposite. Shankar had only known Sub Officer Kyle Hawkins for a few days, and in that brief span of time had deduced very little about him, on account of him actually saying very little. What little conversation did come out of the Hospitaller tended to be questions about procedures and tactics, giving Shankar the impression that it was a lack of confidence rather than a quiet assurance that led to his introverted tendencies.

That aside, Hawkins certainly seemed to illicit suspicion in most of the Fusiliers in her platoon who had, no doubt, heard of the rumors of the zealous, dangerous and fanatical soldiers of the NeoVatican's Holy Orders, even if few of them had ever worked alongside one. A far cry indeed from the tragic, troubled, and selfless heroes of the caricatured, fictitious Order Knights that frequented Maya-series. That seemed to be the opinion of most of her soldiers, at least, but certainly not all. Shankar had already warned three of her female Fusiliers concerning a lack of professionalism around the young Hospitaller, which she understood entirely given his flawlessly handsome face and toned physique.

The final two occupants of the room had arrived less than an hour before. Major Nicholas Barker was the Commanding Officer of A Company, Number One Battalion; a unit made up of three platoons of which Shankar's was one. Barker's short, graying hair and weathered face highlighted him as older than most Fusilier majors, a product of him being promoted to a commissioned officer from the ranks after a fifteen year career as an NCO; a relatively common career path but still far less common than the normal practice of accepting junior officers into the military directly from school or university. Barker wore the same camouflaged fatigues and light body armor as the other Fusiliers, with his light blue beret resting on the table in front of him. Seated next to him was Captain Zofia Waczek, the Company second-in-command, or 2IC. Waczek was a tall, muscular woman in her late twenties whose cropped, short, blonde hair seemed only to accentuate her rather blunt facial features.

"Let's sum this up," Barker leaned forward, placing the tips of his fingers against each other. "Sub Officer Hawkins, you were on sentry duty when you saw an unidentified unit. You issued a challenge and opened fire."

"I… Well, sir, as I said in my recorded statement, I don't recall issuing a verbal challenge… I definitely remember the thought crossing my mind, but everything happened very quickly. I'm afraid with my armor being hacked, there is no recording of what I sad."

"He did issue a challenge, sir," Cochrane drawled, suppressing a yawn. "I spoke to the guys after the exchange of fire. One of the other sentries distinctly remembers hearing the sub officer shout out a challenge. I can't for the life of me remember who said they heard it, but somebody definitely did."

Hawkins looked across at Cochrane, his pale face a mixture of surprise and relief.

"Good thing, Sergeant," Barker smiled, "because this incident is escalating rapidly, and it would not look favorable if a sentry did not issue a verbal warning before firing, without good reason. But that was not the case, so nobody needs to worry."

Hawkins took a pace forward.

"Should we ask the other sentries again, sir?" the young Hospitaller asked, sweat glistening on his short, dark hair. "I really don't remember issuing a verbal challenge, and it might be best to make sure there hasn't been a mistake."

Cochrane shook his head grimly. Waczek leaned back in her chair and folded her arms. Shankar looked up at the Hospitaller, her feelings mixed over his clear display of both total honesty and naivety over the admittedly dishonest lifeline Cochrane was throwing to him.

"I don't think it will be necessary, Sub Officer." Barker shrugged. "Sergeant Cochrane has interviewed the other sentries and officially reported that one heard a verbal challenge. We don't need to dig any deeper than that. So, you fired your weapon and then advanced on what you say looked to be two or three figures in the jungle. According to your statement, you advanced into the jungle to close with the enemy whilst the platoon was mobilized."

"Yes, sir."

Barker turned back to Shankar.

19

"Priya, whilst all this was going on, you were off duty and asleep. On being woken by gunfire, you equipped yourself for the engagement and moved to this room to coordinate the platoon."

"That's right, sir," Shankar nodded.

"By the time the platoon secured the site's perimeter, there was no sign of the enemy. Post the incident, it was revealed that elements of both the perimeter security and Sub Officer Hawkins' armor had been hacked. Further evidence of hostile acts was confirmed in a perimeter sweep, where six expended rounds of nine point five millimeter ammunition were discovered; a caliber not used by any weapon at this site."

"That's about the size of it, sir." Cochrane leaned back in his chair, his hands behind his head.

Barker looked across at Waczek. The stern woman nodded a confirmation that the details were recorded.

"That's the formalities taken care of," Barker sighed, before turning to Cochrane. "Jim, you have a background in this sort of thing. Tell me what you think happened here."

"Pretty simple, sir." Cochrane rocked back and forth on his chair. "We're ordered to maintain security on site made up of a privately contracted civilian research company. They're looking at this Cosmolite. Every day they are digging into evidence of alien technology, and that's hugely attractive to every other player in the Human Sphere; state actors, nomads, mercenaries, the lot. Somebody decided to come and take a closer look at what was going on. My guess is that they've been watching us for a day or two now."

"Why?" Waczek suddenly demanded. "Based on what?"

Cochrane nodded at Hawkins.

"Him. If I was in an SF Fireteam of five guys – and I'm pretty sure that's what was here tonight – and suddenly the regular sentry was replaced with heavy infantry in an armored suit that was particularly vulnerable to hacking, I'd make a move there and then. Those guys would have been pissing themselves laughing. Hackable sentry takes over right as the sun is setting? They took the opportunity to hack the sub officer and the perimeter sensors, then quickly made a move to slip past to try to get inside the perimeter and see what we're up to. Problem was, the sub officer saw them and started shooting."

"At that point it's all for naught, I'd imagine," Barker added.

"Spot on, sir," Cochrane said, "and that's why we found a nine point five round. That's been ejected from an assault pistol – a single-handed weapon. Whoever fired at the sub officer here was retreating and possibly trying to do something with the other hand – another attempt to hack or to activate long-range comms, maybe. Possibly even holding a dressing against a wound. Something that stopped him going for his rifle. Those guys are long gone. Back over the border into Yingxian."

Barker's dark brows raised.

"You think this was a Yujingyu SF team?"

Cochrane shrugged nonchalantly.

"We're what, less than fifty miles from their border? A PanO research base within spitting distance of their line? Gotta be them, sir. This jungle is so dense that it's stopping our sensors from working effectively. That stops their kit from having a proper look at what we're up to, but it also gives them the cover they need to sneak into our territory to take a quick peek."

"Seems a bit presumptuous," Waczek declared. "As you yourself said, Sergeant, this site is of interest to everybody. We have no evidence that this was a Yujingyu operation."

"But I asked the man for his opinion," Barker cut in assertively, "and that's what he's giving me. The colonel will want to hear that opinion, too. That's where I'm off to next."

Barker stood and pulled his blue beret onto his head. The room's other occupants all stood as one to attention before the company commander held his hand out to stop them.

"S'alright. Priya, let's have a quick chat."

Shankar pulled on her own beret and followed Barker out of the HQ block, leaving Waczek, Hawkins, and Cochrane behind. The first rays of dawn sunshine greeted her as a fiery orange glow illuminated the horizon. Color slowly bled back into the world, with a hundred shades of green and yellow bursting into life from the darkness of the long night. Shankar looked around the encampment, her field of view restricted by the haphazard scatter of container accommodation blocks. Visible not far to the north, a trio of scientists from the MagnaObra company waited by the doors of the smooth, white research building built over the top of the exotic, subterranean alien Cosmolite; the site housing evidence of a long departed alien race. Even from this range, their body language betrayed their fear and anxiety to Shankar. She did not blame them.

"Good job here last night, Priya," Barker said, his hands thrust into his pockets as he stared out at the rising sun. "This could have gone to shit quite badly."

Shankar folded her arms across her narrow chest and bit her lip. The early morning rays of sun were already warming the air. The sound of trickling water from the stream on the other side of the Platoon HQ block seemed purposefully intended to calm her nerves from the night's events. The planet of Paradiso did, in so many ways, deserve its name.

"Sergeant Cochrane had it under control by the time I was up and running, sir," Shankar admitted. "I just crossed the Ts."

"Yes, well, he's a good man."

Shankar winced at the statement. Unfortunately, it was just at the time

Barker turned to face her. He smiled sympathetically.

"Jim's a bit of a brutish character," the major continued, "but he's very good at what he does. That's why I chose him specifically to be your platoon sergeant. A platoon needs almost parental care from its leaders sometimes. It also needs a firm, solid kick up the arse sometimes. The two of you have all bases covered between you. I've known Jim for years. Beneath all the posturing and flexing, he has a good heart."

"Yes, sir," Shankar shrugged with a forced smile.

"Well, I need to see the battalion commander before the two of us go to brief the colonel," Barker continued. "What happened here last night is already being briefed at governmental level. This place is going to change a lot over the next few days. Number Two Platoon is already on its way here; Number One Platoon has been recalled from leave. I've got four dronbots being delivered to the strip in a few hours to be driven across to you here. Sierras. Having a dronbot with a machine gun on each side of the perimeter around the clock should help no end."

A few birds erupted into their morning songs from the surrounding trees – shrill, harsh, almost aggressive warbles when compared to the gentle chirps she remembered from her parents' house back home.

"Also," Barker continued, "the colonel has already spoken to Divisional HQ. A defense consultant is on the next flight in to provide advice and assistance with this site's security. Major Beckmann. Show her some Fusilier hospitality and meet her at the strip when she lands, would you?"

"Will do, sir."

"That's it, then, for now," Barker said, "I'll leave Zofia here with you. As the Platoon 2IC, she will be in command until I get back. The whole company will be defending this site from now on. Orders from battalion. Might be a few days 'til I'm back, though. Oh, and one more thing. I don't suppose you have thought to check your mail today, with all that has happened?"

Shankar narrowed her eyes in confusion, bringing up her comlog to activate her inbox.

"No, sir?"

"You remember today's date? Annual issue of the promotion signal?"

Shankar's eyes widened. She quickly scanned her eyes across the titles of the mail in her inbox. One communication jumped out, enough for her heart to beat quickly enough for her to feel it in her temples.

** Notification of Promotion ** Shankar, Priya. Lieutenant to Captain.

An entire lungful of air escaped Shankar's lips. Barker smiled and held out his hand.

"Congratulations, Priya," Barker said, shaking her hand warmly, "it's well deserved."

"Thank you, sir," Shankar managed. "Thank you… for writing such a complimentary annual report on me."

"I only told the truth," Barker said. "You earned this promotion, not my penmanship. But look, it will be a tough nine months ahead of you now. You know you have been promoted to captain on merit; you know you are good enough to wear the rank. But for the next nine months, you are still a lieutenant, right up until the common promotion date. So keep your mind on the job, alright?"

"Yes, sir," Shankar replied, failing to suppress a smile, her heart still thumping in excitement.

Barker turned to walk back toward his parked Uro utility vehicle but stopped after a few paces before turning back.

"Keep your platoon on their toes, Priya. I'll see you in a few days."

Shankar stood up straight and saluted. Barker checked warily around him and then casually returned the salute before opening the door to the squat, angular Uro. Shankar watched the company commander drive away, bouncing on the balls of her feet in excitement at the thought of her first promotion on merit. Then she remembered her last conversation with David, her fiancé, and the glowing pride within her was instantly replaced with the heavy nausea of deep anxiety.

***

Leaving the meal hall behind him, Cochrane stepped back out into the furious morning sun and pulled his indigo beret on over his wavy, brown hair. Now off duty, he had shed his body armor, leaving him in his combat trousers, boots, and a t-shirt of light blue with a faded blue and white crest of the Fusiliers on his left sleeve. He quickly brought up the site's security status on his comlog and, satisfied that Number Three Section was handling the perimeter competently and correctly, he logged out again and walked briskly over toward the research building.

Cochrane's interest in the research building was twofold. First off, whilst the majority of the Fusiliers stationed at research site Alpha Four-Four could not have cared less about what they were defending, Cochrane found himself fascinated by the thought of ancient alien technology only a few paces away. It left him uneasy, when he stopped to actually think about it, that only seconds away were items of immense historical significance, perhaps even a key to understanding the mysterious Tohaa or the deadly Combined Army of the Evolved Intelligence; a highly advanced alien race that Cochrane had faced on more than one occasion in open confrontation. Perhaps it was something even more ancient than the two of them.

The conflict raging between the Tohaa and the EI's Combined Army affected events on all planets of the Human Sphere, and the Cosmolites discovered on Paradiso were theorized to be a potential key in explaining the bitter war raging between the two great alien civilizations. As it stood for now, the forces of the Combined Army occupied a significant foothold on the planet of Paradiso in the area around ZuluPoint. Even Cochrane found himself snorting in derision as he briefly contemplated the folly of humankind. With a violent alien empire occupying part of this very planet after a brutal and bloody invasion, the three great empires of humanity – PanOceania, Yu Jing, and Haqqislam – were still involved in political squabbles and even outright hostility, just as nations were back on Earth hundreds of years ago.

The second interest Cochrane had in the research building was more specifically aimed at one of its members of staff; Doctor Marcia Gamble. She first caught his eye when she arrived a few days after the initial contingent of scientists, and Cochrane had engineered the duty roster to ensure his meal breaks coincided with hers. However, today he found her notably absent from breakfast and so now found himself heading across to the restricted building with renewed purpose.

The building itself occupied a square footprint in the sandy ground, with smooth curves leading down from its flat roof to thick, tapered walls. There was only one entrance into the research building; security was provided by a simple but highly encrypted scanner that opened the doors only for those whose biometric data was recorded on the system as worthy of access. Cochrane, as with all of the site's military personnel, was not deemed worthy. As he approached the doors, he saw Doctor Sam Adebayo; a researcher of a similar age to Cochrane and one of Gamble's colleagues. Adebayo saw Cochrane as he approached and diverted his path to walk out to meet him.

"Morning, Jim," Adebayo greeted, his white lab coat folded neatly over one thin arm, a neatly trimmed goatee beard adding definition to his smooth, dark-skinned face. "What the hell was all that racket about last night? One of your lot said we were under attack, but then Priya came around later and said there was nothing to be concerned by."

"Bit of both, mate," Cochrane shrugged, "no point in keeping secrets from you. We're all on the same side out here, after all. Somebody came to take a look at the site. Tried to hack the perimeter security. So we popped off a few shots and they buggered off. How's things here with your lot?"

"A few shots?" the slim scientist exclaimed. "It sounded like the Neo-Colonial Wars were starting up all over again!"

"Nah, mate," Cochrane drawled, "that was nothing. One of our guys got carried away with a machine gun at one point, but the rest of it was just a few rifles snappin' away. No biggie, so don't you guys worry. We've got you covered. As I said, all on the same team. You do your thing in there; we'll keep prowlers away from you. You're safe as, mate."

Cochrane checked Adebayo's expression – subtly, he hoped – to see if his continued attempt to build bridges between them was solidifying. Adebayo was, after all, immensely useful as an ally in both of Cochrane's scientific interests; finding out what was going on inside the research building and getting Marcia Gamble into bed.

"We're lucky to have you and your lot keeping an eye out." Adebayo scratched the back of his head. "I… I really wasn't expecting anybody to come here and start shooting! I think we all thought your unit was just a show of power. A formality."

Cochrane glanced past the scientist and through the reinforced, shaded glass panels of the double doors behind him. He could just about make out an entrance foyer, but nothing that gave him even a hint of the work that was being carried out inside.

"Don't you worry about it, mate!" Cochrane repeated. "We're all over this! Anyway, enough about me. How's it all going with you guys in there?"

"Oh, fine! Fine!" Adebayo forced an insincere smile. "Life goes on even past the shootouts! Work continues! Progress is slow but steady."

"Does it look like all the others?" Cochrane asked. "The Cosmolite, I mean? Does it look like the ones at ZuluPoint? I mean, I've seen pictures. They just look like rocks."

"Well, in many ways they are." Adebayo bit his lower lip. "Don't believe the horror movies about them! They're certainly not alien eggs! It's more what is *beneath* them that is of interest. The tunnels and the rooms, I mean."

Cochrane's brow lifted.

"Tunnels?"

"Yes, a network of them. The Cosmolite and this site is just the surface entrance. Anyway, I'd really better get to work, I'm running late."

"Yeah, sure thing, mate." Cochrane grinned. "You go on ahead. I've got to drive the boss to the airstrip to pick up some security advisor, anyway."

Adebayo flashed a friendly smile, moved to turn away, and then looked back.

"Jim? One other thing…"

"Yeah, mate?"

The scientist's smile was already gone.

"It's not easy for me to say. It's… about Marcia. Look, I know you could literally crush my skull like an egg, so I'm really uncomfortable saying this, but… Marcia asked me to ask you to back off a bit. You… intimidate her."

"I intimidate a lot of people, Sam." Cochrane winked.

"Not in a good way," Adebayo managed through gritted teeth, his thin shoulders hunched nervously. "She's really rather uncomfortable around you right now. Please, Jim, could you..."

"Alright!" Cochrane snapped, stepping back and throwing his hands up in surrender. "Bloody hell! Alright! Tell her I won't bother her again!"

Muttering under his breath, the bitter taste of rejection at the back of his throat, Cochrane paced away from the research center entrance. He checked the time; he was running late for driving Shankar to the airstrip. He swore as he picked up the pace to toward the site's small, dusty parking area. Marcia Gamble was a write off. He would have to content himself with a third turn of the wheel with Natalie Southee.

***

The dusty road meandered along the natural embankment, winding between the colorful jungle to either side. The road, which was little more than a flattened dirt track, took advantage of the naturally formed break in the now thinning jungle to the northwest of Alpha Four-Four. Building a road on such a feature was not merely logical; it was imperative. The jungles of Paradiso seemed almost sentient in their ability to grow rapidly to overcome any human attempt to build and settle. Even the great cities of Paradiso employed teams of civil engineers to constantly dig, burn, and blow up the creeping vegetation – most notably the ubiquitous linger-long weed – to stop their boundaries from being overrun. Out here, Cochrane mused from behind the steering wheel of the tan and green painted Ypsilon Motors Uro, at least the road worked *with* nature rather than *against* it.

That being said, the sky above the road was regularly punctuated with a line of hovering drones, constantly surveying the vital link between Alpha Four-Four and the resupply airstrip at Hill Eight Six. Cochrane had previously thought them to be perhaps a little unnecessary, but in light of the previous night's events, he now welcomed the extra security. For the first time on the drive to the airstrip he wore his body armor, and he ensured the machine gun fitted to the automatic turret on the back of the vehicle was loaded, serviced, and made ready to fire. However, even with the body armor, he had deliberately neglected to pull his combat shirt on over the top of his tight fitting t-shirt. If he was going to be the first to welcome a new woman to Alpha Four-Four, he would be damned if his first impression did not include his carefully sculpted, bulging biceps.

Cochrane checked the passenger schedule for incoming flights to the airstrip. Beckmann's flight was indeed listed, but there were no details of her as a passenger past her name and rank. Cochrane frowned. That was odd. A lack of details was normally associated with Special Forces. More likely some lazy logistician could not be bothered to upload the details as it would have resulted in enough work to take him past a four hour working day.

Cochrane glanced across at where Shankar sat in the passenger seat next to him. The platoon commander stared out of the window at the passing jungle, a smile on her thin lips.

"Oh! I forgot!" Cochrane beamed, suddenly reminded by her grin. "I heard you got picked up on the signal today! Congratulations!"

Shankar glanced across, her smile now even broader.

"Thanks, Jim."

"Will that be you moving on, then?" Cochrane continued as he rounded a corner in the track, gently accelerating up the sandy incline ahead. "Waczek hasn't been here for that long, so I guess there isn't really an opening for a captain in A Company."

"No, it will be C Company, I imagine," Shankar replied. "Ty Molin is overdue a move from 2IC there."

Cochrane glanced across at her again. He was genuinely happy for her and the well-deserved promotion, and he would be sorry to see her go. They did not always agree, they did not always see eye-to-eye, but one thing he could say for Shankar as a platoon commander was that she did at least listen to him. Well, normally, at least; certainly more than some junior officers he had worked with. She might not always run with his recommendations as platoon sergeant, but she did always at least consider them carefully. He felt respected for the most part, and that was why their working relationship ran smoothly.

Shankar had been a good boss. Cochrane definitely had his doubts when they first met; with Shankar standing shorter than average height with a thin, wiry frame, he had predicted she would not prove capable of keeping up physically with the demands of life in the light infantry. However, he soon saw that her build was the result of years of long distance running; she had produced admirable finishing times in high profile marathons.

She was relatively easy on the eye, too. Certainly not a head turner in Cochrane's opinion, but her Indian heritage gave her a dusky, exotic appeal when they first met. That was, at least, until Cochrane had noted the engagement ring on her left hand. Given the abhorrent mess that was the termination of Cochrane's brother's marriage – and, more importantly, the effect it had on the children – women in committed relationships was somewhere Cochrane flat refused to go.

"So, are you accepting the promotion?" Cochrane asked tentatively.

Shankar cocked her head to one side.

"Why wouldn't I?"

"Have you told David?"

Shankar's face fell into a frown. She looked back out of the window. The rising sun illuminated the thinning jungle around them; the sandy ground only now irregularly punctuated with towering, drooping trees and clumps of dry vegetation.

"You should be allowed to do what you want, you know," Cochrane continued as they reached the peak of the shallow incline in the dusty track. "You're allowed to be happy, too."

"I don't want to talk about it," Shankar retorted, "not with you."

"Not with me?!" Cochrane exclaimed. "What have I done?"

"Let's just say that you and I have fundamentally opposing opinions on relationships." Shankar folded her arms.

"What the hell is that supposed to mean?" Cochrane demanded, his temper rising another level as he recalled the words passed on to him outside the research building. "What the hell is this? Kick Jim in the nuts day? You as well, now?"

"Come on, Jim, you're hardly a paragon of traditional virtue and values!" Shankar countered. "You only volunteered to drive me here once you heard that this Major Beckmann is a woman."

"Now, that's not true," Cochrane lied profusely, focusing on the road ahead as he saw dust rising up from approaching vehicles on the horizon.

He quickly dialed into his comlog and brought up an image from one of the overhead surveillance drones. The convoy ahead consisted of an Uro and two trucks. Clearly, Number Two Platoon had arrived at the airstrip on time.

"You're wearing that tight t-shirt," Shankar grimaced, also looking ahead at the small dust cloud. "You do that every time there is a chance of meeting new women."

"Well, you can't blame me there." Cochrane flexed one of his biceps and nodded to his left arm. "I mean, they're bloody works of art, mate."

Shankar burst out laughing and shook her head.

"You're such a dick, Jim."

"I know. But seriously, this whole thing with David telling you that you have to leave. Just… do what you want, Priya. You don't have many people to talk to about it while we're out here, and I can at least try to be a mate. I won't pry any more than that because it's none of my business. Do what makes you happy. That's all I'll say."

The vehicles approaching swam into view.

"D'you want to stop and say g'day?" Cochrane offered.

"No, keep going," Shankar said. "I don't want us to be late at the airstrip."

"We're doing alright for time," Cochrane offered. "When have you ever known aircrew to turn up early for anything except a piss up?"

"Just keep going."

Cochrane continued along the dust road, pulling the vehicle over to hang over the side of the embankment to allow the convoy of vehicles from Number Two Platoon to pass. He recognized Second Lieutenant Howe in the passenger seat of the lead vehicle and briefly exchanged a wave as they passed by. Cochrane and Shankar watched in silence as the small convoy drove on past. The lightly armored trucks, cruising through the dust on their large, off-road tires, would be packed with lines of Fusiliers ready to bolster Alpha Four-Four's defenses. Cochrane shook his head. An entire company to defend a rock. This was escalating quickly.

The remainder of the drive to the airstrip passed by in relative silence, a quarter of an hour spent watching the same trees with the same rubbery, triangular leaves dropping down toward the dry bushes, occasionally dotted with small flowers of vivid yellows and reds. The airstrip itself was little more than an advantage taken of a natural clearing atop a flat plateau, not hugely dissimilar to the site at Alpha Four-Four, just a lot smaller but clearer. Cochrane drove the Uro up the road toward the top of the hill, wincing in discomfort as he heard the roaring blast of jet engines from an aircraft up ahead. They were late, after all. Those bastard pilots had finally turned up early for something.

The road led around the edge of a concrete pad, a few storage containers dotting its perimeter for fuel and basic administration facilities. Cochrane wondered how long it would be before the defenses on this site were increased, too, although it might not come to that. Sneaking across the border to infiltrate a vital scientific research facility was one thing; an overt attack on a military airstrip was an entirely different level of aggression.

"We're on time," Shankar remarked as Cochrane parked up next to the concrete pad, watching as the lean, twin-engined Tubarão aircraft lifted to the hover, turned into wind, and then transitioned away into forward flight with a roar of its powerful engines. A solitary figure stood waiting for them on the other side of the pad. Cochrane and Shankar simultaneously opened their doors and stepped out of the vehicle. Cochrane looked across the pad. His jaw physically fell open.

Major Beckmann, assuming that was indeed the awaiting figure, was – without a shadow of a doubt – the single most beautiful woman Cochrane had ever seen in his life. Or in movies and sensorium games. Tall, slim, and perhaps in her mid-twenties, Beckmann's long, brown hair fell past a tanned face of striking beauty, dominated by eyes of deep, vivid blue. Her attire of fashionably shredded, denim five-pocket trousers and a white vest top accentuated a perfect blend of an athletic physique and femininity; Cochrane's eyes were immediately drawn to the large, perfect breasts accentuated by her form-fitting, cropped vest. Frozen in place, his own eyes darted between her face and breasts, unsure on which he was more drawn to, before settling on the higher of the two. Cochrane grinned and nodded, proud of himself for his display of chivalry in choosing her face.

"Close your mouth before you catch a fly." Shankar rolled her eyes, slamming the Uro's door and striding out to meet the new arrival.

Cochrane eagerly followed. Beckmann slid on a pair of slim-framed, aviator-style sunglasses as the two approached and folded her tanned arms. Cochrane noted a tattoo of a heraldic-style eagle on one of her toned shoulders.

"Major Beckmann," Shankar greeted, "I'm…"

"What you are is late," the tall, statuesque woman snapped, her accent immediately betraying her as not a native English speaker, "so let's get off on the right foot. That's the first and last time you will leave me waiting for you. Clear?"

Shankar swallowed.

"We were told to expect you on the hour, and it is only…"

"So it isn't clear." The tall woman stepped across to tower over Shankar, staring down at her through the shaded lens of her sunglasses. "I'll spell it out for you. I'm here to do a job and I'm not interested in your excuses or your fucking back chat! So let's dispense with the introductions. Carry my bags and drive me to the site. Now."

Beckmann picked up a rucksack from her feet and threw it into Shankar with enough force to knock her back a pace. Cochrane failed to suppress a wide grin. He liked pretty faces, foreign accents, huge tits, and attitude. She was literally perfect. Beckmann picked up her second bag – a long, camouflaged kit bag that Cochrane noted with interest was the right size to safely transport a long-barreled weapon – and held it out toward him.

"And you, Sergeant."

Cochrane, still grinning inanely, dashed across and took the heavy bag, slinging it over his shoulder.

"Right you are!"

Beckmann's head tilted to one side.

"What is this? Fucking amateur hour? I hold the rank of major! Marks of respect, Sergeant!"

Cochrane tried to stop smiling but again failed.

"Yes, ma'am!" he replied enthusiastically.

Cochrane watched as the major paced past him, leaving them both with her baggage. Cochrane remained rooted in place, staring at her as she walked away. The back was just as perfect as the front. All other objectives in life faded away to nothingness as he stared lustfully, lost in thought.

"What the hell was all that about?" Shankar muttered quietly. "We're not even late!"

"Perhaps she just gets air sick?" Cochrane offered as he lugged the heavy kit bag over to the Uro.

The first five minutes of the drive passed in an awkward silence, with Beckmann staring out of the window from the back of the vehicle whilst Shankar fidgeted uncomfortably in the passenger seat next to Cochrane. Cochrane watched the dark-haired major in his rear view mirror. The beautiful woman shifted in her seat and thrust her hips up to allow her access to the pocket on her hip. She produced a crumpled packet of cigarettes and an archaic, chrome plated Zippo lighter. After lighting one of the cigarettes, she took in a long drag and blew out a small cloud of pink-red smoke that filled the vehicle with the scent of strawberries.

"Did you have to travel far, ma'am?" Shankar asked.

"Does it matter?"

Another leg of the journey passed in silence before Cochrane tried to ignite the conversation.

"You... erm... briefed up on the site, ma'am?" Cochrane ventured. "We were told you'd be advising on increasing security measures, now we're bumping our permanent presence here up from platoon to company level."

"Acting as an advisor is my secondary role, Sergeant," Beckmann replied coolly.

"How do you know I'm a sergeant?" Cochrane queried, covering the brake pedal as the Uro rounded a crest in the road and slowly accelerated downhill. That was twice she had referred to him by his rank, yet he was wearing no rank insignia.

"Being able to quickly determine the command structure of a military unit. That's my primary role," the young woman answered.

"Really?" Cochrane flashed her a grin in the rear view mirror. "I thought you were a defense consultant. What's your main job?"

"I'm a... tactical operative for Strategic Security."

"Ha!" Cochrane flashed a smile across the vehicle at a still sullen Shankar, reveling in his ability to generate conversation with the new arrival. "That makes you sound like you're a Hexa!"

"*Ja*," Beckmann blew out another mouthful of strawberry scented smoke, "Garkain."

The vehicle lurched forward as Cochrane instinctively nudged the brake pedal, his stomach churning up in knots at the mention of that single word. Shankar looked across at him inquisitively.

"Sorry," Cochrane breathed, allowing the Uro to accelerate to the bottom of the hill before turning the corner onto the next level stretch of track.

Shankar turned in her seat to look back at the tall woman.

"So, you're a Hexa operative then, ma'am?"

"I'm part of a sub-division," Beckmann said.

Shankar looked dead ahead and swallowed. Cochrane shook his head. Sure, Shankar thought she knew a little about Hexas; operatives of PanOceania's Strategic Security Division responsible for covert, unconventional military operations. Hexas were not in the business of legitimate military tasking; from what Cochrane had seen and heard in his time in Spec-Ops, Hexas operated outside of the normal law of armed conflict. Assassination, sabotage, political destabilization – he had heard it said that war crimes were part of their daily running. That was Hexas. Garkain was something else. A word he had only heard used a few times before.

The remainder of the drive back to Alpha Four-Four passed by in silence. Cochrane glanced periodically in the rear view mirror, his captivation and lust now completely replaced with fear and anxiety. The young woman stared silently out of the window at the passing trees, the harsh, barely audible thud of hard rock music emanating from a hidden earpiece.

"This is it, ma'am," Shankar said as Cochrane parked the Uro outside the Platoon HQ building. "I'll find out where you are staying and have your bags taken across. Major Barker tells me that we have new accommodation blocks arriving in two or three days, but with a second platoon now here, I'm afraid that even the officers are having to share rooms for now."

"No," Beckmann said coldly, "I've traveled half a damn planet to get here in a rush, and I'm the ranking officer on this base. Get me my own room, even if somebody else has to sleep up a tree. Or you will see me properly fucking angry."

Beckmann stepped out of the vehicle, slamming the door behind her before pacing off toward the eastern edge of the site, a pair of Fusiliers from Number Two Platoon staring wide-eyed at her as she barged past them. Shankar turned to look across at Cochrane.

"What's Garkain, Jim?" she demanded.

Both hands still on the steering wheel, Cochrane stared ahead as he mentally filtered a jumble of memories from what now seemed to be a previous life.

"I only once worked with a Hexa," Cochrane recalled. "It was on Dawn. The... details don't matter so much. We'd been tasked to take a look at a power plant that Command thought would be a primary target in case of things getting kinetic between us and Ariadna. This guy, this operative was sent in with us. We were told to keep him in one piece, get him past the power generator and not to ask any questions. This guy, the Hexa... he killed anybody who got in our way. We had so many chances to bypass security checkpoints, to incapacitate people who were in our way. But he just killed and killed and killed. We were even talking about taking him out ourselves at one point."

"And he was Garkain?" Shankar asked.

"No," Cochrane shook his head, goose bumps rising on his forearms as he recalled details of that past experience. "He was a part of the regular Strategic Security Division, if you can call them such a thing. But the thing was... when we got to the power generator, of all the things to be happening there was a school trip. Can you believe that? A bunch of kids on some science field day getting shown around the power plant. We all thought the Hexa was gonna kill them. But he didn't. When my team leader asked him why he drew the line there and didn't kill those kids, he looked across at us and laughed. He said: 'What d'you think I am? Garkain?' That's one of the only times I've ever heard of that unit before. Hexas, they're loose cannons working directly for the government. All I know about the Garkain lot is that they are military, through and through. Trained to do the fucked up shit that Hexas do, just specializing exclusively on the battlefield or close to it."

Shankar raised one hand to her head, wincing and rubbing at her temples. She looked back at Cochrane.

"That whole thing she said about knowing I was a sergeant," Cochrane continued, "about that being her job. Her job is to stalk people like you and me. To watch a platoon, work out who the high value targets are, then start killing them from the top down. That's how she knew what I was. She knows exactly what to look for."

Shankar took in a deep breath and nodded.

"Jim," she began, "I'm going to talk to Captain Waczek to make sure Major Beckmann has her own room. In the meantime, you get around our platoon and you make sure everyone, *everyone* steers clear of that woman. I don't care that she looks like a damn underwear model, not one of them is to engage with her in any way. They're not even allowed to look at her. Got it?"

"Got it, Boss," Cochrane said, opening his door and stepping out of the parked Uro.

Chapter Three

Chapter Three

The moment Kyle Hawkins began training as a Knight Hospitaller, he was convinced that he would fail at some point. Now, unable to sleep after the events of the previous night and resigned to jogging lap after lap of the inner perimeter of Alpha Four-Four, he was left with ample time to reminisce on the past and those harsh days of training at the fortress monastery. His childhood friends had all moved on to university after their last year at school, and Hawkins applied to several middle of the road universities that his decent but not spectacular grades would have allowed admittance to. But higher education was, to Hawkins, merely a stepping-stone in his life-long plan to obtain a commission and join the military as an officer. His sights were set on a career as a TAG pilot, but not firmly; any front line role would suit him.

Hawkins rounded the corner of the dining hall at the northeast tip of the site and accelerated down the slight gradient forming the eastern perimeter. A Fusilier on sentry duty – a tall youth with dark skin and a neat beard who Hawkins did not recognize – watched him jog past, offering him a polite nod and a slight smile. Hawkins returned the gesture as he passed before focusing on the path ahead, the relentless sun beating down on his back as he ran.

Hawkins' decision at the age of eighteen to apply to join the Holy Order of Saint John seemed to shock everybody with the exception of his school headmaster.

"You took your faith seriously." The frail, ageing teacher smiled on Hawkins' last day of school. *"You were always heading toward something like this. I'm proud."*

But even though he clawed his way through the Hospitallers' strict application process; entrance examinations and grueling tests of faith, intellect, and physical ability; Hawkins was convinced he would not pass the four years of training. At some point, he knew he would have to go home in shame, having failed to make the grade. Each phase of training was a short term push to achieve; to pass one more phase so that his head could be held just that little bit higher when he was sent home.

"I passed elementary training, but I failed basic," gave way to, *"I passed basic training, but I failed advanced."* Each six months that passed by saw more knight aspirants fail, pack their possessions, and go home. Somehow, Hawkins was never one of them. By the time he was in his fourth year of training as a senior aspirant, even he began to believe he might graduate and receive his commission.

Hawkins reached the southeast corner of the site and, satisfied that he had completed ten laps in a decent time, abandoned his run. Dripping with sweat, his feet aching within his lightweight infantry boots, he walked back toward the center of the site to where the picturesque stream babbled gently across the top of the plateau. Attempting to drag his mind away from thoughts of the past, he briefly thought on the feelings he experienced after returning to his bed in the early hours of the morning.

It was like training all over again; that need to achieve *something* before failing and going home. And it was with that in mind that Hawkins, suddenly ashamed of himself as a man of God, found that he was somehow glad that he had fired his rifle at another human being. He also found himself glad that, even though there was an even chance it was friendly fire, he saw a dark smudge of impact damage on the thigh plate of his armor after the confrontation. It somehow added a note of validity to his existence, as if a call would arrive at any moment to tell him that a medical exam had picked up some flaw or ailment that made him invalid to continue in the military. At least now, if something went wrong, he could go home and say that he once shot at an enemy of PanOceania and once took a hit without falling. But that should not be at the forefront of the mind of a man of God.

Hawkins reached the small stream. The clear water flowed smoothly over a sandy bed, broken only by a few smooth stones and an occasional patch of vegetation. Hawkins unlaced his boots and removed them. He lowered himself into the fresh, cooling stream and lay back to sink momentarily beneath the water. Sinking down to the sandy bed, he held his breath for a few moments as the water washed away the sweat, before jumping up and out into the blazing heat of Paradiso at midday. The water was already drying off him as he hauled his boots back on.

The unmistakable sound of traditional hard rock music snapped Hawkins away from thoughts of his past. He finished lacing his boots and stood up, turning in place to identify the source of the thundering music that cut out the constant but somehow soothing racket of insects in the surrounding jungle. Following the familiar riffs of thrashing guitars, Hawkins was surprised to see a lone figure stood by an upturned ammunition crate in an area of empty ground halfway between the Platoon HQ block and the research staff accommodation area.

The figure was a woman, tall and slim, with dark hair tied up at the back of her head. She wore the tri-color camouflaged trousers of the Fusiliers, with the blue beret of the PanOceanian military, and a tightly fitting vest top of the same color. On the improvised table in front of her, next to the blaring portable speaker, the tall woman was assembling a Sinag MULTI Sniper Rifle.

"Excuse me…" Hawkins began.

The woman span around to face him. Her blue eyes were half-closed, her face twisted in anger. Her eyes met his and she paused. Her features softened. A warm smile lit up a face more beautiful than Hawkins had ever seen. The tall woman thrust her hands into her trouser pockets and pushed her hips out to one side.

"You're not here to tell me to turn my music down, are you?" she smirked.

Her accent was heavily Germanic, placing her possibly as a native of Svalarheima.

"Oh, no!" Hawkins held up his hands. "I'm ever so sorry if that's how I came across! I just... my dad used to listen to this band. I grew up with this music."

The beautiful Fusilier's smile grew.

"You like MCA?" She laughed. "I thought I was the only one under the age of fifty who listened to these guys!"

Hawkins took in more details of the dark-haired woman. She was perhaps three or four years older than him, with a tattoo of a medieval-styled heraldic eagle artistically drawn on one tanned shoulder. Her beret was worn stylishly tilted on the back of her head, against clothing regulations; the blue and white badge of the Fusiliers was notable in its absence. She also wore archaic, imitation identity discs dangling on a thin, metal chain around her neck.

"I... I used to love this stuff," Hawkins said. "I'm a bit out of touch with it all, really. Perhaps I should get back into music. Are you here with Number Two Platoon? The chaps who just turned up today?"

"Something like that." The woman shrugged, still smiling warmly. "And you're the Hospitaller attached to Number Three Platoon?"

Hawkins' eyes widened.

"How... how did you know that?"

"I spy on people so I know who to kill," the woman said huskily with a sarcastic tone and a glint in her eyes, before resting a finger on his chest. "Plus, you've got a white Maltese cross right here on your shirt, which is something of a giveaway."

Well-accustomed to speaking without thinking and looking stupid as a result, Hawkins passed the remark off with a brief, uncomfortable laugh.

"I'm Kyle," he managed to break the silence. "I'm the Hospitaller. Well, I've been qualified for a few days. I'm still finding my feet."

"Beckmann," the woman introduced herself.

Hawkins looked past her at the partially assembled rifle behind her.

"You're the Number Two Platoon marksman?" he asked.

"Not quite," Beckmann replied, turning to look down at the weapon. "Have you ever fired one of these things before?"

"No," Hawkins said, "never. We train in weapons more for close quarter fighting."

"Well," Beckmann said, lifting up the weapon's housing and sliding the long barrel in before twisting it a quarter turn to lock into place, "I can't fire it here because people might get the wrong idea. But come and have a look, I'll

***

Captain Zofia Waczek leaned over the table in the center of the command block, now redesigned from Platoon HQ to Company HQ following the uplift of Fusiliers at Alpha Four-Four. Packed around the table were the two platoon commanders, their respective sergeants, and Major Beckmann. Stood opposite Shankar and Cochrane was 2nd Lieutenant Rory Howe and Sergeant Dev Bakshi of Number Two Platoon. Howe had joined A Company straight from training and was the battalion's least experienced officer; his grizzled sergeant, however, was second only to Cochrane for actual combat experience.

"The first of two issues, is base security," Waczek began the evening brief, tapping her comlog to project a holographic image of Alpha Four-Four and the surrounding terrain, accurate to every last tree and container block thanks to scanned imagery from the overhead surveillance drones.

"We've got more mobile blocks coming in via truck over the next few days," Waczek continued, "to sort out the uplift in accommodation, supplies, and administrative facilities. We'll even have a medical block now, although we won't have anybody better qualified than the two platoon medics. What we need is a robust plan for increased security."

"Defensive structures," Sergeant Bakshi answered immediately, "I doubt we'll have proper bunkers and pill-boxes suddenly appear, but right now we're relying on sentries walking the perimeter. Our guys and girls need cover. Even if it's just sandbags to protect against shrapnel and some shallow trenches, it's better than nothing. A handful of those cheap, mobile bunkers would be a good start."

"What you need is clear fields of fire," Beckmann leaned over the desk and gestured at the surrounding jungles. "If I wanted to break into your research building, I'd be laughing my way through these trees leading right up to your perimeter. You need to knock these back. You need open ground around you so you'll see your enemy a mile off."

Waczek stood up straight and folded her arms.

"Have you ever tried to cut down trees in Paradiso, Major?"

Beckmann produced her lighter from her pocket and lit a strawberry scented cigarette.

"Not personally, no," she mumbled as she drew in a lungful of sugary fumes. "I'm not really the horticultural type. But if you're talking about getting defensive installations constructed here, that means you are expecting engineering assistance. And if you have engineers, you can use explosives and flamethrowers to beat the jungle back. And you will need flames for the linger-longs."

38

Waczek looked across the table at Cochrane.

"Sergeant?" she asked. "Do you agree?"

"You don't need to ask him!" Beckmann snapped. "You need to ask me! That's why I was sent here! If we wanted to infiltrate an enemy research facility to steal their data, I would be sent in to do the job, not him."

Cochrane nodded slowly and exhaled.

"The major is right, ma'am," he said quietly, "infiltrating a place like this would fall to Strategic Security; not Indigo Spec-Ops. And yeah, we do need better fields of fire."

The blonde captain held up her hands in exasperation.

"Fine. Fine. I'll inform Major Barker that engineering assistance should be one of our priorities. In the meantime, Number Two Platoon will be staying here to provide ongoing security to the site. Rory, that will fall to you. I'll be coordinating the Company's overall plan until Major Barker returns, but day to day security will be you and your lot."

Howe glanced across at his sergeant and then back at Waczek.

"Understood, ma'am."

Waczek turned to face Shankar.

"That leaves Number Three Platoon," the short-haired woman continued. "The battalion commander was in touch about an hour ago. We've been ordered to commence patrols of the area beginning tomorrow at dawn. Priya, that'll be down to you."

Shankar looked down at the holographic map as Waczek panned out, altering the scale until the hazy projection depicted the surrounding area for a hundred miles in every direction. A blue arrow slowly animated itself across the map.

"Here's your route," Waczek pointed along the jungle spanning to the east, "about forty miles out to the east and back, so you'll be gone a good couple of days."

Shankar copied the route details onto her own comlog. She frowned as she registered a vital detail about the patrol route's final destination.

"That takes us very close to the border with Yingxian," Shankar observed. "Might seem a bit inflammatory."

"Bloody hope so," Sergeant Bakshi commented, "I'd bet anything it was those Yujingyu bastards that had a pop at us in the first place."

"I dunno mate," Cochrane shrugged, "could have been anybody."

"Come on!" Bakshi frowned. "Nine point five mil ammunition expended at the scene of the crime! Attacking force retreated east? This is pretty open and shut!"

Cochrane folded his arms and shook his head.

"A lot of different militaries use nine point five," he countered, "and they would have scouted our entire perimeter. Just because the firefight occurred when they were on the east side doesn't mean they arrived from the east."

Waczek zoomed in to a point on the patrol route, about halfway between Alpha Four-Four and the Yingxian border.

"Following on from that," the Fusilier captain continued, "our Intel guys have analyzed ever iota of surveillance data we've got from the last week. They didn't find much, but they did find this: two nights ago, one of our drones picked up what could have been a transmission from this area. The signature is so weak that the drone assumed it to be an atmospheric disturbance, but it is possible that it was an encrypted data burst. If that is the case, it was emitted from a point that would support the theory of an SF team crossing the border from Yingxian."

Shankar looked across at Cochrane. The big man shrugged, one eyebrow raised as if happy not to discount the theory yet.

"That's it for now," the captain concluded. "Priya, Jim, go brief your section leaders and then be ready for an update at zero five hundred. You'll be heading out straight after that. Best you all go get some sleep."

Shankar took a step back from the table as it was powered down and pulled her beret out of her pocket. She turned to speak to Cochrane about briefing their section leaders when Beckmann spoke up.

"I'm going on that patrol with Number Three Platoon," the tall woman declared.

Waczek seemed to barely manage to suppress rolling her eyes.

"Ma'am," the blonde captain began warily, "we were told that you had been sent to us as a security advisor. We could really do with you here whilst we address our security issues at the site."

"Bullshit," Beckmann planted her fists on her hips, "my primary role is to bolster defense directly, and the best way to do it is to ensure that patrol hits hard if it encounters anything. Lieutenant Shankar, I'm attaching myself to your platoon. You will retain full command, naturally. I'll see you at the brief at five in the morning."

Without giving any of the Fusiliers a chance to respond, Beckmann positioned her blue beret over her head, tilted it back and dragged a few strands of hair stylishly across one eye, and then paced out of the briefing room. Waczek shook her head in disgust.

"Who the hell does she think she is?" the captain spat. "And can somebody explain to me why the hell she is wearing our uniform? Who authorized that?"

"Give me a second," Shankar offered, finding Waczek now all the more agreeable with them sharing a common foe, "I'm going to go and have a word."

"Ma'am!" Cochrane warned her as she stomped over to the briefing room door.

Shankar held out a hand to stop Cochrane. She did not believe in the horror stories that he was clearly spooked by. All she saw was an arrogant, vain, narcissistic beauty pageant queen playing dress up as a soldier. She shut the door behind her and jogged to catch up with the towering security operative.

"Major!"

The tall woman stopped and turned to face Shankar. The light on the faded, blue container block next to the two women was swarming with insects and cast long shadows from them both as they faced each other. Shankar looked up into Beckmann's impassive, cold eyes. Confronting her immediately seemed to be a bad idea. Then she remembered the promotion signal. Shankar was a captain now; or at least, as good as one for the nine-month wait to wear the rank. She had proven herself capable of the role of Company Second-In-Command in the PanOceania Fusiliers. Would a captain stand for this? Shankar drew herself up to her full height and clenched her fists.

"Major," she began, "there was no way it would escape our attention that you have chosen to wear the attire of a PanOceanian Fusilier. First off, you have not earned the right to wear that uniform. Second, the liberties you have taken with how you have chosen to wear our uniform are unacceptable."

The taller woman slowly narrowed her eyes and folded her arms.

"Go on," she said quietly, "I'll let you finish before I go. Liberties with wearing uniform?"

Shankar pointed down at Beckmann's clothing.

"Well, I shan't criticize you for your choice in following this ludicrous tight leggings fad some of the women are now going for. It's technically not against regulations, but I don't think it reflects well on anybody who chooses to do it. Second, vest tops are for physical training; they are not acceptable working dress. Third, dress regulations state the make up is to be kept to a minimum. Your make up would perhaps pass as minimal for a catwalk model, but not a soldier. Finally, you should be wearing your beret properly and in a soldierly manner, not like a fashion accessory for posing on the cover of a punk album..."

Shankar's tirade faded away as she saw Beckmann tap her comlog controls and then her eyes rapidly scan from side to side as she read through some document on her contact lens, unseen to the shorter woman.

"Shankar, Priya Saanvi, Lieutenant, 50614257," Beckmann recited, "five years service... You've done peace keeping, disaster relief, military aid to civil powers... No, I can't see anything in here about you having any actual combat experience. But you were on the promotion signal to captain this morning, so that explains a lot."

Shankar's teeth gritted.

"You're… reading my service record?"

"Strategic Security," Beckmann said, looking down at Shankar again, "I have access to everybody's service documents. So, you've just made captain. Which, coupled with a background of only moderate wealth and a childhood spent being academic, short, and not particularly good looking leaves you, no doubt, with some confidence issues. And now you know that captaincy is just around the corner, you come squaring up to me to prove something to yourself, no?"

Shankar's face dropped. Her arms slumped to either side. Beckmann's brief, scything précis seemed to sum up Shankar's entire tragic existence in one go.

"You look hurt, Lieutenant," Beckmann smirked, "and I haven't even started analyzing you on that engagement ring yet. Now, I've got some respect for you coming here to try to face me down. That's why I'm going to give you a decent, mature answer to your points instead of kicking the living fuck out of you. Alright?"

Shankar said nothing. Beckmann took a step forward, her annoyingly perfect chin held arrogantly high as she looked down her nose at Shankar.

"I'm wearing this uniform because I don't want to wear the somewhat distinctive garb of a Strategic Security operative," Beckmann continued. "You see, under your 'leadership' this facility has already been nearly compromised, due in part to you personally authorizing a soldier of a Holy Order, complete in full heavy armor and surcoat, to patrol your perimeter. There's somebody out there, watching this place. And now they know the NeoVatican has a direct interest in the defense of this facility. Because of you. I'm not willing to identify myself to whoever is out there, so I'm dressed in clothing similar to you and your dumb fuck light infantry. With me so far?"

Shankar swallowed nervously. The legitimacy of the answer, regardless of the manner Beckmann delivered it in, left her feeling more stupid than she had in a long time.

"But let's move onto the uniform itself," the sneering operative continued, "the 'hallowed blue beret' of the Fusiliers! First off, the blue beret is a generic item of uniform for many units within the PanOceanian Military Complex. You'll note that I am not wearing a beret badge. That's because I'm entitled to wear a blue beret, but don't think for a moment that I'm avoiding your badge because I haven't earned it. It's because I'm too fucking embarrassed to. You see, you're not an elite force. You're the butt of ninety percent of jokes within the military. When some kid leaves school and it's all gone to shit, so much so he can't even get a job in sanitation, he thinks, 'well hell, it'll have to be the light infantry, then.' You still with me, Lieutenant?"

Shankar closed her eyes for a moment and winced as a dull throb of pain pounded at her temples. She nodded.

"Yes, ma'am."

"So finally," Beckmann concluded, "you object to me wearing a vest. It's forty degrees in the shade at midday here. What the fuck is your problem? Getting in my face about not covering my arms up, like I'm dressed like some skank from the Tech-Bees? Fuck off! So now I know where you stand, you know a little about where I stand, and I'll see you at the brief at zero five hundred. And next time you challenge me in *any* way, you'll be on your hands and knees, crying, scrabbling around in dirt and blood to try to find your own damn teeth. We clear with each other?"

Her heart pounding as the sickening claw of anxiety seemed to constrict her throat, Shankar watched Beckmann pace away and disappear into the darkness.

***

"Three-One from Zero-One, sitrep."

Cochrane's entire world faded into darker shades as he took a pace forward into direct sunlight, his reactive lens automatically compensating to reduce the glare from above. In the rapidly changing jungle-scape of Paradiso, the foliage once again grew denser around the Platoon HQ team as they continued their slow trek to the east. Despite the tireless work of the four-limbed, bulky Mulebot remote that opened a pathway ahead with its defoliating kit, the first three hours out of Alpha Four-Four had been painfully slow as the platoon was forced to hack their way through the dense jungle with blades, each step seemingly punished by the very jungle itself for their intrusion. Then came the respite, with the thick trunked trees opening out with meters between them, the platoon's path taking them along a shallow river whose sandy, sunlit banks looked as close to paradise itself as Cochrane ever expected to see.

Now, with a surveillance drone somewhere above the rapidly closing canopy of green, the Fusiliers' advance slowed once more as each of the four soldiers on point was forced to draw their blades and resume the tiresome process of hacking through the dense, colorful bushes and mossy, entwined, tentacle-like vines.

Cochrane checked the map projected on his lens again. The contour lines showed a gentle change in the gradient up ahead, and the shades of green indicating the foliage denseness seemed to paint an optimistic picture of what lay to the east, given their current struggles. One Section advanced steadily eastward from perhaps two hundred meters to the north, Two Section had the center, whilst Three Section wallowed slowly to the south. Cochrane and the HQ Team advanced slowly behind Two Section; close enough to join them if required but not so close as to maintain visual contact.

"Three-One from Zero-One, sitrep," Cochrane repeated.

"Zero-One, this is Three-One," answered Corporal Rossi, the leader of Number Three Section. "We're still proceeding east, we're… about a quarter of a K south of you. Just getting slowed down by the terrain."

"Zero-One, roger," Cochrane acknowledged.

Cochrane paused for a moment, watching as the rest of the Platoon HQ Team advanced slowly through the jungle. Aida Castillo, the team's hacker, advanced at the head of the column, picking her way through the thin trail of butchered foliage left in the wake of Number Two Section. Shankar had agreed to send Hawkins up to support Number Two Section after he volunteered to help, mainly because they were encountering the worst of the jungle's natural obstacles and Hawkins carried with him a huge, straight-bladed sword as issued to all Hospitaller Knights. Whilst the weapon did, in most respects, look more suited to a museum than the modern battlefield, it was the soft, blue glow of the blade that betrayed its hyper-modern, cutting edge technology. It would, no doubt, make short work of the jungle obstacles.

Stefan Mann was second in the column, moving steadily behind Castillo. Selected as the platoon marksman due to his patience, uncanny eye, and rather detached view to the unpleasantries of conflict, he carried his long-barreled, 6.40mm Sinag MULTI Sniper Rifle across his chest. As the platoon had departed Alpha Four-Four, Cochrane noted that Major Beckmann carried a similar variant of the CineticS sniper rifle. She insisted on moving alone, detached from all four teams in the platoon, currently showing on the map as some way off to the north, using the rather laughably theatrical communication call sign of 'Eagle One'.

Shankar followed on in the center of their group of five with Cochrane just behind, leaving Ed Carson – the HQ team's medic – at the rear. Cochrane turned to check on the lanky soldier, just in time to see him quickly raise his Combi Rifle and point it at a colorful patch of purple foliage to their left. The bushes rustled and a dog-sized creature quickly pelted off to the north, away from them. Cochrane filtered through his visual settings and recognized its outline as a Tooba Lizard; a surprisingly quick and agile reptile native to Nortstralia.

"Easy, Ed!" Cochrane grinned.

"I thought it was a cauchemar cat!" the wary soldier commented, still staring ahead.

"Use your bloody head, mate!" Cochrane drawled. "One of those? This far south? If you want to worry about something, keep an eye out for scorpionettes. Those bastards are common around here, and they'll sting you if you startle 'em."

The painfully slow trek through the dense trees continued, the jungle alive around them with rattling insects; hidden, hissing lizards and chirping birds unseen in the shadowy canopy above. Pillars of light penetrated the ceiling of leaves, painting diagonal lines of misty sunlight like hazy spot lamps from the unseen heavens above.

"Broadsword-One from Zero," Cochrane heard Shankar transmit to Hawkins across the tactical communications network, "you okay? I've got a warning here for a high heart rate."

"Zero, Broadsword," Hawkins replied from his position somewhere up ahead with Number Two Section, his voice noticeably breathless over the comm network. "Yes, yes... I'm fine... All good here."

"Two-One from Zero," Shankar called Corporal Garcia, "rotate your point man. Get somebody else up front backing up the Mulebot and get your medic to look over Broadsword-One."

"Copied, Boss," Garcia replied.

Shankar held up a hand above her head to signal the Platoon HQ team to halt. Castillo and Mann sank down to sit on a flat rock jutting out of a sandy embankment, whilst Carson took a series of short sips from his water canteen. Shankar paced over to Cochrane, wiping sweat from her brow and adjusting her rifle's position where it was magnetically attached to her body armor. She shook her head as she approached, checking over her shoulder to ensure the others were out of earshot.

"Jeez," she began, "ten hours we've been at this now! Ten! D'you get the feeling that this is just some ludicrous, token effort so that the colonel can tell some general we have carried out responsive measures to the attack? There is nothing around here for a hundred miles! We are just chopping our way through a jungle for absolutely nothing! And we're not even halfway out yet!"

Cochrane grinned as he reached for his own water bottle.

"Are you seriously asking me if I think most of what we do in the light infantry is utter bullshit, just to impress some..."

Shankar held up a hand to cut Cochrane off mid-sentence and pressed her other palm against her ear. After a brief pause, she looked back up at Cochrane.

"It's Danni Mieke from Number Two Section," Shankar said. "She's just checked Hawkins over. He's dehydrated quite badly... Turns out he hasn't switched his armor's cooling system on."

Cochrane spat out his mouthful of water in surprise.

"What the bloody hell has he done that for?"

Shankar shrugged in wide-eyed astonishment, one hand still pressed to her ear as she continued to listen to the report from the medic.

"That's just a new level of stupid!" Cochrane continued, "I mean, you can't do that accidentally! Did his bloody pope tell him to do that? Some sort of self-flagellation thing? I mean, I'm still impressed! He's spent all day hacking a jungle down wearing enclosed armor in this heat! He should have dropped dead hours ago! The Hospitallers know how to toughen a guy up!"

Shankar turned her back on Cochrane and took a few paces away to listen more clearly to the update before mumbling a response to the medic over a private channel. She turned back to Cochrane.

"Danni says she can get him fixed up, but he needs to stop for a while."

"Fair enough," Cochrane nodded, "probably best we all take a break for a bit anyway."

Cochrane took another swig from his water bottle before returning it to its magnetic stowage point on his webbing belt. He took off his beret and ran a hand through his sweat-drenched hair. Shankar's words about the point-lessness of most peacetime infantry tasking – very uncharacteristic of her, he noted – swam around his mind for a few moments as he remembered life in Indigo Spec-Ops. Never a dull day, never a task without a critical point. He sighed and shook his head, recalling the tragic terms of his leaving Spec-Ops to return to the regular infantry.

His attention was brought back to the here and now when Shankar clicked her fingers multiple times to attract his attention whilst she held her other hand against her earpiece again.

"Shit," Cochrane drawled, "he's not dead, is he?"

"It's Company HQ," Shankar looked up at him, her face serious, "they've had an intelligence alert from surveillance drones up near the border. A Yujingyu force has just crossed the border due east of here. They're tracking straight toward us."

Chapter Four

Two full moons sat high in the night sky, a necklace of twinkling stars surrounding their pale glow. The moonlight reflected across the smooth, undisturbed water of the lake, lines of white shimmering on the gentlest of ripples. Dense rows of trees and vegetation surrounded on all sides save the south, where a gentle, sandy beach swept up from the mirror-like water to the black jungle. Number Three Platoon had stopped for the night, with Number One Section guarding the small encampment perimeter whilst the other sections maintained their equipment before setting up for sleep.

Hawkins sat at the edge of the beach on the lowest of a set of smooth, step-like rocks leading up to the higher ground to the west. His helmet and MULTI Rifle lay next to him as he flicked through the Old Testament on his lens, searching for some guidance or inspiration in the familiar chapters and verses projected into his eyes. He smiled when a section of Ecclesiastes he knew fairly well practically leapt off the virtual page at him.

"What does a man get for all the toil and anxious striving with which he labors under the sun? All his days his work is pain and grief; even at night his mind does not rest...A man can do nothing better than...find satisfaction in his work...To the man who pleases him, God gives wisdom, knowledge and happiness."

Hawkins smiled broadly as he read the words, feeling less alone as the ancient wisdom of the lines swam through his mind. Twice now he had volunteered to do something helpful for the men and women he worked with. Twice he had made a mistake and embarrassed himself. The more he thought on the shots he fired two nights before, the more he was sure he forgot to shout out a challenge. Cochrane was lying about hearing another soldier say he heard that challenge. Why, Hawkins was not sure.

Then there was helping clear the path through the jungle earlier that day. It had been hammered home that the heating system of a knight's armor was to be used for survival and survival alone; it was not a comfort device. Surely the same, therefore, was true of the entire system, and the cooling function with it? Hawkins had not used the internal environmental controls once since he was first instructed in their function back at Skovorodino.

"You okay, Kyle?"

Hawkins looked up from his reading as Lieutenant Shankar walked down from the top end of the gently sloping beach. He stood up as she approached and offered a courteous smile.

"Hello, Priya," he began, "I'm so sorry about the trouble I caused today, I…"

Shankar held a hand up to stop him.

"I was coming to see how you are, not to tell you off!" She smiled. "Are you feeling better? Ten hours of hacking vines in this heat whilst encased in metal… Everybody else is rotating around duty on point. Thirty minutes at a time. Why did you stay at the front for so long?"

Hawkins winced and hung his head for a moment's thought before looking up again.

"Because I can?" he offered. "Because… I'm here encased in metal that gives me a better than fifty-fifty chance of surviving a direct rifle shot, so I think that it's my duty to be the one at the very front. Nobody else can take a bullet like I can, wearing this. It's only fair I take the front. It's the right thing to do."

Shankar smiled sympathetically.

"It was very kind of you, but please look after yourself. As you saw, a noble gesture backfired, and we all had to stop to wait for you. If anything happens to you, I'll have a lot of explaining to do. You're attached here from the NeoVatican; you're not under my command. You are using your armor's cooling system now, I hope? It's not a luxury, it's a necessity. We need you fighting fit."

Hawkins nodded, the comfortable temperature pads pressed against his torso gently cooling his body's core whilst simultaneously leaving him with a chronic sensation of guilt, knowing that no other soldier there could enjoy such an extravagance in the punishing heat.

Shankar took a step back and nodded.

"Try to get some sleep, Kyle. You heard what I said in the evening brief. At the rate we're moving, we'll be face to face with Yujingyu forces by late morning tomorrow. Intel says we're expecting to run into a full platoon of Zhanshi. I hope it will be the normal chest puffing and posturing that seems to occur so often between us and them, but if it isn't… well, you'll definitely get your chance to help then."

"Right oh," Hawkins said. "Good night, Priya."

Shankar moved on to the far side of the beach where Corporal Lanne's Number One Section were sorting themselves for the night, dropping to one knee at the edge of the group of soldiers to join in their conversation. Hawkins had overheard them joking some time before about sleeping so close to the lake, referencing some famous horror movie he had never seen and a horrific, tentacled monster that dragged teenaged lovers below the water to their dooms. The conversation naturally then moved on to the ill-fated termination of the notorious Maya-series 'Tracking the Beasts' – the root of much of the recently restored media interest in the deadly wildlife of Paradiso. Hawkins chuckled at the jokes he overheard – even the risky ones – but knew better than to join in. He was not one of them. He would do best to respect that and keep his distance.

In a way, Hawkins mused to himself as he watched the soldiers prepare their simple sleeping shelters, a confrontation with Yu Jing might do him some good. It took about four months to train a Fusilier with over ninety percent of recruits successfully passing training. Comparing that to four years to train a Hospitaller Knight with less than a fifty percent pass rate and a far higher entry standard required to start with, all odds would surely dictate that Hawkins would do something impressive in his first confrontation! He mentally chastised himself at the thought. War brought death – even the invention of Cubes left the possibility of resurrection being somewhat remote, thanks to the crippling financial costs involved – and a Holy Order soldier's job was to protect life first and foremost; killing an enemy was, in Hawkins' mind, a regrettable necessity to achieve this aim and only as a last resort.

Hawkins was about to return to his Bible when he caught an aroma; a scent in the air that had no place in the jungles of Paradiso. Strawberries. He turned around and saw Beckmann sat on the rocks behind him, watching him from the shadows as she drew on a flavored cigarette; a thin stick of various chemicals marketed at teenagers who wanted to emulate the look of the cigarettes from a bygone era – but without the foul scents and with only minimal health risks.

"Hey," the tall major issued a slight smile.

"Ma'am," Hawkins stood up straight respectfully, eager to redress the lack of formality he presented her with on first meeting her, now that he knew who she was and what rank she held.

"Don't worry about that shit," Beckmann said, hopping down from the rocks to the sand below before leaning back against one of the trees behind her and propping one foot up against the trunk. Hawkins could not help but notice the enticing woman's change in attire, her standard combat fatigues now replaced with tight overalls of what almost looked to be glossy, black leather. Her feminine form was broken up by light, high leg combat boots, a belt of webbing pouches hanging from her waist, and a large, drop leg holster on one thigh whose size could only house a heavy, high caliber pistol. A thin fighting knife was strapped to the opposite thigh.

"Are you alright smoking that here, ma'am?" Hawkins asked tentatively. "I mean, the light might stand out and even I caught the smell."

Beckmann's face lit up with an amused smile. She nodded to where Shankar sat with one of the sections of Fusiliers further down the moonlit beach.

"With the amount of noise they're making, I don't think it matters," Beckmann replied. "It's like going camping with the fucking scouts. Anyway, forget about that. You okay? I heard you ran into some trouble earlier."

Hawkins involuntarily turned away and then sank back to seat himself on the rock by his helmet and rifle.

"Yes," he said quietly, "all fine. Just another stupid decision."

Beckmann stubbed her cigarette out and tossed the butt away before walking over to sit down next to him. She leaned forward, her folded arms resting on her knees, and stared out across the lake.

"D'you learn from it?" she asked quietly.

"Yes," Hawkins replied, "I learned something from it."

"Well, then."

A minute passed by in comfortable silence, both soldiers staring out across the tranquil lake. Hawkins glanced across at her. His eyes were instantly drawn to where Beckmann had left her overalls unzipped to nearly halfway down her chest. He quickly looked up at her face and said the first thing that came to his mind.

"How does that suit work?" Hawkins asked. "The reactive camouflage, I mean."

"Well," Beckmann shrugged, still looking out across the lake, "the whole thing is connected together – the boots, the webbing, the day sack – even the rifle. This stuff costs a fortune, apparently. This suit is an older model, but I prefer it to the newer one."

She pointed to the slightly padded shoulders, elbows, and knees of the black suit.

"These bits have some light armor," Beckmann explained, "but they also have a micro image capture device – a camera, basically – that analyses the wearer's surroundings and then transmits that image onto the material."

Beckmann tapped on the comlog on her wrist, and instantly the black material of her clothing faded into a match of the rocks behind her; the colors exact and the pattern similar enough to break up her form.

"That's the normal setting," she continued, "it doesn't draw much power so you can keep this going for hours. This bit now is the real trick."

Beckmann peeled open the outside of the collar of her suit and pulled a thin hood over her head. Then she vanished, entirely.

Hawkins leapt to his feet and stared down at the rocks where she sat a second before.

"Ma'am?"

He felt a tap on his shoulder and span around. Nobody was there. He turned again and saw Beckmann sitting on the rocks once more, cross-legged and smiling up at him.

"That's incredible!" Hawkins stammered. "I'd heard of optical disruption before but never seen it!"

"*Ja,*" Beckmann nodded, "works across all spectrums, not just visual. That mode uses a hell of a lot of power, and as soon as you move, the image capture loses its lock. It's incredible what the human mind can achieve. Just a shame we use this stuff to kill each other."

Hawkins looked across at the forlorn, beautiful woman as she stared out across the lake. He tried to think of something to say but failed.

"You should get some sleep," Beckmann said. "It could be a big day tomorrow."

"What about you?" Hawkins asked.

Beckmann shook her head.

"I'm not entrusting my life to these idiots while I sleep," she grimaced, standing up and retrieving her rifle. "There's a spot up on the ridge over there that overlooks this area for miles around. I'll set up there for the night and keep an eye on you all. Go get some sleep, Kyle."

Beckmann threw Hawkins a slight smile, hauled her pack over her shoulder, and walked off toward the top end of the beach.

***

"One mile," Shankar looked up at Cochrane, her voice hushed. "Jim, they're only a mile away. Just on the other side of that little valley up ahead."

Cochrane shrugged and issued a single nod of his head, fidgeting uncomfortably in his wet fatigues. A brief spell of rain moved through the area during the morning, adding a stuffy, humid misery to the decamping process, but it was certainly nothing compared to the torrential downpours Cochrane had experienced in the area around ZuluPoint. Somebody had once explained to Cochrane that it was something to do with air picking up moisture whilst crossing the sea and then being forced upward by hills, but Cochrane had paid little attention at the time.

The platoon was again separated into its three sections to cover more ground whilst the HQ team moved steadily behind them, this time with Hawkins in tow on Shankar's request. Regular intelligence updates were flowing in from Company HQ, providing a steady stream of data regarding the position of the Yujingyu force trespassing through PanOceanian territory.

"What does HQ want us to do?" Cochrane asked.

"Confront them," Shankar replied, "move directly out to oppose them and then escort them back over the border."

"They'll claim it's *us* who are in *their* territory," Cochrane warned Shankar as they hacked their way through the jungle, "they'll claim some bullshit about disputed border lines after the Rilaspur Accord. You watch."

Shankar folded her arms and looked down at the dusty earth by her feet. The other members of the HQ team glanced over from the other side of the small clearing they had stopped in.

"Surveillance still thinks it's a single platoon of Zhanshi," Shankar said quietly. "Their Platoon HQs tend to be quite small, so at least we'll outnumber them by a small margin."

"They sometimes overman their squads, though," Cochrane warned. "Twelve soldiers in a squad compared to ten in our sections, if they've come out upgunned. These guys like their missile launchers, too."

Shankar's eyes flickered to one side briefly as her attention was grabbed by an unseen distraction.

"Another alert from HQ," she told Cochrane, "counter surveillance says their drones now have visual contact with us. They know exactly where we are."

"Alright," Cochrane said, projecting a local area map from his comlog to both his own and Shankar's visual displays. "I'd recommend we move Two Section to the north and Three Section to the south; they can cover the flanks on the high ground whilst we move up the valley with One Section to confront them."

"Sounds feasible," Shankar agreed, "but we've lost visuals on them due to the density of the trees again. I want to send Stefan up ahead to get a look at them, make sure they're not doing something we're not expecting."

"Stefan?" Cochane grimaced. "The guy's only a platoon marksman. He's a good shot, but he's got no experience in tactical surveillance. Send that bloody Hexa psychopath up there. She can do it."

The young lieutenant closed her eyes and massaged her temples with her forefinger and thumb – a tell Cochrane had noted in her when the pressure began mounting – before activating her comlog.

"Eagle One from Zero, request you move to Marker Alpha to commence surveillance on inbound force."

"Eagle One acknowledged," Beckmann replied coolly, "going dark."

Cochrane saw Beckmann's blip on the map fade to nothing. He momentarily worried about the potential for a repeat occurrence of when Hawkins was shot at during the incident at Alpha Four-Four, but he then figured that a Hexa being accidentally killed by friendly fire would not be the worst thing in the world. Three new markers appeared on the map as Shankar selected waypoints for each of the three Fusilier sections to advance to.

"Right," she flashed an unconvincing smile at Cochrane, "let's be going, then."

The soldiers of the platoon HQ moved on. Cochrane checked his map display and saw all three sections continue on toward their objectives. Up on point, Aida Castillo, the team's hacker, cut a path through the trees and bushes as the Fusiliers advanced in single file. Cochrane tightened his grip around his Combi Rifle. It had been some time now since he last fired a shot in anger. That had been at the merciless bastards of the EI's Combined Army during their assault on the Headquarters of the Teutonic Order during the Third Offensive.

He had seen there how well the Teutonic Knights could fight. Grim, dedicated, brutal bastards – every bit as bloody as their alien opposition. Cochrane glanced across at Hawkins and suppressed a choked laugh. Perhaps they all started out as timid and useless as that boy. Perhaps the Hospitallers were just a different breed entirely from their Teutonic cousins.

"Eagle One, hostiles visual, transmitting imagery," Beckmann's voice reported over the comm net.

Cochrane's mind snapped back to the present. He swore at himself under his breath for losing focus for a good few minutes as the opposing forces closed, the Fusilier HQ team advancing through the jungle as it mercifully began to thin out again. Shankar looked back at Cochrane.

"Hostiles?" she queried. "Are we at war now?"

Cochrane exhaled and shook his head.

"All teams from Zero," Shankar transmitted. "Yujingyu force is not to be considered hostile. I say again, Yujingyu force is not hostile. Close to your markers and keep your weapons safe."

Cochrane brought up the imagery from Beckmann's riflescope. A column of soldiers advanced cautiously through the clumps of jungle trees, clambering up the hill to the north of the shallow valley. Their appearance was unmistakable; black uniforms worn beneath body armor of metallic orange-yellow. Their armor was lighter, less angular, and more curved than the body armor of the PanOceanian Fusiliers but certainly no less effective. The column of twelve soldiers, complete with a Heavy Machine Gun and a missile launcher, followed the contour of the sandy ground up toward the crest of the hill, where a map marker signified the destination of Two Section.

"Boss," Cochrane called over to Shankar, "you watching this? They're not following the valley. They're going to higher ground."

Shankar rapidly moved and reallocated markers on the platoon's map.

"All teams from Zero," she called, "new destination markers established. Opposing force now five hundred meters away. Move to markers and hold position."

Cochrane checked the map. Shankar had shifted the platoon's battle line north to face the new path of the Yujingyu force.

"Boss, we need to get a move on if we're going to catch up with One Section in the middle," Cochrane advised.

The five soldiers of the platoon HQ, plus their attached Hospitaller, picked up their pace to a fast jog through the sun-scorched trees. The rattle of insects and the hiss of hidden lizards seemed to grow louder as rays of sunshine poured through the gaps in the trees above, lighting up patches of sandy yellow earth.

"Two Section, in position," Garcia reported. "There's a Yujingyu unit two hundred meters east of us. They're fanning out and taking cover."

"Three Section, at Marker Charlie in the valley," Rossi called. "Likewise, we've got a squad of twelve Zhanshi just ahead of us. I'm marking it up on the map as Marker Delta."

Cochrane saw Corporal Lanne's section halted at the edge of a stream a few dozen meters ahead, just as Lanne was designating their position on the map. He followed Shankar across as she jogged over to the section leader.

"What can you see, Jonny?" she asked as she approached.

"Nothing more than Eagle One has sent across," Lanne reported. "There's a Yujingyu section just on the other side of the clearing up ahead. The ground slopes down, so they've got some natural cover. I can't quite make out how many of them, but it looks like a full squad. Drones still can't get a solid picture through the trees, just isolated shots of movement. Definitely Zhanshi, though."

Cochrane grimaced. He had faced Zhanshi before on several occasions. In many ways, the Zhanshi were the Yujingyu equivalent of PanOceania's Fusiliers; general light infantry, forming the core of the Yu Jing Ministry of State Defense's fighting strength, divided between eight separate armies. Cochrane knew them well from several border disputes and skirmishes in the past. They hit like a hammer in close assault and were highly disciplined. But from Cochrane's experience, they couldn't fire a rifle for shit.

"Ma'am," Lanne called, pointing across the small clearing separating the two forces, "look at this."

Cochrane looked across the clearing. Walking as calmly through the trees as if taking a stroll along a picturesque promenade, a Yujingyu soldier paced across the clearing toward them with his hands clasped at the small of his back. A second soldier, wearing hulking heavy infantry armor of pale green walked out after the first soldier, a bulky weapon held across his armored chest. The two Yujingyu soldiers walked out to the center of the clearing and stopped, staring ahead at the PanOceanian line expectantly.

***

Shankar looked across the clearing at the two soldiers waiting motionlessly for her. Her temples throbbed and ached. Her throat was dry. Why couldn't this be like military aid to civil powers? Disaster relief? There were no villains there, no conflict, just the simplicity of doing all one could to help the people who needed it the most. One Section lay prone along the bank of the stream, their weapons at the ready but held low, in non-threatening positions. The HQ team waited only a few paces behind. Shankar turned to face them.

"Right," she nodded, fighting to keep her voice steady, "I'm going out to talk to them."

"Not without me, you're not," Cochrane grunted. "C'mon, let's go see what these pricks have got to say for themselves."

"Not now, Sergeant," Shankar said quietly, "you stay here. Just in case."

"Just in case of what?"

Shankar span to face the tall soldier.

"Just in case you need to lead the platoon!" she hissed under her breath, "If this goes south and we both get shot, then what?"

"I'll come with you."

Shankar jumped as Beckmann appeared next to her, her MULTI Sniper Rifle held casually over one shoulder. Shankar looked up at the cool, blue-eyed woman.

"Ma'am, we might need a sharpshooter. I would appreciate you staying here and covering me."

"Their officer has taken somebody," Beckmann replied, "a soldier of the Jujak Shock Infantry, by the look of that flamethrower. They're trying to intimidate us. You should do the same. I'm coming with you."

Shankar felt bile rise to the back of her throat at the mention of the flamethrower. In this day and age, whilst mankind conquered the very stars, the fact that such a horrific, barbaric weapon could still exist was abhorrent to her.

"I'll go," Hawkins stepped out from the HQ team. "Sergeant Cochrane needs to stay here. Major Beckmann is most useful in a sniping position. I'm not doing anything. I'll come with you, Priya."

"Sir, would you please stop volunteering for everything!" Cochrane snapped. "We need to make a decision! Because right now we're looking pretty bloody stupid with them waiting for us!"

Shankar looked across at the grizzled Spec-Ops sergeant, the cool Hexa killer, and the idealistic Knight Hospitaller. Hawkins was right. In its most callous terms, he was the least useful to be left behind.

"Come on, Kyle," she exhaled nervously, "let's go."

***

Hawkins watched as Shankar and Cochrane rapidly set up markers on the map to present options for advancing and falling back should a firefight begin. He took off his helmet and allowed the piercing rays of sun to warm his face, closing his eyes and tilting his head up toward the heavens. His left hand began to shake.

"Sub Officer."

Hawkins looked up. Beckmann looked across at him coolly and beckoned to him.

"Come with me."

Hawkins followed the Hexa major a few feet away from the others until she turned to face him again. Her eyes were serious when they met his.

"Listen to me, Kyle," she said, leaning in. "Whatever is going through your head right now about Christian virtue and the sanctity of human life, you need to park that to one side. Forget it. I know the Yujingyu. They don't see things the way we do. They are stood there, ready to kill you. They won't bat a fucking eyelid. So you walk out there with Shankar, you stand tall, and you look them dead in the face. They don't know you're new to this under that helmet. They just see a Knight Hospitaller, and that scares them. So you stare them down, stand ready, and if bullets start flying, you fucking kill them. Alright?"

"But... we... we should be talking them down, ma'am! We should be diffusing this situation..."

Beckmann placed a hand on Hawkin's arm and shook her head.

"You shouldn't be out in this," she said softly, "not straight out of training. This is the real world now. Be ready. Just... don't worry, okay? I've got your back. I'm watching out for you. Both of you. Go on."

Beckmann stepped back away from Hawkins.

"Hey," she threw him a cocky grin and a wink, "don't worry. I'm just a shot away from you."

Beckmann pulled her hood up over her head, and her overalls instantly changed to match the surroundings until she had completely disappeared from sight. Hawkins pulled on his helmet and looked across at where Shankar waited for him by the stream.

"Let's go," she nodded.

Chapter Five

Hawkins stepped up and out of the stream, following a pace behind and to the left of Shankar as she walked across the clearing. Trees sprouted up from the dry earth in twos and threes, breaking up the ground between the two lines of opposing soldiers. As Shankar and Hawkins walked out to meet the two Yujingyu soldiers, Beckmann's words raced around Hawkins' mind over and over again.

"They don't see things the way we do... if bullets start flying, kill them."

Was that not the source of so many evils of the past? Was not seeing things the same way really a cause for war and bloodshed? A single line from Saint Paul's letter to the Romans followed on from Beckmann's words, again and again as Hawkins drew nearer to the two men who he had been told were his enemy:

"...is God the God of Jews alone? Is he not the God of Gentiles also? Yes, of Gentiles also..."

Hawkins had used that line to justify his attitude toward pacifism on multiple occasions during debates in the fortress-monastery. Some Hospitallers agreed with him. Others told him that he was being selective with the words he quoted; twisting their meaning to support his own point of view. But in Hawkins' mind, it was all clear enough; God loved all. Who was Hawkins to choose life and death for others?

"Put your rifle away, Kyle," Shankar said. "I'm still hoping we can deescalate this."

Hawkins clipped his MULTI Rifle onto his back. His left hand clasped onto the top of the scabbard at his waist; partially to hold it in place should he need to rapidly draw his sword, partially for comfort. His heart thumped in his chest as they drew closer to the Zhanshi officer and the armored Jujak shock soldier that stood next to him. He had seen them both in a hundred simulations; shot them and cut them down with his blade in the make-believe world of assessed training exercises. Yet now, standing before him, they were here for real. He ran a built-in test function on his armor's power distribution system again. Not that it mattered now. If it detected an error, he could hardly turn around and walk away.

Shankar stopped a few paces in front of the Zhanshi officer. The man was shorter than Hawkins, perhaps in his mid-twenties with long, dark hair tied in a topknot and accompanied by a thin moustache. Next to him, the Jujak trooper's helmet enclosed face turned to look up at Hawkins. Unseen eyes gauged him from behind the shaded, orange visor that dominated the trooper's entire face. The Jujak tightened his grip around his flamethrower. The blue light of the igniter at the end of the weapon hissed angrily.

"I'm Lieutenant Shankar of the PanOceanian military," Shankar began, her tone formal and unyielding. "You are…"

"*You,*" the Zhanshi lieutenant cut her off, his words accented but perfectly clear, "are trespassing on the wrong side of the border agreed and ratified by O-12 at the Rilaspur Accord. This is an armed incursion, carried out illegally by an overt military force. You are to surrender your weapons and accompany us for detention until this matter can be resolved."

Shankar's eyes narrowed. She remained silent for a long, uncomfortable moment until finally responding. Hawkins stared incredulously at the map projected in front of him. Surely this was an attempt at deception? Their interpretation of the border was inaccurate by over a dozen miles. Then again, if there was a discrepancy between the two sides' interpretation of just a single way point…

"The Rilaspur Accord clearly defined the border in this region," she countered, "and you have crossed it. My orders are… less hostile than yours. I am instructed to escort you back across the border, where…"

"I'm not interested in your orders or your deceitful interpretation of the accord. You are well, well over our side of the border. Armed to the teeth."

The Zhanshi lieutenant held out his arm and projected a holographic image of a local area map above his wrist. The marked border on his map did not reflect that of the map Hawkins had been working to for the past few days. The Jujak trooper tilted his head slowly from one side to the other, his eyes still fixed on Hawkins. Shankar held up her own wrist and projected her map.

"Your mapping data is in error," she began. "You…"

Even with his hearing augmented by the suite of sensors in his helmet, Hawkins was unable to process and clarify the series of events that occurred in the next few seconds. He heard a rapid, low howl that increased in pitch into a whine in the briefest of moments and the crack of a sniper rifle – he was not sure what came first. A Zhanshi soldier by the trees ahead of Hawkins was flung back. Almost instantly, a second shot and a howl echoed out, and the Zhanshi lieutenant stood only paces away from him braced up as blood erupted from a gaping hole in his chest before he crumpled sideways to the ground.

The world exploded into chaos. Rifle and machine gun fire erupted from ahead and behind. Dull thumps announced the detonations of missiles and grenades from launchers. Bullets tore across the clearing, hacking into trees and sending foliage twirling up into the air in clumps. Handfuls of sand erupted by Hawkins' feet. The Jujak swung his flamethrower around toward Shankar and Hawkins. Hawkins instinctively reacted.

In one smooth motion, Hawkins dashed forward and unsheathed his sword, straight into an upward cut. The blade lashed out and slashed across the Jujak's chest, just as the Yujingyu soldier was attempting to simultaneously bring his flamethrower around and avoid the deadly sword attack. The heavy sword cut easily through the armor, and an arc of vivid scarlet arced up into the air. The flamethrower ignited and sprayed burning chemicals off to Hawkins' right. He swung the blade back around to hack down into a second neat, powerful strike that half-severed the man's torso. Blood spattered across Hawkins' visor and the white cross on his chest. Then the world stopped for a moment as the immediate realization kicked in that he had just taken a human life.

Hawkins instantly snapped out of his brief moment of bitter self-reflection when a fist smashed into his left shoulder with enough force to half spin him in place. Pain seared across his arm from the impact. Another unseen strike punched him in the hip, dropping him to one knee. His helmet exploded with a cacophony of noise as multiple people shouted and screamed across the platoon's communication network. Slow, far too slow, Hawkins realized that nobody had punched him. He had been shot. He looked around to either side and saw Shankar lying on the ground next to him, her teeth gritted as she clutched the burnt, blackened flesh of her left arm. Hawkins grabbed her by the collar and dragged her along the ground to the relative cover of a copse of trees a few paces to the left.

"Kyle!" Shankar yelled up at him. "Get down! You're getting shot to shit! Get down!"

Hawkins dropped to one knee behind the thick trunk as the entire tree banged, tremored, and buckled with the near constant impact of bullets. He grabbed his MULTI Rifle from his back, brought the weapon to his shoulder, and leaned around cover to fire off a retaliatory burst at a group of enemy soldiers lying behind the cover of a lip of earth a few dozen meters ahead.

***

Cochrane watched in wide-eyed horror as the sniper's bullet cut down one of the Yujingyu soldiers on the far side of the clearing. In the time it took him to activate his comlog and open his mouth to order a ceasefire, a second round zipped out to plummet straight through the Zhanshi lieutenant stood opposite Shankar. Then all hell broke loose. Muzzle flashes sparkled from the tree line on the far side of the clearing; rounds whooshed audibly past Cochrane to either side; branches and leaves exploded up into the air around him, twirling through the pillars of sunlight permeating the jungle canopy above as Cochrane dove to the ground.

"One Section, open fire!" Corporal Lanne barked over the comlog.

Combi Rifles erupted into life ahead of Cochrane, sending lethal rounds back across the clearing in response to the Zhanshi fire. Cochrane

quickly brought up his map and checked the positions of the three Fusilier sections by their IFF emitters. Each side's three sections faced each other almost
evenly, with Cochrane and the Fusilier HQ team caught just behind the middle
of the PanOceanian line. Cochrane grimaced as alerts began scrolling down
the side of his lens. They were already suffering casualties. Red blips appeared
on the map as each section's forward observer set about highlighting priority
targets for their comrades. Enemy soldiers to the north were already moving
in an attempt to get around the side of the PanOceanian firing line. The ground
shook as a missile from Lance Corporal Dubois' support team impacted into
the Zhanshi line.

"Two Section from Zero-One!" Cochrane shouted. "Enemy is moving
to outflank you! Reposition to cover the north! One and Three Sections, hold
position and lay down suppressing fire! Section leaders; take charge of targeting priorities!"

To Cochrane's left, Fusilier Marinho's Heavy Machine Gun opened
up with long bursts of fire, the air around them filled with the weapon's distinctive, guttural thudding. Cochrane brought his own Combi Rifle up to his
shoulder and peered through the scope. Ahead, he saw the bodies of the dead
Zhanshi lieutenant and the Jujak Shock Trooper; the latter hacked bloodily
apart. To their left, he saw Hawkins and Shankar taking cover behind a clump
of earth at the foot of a trio of tall trees. Hawkins returned fire at the Yujingyu
positions whilst Shankar, teeth gritted in pain, struggled to unholster her pistol.
Cochrane checked the casualty notifications again on his screen. One of them
was Shankar – wounds to the left arm.

He glanced across the clearing again and quickly formulated a viable
plan. The trees were dense enough to the north side, with good arcs of fire
where Lanne's Number One Section was set up.

"Zero from Zero-One!" Cochrane called. "Hold position, we're advancing to you! One Section support team: continue covering fire at Marker
Echo! One Section rifle team, HQ team: on me!"

Cochrane quickly plotted a route on the platoon's shared map to highlight the plan of advance to the soldiers he had designated and then shot to his
feet to sprint to the left of the clearing.

***

Hawkins fed a fresh magazine into his MULTI Rifle, cocked the weapon, and then raised it to his shoulder again. Next to him, Shankar's pistol
snapped away as she speculatively fired at the line of perhaps ten Zhanshi
soldiers in the trees ahead of them. Automatic fire continued to roar from both
ahead and behind them, with tracer rounds ripping across the clearing in both
directions in lines of glowing white. The comlog was alive with confusing

shouts of orders. Hawkins' focus remained on the enemy soldiers ahead, his mental capacity sapped to the point that the voices in his ears all merged into one long, indecipherable transmission. He picked out a Zhanshi soldier and fired again, his rifle thumping back against his shoulder and his field of view obscured by the smoke hissing up from his weapon's barrel.

"Kyle!" Shankar shouted from his left.

Hawkins looked across, the realization only now sinking in that it was the third time she had called to him. Smoke still wafted up from the burnt flesh on her arm. The image of her attacker – the soldier who Hawkins had bloodily cut down and now lay dead only paces behind him – briefly flashed into his mind. Shankar pointed to the north of the clearing.

"Sergeant Cochrane is moving a Fireteam up to support us!" Shankar shouted, ducking down as a grenade detonated on the other side of the earth bank. "Get ready to run for those trees when he gives the signal!"

Hawkins nodded and turned his attention back to the line of enemy soldiers in the trees ahead. Out of the corner of his visor, a target previously highlighted by one of the forward observers suddenly moved to the right in a clear attempt to mirror the advance of the Fusiliers by outflanking to the south. The soldier had a missile launcher. Hawkins immediately fired a long burst at him but succeeded only in blasting away at the trees around him. Then came another low howl rapidly changing pitch into a whining scream, and a sniper bullet slammed into the side of the Zhanshi soldier's head, blowing off the back half of his skull.

"Zero, Broadsword-One!" Cochrane's voice cut through the chatter in Hawkins' ears. "We're north of you at Marker Hotel! On my mark, retreat to our position!"

"Copied!" Shankar replied, loading another magazine into the grip of her pistol and pulling back on the top slide to house the first round.

Then a dull thud shook the ground and a column of smoke rose up from the trees to the south. Hawkins' visor was filled with a scrolling line of casualties. He checked his map. Half of Corporal Rossi's Number Three Section was gone.

***

Cochrane leaned quickly around the trunk of the tree and fired a short burst from his Combi Rifle into the ditch at the east side of the clearing, forcing two of the Zhanshi soldiers to duck back down into cover. Behind him, Lanne's Fireteam lay prone and fired at the same position whilst Fusilier Carson knelt over Aida Castillo, quickly administering first aid to a bloody wound on one of her shins. Now parallel with Shankar and Hawkins, Cochrane was close enough to affect a retrieval.

"Zero, Broadsword-One!" he shouted. "We're north of you at Marker Hotel! On my mark, retreat to our position!"

"Copied!" Shankar replied, the relief in her eyes clear even from this position as she hunkered down behind the cover of the copse of trees atop the earth bank.

An explosion erupted from the south. Smoke wafted up from the far side of the clearing. Cochrane checked his comlog – casualty reports began scrolling in from Number Three Section.

"Shit!" Cochrane snapped.

That would be his next problem to solve. Right now, he needed to win the fight in the center, and successfully retrieving his platoon commander and the Hospitaller was part of that plan. The sheer weight of fire from Lanne and his Fireteam, and from Lance Corporal Dubois' support team, was forcing the surviving Zhanshi to stay in cover.

"Priya!" Cochrane shouted across. "Now! Leg it!"

Shankar shot to her feet and sprinted rapidly across the clearing before diving into cover next to Cochrane. She collapsed to one knee, her face covered in sweat as she panted, raw burns spanning the length of one of her arms. One down, and they perhaps had the edge in the firefight. Looking at the map, it appeared there was a stalemate to the north; the Fusiliers had a clear advantage in the clearing in the center, but they were being overrun to the south.

Cochrane looked up again. Hawkins remained frozen in place. Cochrane watched him incredulously. Was the boy so stupid that he assumed Cochrane's shout of 'Priya' excluded him from also running to safety?

"Broadsword-One! Move to cover! Move to Marker Hotel!"

The Hospitaller, still hunkered down behind cover, looked across to Cochrane. Then he twisted in place and looked south at the pillar of smoke rising from Number Three Section's position. He looked back at Cochrane. Then south for a second time.

"Don't be a dick!" Cochrane yelled. "Sir! Get over here to us!"

"Broadsword, from Zero!" Shankar shouted. "Move to my position!"

"Kyle, do what you're fucking told!" Cochrane heard Beckmann's voice over the comlog.

Hawkins stood up and sprinted out into the open ground, rapidly heading toward the southern tree line and away from Cochrane and safety. After only four or five paces, he was immediately caught in a burst of fire from the Zhanshi line and crumpled to the ground. Cochrane saw the Zhanshi shooter clearly for an instant, rapidly raised his Combi Rifle to a firing position, and shot the Yujingyu soldier through the side of his torso, sending him falling limply back into the ditch. In the clearing, Hawkins staggered back up to his feet and stumbled on for a few paces before regaining his composure to pick his pace up into a sprint.

***

His armored feet kicking through the fine sand as he stumbled down the shallow incline, Hawkins allowed himself a brief breath of relief as the buzz of bullets around him stopped. The marker on his map up ahead showed the position of Number Three Section, split into their two Fireteams and facing a near equal number of Zhanshi soldiers attacking from the east. Pain flared up from Hawkins' shoulder and arm; he ran a diagnostic check on his armor that highlighted some superficial damage to his heat sinks but nothing more. No penetrating shots – he was only feeling the severe bruising of the impact itself.

The shouts and replies between the Platoon HQ and various Fireteam leaders continued over the comlog as Hawkins rapidly closed with the battle raging between Number Three Section and their Zhanshi adversaries. His MULTI Rifle held ready as he rapidly threaded his way through the sun-drenched trees, Hawkins saw markers on his visor that highlighted friendly and enemy positions. The pillar of smoke he saw earlier was dissipating now, but up ahead he saw a small, blackened crater in the ground. Bodies of Fusiliers lay around the crater.

"Three-One from Broadsword," Hawkins called as he approached. "Three-One?"

"Broadsword, this is Three-Five," an unfamiliar voice responded. "Rifle team took a direct hit from a heavy weapon; Three-One is down."

Hawkins looked to his left and saw a Fireteam of five Zhanshi crouched behind the cover of a fallen tree trunk. Without thinking about the tactical consequences of his actions, Hawkins raised his MULTI Rifle and fired a long burst in their direction. He was immediately greeted with rapid shots in reaction, bullets tearing through the air to either side. He flung himself to his right and crawled for cover, his visor highlighting red squares around the enemy threats who were targeting him directly.

"Three-Five, this is Zero," Hawkins heard Shankar's voice, "hold your position, we're moving around to Marker Juliet to set up a firing line."

Hawkins glanced quickly at his map but saw only a confused jumble of blue and red blips, and white diamond position markers. For a moment, he wondered if he was being hacked again before he realized that it was far simpler and far worse. He was panicking. Hawkins took a deep breath. He checked his ammunition counter. He placed a hand over the cross on his chest.

"God, help me," he whispered.

Trusting in God and praying for his armor to hold, Hawkins sprinted out past the cover of the tree and ran toward the crater, firing his MULTI Rifle at the Zhanshi position ahead. Rounds came across from Number Three Section's support team hidden in the trees further to the south, diverting the attention of the Yujingyu soldiers. Hawkins reached the crater and threw himself down into what little cover it provided. The smell of burnt flesh immediately wafted through his helmet's nasal filters. He looked up at the carnage of body parts around him. His visor locked onto the dead and wounded Fusiliers' IFF emitters.

- *Corporal Lucia Rossi – severe wound, cranial*
- *Fusilier Gordon Burke – dead*
- *Fusilier Franc Clark – dead*
- *Fusilier George Trent...*

Hawkins clipped his rifle onto his back and grabbed two of the wounded Fusiliers, each by their body armor at the scruff of the neck. Half-squatted over awkwardly, his teeth gritted in exertion even with the benefits provided by the augmented strength of his armor, Hawkins dragged the unconscious soldiers over the lip of the crater and toward the safety of the west. Almost immediately, a burst of fire clanged into his back, knocking him over onto his face. Hawkins struggled back up, grabbed the two injured soldiers again, and carried on.

***

The pain from Shankar's burnt arm seemed somehow to intensify. She looked across at Ed Carson and momentarily considered asking the medic to run over to aid her but then thought better of it. Carson could even shoot her with a dart from his medikit's needle gun from range to provide her with some basic medical assistance, but Shankar figured that others would soon need his help far more than she did. She was still in the fight; better to get the job done.

Shankar turned her attention back to the map. Angelo Garcia's Number Two Section to the north was still locked in a stalemate against a Zhanshi squad, with only a handful of minor injuries. The push across the central clearing had been a resounding success, with the Zhanshi forces now in full retreat. Down to the south, the PanO casualties were the heaviest. From his position a few paces away crouched low behind the cover of a pair of sandy yellow rocks, Cochrane ducked down to reload his Combi Rifle.

"Ma'am!" he called across to Shankar, back to using the formalities of her rank now it was in front of the other Fusiliers. "We've just had a message from Company HQ! We've got Tubarãos inbound! They've given us a marker about a mile west of here for extraction!"

Shankar brought up her messages and quickly read through the update to her orders, noting the position of the extraction marker set up for the incoming aircraft.

"They can't land there!" Cochrane shouted. "They'll only be able to winch up our wounded!"

Part of Shankar wanted to carry on the fight. Part of her was raging at the fact the Yujingyu had crossed into PanO territory – knowing *full well* where the border lay – and then lied to her face. Part of her wanted to press home the slight advantage her platoon had to turn a marginal victory into a rout. The other half of her was exhausted, scared, and in pain. That was the part that won.

"Sergeant!" she called back. "I want Number Two section to fall back to the clearing! We'll head to Marker Oscar to provide covering fire for Number Three Section, then we all fold in to regroup before heading to the extraction point!"

Cochrane's eyes moved away as he looked through the plan on the map and then nodded.

"Got it, Boss!" he replied, markers and orders to section leaders already appearing on the platoon's shared tactical map.

Shankar found herself now able to hear individual rifle shots. The battle was dying down. The near ceaseless hammering and thudding of gunfire and explosions gave way to the sounds of the dry, insectoid sounds of the jungle.

"Zero from Two-One," Garcia transmitted from his position to the north, "we're falling back to the clearing. They're not following us. I think they've had enough."

***

Leaning forward over one knee, Hawkins let out a gasp of relief when he saw the approaching soldiers were Fusiliers. He lowered his rifle, tore off his helmet, and took in two long, lungfuls of fresh air. He recognized the soldiers as they approached; Corporal Lanne's Number One Section.

"Y'alright there, Boss?" Lanne called as he jogged over, four of his soldiers only paces behind him.

Hawkins nodded, sweat pouring down his face.

"These two," he gasped, nodding at the two injured Fusiliers he had dragged from the crater, "they need help…"

Lanne nodded at Byron, his Section medic, who darted over with his medikit. Southee jogged over to Hawkins and helped him to his feet. Rifle fire continued to crackle away from somewhere off to the east.

"We're falling back," Lanne told Hawkins, "there's an extraction point about a mile away. We've got them on the run, but they're regrouping to the east. The boss says we've had an intel report saying there's a second platoon of them on the way."

"What about the wounded?" Hawkins asked. "I moved who I could, but…"

"The others are all dead, sir," Lanne said grimly. "The rest of Three Section has already fallen back. We've got to go."

Hawkins looked down at where Byron quickly checked over the two wounded soldiers he had retrieved. The medic looked up at Lanne.

"We've got to move them both, Jonny," Byron said sourly.

Hawkins reached down and lifted one of the limp soldiers over his shoulder before retrieving his helmet with his other hand, whilst Byron picked up the second casualty. The group of Fusiliers moved steadily westward as the gunfire behind them finally halted, Corporal Lanne leading them on converging headings on the map to meet up with the rest of the platoon. In only minutes, they emerged into another tight clearing by a delta in a fast running stream and saw the Platoon HQ Team up ahead. Shankar and Cochrane immediately made their way over.

"Jonny," Shankar called as she approached, "your people all okay?"

"Yes, ma'am," Lanne replied. "We've got Lucia and George from Three Section. They're not so good."

"We're moving to the extraction point now," Shankar breathed before turning to Hawkins. "Somebody take Corporal Rossi off the sub officer, please."

Fusilier Fischer moved up to gently lift Rossi from Hawkins' shoulder. The majority of soldiers quickly moved on, leaving Shankar and Cochrane behind with Hawkins. Wiping another face full of sweat away, Hawkins looked apprehensively across at Shankar.

"Kyle!" she hissed as soon as the others were out of earshot. "What the hell was that? I told you to follow me! This is my platoon! I can't afford to have rogue soldiers shooting from the hip!"

Hawkins swallowed.

"I… I'm sorry, Priya."

"It's not how we do things!" Shankar continued. "We don't run around like headless chickens when we take casualties! We work as a team to secure an area, we don't run off into enemy fire in the open just because we've taken a few hits! Next time, do what you're bloody well told to!"

Shaking her head, Shankar turned and jogged after the others. Hawkins looked up at Cochrane. The muscular sergeant grinned broadly.

"I don't want to undermine the lieutenant's words," Cochrane said, "because she's got a good head on her shoulders and, by and large, she's right. We should follow the rulebook, sir, most of the times anyways."

"Right," Hawkins nodded wearily.

"But sometimes," Cochrane continued, "there is a time and a place to deviate from the play book. Every time you do, you flip a coin. Heads: you're a bloody hero. Tails: you look like a dick and you're dead. Today, sir, you were a bloody hero. My recommendation would be that you never do that again."

Hawkins and Cochrane quickly caught up with the rest of the platoon, just as the final, limping survivors gathered together. It was now only half a mile to the extraction point, where the injured could be winched to safety and flown to a proper medical facility. Hawkins moved across to regroup with Shankar and the HQ team, just as another friendly IFF emitter appeared on his map. Beckmann stepped out of the trees ahead, her overalls turning from jungle greens and yellows to glossy black. She paced angrily over to the HQ Team.

"Major," Shankar greeted, "I…"

Beckmann pushed Shankar aside and stomped over to stand a pace from Hawkins.

"What the fuck was that, Sub Officer?" she snarled.

"Ma'am," Hawkins swallowed, "I…"

"You were ordered to move to safety by your platoon commander!" Beckmann yelled, pointing a finger at Shankar. "You were ordered to move to safety by Sergeant Cochrane, the most experienced soldier in the platoon! You were ordered to move to safety by me!"

The last statement was accompanied by Beckmann shoving Hawkins back a pace with both of her hands.

"And what about you!" Cochrane growled in accusation.

Beckmann turned to face the sergeant.

"*Vas?*"

"Why the hell did you start shooting?" Cochrane demanded. "You fired the first shot, not them! I've got four dead Fusiliers and nine wounded because you went fucking psycho!"

"Sergeant!" Shankar shouted. "Enough! Not now!"

"No!" Beckmann paced over to Cochrane, rage in her blue eyes. "You've got something to say, you fucking prick, then you damn well say it! Yes, I fired the first shot! One of those bastards went for his weapon!"

"Bullshit!" Cochrane yelled.

Beckmann's fists clenched and she paced forward purposefully, her raging eyes locked on Cochrane. Shankar dashed across to stand between them.

"Sergeant! Ma'am! We need to get the casualties to the extraction point! Please! We have to move!"

Cochrane took a step back and held up his hands passively whilst the soldiers of the platoon watched the altercation from a semi-circle around the command team. Beckmann paced slowly back and forth, her fists still clenched and her eyes still fixed on Cochrane.

"We're moving," Shankar ordered, "now. Company HQ says a second platoon of Zhanshi has crossed the border. We're not facing twenty survivors from the platoon we just fought with; we're now looking at fifty of them. We get to the extraction point, secure the wounded, and then I'll lead us back to Alpha Four-Four on foot."

"Ma'am," Cochrane said gently, pointing to her blackened arm, "you need to go, too. I'll lead the boys and girls back. You get yourself to hospital with the other wounded."

"I can walk as fast as..."

"Ma'am," Cochrane interrupted, "please. I've got it now."

Hawkins watched as Shankar looked around the semi-circle of assembled soldiers. Most of the younger Fusiliers seemed nervous; some on edge and even excited. Shankar shook her head and walked quickly off toward the extraction point. The rest of the platoon was quick to follow. Hawkins watched as every last soldier moved onward, with the exception of Beckmann. The tall woman checked over her rifle and then walked off toward the west and the advancing Zhanshi.

"Ma'am?" Hawkins called after her.

Beckmann stopped and looked over her shoulder.

"You've got walking wounded, Kyle," Beckmann said, "and an extraction point to secure. Those bastards out there will catch you up. I'm going to slow them down."

Hawkins let out a breath and searched for the right words but found none. He watched her melt away into the jungle and disappear.

Chapter Six

"Don't stand on ceremony, Jim," Colonel Talau responded as Cochrane stood stiffly to attention, "grab a chair. It's all kicking off down here with A Company, so I thought I'd come and see what was going on for myself."

Cochrane wearily walked across the metallic floor of the HQ block and sat on one of the tan-colored, fold out chairs that normally seemed so uncomfortable, yet today like a warm, loving, plastic embrace against his aching buttocks. Talau sat near the newly installed Company Command Terminal, next to Major Barker. Talau was a broad-shouldered, squat man in his fifties whose muscular frame stood as proof of an individual who took fitness just as seriously in a staff job as he did as a young platoon commander. His olive complexion and broad nose suited him well and spoke of a Polynesian ancestry. As regimental commander, he was in charge of two battalions each made up of five companies. He was effectively Major Barker's boss' boss.

Alpha Four-Four's HQ block had expanded in the few days that Number Three Platoon had been in the jungle; it was just one of many changes that greeted the survivors upon their return to the jungle base. The footprint of the base had perhaps doubled, with large segments of jungle burnt and hacked down around the bottom of the plateau. The base now had two lines of defense; a perimeter made up of ballistic barricades fitted with machine guns and sensor posts, patrolled by dronbots who stomped mechanically along hastily established cutting foam fences. The second line of defense stood atop the plateau consisting of ugly, quickly deployable reinforced bunkers at each corner of the base, housing Fusiliers with support weapons and defending another line of automated sensors.

Talau glanced across the HQ block to where a lance corporal from Number Two Platoon manned the Perimeter Security Control terminal before looking back at Cochrane.

"I bumped into your dad last week," Talau grinned. "I'm sure the old bastard would want me to pass on his regards."

"Tell him to get off his arse and check his mail once in a while if you see him again, would you, sir?" Cochrane replied.

Talau let out a short laugh and nodded.

"Well, Sergeant," Barker said, "it wasn't long since you and I were sat in these very chairs, talking about your last shoot out. Not as much to discuss this time; we've had two days to analyze the footage from your platoon's lenses and scopes, so we've got a very good idea what happened."

"It'll be no surprise to you that this is going to the very top," Talau interjected. "No surprises that Yu Jing is claiming we were in their territory and we shot first. O-12 is wading in, as always. Our government is stating the facts

72

– there was an armed incursion by Yujingyu forces in PanOceanian territory and an armed force was sent to escort them to their own border, using the least possible level of force. But none of that is your problem, Jim. We'll leave that to the politicians."

Cochrane leaned forward in his chair. The dirt repellent smart fabric of his combat fatigues could only cope with so much jungle grime and perspiration. Even he was aware of how badly he smelled.

"Who fired first, Jim?" Talau asked suddenly.

"We did," Cochrane replied without hesitation.

"You sure?"

"Defo. It was that bloody Hexa. Went crazy and started shooting."

Talau and Barker exchanged brief glances.

"And you left Major Beckmann behind?" Barker asked.

"She elected to stay behind," Cochrane replied, aware his tone was slightly defensive. "Said she would slow them down so that we could escape. We haven't heard from her since."

Barker scratched idly at his graying moustache.

"Four dead from your platoon, Sergeant," the company commander said quietly. "I know it's a bloody cliché to say that they were good people, but it's still true. Major Beckmann marked up their bodies. A team was inserted yesterday and they have been successfully recovered."

Cochrane nodded slowly, his eyes fixed on the grated floor ahead of him. Two days for the fit and the walking wounded to return. The dead were home even before that. He was glad, of course, that the bodies were recovered; at best, they could be resurrected from the information stored in their Cubes. At worst, they would at least have a decent burial.

"Glad to hear, sir," Cochrane said. "That was quick."

"We would have gotten you out if it proved practical, or if we thought you were at considerable risk," Talau said, "but once you had broken contact, it was just the walk back here. As you know, we can winch up a handful of soldiers with an aircraft in the hover, but with no place to land, then it is a different matter entirely trying to winch up an entire platoon. Too risky."

Cochrane, tired though he was, did not find himself disagreeing with that decision. Resources were always tight, always in demand. Other things were on his mind, anyway.

"How's Lieutenant Shankar, sir?" he asked.

"She's fine," Barker replied, "she'll be back with us in a couple of days. Until then, you have command of Number Three Platoon. With four dead and five still recovering from wounds, you'll be a full section down. But there's not much time to rest, Sergeant. One Platoon is still out there, dug in to stop any further advances from the Yujingyu. Two Platoon have patrol duty tomorrow, so your lot will have one day to themselves and then it's straight back in to perimeter security."

"Right," Cochrane replied, shifting in his seat.

His eyes ached from lack of sleep and his right arm still stung from an unfortunate encounter with the thorns of a linger-long only a few hours before.

"No rest for the wicked," Talau leaned forward, "but you've got to see this from the point of view of those at the top. The Combined Army is on a full offensive at Concilium Prima. Even here on Paradiso, the movements of EI forces to the east are considered to be much more of a concern than a border dispute with Yu Jing. I'm afraid four dead Fusiliers haven't really caused much of a stir for those in government, or the lobby groups."

"Understood, sir," Cochrane said, the news coming as no surprising revelation to him.

Four dead soldiers. Meaningless in the grand scheme of things. But it meant something to Cochrane and the rest of Number Three Platoon. To the entire company. They were people. With names. Stefan Mann; cool, kept himself to himself, always the professional. Frank Clark and his ridiculous rally car obsession. Gordon Burke and his flatulence. Bit of a shit thing to be remembered for, but it did seem to define him. Aubin Bacque; eighteen years old, only in the platoon for two months. Cochrane knew he would forget Bacque pretty quickly. He was not proud of himself for it. Bacque was still somebody's son.

"One last thing," the colonel continued. "You've got two outsiders attached to the platoon. How are they both doing?"

Cochrane leaned back and folded his arms. Best to start with a positive, he figured.

"Sub Officer Hawkins seems alright, sir. He arrived here literally days from finishing training, so he is bound to be of limited use until he finds his feet. But, he's trained as well as any of those zealots from the Orders. I saw him cut down a Jujak trooper without flinching. Yeah, no dramas with him. But you've seen their lot before, sirs. Once he shakes off his training wheels and starts to get comfortable with all of this, he'll be as much of a liability as any of those nut jobs kicked out by the NeoVatican murder academies."

Barker looked uncomfortably across at the colonel.

"Alright, Sergeant," Barker winced, "ease off on the..."

"It's alright," Talau held a hand up to stop the major, "let him speak. Go on, Jim, I want your honest opinion."

"He's not my worry, sir," Cochrane carried on, "it's that bloody serial killer from Strategic Security. Beckmann. She fired that first shot and started all of this. I think Lieutenant Shankar could maybe have diffused the whole situation with a few diplomatic words if the major hadn't gone full psychopath and started executing people. Well, if you haven't picked up her IFF by now, hopefully the jungle has got her. With a bit of luck, she's been eaten by a bloodbriar."

Talau leaned back and crossed his legs at the ankles, his hands resting across his belly.

"Well," he began, "as I said, Intel have checked through all of the footage. According to that, Major Beckmann did indeed fire the first shot. But it was at a Yujingyu soldier who was raising his weapon to a firing position. I don't honestly know, Jim. Was the guy spooked by a sudden movement from one of our lot? I don't know what caused that, but the footage is unequivocal. The major shot a soldier who was in the process of an apparently hostile act."

"No," Cochrane shook his head, "no, sir! Bloody Hexas! They can alter footage easily!"

"We captured and stored the footage live, Sergeant," Barker said.

"Furthermore," Talau continued, "and you know I'm not into 'confirmed kills' and all of that archaic fighter pilot bullshit, but the intel report quotes interesting figures. Your platoon suffered four deaths. The Yujingyu platoon lost ten soldiers. You gave them a far bloodier nose than they did us. But in actual fact, your platoon killed four Yu Jing soldiers. The Hospitaller killed two; he shot one of them later on when he moved in to rescue our wounded soldiers, but judging from his biometric reactions, he had no idea he actually hit."

Cochrane exhaled and nodded. The boy had done well. First ever time in a proper firefight, and he killed two enemy soldiers whilst saving the lives of two of his own. Then Cochrane's brow darkened. The remaining math was simple enough. He looked back up at the colonel and the major.

"You're saying Major Beckmann killed four enemy soldiers? By herself?"

"The same number as your entire platoon combined, Jim," Talau said, "so let's hope she hasn't been eaten by the local flora. Now I distrust Strategic Security just as much as you do – especially when they turn up looking like she does – but we need every trigger finger we can get here. Alright, that's all, Jim. Go get some sleep. Good job out there."

Cochrane remained in place in his chair for another few seconds; partially out of fatigue but also as he searched for the words to counter the colonel's opinion. Then he thought better of it and dragged himself to his feet.

"Thank you, sirs," he suppressed a yawn, "g'night."

***

The door to the accommodation block slid quietly open. Hawkins looked inside the rectangular prism, focusing on where his bed was pushed up against the far wall of the converted container block and the few meager possessions inside. Afternoon was already giving way to the evening. The rest of the platoon would be asleep by now; for Hawkins, that luxury had to wait until he had carried out the two-hour long process of cleaning and maintaining his armor before safely stowing it in the platoon armory. By the time he packaged the pieces of armor away, the armory block itself was almost bare. Most Fusiliers had chosen to take their body armor and rifles with them to their accommodation blocks. Even after his armor was cleaned, he still had to exercise and pray.

Hawkins stepped inside his accommodation block. The door closed behind him, shutting out the natural light of the Paradiso evening as the cool, blue lights running around the edge of the block's ceiling flickered automatically into life. The white interior walls seemed lifeless and sterile after four days exposure to nothing but the teeming life of the jungle. Hawkins toyed with the idea of activating the smart wall projector to display something a little more homely, but fatigue overrode creativity, and he immediately abandoned the idea. Hawkins sighed. He knew it was just the beginning. He placed his MULTI Rifle and sword by his simple desk and sat down on the end of his bed to take off his boots, eyeing the small shower cubicle in the corner of the room wearily.

His eyes fell to rest on the framed image of his family on his desk. Like everybody else, he knew he did, of course, have reams of data capturing both still images and audio/motion of memories with his family, but there was something traditionally comforting about the simplicity of a simple, static picture of family. He looked across at the image of his mother and father, in a caring embrace, together with his older brother and older sister; Nathaniel and Sarah. His father worked in business administration for a hospital; not a hugely well-paid job but certainly enough for Hawkins to grow up in a large house and affluent lifestyle. A hospital funded by the Order of Saint John. Hawkins sighed again. A sickness rose to the back of his throat. His four loved ones smiled out of the picture at him. Would they still smile if they knew that he had brutally cut down and killed another man?

Hawkins sank forward and rested his face in his hands. He had always told himself that he would kill as the very last of all resorts; if he really had to resort to arms, it would be a brief burst of fire to the legs to make sure his target was safely incapacitated, but not killed. *Thou Shalt Not Kill.* It was pretty clear. Yes, the NeoVatican's Third Vatican Council had made it very clear what the modern Church's beliefs were regarding Just War and when taking a life was a viable option; and in accordance with those rules, Hawkins had done absolutely nothing wrong. He defended himself and a comrade, using lethal force to suppress a dangerous, legitimate military target. Training kicked in; training provided by a military Holy Order of the Church itself. So if he did nothing wrong, why did he feel so utterly, utterly awful?

Old, experienced soldiers of the Church who taught him combat techniques in training rarely seemed to show regret when they spoke of it. Of course, there was no boisterous boasting or Neanderthal chest bashing, just simple statements of what happened in war without any show of emotion attached to them. Hawkins never wanted to become that person. The day he killed another human being without a shred of remorse would be the day he questioned whether he still had a soul, despite the fact that there was some solace in telling himself that the man he killed would have had his body and Cube recovered, and could be resurrected; no matter how unlikely that was to transpire. Perhaps that took a little edge off the feeling of guilt.

Hawkins sat upright again. Then there was Beckmann. He had somehow thought there was some connection between them, some mutual understanding and sympathy as the two outsiders in the group. Of course Hawkins was aware of Hexas and what others said, but that did not mean it was right to judge her based on her organization's reputation. It was never right to judge at all. But their few brief talks – which had made him feel significantly better inside – suddenly gave way to a tirade of aggression from her, followed by her disappearing into the jungle, rifle in hand, to resume her dark trade of killing from the shadows. Cochrane said on the return journey that he doubted they would ever see her again. By now she would be dead or on the next mission, now that so much had changed at Alpha Four-Four. He found himself hurt by the thought, but not nearly as much as the constant guilt of taking a life that hung around his neck.

Hawkins shook his head and forced himself to jump up to his feet. He changed his combat fatigues for physical training kit before slipping on and lacing up his running shoes. Hawkins may have struggled with command, theology, infantry tactics, and even at times rifle marksmanship during training. But he was consistently both athletically the fittest and the best close quarter fighter – swords or unarmed – in his training course of four years. And four days in the stifling heat of the jungles of Paradiso, half of which was under the constant threat of enemy action, was no excuse to let standards slip. A ten-mile run in laps around the site perimeter and then an hour of sword practice. Then he would allow himself time for evening prayers and some sleep.

***

Cochrane awoke to the sound of the siren. For a moment, he thought it was his alarm and groggily swatted around for his comlog controls. Then he realized that it was an alert alarm from the speaker in the corner of his room. Swearing, Cochrane leapt out of bed and pulled on the vest of his body armor over his bare torso before activating his comlog for a situational update. It was 3:14am. He cycled through the various command channels of the PSC whilst pulling on his combat trousers and armored boots, noting that the base's perimeter security system was completely intact, functional, and seemed to be unthreatened.

"If this is a bloody false alarm…"

Cochrane growled to himself before his verbalized thoughts were cut off by a transmission through the speaker from one of the NCOs from Number Two Platoon.

"Intruder, intruder, intruder. Suspect intruder reported in the Research Hub. All personnel, report immediately to your mobilization areas."

Only half-equipped but confident that the word 'suspect' in the reported alarm did in fact render this whole exercise futile and pointless, Cochrane grabbed his Combi Rifle and headed to the door of his accommodation block. He stopped halfway, remembering the importance of his indigo beret – it simply would not do to neglect to capitalize on the opportunity to remind everybody that he was Spec-Ops trained, especially when he was legitimately wearing no sleeves and Shankar was not around to reprimand him. Cochrane pulled his beret on over his short hair and walked out into the night.

The stars in the night sky above were obscured by a low level of overcast clouds, leaving the air close and humid. The verbal intruder alarm was repeated again, echoing across from all of the speakers along the perimeter of the base and from fixtures atop taller buildings. Cochrane saw a Fireteam from Number Two Platoon sprinting off in the direction of the research facility. His curiosity urged him to follow them but, in the absence of Shankar, command of Number Three Platoon fell solely to him. He activated his comlog and opened a channel to Jon Lanne and Angelo Garcia, his two section leaders.

"One-One, Two-One," he called, "this is Zero-One. Get your sections together at the assembly point outside Company HQ and await further instructions."

"Is this a drill, Jim?" Garcia asked.

"It's not a scheduled exercise, no, mate," Cochrane replied, "but I think it's probably a false alarm. Who needed sleep after the better part of a week in the woop woop, anyway?"

Fusiliers from Number Three Platoon began filing out of their accommodation blocks and rushing off toward the assembly area, fastening up their body armor as they ran. Cochrane saw Fusilier Rob May sheepishly stepping out of Danielle Mieke's accommodation block a few paces behind her.

"Bloody hell!" Cochrane bellowed across at them. "Now? Really? Come on, dickheads! Get to the assembly area!"

The last of the soldiers disappeared off into the shadows of the early morning. Cochrane turned to follow them but stopped when the platoon armory door opened with a heavy creak. Hawkins stepped out, the breastplate of his heavy armor worn over the top of a black t-shirt, his armored boots atop the darker greens of his Hospitaller-pattern combat trousers. He carried his

MULTI Rifle in one hand and sword in the other, both weapons held casually by their mid points.

"C'mon, sir," Cochrane said, "best we get ourselves to HQ."

"Sorry for being late! It takes this long just to get the breastplate and boots on. Is somebody inside the perimeter, Sergeant?" Hawkins asked.

"Doubt it, sir. Most likely a false alarm. The research staff work around the clock, so that place is always manned. One of them must have set off an alarm, either by accident or they thought they saw a ghost. But we'll need to stay on alert until that place is secure, and that could take a couple of hours. If you'll follow me, Boss, I'll introduce you to the single most important experience you'll ever need to know being attached to the Light Infantry."

"What's that, Sergeant?"

"Hurry up and wait."

Again, Cochrane turned to head toward the Company HQ, and for a second time, he was interrupted when the base's loud speakers burst into life again, the same message also repeated across the platoon's tactical communication net both on screen and audio.

"Casualty, casualty, casualty! Casualty in the Research Hub! Security Team is on route to investigate!"

Cochrane and Hawkins both stared at each other wide-eyed.

"Bugger me, there's somebody in there!" Cochrane growled.

"Should we get over to the HQ assembly point?" Hawkins asked.

"Yes, sir, we should," Cochrane nodded, "but I'm going to the research hub anyway. You coming?"

Hawkins clipped his sword onto his back and took the safety catch off his MULTI Rifle.

"Yep," he replied simply.

Cochrane led the Hospitaller in a quick dash across the darkened military base from the accommodation area toward the research building. Cochrane activated his comlog communicator as he did, first opening a channel with Major Barker and Captain Waczek at Company HQ.

"Alpha-Zero from Three-Papa-Zero," Cochrane called, using the more convoluted communication callsigns for talking at company level. "Three Platoon is assembled at the mobilization area. One-One has tactical command. I was right next to the research hub when the casualty alarm sounded, so I'm moving there now with Broadsword-One."

"Three-Papa-Zero from Alpha-Zero-One," Waczek replied, "I've got your IFF on map; you're not that close to the research hub. Stop looking for more medals and fall back to the assembly point with your platoon!"

"Negative," Cochrane heard Major Barker's voice. "Carry on to the research site and take charge of the team from Two Platoon."

Cochrane saw the off-white, curved research hub up ahead; an almost beautiful building when compared to the squat, angular converted storage containers that had been utilized to form the overwhelming majority of the military buildings. Five Fusiliers from Number Two Platoon were gathered by the doors to the research center. Raised voices were audible even from this range. Cochrane jogged up the path to the hub, checking warily to both sides as he approached the Fusilier Fireteam with Hawkins still close behind. An open palm slammed frantically against the armored glass panel of the door from the inside of the building.

"What's happening?" Cochrane challenged as he approached.

A tall, red-haired female corporal from Number Two Platoon turned to face him.

"The building is in auto lockdown, Sarn't," the woman replied, raising her voice over the banging at the door. "It's a MagnaObra facility, we don't have access to the security controls."

Cochrane barged his way past the five soldiers and peered through the thick glass of the access door. Marcia Gamble – the researcher who only days before had demanded a colleague warn off Cochrane regarding his unwelcome advances – continued to slam her hands against the door.

"Get it open!" she shouted, her voice only just audible through the thick glass and over the blaring alarm sounding from inside the building. "There's something in here! Get the door open!"

Cochrane looked past the panicked woman and saw the entrance foyer behind her was packed with another half-dozen members of the research staff. The interior of the building was plunged in darkness, lit only by the flashing red light of the alarm system. Cochrane shook his head in disgust. MagnaObra's security protocols called to have the building locked down in the event of an intruder alarm being activated. Better to sacrifice their own staff than potentially allow an intruder to escape with valuable data. Information was worth more than life.

"Stand back!" Cochrane yelled, pointing to the door with the muzzle of his Combi Rifle. "Get back!"

Another researcher grabbed Gamble by the arms and hauled her away from the door. Cochrane planted his rifle against the locking mechanism and pulled the trigger. The night lit up with the muzzle flash and the eruption of a solitary gunshot. The access panel smashed and sparked, the display unit instantly fading to nothing. The door remained locked in place.

"Sergeant!" Hawkins called. "I'll have a go!"

Cochrane stood aside as Hawkins unsheathed his sword. With one brutal hack, the blade sliced diagonally through the door, buckling the armored alloy. Cochrane leaned in, teeth gritted, and hauled open the shattered doors to allow the research staff to flood out of the darkened building and into the open. Gamble immediately threw herself against Cochrane's shoulder, sobbing hysterically and shaking with terror. Cochrane tried to suppress a grin but failed. Finally, nearly a decade after enlisting with the Fusiliers, he had his action movie star moment. Clad in non-regulation attire with his bulging arms on full display, he had a pretty blonde crying into his shoulder in gratitude for saving her. It was a once in a lifetime moment, and Cochrane took the few seconds he had to relish it with a smug grin. That grin faded quickly when he looked down and saw the sheer, unadulterated terror in the woman's eyes. Cochrane stopped dead, and for what felt like the first time in an age, he thought about what that must feel like.

"What's happened?" Cochrane asked another of the research staff, a balding, olive-skinned man named Jarvis whom he had exchanged words with only once before.

"Automated security system detected an unauthorized system access and locked us in," the middle-aged scientist stammered. "Then… the lights went out… we moved to the door but on the way… we saw…"

"Sam!" Marcia gasped. "He's dead! We saw him… he…"

"Doctor Adebayo's body…" Jarvis sighed, his thin chest heaving. "He was in the main corridor… he…"

Cochrane gently handed Gamble over to the corporal from Number Two Platoon.

"Is there another way out of the building?" he asked Jarvis.

"There's the emergency escape on the roof," Jarvis replied, "but that's locked, too. Unless something came in or out of the tunnels below…"

Cochrane looked back to the corporal.

"Corporal, get two of your diggers up on the roof and cover that exit. The rest of you stay here and watch this door. Sir?"

Hawkins looked across.

"Did your lot train you in MOUT? Room clearance shit?"

Hawkins nodded. Cochrane looked across at Jarvis.

"Gimme a plan of the building, mate."

"What? I can't…"

"I don't give a shit about your company rules. If you want us to go in there and clear this place, you give me a floor plan. Right now."

Jarvis tapped quickly at his comlog and sent a file across to Cochrane. He opened the floor plan, shared it with Hawkins, and quickly plotted a clearance plan for the two to carry out.

"Alpha-Zero, this is Three-Papa-Zero," Cochrane called Barker. "Civilians from the research facility are secured. I'm moving in to investigate with Broadsword-One."

"Copied," Barker replied, "we're monitoring your comms and are aware of one casualty and an emergency exit to secure in turn. A second team will be with you in thirty seconds."

"Copied," Cochrane replied before turning back to Hawkins. "I'm Number One, you're Two. Let's go."

Illuminating his Combi Rifle's infrared lamp and cycling his lens' vision modes to take full advantage of the pool of light created by it, Cochrane moved quickly through the shattered doors and into the research facility. He found himself in a small entrance foyer, complete with an empty reception desk and seating area decorated with an ornate water feature. The whole deserted scene was illuminated with a flashing red emergency light as a klaxon blared out incessantly. Cochrane moved quickly forward, his rifle raised to his shoulder as he systematically cleared every vacant space he encountered, moving past the foyer and into the main corridor leading toward the Cosmolite entrance itself.

Cochrane connected to Hawkins' lens and brought the other soldier's visual picture up in the corner of his own. The young Hospitaller moved quickly and efficiently behind him, his larger MULTI Rifle held up and ready as he advanced in an eerie silence. The two soldiers met a junction in the corridor and took covering positions, back to back, to check down both ends. Cochrane saw nothing ahead but doors leading into office spaces, a conference room, and a recreational area.

"Over there!" Hawkins reported. "There he is!"

Cochrane looked over and saw a crumpled body by the doorway to a small storage room. Even from this distance, bathed in the flashing red lights, Cochrane recognized Adebayo. He advanced past Hawkins, his rifle moving to check every corner and alcove. Once Cochrane took position at the end of the corridor, Hawkins dropped to one knee to check the fallen scientist.

"He's alive!" Hawkins said. "His pulse is fine! Just unconscious."

"Can you wake him up?" Cochrane asked, peering down both ends of the corridor.

"Not really, no..."

"Thought you were a Hospitaller, sir. Doesn't that mean you know medical stuff?"

"You're a Fusilier," Hawkins retorted in a hushed voice. "Do you know how to fire a French musket?"

Cochrane shrugged.

"Fair enough."

The comlog suddenly burst alive with a series of agitated voices hurriedly over-talking each other before Barker shouted over them all.

"Alpha-Zero to Two-Three-One! Comm discipline!"

"Two-Three-One to Alpha-Zero! The emergency escape on the roof has just opened!" A voice from the Number Two Platoon team shouted.

"Hold position! Wait there!"

Cochrane looked across at Hawkins. His desire to find and challenge the intruder was quickly overridden by experience and common sense.

"Let's get him out of here," Cochrane nodded down at the unconscious scientist.

Cochrane slung Adebayo's prone body up over one shoulder and retreated quickly back toward the entrance.

"Alpha-Zero to Three-Zero-One," Barker called Cochrane, "fall back to the foyer. There's a Fireteam waiting there for you. Emergency escape on the roof has now been opened but still no sign of the intruder."

"Zero-One copied," Cochrane responded, backing slowly down the corridor with his Combi Rifle held ready in one hand, Hawkins retreating alongside him.

Chapter Seven

"Gohon-me."

Hawkins bowed his head and took up his stance to commence the kata, his sword held at the ready. Uttering the words of the kendo *tachi kata* he had learned as a child seemed strange, almost disrespectful given the origins of the martial art in Japan, and that ancient nation's integral part in the modern Yu Jing alliance – despite the Japanese Secessionist Army's concerted efforts to break away. As Hawkins slid his feet carefully from stance to stance, smoothly moving his blade through a succession of clinically precise attacks and defenses, he could not help but remember the contempt and criticism that came his way during his martial arts training with the Hospitallers, knowing that he had trained in Asian-originated martial arts as a child.

The morning sun beat down on the small scrub patch of earth behind the dining hall where he practiced, clad in his combat trousers and black t-shirt, emblazoned with a white cross on the left breast. The sounds of construction – now apparently a permanent feature during the daylight hours – continued from all around as new accommodation blocks were fork-lifted on top of the existing containers, perimeter defenses were solidified, vegetation was burnt down, and ground was flattened by engineering dronbots in preparation of a new landing strip.

Even with the events of the early hours disturbing his sleep, Hawkins felt better for some rest. Whoever or whatever had infiltrated the research facility only hours before had escaped without a trace – the source of a thousand rumors and theories across the encampment over breakfast – but the research staff were all safe, and the one casualty had awoken with nothing more than a sore head. Whatever that scientist had to say about his experiences was above Hawkins' meager rank, although given the secretive nature of the fiercely competitive MagnaObra company, he doubted even Major Barker as the ranking military officer at Alpha Four-Four would be privy to what that man saw inside the research facility. Even the message he had received only an hour before, demanding a full written report to be submitted to his seniors within the Order of Saint John, did little to dampen his positivity over his brief role in securing the safety of the hub's scientists. He had no doubt, however, that a more direct conversation with his immediate superior, Father-Officer Valconi, would emerge as a result of his written report. A platoon-level firefight resulting in fatalities, followed by an intrusion in the MagnaObra research hub, would demand it.

Hawkins completed his kata, bowing before returning his sword to his side. He had been aware of prying eyes watching his every move during the latter half of the kata, and he now turned to face his audience. Sat along a pile of empty storage crates, Fusiliers Carson, Southee, and King watched him silently. Hawkins sheathed his sword and offered them a polite nod.

"D'you learn that in your Order, sir?" King asked.

"No, before I joined up. It's Kendo."

"Does it… help, with real fighting?" the young, lanky soldier followed up.

"Yes," Hawkins answered after a reflective pause, "I mean, the Order taught me everything I've needed so far, but certainly a decade spent on three martial arts before joining was very… helpful."

Hawkins considered moving on to mention his childhood obsession with the skilled swordmasters catapulted into fame when their spectacular fights were broadcast into people's homes from the *Aristeia!* tournaments. Perhaps that was too much of a revelation to make to a stranger, although Hawkins found it difficult to stop from boasting that the great Shona Carano herself had complemented him on his skills with a sword when she once visited the fortress-monastery of Skovorodino to inspect the standard of training, declaring him to be the best in his class and even calling him a natural warrior.

"Sir," Carson said, standing up and taking a pace toward Hawkins, "we were talking over breakfast. We just wanted to say… thank you. For grabbing Lucia and George the other day. When they took that hit. They'd have died if you hadn't dragged them away from that crater."

Hawkins narrowed his eyes in surprise. Ever since that exchange of fire with the Yujingyu, the subject of death had not been far from his mind. However, with the benefit of a good few hours' sleep, that subject now felt far less morbid. There was a chance that the man he had killed would be up and running again soon enough, his memories transferred from his Cube into a biosynthetic body. A slim chance. Similarly, if Hawkins had not rescued Lucia Rossi and George Trent, their deaths possibly would not have been the end. A brief comparison between the horrifically wasteful wars that blighted Earth's history and the comparative civility of modern, low casualty conflicts ran through his mind before he realized he had not answered Carson. He turned to the medic.

"It's very kind of you to say. I was just in the right place at the right time to do something useful. I rather thought that I was overdue a useful act."

"For what it's worth, sir," Southee smiled, "everybody noticed. We all know you took a few rounds to help us out. It's appreciated."

"I was encased in some of the best armor that Omnia Research can provide." Hawkins shrugged. "It's easy to play the hero when you're bulletproof."

"With respect, sir," Southee grinned, "I'm gonna call bullshit on that. A four point five can get through ORC armor well enough."

Hawkins looked across at the pretty Fusilier, smiled, and bowed his head in gratitude at her kind words.

"Were you in the hub last night with the sarn't?" Carson asked suddenly.

Hawkins turned back to the medic, realizing that the exchange of words was one of the longest he had had with any of the Fusiliers since he was attached to their unit.

"Yes. That's right."

"D'you see much in there, sir?"

"Nothing, really," Hawkins admitted, "I'd say that we would find out soon enough, but from what Major Barker told me and the sergeant after it all, we're not expecting MagnaObra to be particularly forthcoming with what happened in there. Even more so after I cut their security door in half."

King let out a laugh.

"Word is that there's a load of tunnels and rooms under the hub," he said, his gray eyes alight with excitement. "I heard that something came up through the tunnels! Some fuckin' alien shit stompin' around in there and having a swipe at the scientists!"

Hawkins continued to smile politely and shrugged.

"I honestly have no idea," he said, "the only thing we know for a fact is that one of their scientists hit the alarm after she believed she saw evidence of an attempt to hack their main frame. Then the lights went out, and then one of their staff was knocked unconscious. That really is all that is fact. The rest is just speculation."

Carson nodded for a moment, opened his mouth to say something, thought better of it, and then spoke anyway.

"Have you ever seen *Escape from Paradiso 2*, sir?" he suddenly blurted out. "Is it accurate, at all?"

Hawkins could not help but laugh briefly. He hoped his mirth did not come across as confrontational. Of course he had seen the latest blockbuster holofilm released around the immensely successful Padre-Inquisitor Mendoza brand. Every young Hospitaller had. But that was not an easy question to answer. Many of the old veterans of the Order were overtly hostile toward the iconic Mendoza brand, claiming disrespect or even heresy. But for the younger knights, there was perhaps the realization that, even though the holomovies and HexaDome appearances were stylized and embellished at best – and overly choreographed lies at worst – Mendoza was still a positive role model and brought in a huge amount of good publicity to the NeoVatican's Military Orders. Even if that was a fortunate second order effect that came well after the primary goal of profit making.

"Yes, I've seen a few of Mendoza's outings!" Hawkins smiled. "I'd... take it with a pinch of salt. It's just supposed to be entertaining, it's really not an accurate depiction of life in one of the Holy Orders."

A truck drove past the scrubland by the dining block, rounding a corner in the dusty road threading through the base before disappearing off toward the landing strip building site near the south perimeter.

"What's different?" Carson asked.

"Well," Hawkins scratched his chin, wondering what he could divulge without betraying any confidences of his Order, "the people who make those holomovies and Maya shows really like to dwell on the myths and clichés from the medieval era, rather than the truth of what it's like now. The characters in the show all live in cells in the monastery which look like prison cells. Yes, our rooms are called cells to keep with tradition, but they're perfectly comfortable. We've got modern amenities. We get time off to talk to friends – watch holomovies about heroic Military Order knights – that sort of thing. Nobody would put themselves forward for selection if we actually lived in stone cells with just a block of wood for a pillow and a copy of the Bible."

"D'you have to take vows, sir?" Southee asked.

"Yes," Hawkins replied as four soldiers jogged past the dining block on the perimeter running track, "but they're modern interpretations. The vow of obedience is very similar to your military discipline…"

"What about the vow of chastity, sir?" Southee demanded.

"It's a modern interpretation again," Hawkins explained carefully, "a lot of people think that because we have two ranks and one is religious that it means we are priests. We're not. We're allowed to have relationships, get married, start families, all that. It's just a lot more controlled. If I met somebody, I would have to submit the correct forms to seek approval from my Order for the relationship to be allowed to continue."

Hawkins found even himself nearly convinced by the description he reeled out to the three Fusiliers. The theory sounded good enough. In practice, Hawkins had known of three knight-aspirants who had applied for approval to pursue a relationship with individuals they met during training. All three applications had been rejected by the Order; one resulting in a formal reprimand for pursuing a relationship with a member of the instructional staff.

"Oh," Southee tilted her head to one side, "that doesn't sound as bad as I thought."

"Really?" Carson exclaimed. "It sounds a bit… intrusive, if you don't mind me saying, sir."

"Jeez!" King grinned. "Wouldn't work for me! They'd need a full time clerk to keep up with all of the forms I'd be submitting!"

Hawkins winced, thinking how best to explain to the young Fusilier that the submitted forms were for serious, committed relationships – not a string of one night stands which was in clear contravention of the vow he had only just described. He elected to change the subject instead.

"The vow of poverty limits our pay," Hawkins continued. "For me as a Brother-Sub Officer, I get paid the same as a Fusilier lieutenant as that is the equivalent rank, but whereas you are all getting extra pay for being here – deployment pay for being away from home and being put in harm's way – I'm not allowed to claim any extra benefits. That money all goes directly to my Order for upkeep. Anything extra goes to charity."

Carson looked down for a moment.

"Fancy that!" the dark-haired medic's brow raised. "I just got a message from Jiv Khatri in Two Platoon. He says that Hexa major has just turned up at the perimeter."

Hawkins let out a breath, his stomach suddenly contracting.

"Awesome!" King leered. "She is damn hot! I mean, I know you're the self-appointed platoon hottie, in your own words, Nat, but that woman leaves you way, way behind."

"Oh, piss off, Luc!" Southee snapped.

Hawkins found he had already back stepped several paces away from the three Fusiliers, edging toward the eastern perimeter as soon as he checked the PSC logs on the comlog.

"Would you excuse me, please?" he smiled to the trio of soldiers with a courteous nod of the head before turning and walking quickly away.

Once out of sight of the three Fusiliers, Hawkins picked up his pace to a jog as he headed across to the encampment's inner perimeter. An Uro utility vehicle drove past him on the perimeter track, kicking up clouds of yellow-or-ange sand and dust from its thick, off-road tires. A surveillance drone buzzed gently overhead in the sunlit, clear blue sky; an automated Sierra Dronbot stomped carefully along the outer perimeter track at the bottom of the embankment below, the four-legged machine swiveling its main body slowly from left to right as its Heavy Machine Gun tracked along the open ground between the northern perimeter of Alpha Four-Four and the endless jungle sprawling out ahead.

Hawkins reached the eastern inner perimeter and looked down the embankment to see a single figure walking slowly up the hill. Beckmann held her MULTI Sniper Rifle across her chest, her flawless face streaked with smeared lines where sweat had run across days of grime and dirt. She looked up at Hawkins as she approached. The tall woman stopped a few paces from him and slung her rifle over one shoulder. Her tight overalls faded back to their natural black color but remained covered in yellow dust and green stains.

"Ma'am," Hawkins began, "I thought I should apologize for…"

Beckmann held up a hand to stop him, reaching into her belt to produce a cigarette and chrome plated lighter.

"I owe you the apology," she said quietly as she lit the paper-wrapped chemical stick and drew in on the sugary fumes. "I shouldn't have raised my voice like that. Certainly not in front of lower ranks. It was unprofessional.

More importantly, it was unkind."

Hawkins swallowed, the rattling and buzzing of insects around them providing a constant backdrop against the rumble of vehicle engines and the hammering of construction from the far side of the base. He remembered seeing her turn to disappear into the jungle when they last saw each other, moving back to face the advance of two platoons of enemy soldiers.

"Did you... run into much out there?" Hawkins asked hesitantly.

Beckmann blew out a small cloud of smoke that quickly dissipated. Her eyes were red and exhausted.

"Don't you worry about that," she half-smiled without a shred of warmth or mirth on her lips. "You all made it back here safely, no? Then it was worth me staying out that extra time to slow them down. But right now, I need to clean this rifle, get a shower, and get some sleep. I haven't slept properly in a week now, and I'm feeling it."

"I can clean your rifle if you need some sleep, ma'am," Hawkins offered. "I'd imagine Major Barker will want to catch you up on what you've missed here in the last few days."

Hawkins immediately regretted his words for sounding far too desperate for her approval, so he stood up straighter and folded his arms, forcing his expression to one of utter neutrality. Beckmann shook her head.

"These things are a little more temperamental than Combi Rifles and MULTI Rifles," she nodded to the sniper rifle on her back. "I'd best do it myself. And you don't need to keep calling me 'ma'am,' not when there is nobody else about, at least."

"I... don't know your name."

Beckmann narrowed her tired, deep blue eyes.

"Lisette," she said after a pause, "my name's Lisette."

"Well, it's nice to... I mean... I'm glad you're safe," Hawkins found himself stumbling over his words, still, next to the beautiful woman.

Beckmann finished her cigarette and tossed the butt aside before wiping wearily at her reddened eyes. After a pause, she looked back up at Hawkins again.

"What's the last thing you listened to?" she suddenly demanded.

"Sorry?"

"Music. What's the last album you had on?"

Hawkins reached down to his comlog and checked to see what had played through his earpiece on his morning run.

"Generation Damned," he answered hesitantly.

Beckmann's face lit up with a smile, somewhere between genuinely warm and tragically disappointed.

"Oh... come on, now! If you want psychedelic rock, Dark Move did that way better thirty years ago! You've heard of them, right? Seriously, Kyle, you need to listen to some proper music, not this hormonal kid's shit."

"Right," Hawkins nodded, "I'll try that."

"But not their first three albums. They're shit. Go straight to 'On Rock.'"

Hawkins nodded again. Beckmann turned and walked away toward the platoon armory block. After a few paces, she turned mid-stride, stepping backward but looking across at him.

"Dark Move, On Rock," she repeated, her face lit up enthusiastically and her tone animated. "Seriously, Kyle, it'll blow your fucking mind. Single coil through valve distortion, it's awesome. I'll be testing you when I next see you to make sure you've listened to it."

Hawkins smiled. Beckmann flashed him a wink and walked off toward the armory.

***

Connecting her lens to one of the truck's exterior cameras, Shankar sank forward against her seat harness and concentrated on the sun-kissed jungle sprawling out to either side of the dusty road. From what little she had been briefed after being discharged from the hospital, this would most likely be her last drive from the airstrip at Hill Eight Six, as work was ongoing to complete a landing strip at Alpha Four-Four itself as part of the site's expansion. And that was even before the intruder broke into the research hub in the early hours of that morning. Shankar shook her head. She would not be surprised if a TAG depot sprouted up overnight at the site, given the increasing political attention it was gaining.

Then again, Shankar mused, the back of the very truck she sat in was evidence enough of the military complex's continued commitment to expanding and defending the research site built over the Cosmolite. The front end of the truck's hold was packed with containers housing construction drones, and sat with them was a tired-looking engineering sergeant whose heavy eyes fought to stay open beneath their bushy, red brows. The only other occupants of the truck were three soldiers dressed in the same fatigues as Shankar. However, the circular badge of the ORC Heavy Tactical Group on their shoulders and the distinctively marked containers next to them that housed their heavy armor marked them out as veteran soldiers, a cut above Shankar's Fusiliers, and no doubt sent there to bolster the defenses further still.

A flare of pain shot up Shankar's bicep, reminding her of the injury that necessitated the last few days in the hospital and the layers of cloned skin that had been surgically affixed to her arm. She was one of the lucky ones; the first of the wounded to return to duty from that frantic firefight. Then there were the dead. Shankar had heard nothing about whether any of her four dead soldiers would be resurrected, their consciousness and memories transferred from their Cubes to a biosynthetic body based on their original form; a chance to live again, but nothing like the cripplingly expensive procedure of using cloned tissue to create a superior Lhost. Even the lower cost biosynthetic body was beyond the means of the majority of soldiers. But that did not stop those left behind hoping and wondering.

Shankar was momentarily knocked up off her seat as the heavy truck crested a bumpy ridge in the road before turning a corner to head back down slope. The sudden jolt sent another wave of pain across Shankar's arm, causing her to suppress a hiss. She remembered the call she made to David, her fiancé, from the hospital. *"I took a bit of a tumble in a training accident."* It was a white lie to stop him from worrying, but it was still a lie nonetheless. Shankar shook her head. They were not even married yet and she was already lying to him. Then there was the promotion to captain. She had still not broached that subject, and there was no excuse to tell herself about white lies. It was simple self-preservation. She was avoiding the confrontation; nothing deeper than that.

Up ahead, the familiar sight of Alpha Four-Four became visible from one of the truck's exterior cameras through a gap in the trees. Even from this distance, Shankar could already make out major changes; the surrounding jungle had been cut and burnt back in every direction, allowing a new perimeter to be constructed at the bottom of the plateau. At the top, the number of buildings constructed out of the ubiquitous storage containers seemed to have tripled. Shankar caught a glimpse of the research hub, its smooth, off-white walls standing out in stark contrast to the olive green, rust red, and deep blue storage containers surrounding it.

The Cosmolite within that building now seemed to hold ten times the importance it did when she had last walked away from it to commence the patrol a week ago. Yu Jing's push across the border would not, she thought, have ever occurred if the research station was not so close to their territory. Somebody had broken in to the hub only two nights before, and she was eager to find out more details as soon as she stepped off the truck.

The Cosmolite itself was a physical, direct link from the entire age humanity now found itself within to the ancient unknown. With space travel finally becoming a reality after the discovery of the first viable wormhole, the old superpowers of 20th and 21st century Earth had poured their finances and resources into two vast seed ships to colonize planets beyond the Sol System; the *Ariadna* and the *Aurora*. Their destination was the fourth planet of the Helios system, identified as habitable by probes sent through the wormhole. That planet was named Dawn. Both of the ships were crammed with an entire population of colonists, scientists, and military contingents made up of volunteers from America, Russia, and the European Union.

The *Ariadna* was the first to reach Dawn, and initially, progress was promising. However, shortly after the *Aurora* was enveloped within the dark folds of the wormhole, catastrophe struck. The wormhole collapsed. Contact with Dawn was lost and the *Aurora* disappeared entirely, never reaching her destination. Back on Earth, the old superpowers were left to face a succession of challenges which, partially influenced by the crippling debts of the failed colony ships, they were unable to overcome. New alliances were quickly formed. PanOceania and Yu Jing both arose from the ashes of the 21st century to dominate human affairs.

More than a century later, a PanOceanian scout ship re-established contact with Dawn via a second wormhole, and the nation that had emerged from the Separatist Wars that raged following the violent conflicts that tore apart the societies of the original colonists from the *Ariadna*. But it was the story of the *Aurora* that held more of a captivating mystery. The *Aurora* did survive the collapse of the wormhole. But it arrived at an entirely different destination. It arrived at the planet of Paradiso. And it was only months after that the colonists from the *Aurora* discovered the first Cosmolites – evidence of alien technology – not far from their crash site and first settlements.

Shankar exhaled and leaned back in her seat, looking through the external camera at the research hub once again. Whatever lay within could hold the key to the events leading to the loss of the entire colony began by the ill-fated *Aurora*. That building represented the planet's link to this entire age of humanity; to the dominance of the PanOceanian alliance following the collapse of the United States, the European Union, and the Russian Federation back on Earth. For the first time, looking at that sleek, white building, Shankar began to realize why Cochrane was so fascinated by whatever lay inside, past those cold security doors installed by the MagnaObra company.

The truck drove up the shallow incline on the last leg of the route to Alpha Four-Four. Shankar's brow raised as she surveyed the increase in perimeter security; more regular sensor posts, Heavy Machine Gun emplacements, dronbots, even minefields. The truck stopped outside the Company HQ block, which also now sported a newer, larger array of communication aerials. The three ORC soldiers stood and opened the back of the truck to reveal Captain Waczek and Sergeant Cochrane waiting by the entrance to the HQ. Waczek stepped out to meet the three troopers as they jumped down from the back of the truck.

"Corporal Burns?"

A powerfully built woman with dark skin stepped out to meet the captain.

"Ma'am."

"Welcome to Alpha Four-Four," Waczek winced, "you and your team are attached to Number Two Platoon, under 2nd Lieutenant Howe. He's in the

HQ, so go introduce yourselves."

Shankar jumped down from the back of the truck as the three ORC soldiers filed into the HQ, the drop down leaving her with an ungracious squat at the end due to her diminutive stature. Waczek paced across to her and smiled.

"Hello, Priya! Welcome back. Glad to see you're all in one piece. You doing okay?"

Shankar hesitated, finding herself wary of the uncharacteristic display of warmth from the Company 2IC.

"Yes… all good, ma'am."

"Don't worry about the 'ma'am' when we're away from the troops," Waczek said. "Major Barker told me to apologize on his behalf for not being here to welcome you back, but he's in and out of here every day at the moment, with all that's been going on. He's over at Regimental HQ at the moment but should be back tonight. Look, I've got to speak with the new engineer here about the airstrip build, but I'll catch you later. Jim will fill you in on what you've missed."

Waczek moved across to greet the last arrival from the truck, the engineer NCO who nearly slept the whole journey across. Shankar reached back into the truck to grab her kitbag, eager to retrieve it herself before Cochrane offered to carry it for her. The burly sergeant paced across with a big grin visible between the bristles of his brown beard.

"G'day, Boss!" Cochrane beamed. "Welcome back! You all fixed up?"

"Just about," Shankar gritted her teeth as pain lanced up her arm again as she slung her camouflaged kit bag over one shoulder.

"D'you want me to carry that for you?" Cochrane offered as the two walked toward the Number Three Platoon accommodation area.

"No," Shankar replied, "what have I missed? I heard about the break in at the hub."

"Yeah," Cochrane nodded as two engineers walked past them and began unloading containers from the back of the truck, "predictably, MagnaObra are playing their cards close to their chest on that one. Alarm went off because one of their staff thought there was an unauthorized access to their main terminal. The place went into lockdown, and then another of their staff was knocked out."

"Knocked out?" Shankar repeated.

"Yeah," Cochrane replied, narrowing his eyes as they rounded a corner and both received a face full of the intense ferocity of the morning sun, "don't know what happened there. MagnaObra hasn't shared any security footage with us or allowed us to talk to the staff. I managed to get a few words in from a couple of them after the incident, but it all got locked down pretty quickly. The rumor around camp is that some bloody alien came up through the tunnels below the Cosmolite, but I'm calling bullshit on that."

Shankar adjusted the angle her bag sat on her throbbing shoulder. She knew Cochrane should not have engaged with the research contractor staff, but she was also eager to know what was going on inside the mysterious building they defended.

"What d'you reckon, then?" she asked.

"Well, first off, I can't see why a bloody alien would want to access a research terminal. Second, my experience of fighting aliens is that they don't knock people unconscious. They bloody well kill 'em. So my gut says a Yujingyu operative got in there. Some ninja or something. But..."

Shankar stopped, ostensibly to concentrate on Cochrane's words but actually to swap shoulders with her bag.

"But?" she queried.

Cochrane scratched his bearded chin and shook his head.

"Just... something one of the researchers said. She said that after she raised the alarm... she said she heard her dead mother singing to her. I know that sounds... unlikely. I put it down to panic, you know, a scientist with no experience of coping with danger suddenly being locked in a darkened building with a stranger inside. Maybe it's just that. It just struck me as odd. She was absolutely sure of it. Said she heard her mum singing her the song she used to sing when she was a kid."

Shankar exhaled and shook her head. Whether the story was true or not, the imagery of a dead woman's ghost singing in the darkness was enough to send goose bumps rising across the skin of her arms; both original and bio-synthetic.

"Alright," she said, resuming the walk back toward her accommodation block, "I guess we just wait and see there, although my guess is we won't hear anything else about whatever happened. What else have I missed?"

"With the casualties we took, I've kept us in two slightly larger sections. Number One Platoon is dug in not far from where we exchanged shots with the Yujingyu. They've had a few minor skirmishes but nothing significant. The politics are still ongoing regarding who is trespassing in whose territory, but the news networks reckon that O-12 is siding with them, not us. As for the rest of it, we're just stuck here taking it in turns with Two Platoon for perimeter security."

Shankar saw the collection of accommodation blocks up ahead, scattered haphazardly around a concrete square that had already cracked up to allow weeds and small vines to punch a few inches up toward the sun. Her own block, a dusty, white rectangular prism at the far end of the little complex, suddenly seemed like a true home. She eagerly awaited the chance to shut the door on the rest of the world, even if for only a few minutes.

"And how is the platoon? How's everybody doing?" she asked.

"Mainly alright," Cochrane answered, "Pierre Moulin wants to apply to transfer to the ORCs. Again. I've told him he still isn't good enough. Jack Byron asked for compassionate leave because his parents' dog died, if you bloody believe that. Nat Southee is in a pissy mood because now that we've lost some guys, she thought it was a good time to demand promotion to lance corporal. So I made her the section's machine gunner instead. She wants responsibility; she can lug that little ripper around with her. Oh, and Rob May and Danni Mieke are nailing each other. That's about it. Everybody else is behaving."

Shankar let out a grumble and shook her head. Her temples began to throb.

"Send them all my way. I'll talk to them."

"No need. I've sorted them all out."

Shankar looked up at the towering sergeant.

"Pierre Moulin wants to advance in his career and you've told him he's shit, so he's now disillusioned and resentful. Jack Byron is a soft touch and he needs a friendly ear, not some idiot telling him to toughen up. Nat Southee is a decent soldier, but she's hardly built like a brick shithouse, and you've got her dragging a Heavy Machine Gun around. And what have you done about Rob and Danni?"

Cochrane folded his thick arms defensively.

"I told them both to bloody well keep it in their daks. Or at least be discreet."

"Both of them are hardly impetuous, frivolous types. My concern is that this isn't a fling, it might be serious. In which case they will carry on and I need to transfer one of them out of this battalion."

Cochrane fixed Shankar with a stern stare as she opened the door to her room.

"You're pandering to them, Priya. They're soldiers. They need to do what they're told. We're in command. They don't hold us to ransom with career advancement demands and dead pets!"

Shankar took a step back away from the huge NCO toward the door to her accommodation block. Her arm hurt. Her head hurt. Her eyes ached with weariness. Cochrane's words frayed her already short temper with their patronizing accusations.

"I'm not having this conversation, Jim!" she snapped. "Just send them all my way and I'll deal with them. Trust me, when bullets start flying again, you will be the first soldier in this platoon I turn to for help. But when it comes to the pastoral care of the men and woman in this platoon, you might as well stay out of it because you are absolutely useless sometimes!"

Shankar stormed into her room and slammed the door shut behind her.

***

The sudden and unannounced addition of a small gymnasium block being added to the basic facilities at Alpha Four-Four did a little to raise Cochrane's spirits, but not much. After a late afternoon workout and shower, he now found himself sat alone in the dining block listening to the buzz of the faulty, flickering white lights above his head as he stared at his meal tray with disinterest. The evening sun dipped beneath the horizon, painting the clear sky in a vivid panorama of lilacs and purples as the day creatures of the Paradiso jungles handed over to the night shift. Number Two Platoon still held perimeter guard duty; most of Number Three Platoon would by now be in their own accommodation blocks or crammed into the small recreation room.

Cochrane glanced over at the only other occupied table in the dining hall where three of the contracted research staff shared a quiet laugh over their dessert. Sam Adebayo was one of the three researchers; Cochrane had not spoken with him since their very brief exchange following the scientist regaining consciousness after Cochrane and Hawkins rescued him from the hub. At the far side of the small hall, Corporals Lanne and Garcia slid their trays across the counter of pre-prepared foods, idly picking through what was left of the original selection now that the majority of base personnel had fed and departed. Cochrane glanced down at his own food, his brow raised as he realized how much he now took for granted being able to eat freshly cooked pizza and chocolate cake even on an isolated outpost in the middle of a jungle. That introspection continued as again he found himself ruminating on Shankar's words from earlier. *"Thanks for running the entire platoon in my absence, Jim,"* would have been far more appropriate than the sudden and unprovoked tirade of abuse he had received, Cochrane mused miserably, *"Thanks for leading the platoon safely back to base after I buggered off to hospital by air!"*

"Evenin'," Jonny Lanne flashed a brief smile as he dropped his tray of food noisily on the table opposite Cochrane before pulling up a chair.

"Y'alright, Jim?" Angelo Garcia nodded as he, too, sat at the table.

Cochrane grunted a greeting.

"Highlight of my week," Lanne turned to Garcia, clearly continuing a conversation from when they walked in to the dining block, "and I'm being pretty subtle in scoping her out."

"Subtle?" Garcia sneered. "You sure that word means what you think it means?"

Cochrane glanced across at the two corporals.

"What's that, then?" he demanded.

"The young Hexa major," Garcia shook his head with a sneer. "Jonny's the latest in the long line of our guys who've taken a shine to her. On the one hand, I can't blame him. On the other, he's being pretty fuckin' tragic in how he is trying to get her to notice him. Particularly given that he is repulsive to look at. I mean, look at his face, Jim. He's absolutely hideous."

Cochrane slammed down his cutlery.

"You two need to pack that shit in!" he hissed a warning.

Lanne glanced across nervously, a forced and insincere smile tugging at his thin lips whilst Garcia leaned back in his chair, folding his muscular, tattooed arms across his barrel chest.

"Come on, Jim," Garcia snorted, "you gonna tell me that you're some white knight, now? What's gotten into you?"

"No!" Cochrane sneered, shaking his head in derision. "That's not what I meant! Look, if you want to go letching over some woman whilst you're out here, I get that. Just not her. Got it?"

"Why's that, Jim?" Lanne smiled. "You staking your claim?"

"Piss off, Jonny!" Cochrane retorted, leaning in, checking over at the table of scientists to ensure they were out of earshot. "Absolutely not! I'm telling you to back off from that war criminal, serial killer bitch before you wake up with your throat slit and your balls ripped off! Have you never heard of these bastards?"

Garcia let out a long sigh.

"Come on, mate!" the veteran corporal grunted. "You sound like a bloody Nod! You believe that shit about Hexas? They thrive on the rumors! They generate the myths themselves, just to sound badass! I don't buy it, mate. Not one bit."

"Then you're a bloody idiot," Cochrane folded his arms and rested them on the table in front of him, "because last time I looked, there's only one of us here with time in Indigo, and it isn't you. You think the rumors and myths are bullshit? You're right. The truth is ten times worse, digger. Take my advice and stay well, well away from that psychopath. If she is showing even the slightest bit of interest in any one of you, don't be the sucker who falls for it and ends up as a dead pawn in some Hexa espionage game."

Lanne began to offer a counter argument, but Cochrane immediately lost interest as he saw the three MagnaObra scientists stand from their table and move over to the recycling bins at the far end of the dining block. Ignoring the salacious comments from his two comrades, Cochrane shot to his feet, hurried over to the recycling bins, quickly cleared his tray, and then dashed after the three scientists as they left the building. A blast of hot evening air hit Cochrane as he left the cool dining block behind, the doors sliding smoothly shut behind him.

"Sam!" Cochrane called out. "Wait up!"

Adebayo turned and saw Cochrane approaching. He looked back over at his two colleagues.

"I'll catch you up later," he said to dismiss them.

Cochrane waited until Adebayo's two juniors were well out of earshot and then turned to regard the shorter man.

"You alright?" he began, hoping a demonstration of concern would ease into the conversation on the right note. "I haven't seen you since the break in at the hub."

"Oh, I'm fine, Jim," Adebayo scratched the back of his neck, "just got back this morning. The company wanted to run some medical checks, just in case."

"Yeah," Cochrane nodded, "people can dismiss a knock to the head and unconsciousness as a nothing, but there can be some serious shit underlying it if it isn't checked out. Good that your company is looking after you."

"Oh, I wasn't hit on the head," Adebayo said. "I was choked. Somebody grabbed me from behind. Put me in some sort of lock. That was the last thing I remember about that night."

Cochrane immediately fought to keep a stoic, straight face. Adebayo had been put in a sleeper hold? That led to a hundred follow up questions. But no, Adebayo was an intelligent man. Cochrane needed to play it cool and double back to that point later; otherwise, he would arouse suspicion and shut down his inside source.

"Main thing is that you're alright, Sam."

"Thanks to you and the sub officer from the Hospitallers, from what I hear," Adebayo said, "thank you for that. I gather you both got in a bit of trouble for hacking open the door and freeing us."

Cochrane shrugged. That was not entirely true. From what he had heard from Captain Waczek, MagraObra was furiously attempting to file charges against both the PanOceanian military and the Hospitallers for security transgressions. The word passed down from Colonel Talau was to not lose any sleep over it. The PanOceanian Military Complex's view of prioritizing civilian life over corporate secrets was very clear, and command supported Cochrane's decision.

"Yeah, we're in the firing line," Cochrane lied, "but you know... it was worth it. We're here to look after you guys. Not your fault that your security system wasn't robust enough to keep an intruder out."

"Who do you think it was?" the thin scientist asked.

"I shouldn't really say anything, but I'm fairly certain it was a Yujingyu intelligence operative," Cochrane lied again, his theories moving swiftly away from that avenue now that he categorically knew the intruder took the more difficult option of knocking Adebayo unconscious. It would have been far easier – and certainly more typical of Yu Jing's approach to such matters – to just kill him.

"Just... keep that to yourself," Cochrane muttered quietly, "I could get in a lot of trouble for telling you this stuff. Even more trouble than I'm already in for saving you and your mates."

Adebayo smiled uncomfortably.

"Well, thank you, Jim. Thanks a lot for getting us all out of there. I realize how bad that must look to a non-company man, but we all signed disclaimers to work here. We all know the importance of this project and that, sadly, our safety might sometimes be considered secondary."

Cochrane suppressed a grin. That was the perfect cue. That was his in.

"You're right, I don't get it," he said. "I mean, what's so important about that place anyway? You guys get locked inside at the first sign of danger, we end up in a firefight in the jungle and lose four guys because Yu Jing wants this facility. What are we all taking these risks for?"

Adebayo's face fell. His eyes narrowed.

"Jim, you know I'm not permitted to talk about..."

"And I'm not permitted to break into your facility to rescue you and your mates. Or to answer your questions about what I think happened in there. But I did it anyway, because we're all in this together. Come on, Sam. I'm not asking for files or data or any of that shit. Just a basic overview of what me and my people are risking our necks for. It won't go any further."

Adebayo closed his eyes momentarily and ran one hand across his face. He checked quickly to either side before leaning in a little closer.

"Have you heard of the Ur-Probe?"

This time, Cochrane failed to keep his eyes from widening in amazement.

"You've got the Ur-Probe in there?!"

"No! Quiet! Keep your voice down! Of course not! That thing is long gone. Look, the vast majority of Cosmolite sites are scattered around the ZuluPoint area. Do you think it is a coincidence that the Combined Army landings on this planet were centered there? We've got an alien invasion way off east of here, expanding its foothold over the last three offensives. I know, you're a military man, I don't need to explain this to you."

The Paradiso Front was, indeed, a complex affair. The NiemandsZone – an area around ZuluPoint initially de-militarized by O-12 in an attempt to stop the fighting between PanOceania and Yu Jing, was famed for the high number of xeno-archeological remains hidden in the depths of the dense jungle. Of course it came as no surprise when the EI's Combined Army centered their assault in that region. It was nothing to do with a geographically defendable position. It was all about the Cosmolites and similar sites. The Ur-Probe itself – almost certainly an example of EI tech – was discovered on Paradiso shortly after PanOceanian scout teams first arrived on the planet. Not long after, the remains of the *Aurora* were discovered.

"That probe," Adebayo continued, "it was dripping with nanotechnology. Almost literally. It infected the teams who worked on it. That's why the entire settlement built around the *Aurora* crash site detonated the bomb to wipe themselves out. A cleaner way to die rather than that horrific infection from the Ur-Probe. Or so we thought. That theory... there was always something wrong about it. Something uncharacteristically defeatist about the actions of the *Aurora* settlers."

All pretenses at subterfuge now gone, Cochrane took a step back.

"Have you got nanotech in there?!" he exclaimed. "That VoodooTech shit isn't safe!"

Adebayo held his hands up defensively.

"Jim! Please! We trust you to keep Yu Jing away from this site! We trust you because you are the professionals and you know what you're doing! So please, trust me when I say that you and your colleagues are perfectly safe! There is nothing in that building that can cause harm! The point I'm trying to make is that this Cosmolite is a long, long way from the main clusters around ZuluPoint. It is sat here in complete isolation! And we think the reason is that it is a... back up of sorts. A data repository site. This place wasn't a settlement, it was a scientific facility. The reason we know this is that this site... well, it's in a better shape than any of the other Cosmolites discovered so far. There are things down there that are still intact. Still identifiable."

"But what if..."

"I've already said too much." Adebayo took a step back. "You helped me and my team, and I appreciate that. But I really shouldn't be talking about this. Just... do me a favor and keep this to yourself, would you? I can't stress that enough."

The thin scientist turned around and walked quickly off in the direction of the research hub. Cochrane watched him go, his mind awhirl as he processed the information he had just received. If there was data from alien civilizations stored in that Cosmolite, would the forces of the Combined Army know? Were the Tohaa watching them? Was it even possible that it was a third, as of yet undiscovered, alien race? Would they soon be facing a threat far greater than a company of Zhanshi waiting in the jungle? And then there was the intruder. The sleeper hold.

Cochrane walked slowly back toward his accommodation block, his hands thrust into his pockets, his eyes fixed on the fine, almost powdery sand his boots kicked through. There was a small, gnawing guilt nagging at the back of his mind for exploiting Adebayo's honesty, especially as the motivation behind it was nothing more noble than his own personal inquisitiveness. He reached his block and slid open his door.

"Jim?"

Cochrane turned and saw Shankar standing a few paces away. His keen interest in the secrets lying within the research building was immediately replaced with the bitter sensation of animosity toward his platoon commander for her earlier outburst.

"I'm glad I found you," the young woman said, "I wanted to apologize. For being such an idiot. I snapped at you because I was tired. That's no excuse."

"Oh, that? No wuckas," Cochrane shrugged. "I'm made of tougher stuff than that. I didn't give it a second thought, really."

"Oh, well... good."

His ego satisfied with a sincere seeming apology, Cochrane immediately felt that animosity toward Shankar dissipate. The platoon commander looked up at him uncomfortably. Cochrane had no interest in drawing out that discomfort and was also desperate to talk about what he had just discovered from Adebayo. Checking his surroundings and seeing nothing more than four soldiers from Number Two Section walking off toward the new gymnasium, Cochrane stepped closer to Shankar.

"I've just had a chat with Sam Adebayo. The guy who got knocked out in the research hub."

"Jim. You shouldn't be..."

"He was taken down by a choke. A martial arts move. He remembers it clearly. Somebody deliberately knocked him out when it would have been easier to kill him."

Shankar's features darkened in suspicion.

"Why? That's not the Yujingyu approach to infiltrating a site. Sure, if they can get in and out undiscovered, but if the alarm goes off then they've never been afraid to start killing."

"Exactly," Cochrane nodded, "it wasn't Yu Jing."

Shankar folded one arm across her chest and rested the elbow of the other against it, propping her chin up in one hand thoughtfully.

"Haqqislam?" she mused quietly.

"No. It's just... no. You could choose any of our adversaries – from within the Human Sphere or not – and the answer would be the same. Any of the factions opposing PanOceania are not afraid to kill. It just doesn't add up."

"So what, then?" Shankar asked, her eyes fixed up at the dark sky above. "A rival company? This could be a sort of... industrial espionage, but somebody else trying to get access to the information in there. It must be worth a lot of money. A life-changing amount. What if it was an inside job? One of their lot?"

Cochrane shook his head and winced.

"No, no, whoever did this knew what they were doing. This wasn't an amateur. They escaped without a trace. Priya, I think this was one of ours. I think it was a PanO operative in there."

Shankar let out a long breath.

"You sure? Sounds a bit far-fetched."

"Look, somebody waltzed straight past all of our security measures without getting picked up, then broke into that building. When they were near-ly confronted, that person knocked Sam out. And the only logical reason for that is because his Rules of Engagement didn't permit him to use lethal force. Why? Because it's one of ours. A PanO mission against a private company on PanO soil."

Shankar looked anxiously to either side.

"Do you think... it was Beckmann?"

Cochrane shook his head.

"No, I thought about that at first. But then I remembered she wasn't even here. She didn't get back from the jungle until hours after this all hap-pened. I don't know who it was, mate, but... just keep your eyes out?"

Shankar nodded slowly.

"We should tell Major Barker."

"No," Cochrane shook his head, "nothing to tell him, really. Not just yet, at least."

***

"Brothers, whatever is true, whatever is noble, whatever is right, whatever is pure, whatever is lovely, whatever is admirable – if anything is excellent or praiseworthy – think about such things..."

Saint Paul's words to the Philippians, written thousands of years ago on a planet light-years away, resounded just as powerfully now as they scrolled across Hawkins' lens as they must have done in around 60 AD. It was his sin-gle favorite extract from the Bible; just a few optimistic lines centered around good thoughts that continually proved to be an inspiration to Hawkins in the darker times of his life. And now, as he lay on his bunk in the dimly lit accom-modation block, his hands behind his head as he read through those ancient lines, he needed more optimism than ever.

News had reached him about the second man he killed. He had that morning submitted his report to the Order to update his superiors on the events at Alpha Four-Four and his part in them. Given his decision to break into a secure area belonging to a rich and powerful private company, he had expect-ed to be summoned to explain his actions. The reply came through only hours later;

"Report acknowledged. Continue with regular sitreps. Combat performance noted."

It was only when he had then followed a link to his combat evaluation, sent to the Order by Major Barker, that he saw his gun camera footage and, whilst taking a rapidly aimed shot during his advance to assist the wounded Fusiliers, he had in fact hit an enemy soldier square in the chest and killed him. Yet it was not the blood on his hands that worried him. It was how little it weighed on his heart. He was in a conflict and both men he killed were legitimate military targets of the opposition. It was an action sanctioned by the orders of the NeoVatican. He was doing his job. What else did he expect when he volunteered for a career in the Church's Military Orders? Yet, deep down, he wanted the pain. He wanted the hurt. He needed to feel guilty.

Hawkins sat bolt upright when the door to his room suddenly opened and then shut again just as quickly. He looked over and saw Beckmann stood by his door. The tall woman wore loose fitting, low slung combat trousers and a roughly cropped black t-shirt emblazoned with the name of a heavy metal band Hawkins vaguely remembered from his early adolescence. Her hair was tied up messily in a ponytail, but her scruffy look did nothing to detract from her beauty.

"Hi," she greeted warily.

"Hello," Hawkins replied, slowly standing up.

"Sorry about rushing in so abruptly," Beckmann thrust her hands into the rear pockets of her combat trousers, "it's just that if people see me in here after dark, they're gonna jump to conclusions and talk."

Hawkins shrugged uneasily. He hoped nobody would judge him as so unvirtuous.

"Are you okay? Would you like me to get you a drink?"

"Sure," Beckmann nodded, walking over to perch on the edge of Hawkins' desk as he opened his small refrigerator and poured out two glasses of soda. "I was just sat around, doing nothing. I don't really expect these guys here to embrace me in their evening social lives and I figured that with you being the other outsider, you'd probably be in the same position as me. So you might like some company. I wasn't disturbing anything, was I?"

"Oh no," Hawkins handed over the glass to Beckmann, "I was just reading."

A surge of guilt immediately flooded into the fore of his mind. Had he really just dismissed reading the Bible as a mere triviality, just to entice a beautiful woman to spend more time with him? It was a genuine guilt, but not the guilt he had gone looking for when ruminating over the two lives he had taken only days before.

"*Ja?*" Beckmann smiled. "I just started reading something new a few days ago. Anna, a friend of mine, said to try to read something other than just guitar magazines, so I got this book on pirates from Earth. Blackbeard, Hornigold, Bellamy, all your lot."

"My lot?" Hawkins queried.

"Englishmen," Beckmann said, "your accent. Even the name 'Hawkins' has a bit of history in piracy, hasn't it?"

"Oh, right." Hawkins shrugged. "Yes, I suppose. I'm three quarters English in terms of heritage. My mother is half Irish and really clings to that link. Hence my name; Kyle's Irish."

Beckmann hugged one leg to her chest and rested her chin on her knee.

"What were you reading?" she asked.

"Philippians," Hawkins replied, "the New Testament."

Beckmann jumped to her feet and planted her glass of soda down on the desk.

"I'm so sorry," she said sincerely, "I didn't know this was your time of prayer. I'll get out of your way."

"You're not in my way," Hawkins said. "Yes, there is an amount of time an Order member must set about each day for prayer. But I did that this morning. I wasn't reading the Bible because I have to. I was reading it because I wanted to."

Beckmann sank back down to her perch on the edge of the desk and resumed her earlier position. She reached up to the chain around her neck and pulled it up from beneath her t-shirt. A pair of archaic military identity discs jangled in her grip – an expression of fashion rather than an actual item of issued military equipment. Hawkins looked across and saw a cross neatly engraved on the back of one of the discs.

"Considering the incredible power and might of the church," Beckmann said quietly, "it really feels like there aren't that many of us, sometimes."

Hawkins looked across at her with what he hoped was a kindly smile.

"I didn't realize that you are a Christian."

"I've only started to take it seriously recently," Beckmann admitted. "I've only given it proper thought in the past few years. That's why I stopped to talk to you when I first saw you. You had a cross on your chest and that means something to me. But, well… Jesus' message doesn't gel with the direction and methods of the Strategic Security Division."

"You are your own person," Hawkins offered, "they don't define you."

Beckmann looked into his eyes, her own narrowing a little. Hawkins met her gaze and felt a connection with her for not the first time.

"It's not as simple as that, Kyle. I wish it was."

Hawkins searched for something to counter the statement with, some words of comfort for her. He found none.

"Hey, don't look so sad!" Beckmann smiled. "I'm sorry for bringing the tone down! Don't sit there thinking that I'm some lost cause with nothing outside of the Division. Same as you, I have my own life. I've got my own place, it backs onto a beach. I live there with Chloe."

"Chloe?" Hawkins repeated. "I didn't realize that you…"

"What," Beckmann's smile grew broader, "own a kitten? Chloe is my cat. So yeah, add 'crazy cat woman' to my list of oddities. Look, do you want to watch a movie or something? I don't know, something to just forget about where we are for an hour or two."

Hawkins tapped his comlog and accessed his geist. The AI echoed a warm yet robotic 'welcome' in his ear before assisting him in cycling through movie choices as Hawkins cleared a space in the center of the room.

"Sure," he replied. "What would you like to watch?"

"Something funny," Beckmann replied, "light-hearted, silly… just nothing serious."

Hawkins cycled through menus and selected an arbitrary comedy movie based on its high ratings listed on its Maya reviews. The movie projected its holographic title credits from his lens onto his retina, the space cleared on the floor between the bed and the desk allowing a clearer image to solidify without interference from the background. Hawkins sat down at the foot of the bed, giving Beckmann plenty of space to sit well away from him, lest his intentions be seen as less than altruistic. Beckmann walked over and sat down next to him, leaning slightly to one side until her arm rested against his.

The next hour passed by too quickly, the movie eliciting laughs from them both and brief conversation. All the noble intentions and willpower in the world could not stop him staring at her from time to time, transfixed by the perfect lines of her face and the color of her eyes as she stared ahead, captivated by the story playing out holographically before them both.

And then Hawkins' alarm nagged at him, the chirping tone dragging him out of his sleep. He had no idea when he had drifted off but found himself lying on his bunk, carefully tucked beneath his blanket. He sat up and saw the holographic movie display paused on his floor, finished at the last of the ending credits. He checked the time. 4:30am. The shrill chirp continued to hammer at his head. It was not an alarm. It was a call.

"Yeah?" Hawkins replied wearily.

"Kyle, it's Priya!" the tone of Shankar's voice had Hawkins fully awake in an instant. "You need to get suited up! Yujingyu forces have just mounted an offensive southeast of here, we're briefing in five minutes!"

Hawkins leapt out of his bed and pulled on his boots.

"I'm on my way."

"No, there isn't time!" Shankar said. "Get to the armory and get armored up. That takes you a lot longer than us and we don't have time to wait. We're getting air moved in; I doubt there will be an LZ so probably fast roping down. I'll give you a call as soon as we are out of the brief, just get your arms and armor and be ready to go."

"Got it," Hawkins replied, switching off the call and rushing toward the door.

Chapter Eight

The trio of twin-engined Tubarão aircraft cruised low over the dense canopy of vivid green jungle foliage, spread out in a loose tactical formation. The morning sun rose steadily behind them, silhouetting their aggressive, shark-like profiles to any onlookers on the ground. In the lead aircraft, Hawkins leaned back in his seat and glanced across the rear cabin at Ed Carson, the HQ Section medic, who stared vacantly up at the complex lattice work of mechanical pipelines, linkages, and electrical cables than ran across the ceiling of the Tubarão. The aircraft shot along through the humid sky, the smooth flight occasionally interrupted by the ripple of low level turbulence from the disturbed air above the trees. The angry scream of the engines to either side of the fuselage broke incessantly through into the cabin, despite the built-in Active Noise Reduction.

The rear cabin of the modular-fit aircraft carried two rows of seats, running along the walls of the Tubarão to face each other. A sliding cargo door was fitted to each side of the aircraft, currently locked shut but each with a pintle-mounted machine gun at the ready. An aircrewman clothed in green overalls and a bulbous helmet with dark visor sat by one of the guns, responsible for the safety of the passengers as well as supervising the autonomous operation of the guns as soon as the doors slid open. Hawkins followed Carson's gaze and looked up at the pipelines above; a slow smear of dark brown fluid ran back along one of the thin, metal pipes until it met the left hand side of the cabin, where it dripped down to form a slight pool on the alloy floor.

"Don't worry about it!" the aircrewmen called across from his seat by the right hand side cargo door, watching as the two soldiers eyed the oil leak nervously. "It's just old stuff working through the system!"

"Is... is it supposed to come out of there, though?" Carson asked hesitantly.

"Absolutely not!" The aircrewman's grin was just about visible below his shaded visor. "But don't worry, we've already had it checked! It'll hold out until the end of the day! Probably!"

Hawkins looked down again, bringing up a map on his lens to check their progress. His update from Shankar after the platoon's brief from company HQ was simple but attention grabbing – following the last few days of political posturing between PanOceania and Yu Jing, and with O-12 unable to mediate a solution, a second Yujingyu force had advanced across the border and was now heading toward Alpha Four-Four from the south. An abandoned Minescorp facility some ten miles to the north of the advance had been identified as a defendable position for Number Three Platoon to hold whilst Number One Platoon was occupied with the initial Yujingyu push from the east.

Hawkins looked down at the MULTI Rifle clutched in his hands, the barrel of the weapon pressed down against the floor as was the norm for troop transport in the back of a Tubarão; in case of an accidental, 'negligent discharge' of a weapon, a round fired straight down would do the least amount of damage to the aircraft and its occupants. Hawkins let out a long breath and ran another built-in test of his armor's functions; power source; mobility; visuals; communications; chemical, biological, radiological and nuclear defense... He was interrupted when a tone sounded in his ear, alerting him that he was being hailed privately on a secure communication channel. He checked the upper right corner of his visual display and saw a new line of text within the communication box. 'Eagle One.' He glanced to the back of the aircraft's cabin and saw Beckmann looked across at him. Her face was cold, impassive, devoid of any of the life and warmth from the previous night. Hawkins opened the communication channel.

"You okay?" Beckmann asked.

"Yes. Fine, thank you."

"You don't look it."

"I... I'm wearing a helmet, how can you tell?" Hawkins asked.

The Hexa operative's blue eyes remained fixed on his, her voice clear through his helmet ear pieces despite the whining jet engines drowning out all other sound within the aircraft cabin.

"It's your body language," Beckmann replied. "Look, Kyle, you need to focus now. Leave the nice guy behind in that accommodation block. Be him again when you get back. You're new to this, and I want to see you get through it, so take some advice from somebody older and wiser than you. We're booted and spurred now, ready for war. No room for nice guys here. Time to be a fucking killer. Focused and remorseless. Got it?"

Hawkins swallowed and nodded.

"Yes, ma'am."

Beckmann threw him a wink – again, lacking any warmth or camaraderie – and turned to stare directly ahead, her hands clutching her MULTI Sniper Rifle. Hawkins looked around the cabin at the other soldiers. Shankar's eyes flickered from side to side, no doubt scanning through the latest intelligence updates projected onto her lens. Cochrane looked out of the cabin door window at the jungle below and yawned. Aida Castillo cycled through menus on her hacking device. Ed Carson continued to stare up at the oil leak on the cabin ceiling above. Satisfied that there was nothing more he could do to prepare himself, Hawkins tapped through the menus on his comlog to project Luke's Gospel on his lens, calming himself with the familiar words as the three Tubarãos hurtled across the treetops toward battle.

***

Only three minutes to the mining site. Shankar brought up her comlog again, the nagging at the back of her mind refusing to be silent. Had she compartmentalized the correct set of procedures for leading a platoon with only two sections instead of three? Four years in the Fusiliers, and this deployment was the first time she had ever been shot at. Everybody said that the first engagement was as bad as it ever got, but this one seemed infinitely worse than the last. She knew what was coming. She had time to fret. To panic.

Shankar cycled through the copy of the Light Infantry Tactics Manual projected onto her lens, tapping at her left wrist to filter all search results to contain the words 'reduced' and 'two sections.' In a separate window, she accepted an intelligence update from Company HQ, stating that the expected strength of the enemy force was still a single platoon 'with supporting elements.' Again, due to the density of the jungle and enemy counter surveillance measures, it was still not possible to ascertain exactly what they would be facing. In the lower right corner of Shankar's lens, her biometric data warned her that her heart rate had entered the amber band. She thought of her parents. They had told her not to join the military. So had her brothers. Above all, her fiancé David had insisted it was the worst idea she had ever come up with. It was, perhaps, the only time she had seen him truly, truly angry.

"Two minutes!" the aircrewman called over the cabin communication network.

The aircraft's attitude changed, pitching up to raise its nose as the jets on the end of the winglets swiveled to tilt upward. The aircrewman stood up and walked over to the right hand side cargo door, fastening his dispatcher harness to his waist and magnetically locking his boots to the decking before sliding open the cargo door. The ANR cut out as the banshee screech of the engines filled the cabin, along with the blinding sunlight of the Paradiso morning and the hot air above the jungle. The stench of recirculating exhaust fumes filled the cabin. The aircrewman moved across to the left door and repeated the process before both pintle mounted Heavy Machine Guns automatically swung out of the aircraft to point ahead and below. Shankar saw the other two Tubarãos – one out of each door – formatting loosely to either side.

"One minute!"

Shankar looked ahead and saw the disused mining complex atop a prominent hill in the jungle. Lattice frames of steel supported a multitude of square, metal platforms, scattered around which was an expansive collection of small office blocks, also made up of dull, silver metal and edged in hazard stripes of yellow and black. Even from this distance, Shankar could see orange-brown patches of rust across the platforms and supporting metal frames. Even more prominent were the thick, green vines wrapping around the man-made structures, sprouting up from the sandy earth like the hands of nature itself, intent on taking a firm hold on the evidence of human intrusion before ripping it violently apart.

"Thirty seconds!"

The formation of three aircraft banked around over the top of the site, and a blast of air whipped through the cabin to tug at Shankar's clothing as she looked down into the abandoned, deserted industrial complex. The first Tubarão peeled away from the formation and descended, arcing back around to commence its final run in to the site to position in the hover for a fast rope deployment of its troops. Shankar watched the aircraft straighten its wings and decelerate as it approached the hover, the force of its engines wrenching and thrashing at the trees below.

A panicked shout of alarm sounded across the cabin comm network. Shankar looked up and saw two white trails of smoke shoot up from the jungle to the south of the mining site and hurtle toward the Tubarão. The sky lit up with counter measures as chaff and flare fired out of the aircraft, seducing one of the inbound projectiles away to fall harmlessly into the jungle below. The second slammed into the Tubarão, blasting apart one of its engines with a brief flash of orange before clouds of black smoke billowed back from the stricken aircraft. The cabin comm net erupted with panicked cries from Fusiliers and airmen alike.

"Shit!"

"What the hell was that?"

"They've got Shark Two!"

"Where's the fire from? Where's the shooter?"

"Boss, who've we lost?"

"Get back in your bloody seat!"

"Shooter! Four o'clock low! 'Bout ten feet in from the tree line at the edge of the clearing!"

"Engage! Shoot the bastard!"

Shankar's heart jumped as the gun on the right hand side of the aircraft moved rapidly across to track a target and then opened fire, pouring long streams of bullets down into the trees below as the blazing Tubarão at the edge of the overgrown mining site hurtled forward in a frantic attempt to power away from the incoming fire and the vine-covered metal obstructions ahead. Her heart pounding as bile rose to her throat, Shankar sat helplessly in her seat and watched as lines of tracer fire swept up from the jungle below from unseen enemy soldiers firing up at the three aircraft. The wounded Tubarão limped over the crest of the hill and disappeared from view into the valley on the far side. It did not re-emerge.

"What do you want us to do?"

Her shaking hands clinging desperately to her Combi Rifle, Shankar looked down and saw orange shapes moving through the jungle below, barely visible through the small gaps in the dense canopy of vibrant green.

"Lieutenant!" Shankar blinked and looked up as she realized the voice was addressing her. "What do you want us to do?"

The voice in her ear over the cabin comm net came from one of the two pilots in the cockpit at the front of the aircraft. Shankar looked down again at the scene below as a Fireteam of five orange armored soldiers sprinted out of the trees and below the dense maze of buckled metal platforms in the abandoned mining site.

"Do you want us to abort the run?" the pilot demanded.

"No!" Cochrane yelled. "No! Get us to the north of the site, away from that ground fire! Can't you get lower and use the terrain to mask an approach? We need to get down there and get amongst this shit!"

The Tubarão lurched around into a steep bank and then dropped suddenly, forcing Shankar to let out a gasp as she was flung up half an inch from her seat and suspended by her harnesses in mid-air for a brief moment as the aircraft dropped out of the sky. The horizon out of the cabin door, smoky when viewed from the hot exhaust fumes from the right hand side engine, lurched up and down as the aircraft jinked from side to side in its mad dash down to tree-top height. The guns at both cabin doors continued to blaze away, firing long bursts into the jungle and filling the cabin with the bitter stench of expended, caseless ammunition.

"Site's on the nose!" the pilot called over the comm network. "We're running in now! Be ready to get out, fast!"

Shankar looked up in confusion as a noise not dissimilar to a child's rattle suddenly sounded from somewhere above her. She heard it again, but this time a hole appeared in the aircraft's skin, allowing a thin pillar of sunlight into the cabin only an inch to the left of Beckmann's head. Almost instantly, a second bullet hole appeared to the right of the sniper's face, and then Fusilier Castillo, sat in the next seat along, slumped lifelessly forward, her chest red with blood. Shankar stared at the young woman incredulously as she sat calmly in her seat, eyes focused on the cabin floor beneath her, her rifle dropping from her limp fingers.

Shankar jumped as a hand clamped on her shoulder.

"Priya!" Cochrane yelled. "We've got to get off this bloody thing! You ready?"

Shankar exhaled, shook her head as if that would somehow clear her thoughts, and checked the biometric readouts of her soldiers. Castillo was dead.

"She's gone!" Cochrane shouted. "We've got to go! Come on!"

The aircraft's nose lurched up again as it decelerated in a shallow drop earthward, the smoking door guns momentarily silenced as the Tubarão approached a low hover. Shankar looked across at where Cochrane stared at her

112

from the next seat. She realized that she had not spoken a word since the shooting started. That was what it felt like. To freeze. She had been numbly aware of what was going on, but the whole ordeal had occurred around her, leaving her vacantly watching as a useless bystander. Cochrane had ordered the run in to the north of the site. He was commanding the platoon instead of her. She was failing as a leader. Shankar swore under her breath and then checked her lens for the status of her platoon again.

"HQ Team!" she shouted. "I'm going first! Follow me down and take up firing positions directly below until One Section is with us! One-One from Zero, deploy to my Marker Alpha and be ready to advance to cover!"

Why had she insisted on going first? Her job was to command and coordinate. No time to ruminate over that snap decision now.

The Tubarão's engines increased pitch to an ear-piercing shriek as the aircraft steadied in the hover. The Tubarão's aircrewman moved to the right cargo door and reached up to a small, box-like appendage on the outside of the aircraft and pulled open a flap on the lower side. A thick length of black rope snaked down from the side of the Tubarão. Shankar released her seat harness as the aircrewman hurried across to release the rope on the left side of the aircraft. She fixed her rifle to her back and stepped over to clip on to the rope, securing herself for the drop via the integral harness built into her body armor. She looked down and saw the orange-yellow earth below blasted away from the aircraft in every direction by the tempestuous exhaust of the two engines, forming almost elegant patterns of drifting vortices of sand. The order came across the comlog from the pilot.

"Dispatch troops!"

Shankar grabbed the rope, stepped out of the cabin, and slid down to the ground with her eyes fixed on the horizon. The ground came up to meet her feet with a forceful thump, her legs buckling at the knees with the impact. Training kicked in and her hands mechanically reached up to quickly unfasten from the rope before she ran forward and out from underneath the hovering aircraft. She flung herself to the ground and brought her rifle up to her shoulder as the second Fusilier out of the aircraft rushed off to her left and threw himself down to take up a firing position.

Command and control now needed to wait. Shankar and the soldier to her left, Carson, were responsible for keeping any enemy at bay whilst the remainder of the team dropped down from the hovering aircraft above. No sooner had the thought entered her head when she saw a flash of metallic orange dart in between the rusted, metal frame buildings up ahead. The figure was gone and out of sight before Shankar could react; the briefest blur of movement in a narrow opening between two tall mining platforms. Shankar momentarily moved her fingers across to her left wrist to activate the comlog and report the enemy soldier moving across to flank them from the northeast but then changed her mind. One solitary soldier would not be advancing alone. Shankar tucked her Combi Rifle into her shoulder and settled into a firing position, correcting her aim as the weapon's scope transmitted imagery directly to her lens and then onto her retina.

Another figure in orange and black darted out from behind cover and Shankar squeezed the trigger of her rifle to fire off a burst of three rounds. The momentum of the Yujingyu soldier's movement brought him another pace or two onward, but what looked like two puffs of dust momentarily blossomed up from the trooper's chest and he crumpled down into the dry, sandy earth.

"Got you," Shankar whispered.

She risked a quick check over her shoulder and saw Cochrane, Hawkins, and Beckmann lying prone to form a semi-circle around their egress site, weapons raised as the first Tubarão yawed through a half turn to face downwind before transitioning away from the mining site, back along its original approach route as the second aircraft ran in to the south. The roar of the Tubarão's engines still deafening above them, Shankar jumped and looked across as Cochrane's Combi Rifle boomed out a burst of fire at an unseen enemy soldier in the cover of the buildings ahead.

"We need to get in cover!" Cochrane called to Shankar over a private channel. "There's a couple of them in those buildings ahead, and they'll be more close behind!"

Shankar looked ahead at the mining platforms. Half a dozen tall, boxy buildings made up of long, latticework metal frame legs and simple, flat working platforms with holes cut out of the center where huge mining drills once operated. The buildings were completely open to the elements, with nearly as much colorful vegetation growing in and around them as in the surrounding jungle. To the right, a handful of much smaller, partially enclosed, control room buildings sat on the far side of three large, metal liquid storage cylinders. Shankar set up a marker on her map and transmitted it to the rest of the team.

"Advance to Marker Bravo!" she called.

Shankar hauled herself up to her feet, her body armor suddenly seeming a dozen times heavier in the blazing sun and its stifling heat, and sprinted forward toward the closest of the tall mining platforms. After only a few paces, she heard a crack above her head, and then another just behind her. It took another moment for her to realize that she was being targeted. Shankar reached the cover of the closest of the mining platform's tall, metal legs and dropped to one knee against the construct. Behind her, Carson hunkered down lower and surged faster toward cover whilst Cochrane returned fire toward one of the control room buildings. Hawkins stopped in place, in plain view of the enemy, and raised his MULTI Rifle to his shoulder to return fire. Beckmann had disappeared completely.

"Sir!" Cochrane yelled. "Keep moving! Get to cover!"

As Carson reached cover next to her, Shankar raised her own Combi Rifle and looked through the scope at where Cochrane and Hawkins were firing, but she saw no enemy activity. She quickly brought up the view from Hawkins' visor onto her lens but saw only a blur of orange tinged movement from behind the cover of the rusty, metal control room block. A round slammed into Hawkins with a clang of alloy on alloy, knocking him back half a pace. Clearly thinking better of standing still in plain view of the enemy, Hawkins dashed after the others as Cochrane dove down into cover next to Carson and Shankar.

"Get in cover!" Shankar screamed as the second Tubarão roared in to settle in a steady hover a few dozen yards to the south, one of its door guns blazing away as ropes snaked down from both of the open cargo doors.

The Fusiliers of Number One Section rapidly descended down along the ropes into the swirling cloud of yellow dust below the hovering aircraft. Shankar took a moment to check her map; the first enemy soldier she had missed earlier was still somewhere to the north of the complex whilst at least two shooters were to the south. The enemy force was clearly moving around to encircle the PanOceanian landing area, but Shankar still had no idea how many Yujingyu soldiers they faced, or even what type. As if in response to hearing her thoughts, Beckmann transmitted across the tactical comm network.

"Zero from Eagle One. You have a Zhanshi Fireteam to the south of your position at my Marker Charlie. One Zhanshi to the north of you at Marker Delta, but with another Fireteam moving up to support. A second enemy section is moving through the jungle in an attempt to get around the back of the landing zone to encircle us. I'll move to engage them. How copied?"

"Zero, all copied," Shankar replied, "anything else?"

"Yeah, there are supporting units with the Fireteam moving toward Marker Delta. Heavy infantry – looks like a Fireteam of Zuyong Invincibles and a Yān Huŏ armed with missile launchers."

Shankar's eyes widened in alarm. Invincibles? Facing the Zhanshi line infantry of the Yujingyu was one thing – even a little outnumbered, the Zhanshi were essentially the equivalent of the Fusiliers. But Invincibles of the Zuyong and Yān Huŏ? The famed 'Terracotta Warriors' of the Zuyong were the largest Heavy Infantry Corps in the Human Sphere – whilst not equipped with the best, most state of the art armor, they were still notorious for their harsh training and grim determination in combat. Then there was also the Yān Huŏ – attached to Yu Jing military units as essentially a one soldier artillery force, their gargantuan armor was built to mobilize heavy support weapons; it now made sense to Shankar that the Yān Huŏ soldier Beckmann had identified was almost certainly responsible for the salvo of missiles that attacked the Tubarãos on the way in to the mining complex.

"Eagle One from Zero," Shankar called as she checked her map to see where Beckmann was observing the enemy positions from, "can you mark up the Yān Huǒ as a priority target for all friendly units?"

"Eagle One, negative," the Hexa sniper replied, "I'm not carrying forward observation equipment. Enemy units are marked on your map. I'm moving to engage the section of Zhanshi attempting to encircle us from the southeast."

Shankar looked across at Cochrane.

"You get all that?"

The tall, bearded sergeant nodded as another brief burst of rifle fire clattered and clanged against the green-stained metal of the platform support column above their heads.

***

His focus jumping between the Zhanshi Fireteam to his right and the rapidly populating tactical map projected into the corner of his field of vision, Cochrane quickly assessed their situation and options. The Fusilier HQ Team and Number One Section were now deployed to the northwest of the long strip of the mining site, with enemy forces advancing not only through the site itself, but also in the jungle to both sides. Reduced to only two sections, the Fusiliers were already on the back foot before the appearance of enemy heavy infantry; even a single Fireteam and a solitary one of those Yān Huǒ walking missile batteries effectively placed the Fusiliers as being outgunned two-to-one. Mentally chastising himself, Cochrane quickly surpassed the urge to recommend a withdrawal.

"Priya!" Cochrane called across to Shankar. "I think we should set up a defensive position just west of Marker Delta. Jonny can get his section in cover at the mining platforms and hold the line against their heavy infantry and that second Zhanshi Fireteam. You and Ed can fall back and dig in with them."

Shankar looked across from where she knelt behind one of the platform's supporting metal lattice legs, wincing as another burst of fire clanged into the rusted metal above her.

"What about the enemy section to the south? And the Zhanshi Fireteam shooting at us from the control rooms right now?"

"Beckmann can keep a section pinned in place, that's what snipers do," Cochrane replied, cautiously eyeing the small control buildings only a stone's throw to the southeast, "and as for those bastards shooting at us, me and Sub Officer Hawkins can sort them out."

Cochrane saw Shankar's eyes quickly flickering as she absorbed all of the information on her map. New markers were quickly created and transmitted to the rest of the platoon.

"All units from Zero!" Shankar called, "advance to Marker Echo!

116

I'll lead, One Section to follow! Eagle One, you are free to position under your initiative to engage enemy section at Marker Foxtrot. Zero-One, Broadsword-One, engage enemy Fireteam at Marker Charlie."

"Zero-One, copied," Cochrane replied over the platoon's channel as the third and final Tubarão transitioned away from the northeast corner of the former mining site and hurtled away to the north at low level over the vibrant jungle trees, jinking at random intervals in an attempt to throw off the aim of any enemy units tracking its progress.

"One-One, understood," Corporal Lanne replied, "advancing to Marker Echo."

"Eagle One, positioning to take enemy unit at Marker Foxtrot," Beckmann called coolly.

Shankar glanced back across at Cochrane.

"There's four or five of them in there, are you sure about this, Jim?"

Cochrane flashed a brief grin.

"Sure I'm sure," he winked, "this is where their line is weakest, that's why I volunteered to do this bit!"

Shankar frowned and shook her head.

"Double back to our position as soon as you can. If you get in trouble, just fall back to us. Don't try anything stupid."

Shankar and Carson backed away from the sparse cover of the platform legs and moved off across the open ground toward the very northern tip of the mining site, Lanne's Section advancing not far behind them. Hawkins edged across and dropped down to one knee by Cochrane's side. The firing from the enemy position in the control buildings had stopped. There was a brief lull in the battle, allowing the buzzing and rattling of jungle insects to drift across the sun baked, overgrown mining site. Then the staccato bark of two sniper rifle shots in quick succession erupted from the south, and the treeline near Marker Foxtrot illuminated with muzzle blasts as automatic fire poured up into the mining platforms above.

Ignoring the cacophony, Cochrane glanced across at Hawkins.

"Targets at Marker Charlie," he said quickly, "I'll get their attention so you can get in there. I'll move southeast across what cover I can find and make a lot of noise. You loop around west, get to those control rooms, and then move through them."

"Yes," Hawkins nodded, his nervousness still somehow transmitted through the cold, inhuman faceplate of his armored helmet, "ready when you are."

Cochrane nodded and brought his Combi Rifle up to his shoulder. Tentatively peering over the cover of the short, metal alloy wall by the foot of the mining platform, he stared across at the control room and saw a silhouetted figure move inside. Gunfire erupted from somewhere off to the north. Cochrane lined up his weapon and pulled the trigger of his Combi Rifle. The butt kicked back against his shoulder as he fired a series of controlled bursts, pelting the side of the building but failing to catch his elusive target who ducked into cover.

"Now! Go!" Cochrane shouted to Hawkins.

Cochrane jumped up to his feet and, leaning low, dashed along the wall to his left, firing short bursts of automatic fire from his Combi Rifle as he moved. Muzzle flashes twinkled from the other side of the clearing, and Cochrane heard the familiar snaps and cracks of bullets tearing through the air above his head. He felt a hand yank at his shoulder. Cochrane turned angrily to look for Hawkins and reprimand the young soldier for failing to follow simple instructions, but instead found the source of the pull to be a smoking bullet hole in his shoulder armor.

Swearing to himself, Cochrane continued to move along the wall as he poured automatic fire into the small control rooms. His Combi Rifle bolt snapped shut to signify it was empty. He dropped to his belly behind cover to quickly remove the empty magazine from his rifle to replace it with a fresh one. Cochrane checked his tactical map. Hawkins had moved around to the south, hugging cover, and was now only a short sprint away from one of the control rooms. Grimacing, Cochrane dragged himself back up to one knee and resumed firing on the enemy position.

***

Leaning over so low that her torso was nearly level with the ground, Shankar rushed around the edge of the final mining platform and sprinted across the dusty, open ground toward the neat piles of alloy crates and barrels in the very northerly corner of the mining site. Rifle and machine gun fire punctuated by the occasional grenade explosion boomed and echoed from the south as Shankar's soldiers exchanged shots with the advancing Yujingyu forces. Dashing down to drop behind the first stack of vegetation-covered crates she encountered, Shankar rapidly brought her rifle up to check to the southeast – the most recent position of the closest enemy unit as highlighted on her tactical map. Carson skidded into cover beside her, raising his own Combi Rifle to peer over the edge of the crates, his breathing rapid and labored.

A flash of orange-yellow in the foliage ahead announced the arrival of the Zhanshi Fireteam flanking along the mining site's northern edge. Carson was quick to the trigger, firing a long burst into the green bushes ahead. The response from the advancing Zhanshi was instantaneous, with rifle fire slamming into the alloy crates around Shankar and Carson, soon followed by the thumping whine of a Heavy Machine Gun. Shankar dove to the dirt by her feet, the vine-covered crates that formed her cover tremoring and jolting as round after round slammed into them. Fighting to suppress the panic and fear rising from her gut, Shankar checked her map and saw Number One Section advancing rapidly toward her position.

"One-One, this is Zero!" She yelled above the din of gunfire, "HQ Team established at Marker Echo! We're under heavy fire from enemy forces advancing from Delta!"

"One-One, copied," Lanne replied calmly, "we're moving to engage."

Gritting her teeth, Shankar clambered back to one knee and pulled her Combi Rifle back in to her shoulder before risking a glance around the edge of the cover of the crates. A Zhanshi gun group – four or five soldiers – was set up in the cover of a small lip of earth at the edge of the facility clearing, their HMG barking out fire as a second team of Yujingyu soldiers moved rapidly around in an attempt to flank Shankar's position. She fired two bursts from her Combi Rifle toward the advancing Fireteam in a desperate attempt to make them think twice about advancing to surround her. Carson fired off another burst and managed to gun down one of the Yujingyu riflemen.

A fresh torrent of gunfire exploded from Shankar's right as Lanne's Section took up firing positions, their own HMG pelting away at the shallow earth bank by the Yujingyu unit. Shankar took in a long breath of relief as the Zhanshi gun team shifted their aim toward Lanne's Fusiliers. From their elevated position, the Fusilier HMG was able to sweep down over the Zhanshi's limited cover and tear through their ranks. Shankar almost laughed in relief as Southee's HMG poured long bursts into the Zhanshi team, obliterating their machine gunner and a soldier crouched next to him. Her face twisted in grim determination, Shankar stared down the sights of her Combi Rifle and added her own shots to the crossfire blasting into the Yujingyu position.

Then, around the corner of a tall, industrial platform behind the Zhanshi position, Shankar saw the next enemy group advancing to support their comrades. A towering, heavily armored soldier encased in metallic orange-yellow stomped out from cover, a long-barreled weapon swinging from side to side from a hard point behind each shoulder of the armored suit. Following the movements of controllers in each alloy-encased hand, the shoulder mounted missile launchers of the Yān Huǒ soldier moved to line up with the Fusiliers' position as four marginally shorter and more compact heavy infantrymen charged out to engage. The enemy soldiers – Zuyong Invincibles and the Yān Huǒ trooper – were familiar to her from her training as a warning, a cautionary tale of extreme danger if ever encountered in battle. Now, only meters away, she marveled in horror at the smooth lines of their bulky armor, the bulbous mass of their chest and shoulder plates, and the glint of green lenses set within the angular helmets.

"One Section, we've been targeted for enemy fire!" Shankar heard Lanne shout out over the platoon's com log channel. "Move to…"

Downfall

The corporal's commands were cut off as two howling whooshes erupted from the Yān Huǒ trooper's missile launchers. White streaks of smoke trailed out behind a pair of rapidly arcing missiles that shot up into the blue sky briefly before hurtling down to impact the dry earth amidst Lanne's section of Fusiliers. The entire ground shook with the colossal detonation, and Shankar watched in horror as clumps of earth were thrown up into the sky from amidst the yellow flash of the eruption, accompanied by irregular shapes twirling amidst them. Shankar let out a cry as she realized what the shapes were. Body parts. The limbs and torsos of her dead soldiers. The casualty report began to file across her field of view.

- *Corporal Jon Lanne – dead*
- *Fusilier James Fischer – dead*
- *Lance Corporal Erin Dubois – wounded...*

***

The acrid stench of smoke and the bitter taste of burnt propellant filled the air as Cochrane hurriedly loaded another magazine into his Combi Rifle and pulled sharply back on the cocking handle. Quickly ignoring the list of dead friends and subordinates that scrolled across his lens, he looked back at the squat control rooms only a few paces ahead, their hazy outlines barely visible through the smoke. He heard shouts of alarm from within as he saw Hawkins' symbol on his tactical map move quickly into the far control room from the west. That was as good a distraction as he was likely to get – it was now or never.

His eyes fixed ahead, Cochrane launched himself over the cover of the short wall and sprinted through the dense, gray smoke toward the closer of the control rooms. He heard gunfire from somewhere close ahead but had no idea if it was targeted at him. Then, after a long, exposed few seconds, he was racing through the open doorway and into the small control room, plunging through the smoke and into the shadows of the vine-covered interior. Two Zhanshi soldiers span around to face him, both quickly raising their Combi Rifles up to a firing position.

Cochrane was faster, tucking his Combi Rifle into his hip and gunning down one of the two enemy soldiers with a long burst of fire that sent him sprawling down into the dirt, bloody holes tearing through his armor. With a yell, Cochrane charged into the second Yujingyu soldier, knocking the shorter man's rifle barrel away just before the Zhanshi trooper pulled the trigger, sending a hail of bullets tearing into the wall behind Cochrane. The Fusilier sergeant grabbed his own Combi Rifle by the barrel with both hands and swung it toward the Zhanshi trooper's head. His opponent – a determined looking sol-

120

dier of about Cochrane's age, with long, black hair and a thin beard – brought his own rifle up to block the attack before swinging a knee up to connect with Cochrane's gut. The wind knocked out of him, Cochrane let out a gasp and bent over double before a fist slammed into his face and snapped his head to one side.

The Zhanshi veteran brought his rifle up again, but Cochrane lashed blindly out with one fist, connecting with the Yujingyu soldier's jaw and knocking him back. The Zhanshi retaliated with a feral roar, barging a shoulder into Cochrane. Both men clattered down to the ground, their rifles spinning away. His eyes ablaze with the fury of a killer, the Zhanshi trooper knelt on top of Cochrane and planted one hand across his face, his fingertips digging into Cochrane's eyes and cheeks as his other hand grabbed at a knife on his belt. Cochrane opened his mouth, leaned into the attack, and clamped his jaws shut to bite through the Zhanshi soldier's fingers, tasting blood as he heard the man yell out in pain. Seizing the opening, Cochrane swept an elbow around to connect with the Zhanshi's head and knock him back; he quickly grabbed at the nearest weapon – the Zhanshi veteran's own Combi Rifle – and slammed the butt of it into the trooper's face to break his nose.

Roaring animalistically, Cochrane barged the man back down to the ground and brought the rifle butt down again, cracking open the side of the Yujingyu warrior's skull. Another three or four heavy blows and the Zhanshi's cranium gave way completely, leaving his face as a bloody, unrecognizable pulp. Breathing heavily, Cochrane threw the Yujingyu rifle to one side and staggered back to his feet. His fallen foe's knife fell from still fingers. Cochrane looked down at the weapon; an exquisite, curved blade of snowflake-patterned Bintie steel with a full tang set within a pair of pearled grips. A beautiful knife, definitely not military issue.

"I'll take that, Dickhead," Cochrane snarled to the dead soldier, snatching the knife and its sheath before recovering his Combi Rifle and moving to the far end of the square control room.

He checked his tactical map – Hawkins showed up in the next control room along. Cochrane quickly made his way out of the tiny building and rushed on to the next, rounding the corner of the first building before checking to both sides and then dashing to the second. His rifle tucked into his shoulder, Cochrane barged his way into the next control room. Hawkins stood alone in the center of the room, his heavy blade and the archaic tunic covering his armor spattered in blood. Two dead Yujingyu soldiers lay at his feet in the center of the small control room, and scarlet stains covered the overgrown walls. Cochrane looked up at the younger soldier.

"You alright, sir?"

The red visor within the heavy helmet turned to silently regard Cochrane. His movements almost mechanical within the heavy, blue-gray armor,

Hawkins nodded. Cochrane checked his map again.

"Beckmann's got the Zhanshi section to the south pinned in place but HQ and One Section is taking hits. We need to work our way around to the south of Marker Delta and hit these bastards from behind."

"Understood," Hawkins nodded, "let's go."

***

Fusiliers Nico Marinho and Rob May were the first to reach cover by Shankar, both soldiers diving behind the improvised alloy crate barricade as enemy fire swept across the dry earth just behind them. Flames licked up from the dense, vibrant foliage to the left of the Fusiliers' position where stray explosives had set the dry vegetation alight, causing plumes of thick, black smoke to waft across the battle area. Shankar leaned over the cover of the crates and fired off another rapidly aimed but ineffectual burst into the enemy positions, noticing that the heavily armored Terracotta Soldiers had taken position in the center of the enemy line and that a Fireteam of Zhanshi were again attempting to outflank to the north. Her rifle clicking empty, Shankar ducked back down into cover and pressed her back against the crate barricade, ejecting her spent magazine and grabbing a replacement from her webbing.

Amidst the carnage inflicted by the enemy fire, she saw her soldiers attempting to restore order in the panic and chaos that grew from the missile impact. Ed Carson and Jack Byron frantically attempted to pull wounded soldiers through the smoke and toward safety; Shankar saw Lance Corporal Dubois stagger blindly and erratically as she clung to Byron, blood covering one half of her face. Nat Southee had taken up a firing position on the other side of the small clearing with Rex Smalls, but return fire from the Yujingyu line prevented them from providing anything close to effectual in the firefight. Her heart still thumping, Shankar brought her attention back to her tactical map. The whole thing made no sense. Images and symbols swam in and out of focus, north and south seemed to be reversed, panicked and pained shouts and cries over the communication channels might as well have been in another language.

Shankar took a deep breath. It did not help. Bullets slammed into the cover behind her as her soldiers returned fire against the more powerful enemy force. She looked at her map again. They had entered the fight with only two sections instead of three and then had immediately lost another when the first Tubarão was hit. Now her only section left was reduced to nearly half its strength and they were pinned in place. The fight was lost. Her mind racing in panic, Shankar zoomed out a scale ring on her map to plan a withdrawal. There – half a kilometer to the northeast – a dry river bed they could retreat to and then follow to a clearing for extraction. She marked the position. A second later, a private communication channel opened on her comlog.

"Shankar! You cancel that fucking waypoint!" Beckmann's voice boomed in her ears. "You order a retreat and we're all dead! Now get your machine gunner to a proper firing position and dig in! We're not falling back!"

"I've got dead and wounded, and we're outgunned three-to-one down here!" Shankar cried. "What the hell do you want me to do?"

"I want you to do your fucking job and lead your platoon!" The Hexa major yelled angrily. "Look... just get every gun you have on them right now and give me a few seconds, I'm repositioning!"

Shankar saw Beckmann's Eagle One marker on the map slowly move across one of the mining platforms. Shankar quickly highlighted the enemy position on the platoon's tactical map and sent the marker out to all of her Fusiliers.

"Three Platoon from Zero!" she shouted. "Enemy forces at my marker! Hit them with everything you've got!"

Shankar leant over the cover of the barricade to join Marinho and May, her Combi Rifle jumping in her hands as she fired a series of aimed shots across the small clearing and into the enemy positions by the tiny ridge at the edge of the mining site. The armored bulk of the Invincibles and a trio of Zhanshi returned fire as the outflanking Zhanshi Fireteam moved steadily north along the edge of the tree line. Shankar saw her platoon's fire accurately pummel the ground by the enemy soldiers but fail to pick any of them off. Then, somehow above the cacophony of exchanged rifle and machine gun fire, she heard the characteristic low howl of a high velocity sniper rifle round, quickly increasing in pitch into something almost like a zooming whine. Shattered armor, blood, and brain matter exploded out of the side of the head of one of the heavily armored Zuyong Invincibles. The veteran soldier slumped down, dead.

Instantly, the towering Yān Huǒ missile trooper swiveled in place and tilted his weapons systems to point up toward one of the mining platforms to the southwest of the site. A second howling sniper round cut through the hot, dry air, and with a dull thump, the heavily armored trooper staggered back a step as a crack appeared in his torso armor, his shoulder mounted missile launchers drooping to one side in imitation of the involuntary commands sent to them by the soldier's flailing arms. A fraction of a second later, before Shankar's ears had even registered the whine of another shot from Beckmann's MULTI Sniper Rifle, blood and debris smashed out of the back of the Yān Huǒ trooper's head, and he dropped lifelessly to the ground.

With two of their elite heavy infantrymen cut down by sniper fire, a pair of the Zhanshi broke and turned to flee. They had both taken only a few steps when a long burst of fire from Southee's HMG swept across the Yujingyu position, cutting them both down. In only a matter of seconds, accurate fire from the PanO positions had killed four enemy soldiers and forced the remainder to dive to cover. The fight was not over yet. Shankar quickly brought her map back up and designated a path of advance to create a crossfire.

"Nico! Jack! Rob!" Shankar shouted, abandoning communication protocols in favor of the far more simple use of their names. "Flank left! Get in the trees and advance to Marker Golf! Nat – covering fire!"

***

Hawkins followed Cochrane back up around the edge of the over-grown mining platforms as the Fusilier sergeant threaded his way quickly through empty crates and short walls toward the sounds of gunfire. The tactical map showed the remnants of the Platoon HQ and Number One Section in cover at the northern extremity of the mining site, engaged in a bitter firefight with Yujingyu units to the south. Off on the western edge of the site, a second section of Zhanshi were pinned down in the jungle just outside the site's perimeter. His MULTI Rifle held up to his shoulder and ready to fire, Hawkins watched as the veteran Indigo sergeant ahead of him led him around toward a position where they could fire into the back of the enemy unit engaged with the HQ and Number One Section. What Hawkins marveled at as they ran was that it was suddenly all crystal clear.

His first engagement, a few days before, had been a confused affair of explosions, shouts, screams, and utter confusion. He briefly recalled that hazy, confused restriction in his mental capacity to fully understand his situation, but four years of live fire training kicked in to see him through. Now, he once again appreciated and fully understood his tactical map. Any areas of uncertainty that could hide a hostile soldier seemed to leap out at him, warning him to proceed with caution and be ready to dive for cover or open fire. It was like the difference between his very first combat exercise in training and his very last.

Up ahead, Cochrane held up one hand and signaled for Hawkins to move off to the right. Cochrane dropped down and took cover behind an ancient looking, rusted barrel. Hawkins took position next to him, leaning over the sights of his MULTI Rifle.

"Targets front!" Cochrane shouted over the perpetual din of gunfire. "Hit the big bastards! Don't worry about the Zhanshi!"

Hawkins looked ahead and saw a quartet of Zuyong Invincibles facing away from him, desperately trying to hunker their orange-yellow armored bulks – seemingly crude in comparison to Hawkins' armor – down beneath a lip of earth as they exchanged fire with Fusiliers to the north and a Heavy Machine Gun position outside Hawkins' field of view. A little further ahead, a Fireteam of five Zhanshi were locked in an exchange of fire with three Pan-Oceanian Fusiliers who were highlighted on Hawkins' lens as blue for friendly. Cochrane shot a burst of rounds into the back of one of the Invincibles, knocking the Yujingyu soldier down onto his face but failing to penetrate the thick battle armor. Hawkins lined up his sights, held his breath, and fired off three aimed, single shots into the next enemy soldier along. His first flew wide of the mark, a second round sent a red mist erupting from the back of the trooper's thigh, and the third caught him dead center in his back.

A second series of shots from Cochrane dropped a second Invincible, but the remaining pair turned to face Cochrane and Hawkins to return fire.

"That'll do, sir!" Cochrane yelled. "Fall back!"

Fuck that. Hawkins gritted his teeth and fired a long, continuous burst into the enemy position. A double bang snapped above his head as two rounds from the Yujingyu shooters narrowly missed him before a third slammed into his bicep and span him half around in place but failed to punch through his thick armor.

"Kyle!" Cochrane shouted, grabbing him by the shoulder. "We need to reposition! Follow me!"

Cochrane dashed off back behind the cover of the closest mining platform leg, bullets whizzing and zipping through the lattice work metal frame as Hawkins followed him.

"Zero from Eagle One," Hawkins heard Beckmann's voice, "enemy unit at Marker Foxtrot is falling back."

"Got it!" Shankar yelled in reply. "They're retreating at this side as well!"

Hawkins looked across to his right to where the abandoned facility met the relentless jungle and the enemy's only viable avenue of escape. He quickly plotted a marker and a route to it.

"Sergeant!" Hawkins called. "We can cut across the broken ground between here and the next set of platforms to cut off their retreat! That way we can..."

"Woah! Woah!" Cochrane held his hands up. "Hang fire, sir! Let 'em go!"

Hawkins' eyes widened in surprise.

"What? We haven't just been through all of this to let them out of here without a fight!"

"Ease off the gas, sir!" Cochrane warned. "Remember our orders! The mission briefing was clear; set up a defensive position at the Minescorp facility and stop the enemy advance. There was nothing about chasing down fleeing soldiers into a jungle and who knows what else!"

"But we've got..."

"Look!" The older soldier's face twisted angrily. "We chase those bastards down and we maybe kill two? Three? Four? Let's say we lose another one of our guys or girls. One more dead. Is that worth it? You're happy to exceed our orders without authority and watch one of our lot get a bullet in the head? Stop! Just bloody well stop! Let them go."

A few isolated rifle shots crackled across the old mining site. Sinking down to sit behind the cover of a low, alloy wall, Hawkins rested his MULTI Rifle across his lap as smoke wafted up from the end of the barrel. He took off his helmet and ran a hand through his short, sweat-soaked hair as rays of unfiltered sunshine caused him to wince in discomfort. He took a few deep breaths before clambering back to his feet and following Cochrane back to the northern end of the site to rejoin the main force.

Chapter Nine

"Stay focused," Shankar warned, the outstretched fingers of one hand gesturing pointedly at her two soldiers, "you've got the responsibility for anything coming from the south until we have a better idea of what's going on. You understand?"

Fusiliers Vesilin and Southee briefly exchanged glances, concern painted across the features of the tall, heavy set soldier and the short, brown-haired woman. The panoramic perspective from the top of the mining platform allowed a spectacular view of the ubiquitous, dense jungle in all directions, the green canopy rising and falling over the undulating ground leading back to Alpha Four-Four and to the Yujingyu border to the east. Southee looked across at where the HMG was set up behind an improvised barricade, pointed down to the tree line to the south.

"Got it, Boss," she nodded, "anything comes our way, we'll knock it down."

"Any... idea on how long we'll be out here?" Vesilin asked, his thin features pale and drawn.

"You'll know as soon as I know," Shankar replied honestly, blinking as another bead of stinging sweat rolled into her left eye. "If you think you see anything, get straight on the comlog and let everybody know."

Shankar walked to the edge of the alloy platform and lowered herself onto the rusted, bent frame of the ladder leading three stories down to the dry earth below. A warm breeze swept past her, unopposed by the trees at this height above the ground. The metal ladder creaked and swayed a little as she slowly lowered herself back down toward the ground, thoughts racing through her mind of how ridiculous and embarrassing it would be to fall to her death from a snapped, ancient ladder only minutes after the end of a firefight that had resulted in the deaths of some twenty soldiers.

A brief sweep had recovered the bodies of fourteen dead Zhanshi troopers and their supporting heavy infantry. In exchange, Shankar had lost five of her own soldiers in the fight as well as an entire section of ten Fusiliers when the Tubarão carrying Number Two Section was shot down. Of her original platoon of thirty-five soldiers who arrived at Alpha Four-Four only weeks before, she was now left to defend the mining site with nine, of which one needed medical evacuation.

Reaching the foot of the ladder, Shankar took a few paces before she stopped in the unbearable, late morning heat. She removed her beret and tilted her head back, her eyes closed as the blazing sun beat down on her. Nausea scrambled up toward her dry, tight throat as the adrenaline from the fight washed away, leaving her hands trembling. Fifteen dead. Ten gone in an instant, and then Castillo, Lanne, Fischer, and Rodriguez shot down in front of her. Shankar buried her face in her hands. The guilt of pacing around the now silent mining site without a scratch when fifteen men and women she was responsible for were now dead was something she would have to address at some point. She had not even started to process her feelings over the enemy soldier she had shot dead. Now was not the time.

Shankar opened her eyes again. The piercing blue sky, the warmth of the sun, and the melodious buzzing of the jungle insects reminded her in that moment of her most memorable vacation with David, nearly two years ago now. They had visited Mauritius on Earth for a perfect week without interruption or even so much as a single cloud in the sky. It had been there that he, wearing a suit of white linen, had dropped to one knee in the surf of an idyllic beach to ask her the question.

"You alright?"

Shankar was wrenched from that perfect memory and back to the humid, deadly jungle. She looked across and saw Beckmann a few paces away. The tall woman had the arms of her jumpsuit tied around her thin waist to reveal her annoyingly perfect figure, barely covered by a skintight cropped vest of white. Shankar felt her temper rising. The long-barreled, deadly MULTI Sniper Rifle that Beckmann had used to such violent effect less than half an hour before was carried in one hand by her side. Her dark blue eyes regarded Shankar from beneath a few locks of perfectly positioned hair. Everything about the woman was perfect. She did not even look as though she had broken a sweat in the punishing heat and deadly exchange of fire.

"Are you alright?" the Hexa sniper asked again.

Shankar folded her arms and glared up at the taller woman, biting back a response.

"Why wouldn't I be alright?" Shankar managed, not as loud and as confidently as she would have liked.

"Well," Beckmann shrugged, "I don't think any of us were expecting to jump straight into something like that."

"Right," Shankar grunted, "I suppose now you can tell me all about how hard it is to lose people under your command, how difficult leadership under fire is... all the bullshit that you've done for years and are an expect at, and I know nothing about? Is that why you're here?"

Beckmann's eyes narrowed in confusion, her head tilting a little to one side. She slowly slung her rifle over one shoulder and took a step back.

"I was just seeing if you are holding up okay after all that," she said, her tone low, "that's all."

"What, like you care?" Shankar snapped. "Like you care about anything? You blow people's bloody heads off without even flinching! Twenty lives gone in minutes, but as long as you get to prance around and remind

129

everybody how good you look in the interval, why would you care?"

Beckmann blinked, took another step back, and then turned away. She took a single pace and then stopped. She turned back to face Shankar again. What little compassion had formerly highlighted her flawless features was now replaced with a purposeful glare and grimly set jaw.

"You filed your casualty returns to Company HQ?" Beckmann demanded.

"Yes."

The tall sniper flicked a finger across her comlog, her eyes flicking from side to side as she quickly read through data on her lens.

"James Fischer," Beckmann said coldly, "when was his birthday?"

"What?"

"How many brothers and sisters did he have? What were his hobbies? Was he in a relationship? Did he like sports? Music?"

Shankar felt her face contort in confusion.

"Why the hell are you asking me…"

"You don't fucking know, do you?!" Beckmann boomed, striding forward purposefully. "You have no idea! You *dare* to judge *me* and hide behind the damn sob story of losing men and women under your command, and you don't know the first thing about them! About any of them! They were human beings! How long was James Fischer in your platoon? How many opportunities did you have to spend five fucking minutes talking to him about his life?"

Beckmann towered over Shankar, planting her hands against the shorter woman's shoulders and shoving her back aggressively. Every accusation came with a terrifying glare and another powerful push.

"Cali Rodriguez! What do you know about her? Nothing! You dare pretend you care? Fuck you! They weren't men and women with lives to you! They were rungs on your promotion ladder! For you to step on!"

Shankar opened her mouth to deny the scything allegations but found herself pushed back again and again, steamrolled over by the powerful woman glaring down at her. She remembered the feeling, that awful, indescribable feeling of being bullied as a child. Suddenly she was twelve years old again, being pushed and taunted by her older sister's friends in front of a packed youth club of fifty adolescents.

"Are you fucking crying?!" Beckmann leaned in until her rage-filled eyes were only an inch from Shankar. "And you call yourself a soldier?! A leader?! You really are nothing more than a waste of space!"

"Ma'am," a stern voice demanded, "is there a problem here?"

Shankar had never been so glad to see Cochrane. The broad sergeant paced over and stood by the two women, his thick fists planted against his hips, the sun behind him casting his face in long shadows. He eyed Beckmann without flinching. The Hexa major stared back at him in silence for several long, uncomfortable minutes.

"What's going on here?" Cochrane asked.

"Ask her," Beckmann sneered, "I think her care and compassion has just overspilled a bit."

The tall Hexa operative turned and paced away.

"Where are you going, ma'am?" Cochrane called after her.

"South," Beckmann pointed, "after those bastards. To make sure they don't come back here any time soon."

"Our orders were to defend this site, Major," Cochrane replied coolly.

"*Your* orders," Beckmann corrected, pulling her coveralls back up over her arms and shoulders, "not mine. I'll cut my own fucking detail."

Shankar let out a long breath as Beckmann paced away from the dusty clearing and disappeared from view. She wiped the streaming sweat from her eyes and cheeks.

"What was that about?" Cochrane asked.

"Nothing, just... I lost my temper and said some things that were ill-advised."

The burly sergeant opened and closed his mouth, pointing after the Hexa sniper, his face a picture of confusion.

"Don't tell me you're saying whatever that was was your fault? Don't take shit from that bloody psychopath, Priya! I guarantee you that you've done nothing wrong here."

"Nothing?!" Shankar exhaled, bile rising into her throat. "Nothing wrong? There's eight of us left who can hold a rifle!"

Cochrane folded his muscular arms and raised one eyebrow.

"Not now, Priya. Not now. Think that through when we get back home. But not now. Come on, come with me."

Her temples aching and her throat dry, Shankar walked after Cochrane as the tall soldier paced back up toward the north end of the site.

"If we had enough people, we could secure this place on all sides," Cochrane began, "but with a single understrength section, there is very little we can do. I reckon we concentrate in the center. That gives us as much clear space and fields of fire as possible to address an attack on any side. We'll need to spray out a good few lines of cutting foam, too. Their heavy infantry will barge straight through that, but it'll make those Zhanshi think twice about charging in here, at least."

"I'll get in touch with Company HQ again," Shankar nodded, the sickness in her throat refusing to die down. "I'll see if we can get increased surveillance cover from overhead to at least give us more advanced warning of any hostile force approaching. I need to get Erin Dubois out of here, too. Ed says that head wound needs proper attention, more than he can give out here."

As if on cue, Shankar's comlog alerted her to an incoming call from the Company Command Post at Alpha Four-Four. Shankar accepted the call, quickly adding Cochrane in to the channel.

"Three-Zero, this is Alpha-Zero-One," Waczek's voice fizzled in to Shankar's ears.

"Alpha-Zero-One, Three-Zero, loud and clear."

"Yeah, Zero, I've finally got some good news for you. Your Number Two Section is inbound to you by air, ETA five minutes."

Shankar's eyes widened in surprise. She looked across at Cochrane, astounded.

"Zero-One, say again?" she blurted over the comlog.

"Your Number Two Section," Waczek repeated, "their Tubarão made it back for a forced landing at the Hill Eight Six airstrip with one engine. I diverted another aircraft out there and your section is all onboard and on their way to you."

Shankar let out a short laugh of delighted surprise. Ang Garcia's entire section was in one piece. That was ten less deaths weighing on her conscience. She looked up at Cochrane again, beaming. The gruff sergeant merely raised his brow ever so slightly, the only indication that he was either surprised or happy to hear the news.

"Well, that's great!" Shankar responded, "I... Zero-One, Three-Zero, that's excellent. I... we can't guarantee this facility is secure for a hover deployment. Recommend they deploy to the marker I am sending you now and move in the last half kilometer on foot."

Shankar quickly identified the point she had found when she had considered falling back during the earlier firefight and sent it to Waczek. She was only then aware that Cochrane was attempting to grab her attention with a wave of one hand. She looked up at him and he mouthed a word. Shankar shrugged. He said the word a little louder.

"Wounded."

Shankar nodded.

"Alpha-Zero-One, we've also got one walking casualty for extraction, will get her to the deployment point. They'll be a ten minute delay for the Tubarão."

"Copied," Waczek said, "I'll get them to drop off the section and then come back later. Can't afford to keep an aircraft flying in circles for ten minutes with all we've got going on. Hang in there, Priya, I'll be back in touch to talk through resupply as soon as I can. Alpha-Zero-One, out."

Cochrane allowed himself a brief smile.

"Things are a bit better," he nodded, "we're doubling our numbers. Maybe we can hold this place after all."

"There's still more of them out there than us," Shankar said as she picked up her pace, walking briskly past the battered control rooms toward where she had last seen Dubois, "we're still outnumbered."

"But," Cochrane countered as he walked alongside her, "now we know Ang's section are all okay, that means we were dropping those bastards at a rate of about three-to-one in that last fight."

Shankar stopped. She looked up at the tall sergeant.

"No. We weren't. *You* were. And Hawkins. And... her."

Cochrane shrugged.

"Yeah, well, Indigo and Hospitallers, we're supposed to be force multipliers. Look, things are looking better. I'll get Erin to the extraction point and be back here before..."

Shankar held her hand up.

"No. You look after things here, Jim, I'll take her to the Tubarão."

Cochrane shook his head.

"This is your show, Priya. If anything happens, it won't look great if you weren't here. I can be spared."

"I know what the Platoon Commander's Handbook says, Jim," Shankar replied, "I know I *should* be here. But both you and I know that you're more than capable of running this – more capable than I am. I've just watched five men and women lose their lives reacting to my orders. The very least I can do is keep an eye on my wounded."

"Is this because of what that Hexa bitch said to you?" Cochrane growled.

Shankar shook her head.

"No," she lied, "it's just the right thing to do. Get the defenses in place here, I'll be back soon."

***

Still glancing warily from side to side at the dark, ominous tree lines flanking the old mining site, Hawkins picked up his pace to catch up with Beckmann. The tall, slim woman paced determinedly off toward the southern end of the site, her rifle slung over one shoulder. She unholstered her heavy MULTI Pistol, broke it open at the hinge just in front of the trigger guard, inspected the cylinder, and then snapped the weapon shut again before shoving it back in her thigh holster.

"Major?" Hawkins called out as he closed the gap between them, the two walking through a narrow passageway between two old lines of palleted crates, beneath the shade of one of the tall platforms above.

Beckmann did not respond. The two walked out into the sun again, in a dry, weed strewn clearing near the end of the installation.

"Lisette?"

Beckmann stopped in her tracks. She turned to face Hawkins, her eyes narrowed and her lips set in a snarl. She planted her fists against her hips.

"What is it, Sub Officer?"

Hawkins stopped. He winced, the sun beating down against his brow painfully without the benefit of the visor built into the helmet dangling from his belt.

"I... well... are you alright?"

"I told you to leave the nice guy behind, Sub Officer. There's no place for it out here."

"I know," Hawkins said quietly, "but... are you okay? You look... distressed."

"I'm not 'distressed,' Kyle, I'm fucked off!" Beckmann snapped, folding her arms. "I'm here to support a platoon of amateurs led by a career minded idiot who couldn't lead her way out of a wet paper bag! Did you see what happened back there? She froze! I don't know how many times!"

Hawkins clenched his teeth uncomfortably as he quickly worked through options for a passive, non-confrontational response. He had every sympathy for Shankar freezing, given her lack of experience and the immense weight of responsibility suddenly placed on her. Beckmann continued before Hawkins could offer an opinion.

"She tells me to set up and stop an entire section dead in its tracks – which I do – and then next thing I know, whilst I've got eight angry Yujingyu fuck heads shooting at me because I've just killed two of their friends, is that she is planning to retreat! So now I'm stuck on top of a platform, alone, in open view, swinging from side to side whilst I'm trying to shoot down a section of Zhanshi in one direction and simultaneously dig her out of the pile of shit she has created in the other!"

"Well, the rest of us are all very new at this, Major," Hawkins offered weakly.

"That's not what's pissed me off!" Beckmann growled. "Shankar being an incompetent prick is forgivable, given the fact she has spent the last five years on ceremonial duties and drinking pink gin in the Officers' Mess! What isn't forgivable is that I still went to check on her, to see if she was holding up okay, and she damn well bit my head off! Me! As if I'm the fucking villain in all of this!"

"I'm sure she didn't mean it to come out that way," Hawkins said, "I mean, maybe she just..."

"Like you care about anything? You blow people's bloody heads off without even flinching! As long as you get to prance around and look good in the interval, why would you care?"

Hawkins stopped dead. It was not the words that Beckmann repeated from her earlier confrontation with Shankar that bothered him. It was the accent. The mannerisms. The delicate, subtle evidence of Indian heritage combined with the precise, almost nervous jerks of the shoulder and jaw. Beckmann's impersonation of Shankar was not just good. It was absolutely flawless. Hawkins eyes narrowed. He took half a pace back. That was what Hexas were, was it not? Assassins. And if an assassin wanted to get close to a target, an uncanny ability to adopt any accent or persona to melt into any situation would be of immense value.

Hawkins looked up at Beckmann again. He did not see the vivacious, charismatic and beautiful woman he knew he was rapidly and uncontrollably developing feelings for. He saw a cold blooded assassin. He wondered at that moment if Lisette Beckmann was really a person or just the figure stood in front of him's latest fake persona. Beckmann raised her hands to her face and took a deep breath. Her perfect features softened.

"Look... I'm sorry, Kyle. I just... it's been ten years of this, you know? Ten years of every man I meet wanting to screw me and every woman I meet being a bitch because she's jealous. I was just trying to be friendly. It got thrown back in my face, and I'm sick of it. I'm sick of being judged. I'm sick of strangers just seeing the face and the body, and the people I know just seeing the kill tally. I'm more than either of those, but nobody ever gives me a chance."

Hawkins felt his suspicions and feelings thawing again, but he remained silent. Beckmann took a step closer to him.

"Except for you," she said softly, "you give me a chance. You talk to me like a human being. Everything about you says you shouldn't, but you do. A guy as good looking as you should be a shallow, self-absorbed prick, but you're not. A guy who has been through four years of religious indoctrination should be a judgmental asshole, but you're not. That's why I can talk to you."

Hawkins smiled in genuine sympathy as he felt a warmth within him, generated both by her kind words and the compassion he felt for her situation. He also felt shame, for doubting her sincerity and for judging her. It was not his place to judge. He, too, took a pace toward her.

Beckmann's face immediately hardened into a mask of cold professionalism. She took a pace back, away from him.

"You need to get back to the Platoon HQ, Sub Officer," Beckmann said, her tone cool. "We're outnumbered and outgunned. Hopefully the damn idiot running this show will rely on some actual experience from Sergeant Skippy Mc-Fucking-Sheep Dip or whatever his name is, but you need to get involved, too. You might not have much experience, but your training was ten times longer than these amateur hour comedians. We may have scared those bastards off for now, but they'll be back here. And soon. That's why I'm going out to give them another scare."

"I'll come with you," Hawkins said determinedly, grabbing his MULTI Rifle from his back.

Beckmann held up a hand.

"You're good in a close quarters fight, but not at what I'm off to do. You'd slow me down. Wait here. If I'm not back by twenty one hundred, I'm dead. Don't come looking for me or anything stupid like that."

Hawkins lowered his rifle again. He looked across at Beckmann and then at the dense, forbidding jungle behind her. Having just seen the ferocious impact of Yujingyu firepower and heard the tales of the dangers of the jungles of Paradiso, he did not appreciate Beckmann talking of her own death.

"You shouldn't go out on your own."

Beckmann smiled and offered him a cocky wink.

"Dense cover? Vegetation that masks even the most modern sensors the enemy has? Clear delineation between friendly forces and hostiles? Boy, this is my fucking playground! Don't worry about me. But seriously, do not come after me."

Hawkins watched in silence as Beckmann turned and took a few paces away from him. She stopped again. Her face sullen, she looked over one shoulder and met his eyes with hers.

"If I'm not back by this evening, leave me be. I'm DNRR, so it wouldn't be worth it anyway."

Hawkins frowned in confusion.

"DNRR?" he queried.

"Do Not Resuscitate or Resurrect," Beckmann explained, "it's what I've declared on my medical records. I've already died once, Kyle. I'm never going through that again."

His heart already heavy with worry before she was even out of eyeshot, Hawkins watched as the tall woman unfolded her hood from her collar and pulled it over her head, her camouflaged jumpsuit morphing into the surroundings as she melted into the boiling, humid jungle ahead.

Chapter Ten

The moons and a swirling panorama of stars were already visible in the darkening azure sky before the sun had retreated beneath the horizon. The rattle and buzz of the day's jungle insects gave way to the lower humming and crackling of their night counterparts as twilight fell across the abandoned mining site. The backdrop of jungle creatures was accompanied by the low thrum of solar generators, miraculously nursed back into life by Fusilier Kapsis, Number Two Section's hacker. With partial power restored to the facility, electrical field windows and climate control now provided some respite from the stifling temperature in the small control rooms, and floodlights now pointed out into the surrounding jungles to enhance the night vision lenses of the platoon's sentries for the long night that lay ahead.

Cochrane sat alone in the central control room, now designated as the Platoon HQ, slumped back against one of the low walls below the level of the gently buzzing electrical barrier window that linked the wall to the roof above, reveling in the relatively cool, dry air provided by the last dregs of the facility's climate control. With eighteen Fusiliers, a Hospitaller, and a Hexa sniper, they now had a chance of defending the site; but left alone with his thoughts, he found his mind wandering back to the main research hub at Alpha Four-Four and what exactly this was all about. Having risen to the ranks of corporal within the Fusiliers, Cochrane had still seen little actual combat until he passed selection for Indigo. PanO's relationship with Yu Jing was very much a cold war at times, with hostility between the two factions erupting into actual shooting only at the peaks of poor political relations, and even then, normally hugely restricted by the threat of O-12 intervention. Casualty statistics were often falsely reported and hidden by all concerned. Cochrane had known of a lot of soldiers who lost their lives in 'training accidents' as far as families back home were concerned.

Yet, even with his time involved in Indigo and the clandestine activities that came with it, it was very rare for full platoon-sized firefights to overtly erupt. This was big, whatever it was all about. Whatever lay within that research hub. And the more Cochrane thought about the night he and Hawkins had swept through the hub, searching for that invisible intruder, the more he was convinced that whoever was in there with them was not Yujingyu. There was another player at work in this little corner of the game.

Cochrane's thoughts were disturbed when Shankar and Garcia entered the control room together. Cochrane considered standing as a mark of respect to his Platoon Commander in front of a junior rank but decided that presenting a clear shot to any enemy sniper potentially watching from the jungle behind him did not outweigh the benefits of maintaining standards. Shankar glanced across at Cochrane and pointed to her ear to signify that she was on a call, and then she sank down in the opposite corner of the small room. Corporal Garcia sat down next to Cochrane. Whilst Cochrane would never admit it to Garcia, he was genuinely relieved to see the stocky, olive-skinned section leader alive and well.

"What happened then?" Cochrane asked, keeping his voice low so as not to disturb Shankar's call.

"The Tub took a missile when we came to the hover," Garcia explained. "Next thing I know, the pilot is practically standing the thing on its nose to accelerate away. Guess he bottled it."

"No, mate," Cochrane shook his head, recalling a similar occurrence from his participation in a counter terrorism incident two years previously, "those things need a shit load of power in the hover. When they lose an engine, they have to accelerate or they pile in to the ground. The pilot was just trying to get speed on so he could fly the thing on one engine."

"How does that work?" Garcia asked.

Cochrane pointed to his own head.

"D'you see a shit load of hair care products here, digger? No! 'Coz I'm not a pilot! How the hell should I know! Something to do with aerodynamics."

"Well anyway," Garcia continued, "they flew us back to the strip at Hill Eight Six. I reckon we were doing close to a hundred miles an hour when we landed."

"Bullshit."

"Seriously. I could actually smell shit from one of my guys, it was so terrifying. Give me a shooting match or a knife fight any day over that bullshit. At least I've got some control over events then. That was just being strapped in a metal box with a missile hole in the side, hoping the two pretty boys driving the thing knew what they were doing. Anyway, they sent another Tub up to pick us up and then brought us here. Bloody hell, Jim, it looks like we missed a hell of a dust up."

Cochrane raised his brow and issued a slight shrug. He looked across at Shankar. Judging by her nodding and repetition of the words "yes," and "understood," he figured her conversation was drawing to a close.

"Jim," Garcia said, his tone still hushed but suddenly more serious, "about Jonny. I know now's not the time... Was it quick?"

Cochrane slowly turned his head to look down at Garcia. Whether his face portrayed confusion or disappointment, he was not sure.

"I knew him for eight years!" Garcia hissed. "We went through basic together! I know his parents will get the visit, but it's me they'll come to for a face to face explanation!"

Cochrane blew out slowly and nodded his head. That made sense. He, too, was sorry to see Lanne gone, but it was not the first comrade he had personally shoveled into a body bag, piece by piece, and it would not be the last.

"Instantaneous, mate," Cochrane replied. "His team got hit by a fragmentation missile. Here one second, gone the next. He wouldn't have felt a thing."

"That the truth?"

Cochrane turned back to face the shorter soldier.

"Yes! It's the bloody truth! You're a corporal in the Fusiliers! Not a bloody space cadet! If he had suffered for a whole hour, I'd still tell you! I'm not going to wrap it in cotton wool for the likes of you, am I?"

Any response from Garcia was cut off as Shankar made her way across to crouch down by the two NCOs. Cochrane looked across to her expectantly.

"That was Company HQ," Shankar said, "Major Barker is back at Alpha Four-Four. The political situation is deteriorating. Yu Jing now claim that not only is our declaration of the border here inaccurate, they also say that the research site at Alpha Four-Four is on their side of the border and have demanded it is handed over."

"Well, that's bollocks," Cochrane grunted.

"Regardless," Shankar continued, "O-12 seem to be drifting closer to their side of the argument. There's talk of an O-12 delegation coming to investigate the site."

"Sounds a lot more like O-12 exploiting this for their own end." Garcia tutted. "So what happens now?"

Shankar pressed a clenched fist against her chin and looked down at the grimy, weed- and vine-covered alloy floor plates. Only now did Cochrane notice how exhausted she looked.

"Number One Platoon is dug in closer to the border," Shankar said, "near where we first encountered the Yujingyu advance. It sounds like they've been involved in fighting even heavier than here. Understandably, most reinforcements we have are being sent their way. The major says he can send us a couple of Sierra Dronbots when we are resupplied at dawn tomorrow. That's about it for now. We're to hold position."

Cochrane cleared his throat as he nodded his head in thought. Two Sierras were far better than nothing; a bit of firepower for their perimeter and some automation to allow some of his soldiers to get some rest was appreciated. The problem was that he expected reinforcements would also be on their way to their enemies. The conversation was interrupted as Beckmann appeared at the entrance to the control room. The lithe soldier dropped to one knee by the three Fusiliers, placing her long MULTI Sniper Rifle down next to her. Her face and chest were streaked with green-tinged grime and sweat, which did nothing to stop Cochrane staring at her cleavage, almost forgiving her many, many flaws by her decision to leave her camouflaged jumpsuit left

140

partially unzipped. A reddened bandage was hastily wrapped around a trio of small wounds on one arm, the pattern indicating that the injury was most likely caused by a careless encounter with a Karava vine rather than the enemy.

"They've set themselves up in a small clearing about two K to the southeast of here," Beckmann said, sharing a marked map image with each of the three Fusiliers. "Half a platoon of Zhanshi with a couple of Invincibles made it out of the fight. They've already been met by another section of reinforcements."

"That about evens us out," Garcia offered, "although we're getting dronbots to reinforce…"

"*Ja,* I know," Beckmann interrupted, "my chain of command has already informed me independently. I've set explosive charges at these markers between us and them. They're set both to proximity and on timers. Here are the timings the explosives will detonate. They're just small anti-personnel charges, it's all I had. If those bastards don't come back here and set them off, the timers will at least keep them guessing every hour or so for the rest of the night."

"And stop my soldiers from getting any sleep, ma'am," Shankar added bitterly.

Beckmann looked across at the Fusilier lieutenant incredulously.

"You're in a fucking war, Cupcake, your beauty sleep will have to wait. Although it certainly looks to me like you could damn well use some."

Cochrane opened his mouth to defend his platoon commander but decided against it. As much as he objected to the Hexa operative's presence, in this case, she was correct.

"I took out one of their sentries to keep those bastards on their toes," Beckmann continued, "if they know we can get inside their perimeter, they'll think twice about another attack any time soon."

"I didn't hear any shots fired," Cochrane folded his arms.

Beckmann looked up at him and patted the thin fighting knife on her thigh.

"I didn't shoot him. In my experience, people are even more scared about being infiltrated and having their throats slit than they are about snipers. I also got close enough to hear half a conversation being transmitted to their platoon commander."

"You hacked their comm network?" Garcia asked.

"No, I don't know how to," Beckmann replied. "I don't know how to hack. I did it the old fashioned way; getting close enough to hear him talking. They've got reinforcements inbound for another attack here. They've also cleared a narrow path to their base. They couldn't get a vehicle through to resupply, so I'm concerned they're going to try to bring up something else entirely."

Cochrane's eyes widened at the suggestion.

"You think they'll try to bring a TAG up here?"

The introduction of Tactical Armored Gear – hulking, battle suits dripping with weaponry and standing over twice the height of a heavy infantryman – would leave a position defended by less than twenty Fusiliers almost certainly doomed. Garcia looked across at Shankar.

"Ma'am, we need to report this to Company HQ," the muscular corporal blurted. "See if we can get a Cutter down here to…"

"Wait, wait, wait," Shankar sighed and held up a hand, "we'll do no such thing. I've just finished talking to Major Barker. We have our orders. Number One Platoon is bearing the brunt of this. I'm not going crying off to the major to demand more reinforcements based on a path cut through some trees. That may or may not be there."

Beckmann's face twisted into a scowl.

"Are you calling me a fucking liar?!"

"Well, it is your job, isn't it, ma'am?" Shankar glared back. "To use deceit to get close to your targets? Do you have any surveillance imagery of this enemy camp you claim to have infiltrated? Literally any proof you've achieved anything in the eight hours you've been gone?"

Beckmann unsheathed her stained, twin-edged fighting knife and slammed it down to stick in between two of the alloy floor plates.

"I've got blood on my blade, which is more than I can say for you, you useless bitch!" Beckmann snapped. "Are you honestly telling me that you are going to risk the lives of your platoon and your mission objective by refusing to act on the intelligence I've provided, for something as immature as the fact that you don't like me?!"

Shankar flicked her dark eyes across to Cochrane.

"Your thoughts, Sergeant?"

Cochrane wrapped the thick fingers of one hand around the clenched fist of the other. A nocturnal jungle animal let out a shriek from only a few paces past the tree line to the west. He looked across at the other three soldiers.

"I don't doubt what the major saw," he finally said, "but I agree with Lieutenant Shankar. We can't just go calling up Company HQ and demanding reinforcements are redirected away from where they are needed because there's a path in the trees."

"Do you two hear yourselves?" Beckmann growled. "We're not in a nature reserve! If there is a path there, that means it has been cut recently! And those bastards don't have mulebots programmed to clear a way through, so it's even harder for them! That's a metric ton of effort, it's right on our doorstep, and this place would be an ideal staging post for an attack on Alpha Four-Four! It's even got power generators! Your Number One Platoon isn't bearing the brunt of the Yujingyu assault! They're taking the feign! The more I think about

142

it, the more I think the main attack is coming this way!"

"Well," Shankar shrugged, "I still fail to see how you've jumped to the conclusion that we're at the epicenter of an entire assault because you saw a pathway cut in the trees. And by your own admission, you are a sniper, an infiltrator, an assassin. You're not an infantry officer. So you'll excuse me if my decision remains. I'll follow my orders. I don't need to go rogue based on a hunch when there are lives on the line."

Beckmann let out a string of obscenities in her native tongue, snatched up her knife, and shoved it back into its sheath. She stormed back to the entrance to the cramped control room but stopped before disappearing into the night to turn around again. She pointed a finger in accusation at Shankar.

"You follow your orders," she whispered venomously, "but don't pretend for a second that you are concerned about the lives of the soldiers here. You're just worried about how this reflects on you and your career advancement. So fine, sit there and do nothing. I'll carry on using my experience and initiative; two things you do not possess. I'll contact your major myself."

Cochrane watched as Beckmann stomped angrily out into the darkening evening. Shankar silently turned away. Garcia looked across quizzically at Cochrane. He could only offer a shrug. Odds were that Shankar was correct, but if Beckmann was right, then the repercussions would be cataclysmic. That was more than enough to concern him deeply.

***

His mouth dry and his head throbbing with a dull pain, Hawkins slowly opened his eyes. His ears quickly adjusted to buzzing on two very different frequencies – one was the electric barrier windows of the small room, the other was the insects in the jungle outside – as he slowly sat up. Hawkins had slept on a borrowed roll mat, clad only in the black combat trousers and vest he normally wore beneath his heavy armor. His bare feet pressing against the cold alloy plates of the floor, he clambered wearily up and took in his surroundings.

The early morning sun sat a few inches above the horizon, scorching the jungle surrounding the overgrown mining site. Another cloudless sky and another sunny day in Paradiso, reminding Hawkins of family vacations as a child where he spent three or four days with a glimpse of what luxury his father could temporarily afford, followed by three or four days counting down to the return journey to a gray, rainy home and a childhood wondering what he would one day have to do for a life in the sun. Hawkins issued a quiet laugh to himself. Getting shot at in a jungle was not what he had in mind as a child when he decided he needed to move away from the rain and fog of his parents' home.

A slight rustle behind him reminded Hawkins that he had not slept alone. Lance Corporal Abby Reid, the second-in-command of Number Two Section, hesitantly opened her eyes from where she was packed into a sleeping bag in the far corner of the small room. The soldiers had been stood down for sleep, two at a time, and it had been Reid who had shared Hawkins' stint on perimeter guard duty. The ginger-haired, freckled woman muttered to herself under her breath and unzipped her sleeping bag, reaching next to her to grab for her combat trousers.

"Oh... I'm sorry, I'll wait outside," Hawkins offered embarrassedly.

"Don' worry about it, sir," Reid drawled, pulling on her trousers, "I reckon with you being a monk and all, you're probably a lot more embarrassed than I am."

Hawkins found that he did not have the energy to correct her, but it did remind him about the need for morning prayers. Technically, given that he was now very much on front line operations and liable for combat at any moment, the rules of his Order did not mandate a requirement for prayers and exercise. It was left to the individual's discretion. But, Hawkins figured, given how quiet it was outside, the very least he could offer was ten minutes of concentrated prayer and solid reflection before venturing back out.

After prayer; washing and shaving with spray-on cans; and the lengthy process of hauling on each component of his armor, connecting them, running the built-in test function, and then retrieving his weapons, Hawkins stepped outside. He noted again a cracked plate of armor from the last firefight but, with his basic maintenance kit being back at Alpha Four-Four, even that simple replacement would have to wait. He suppressed a yawn. Two hours sleep had both seemed to last an eternity and left him feeling somehow even more tired, but as he vacated the old control room with Reid, he found May and Smalls eagerly waiting their turn for a brief respite from guard duty.

Hawkins looked around the mining site. Shankar and Corporal Garcia walked toward the ladder leading up to the HMG position atop one of the mining platforms. Cochrane and another of the Fusiliers Hawkins could not name were in the Platoon HQ control center next to the room designated for off-duty sleeping. Carson, the Platoon HQ medic, crouched next to where Beckmann sat on an alloy crate, inspecting a wound on her arm. Grateful of the cool air circulating around his armored suit now that he had thoroughly given up on the idea of switching off his suit's temperature control support in a blazing jungle, Hawkins walked across to the Platoon HQ.

Cochrane looked up as Hawkins entered the small HQ room - identical in every proportion to the next squat building along that was used to allow soldiers to sleep within the coolness of a controllable environment.

"Morning, sir," the tall sergeant greeted, tapping one ear, "just on a call to Company HQ."

"Right," Hawkins replied quietly before exchanging a smile and a nod

144

of greeting with the second soldier – a swarthy, black-haired Fusilier with a neat, thin beard that Hawkins' comlog identified by his IFF as Giorgos Kapsis. Hawkins made a note to remember the name; it was the very least he could do for the men and women he was working alongside. Hawkins waited patiently as Cochrane replied monosyllabically to the caller at Company HQ before ending the conversation just as Shankar walked into the HQ, taking off her blue beret and placing her Combi Rifle down by the door.

"Good timing, ma'am," Cochrane greeted, "that was the 2IC with a sit rep. Number One Platoon is still locked in place against a platoon of Zhanshi. They've been exchanging fire on and off all night. Light casualties, but they've lost a couple of guys. Number Two Platoon is still guarding the perimeter at Alpha Four-Four. Our two dronbots are on the way and expected at any minute, along with ammunition and water. I've let them know that we've had a quiet night and no updates since yesterday morning."

"And long may it continue," Shankar muttered, unclipping her water bottle from her waist.

She glanced across at Hawkins, seemingly acknowledging his presence, but said nothing.

"Any direction on what they want from us?" Shankar asked wearily.

"No update," Cochrane replied, "orders remain to hold and prevent any advance by enemy forces whilst the politicians duke it out and decide whose maps are correct out of us and them. I'll get some coffee going."

"In this heat?" Shankar snorted.

"You can have it cold, if you want," Cochrane beamed, his beard bristling around his thick lips.

Cochrane took his own water bottle from his belt and fished out a small sachet from one of the pouches of his daypack. He looked up at Hawkins as he set about preparing the coffee.

"Y'see, sir," he began, "a lot of the diggers 'round here will tell you their secrets to the perfect coffee with limited kit to prepare. Get the heat right first before you add the powder, don't burn the milk... but I've got my own secret. To me, the perfect cup of coffee on the move lies in accepting the very worst of standards and simply not giving a shit. Fancy one?"

"Erm... yes?" Hawkins ventured, grabbing his own water bottle and detaching the cup lid. "I'm normally a tea drinker, but your sales pitch was really rather good."

Cochrane half-filled Hawkins' cup with a trickle of worryingly odorless coffee, accompanied by an almost sinister smile.

"Thank you."

"Quite alright, sir."

Hawkins sank back into the corner of the room and looked down into the steaming cup before his eyes wandered back up and out across the jungle.

The rusted metals of the mining site half re-conquered by the jungle were blurred in places due to the heat haze. A small flock of purple-pink birds took to the skies from the lime-colored trees to the west. It seemed incredulous to Hawkins that he had graduated from his four years of training in the icy, unforgiving surroundings of Skovorodino less than a month before. He had even foregone his post-graduation leave to volunteer for the Paradiso job. It had been over six months since he had last seen his parents at their home.

The thought reminded Hawkins of sitting at the window of his childhood bedroom – now his father's study – looking out over the muddy fields below gray, leaden skies and at the fences running around the school he was educated in up until the age of eleven. The same dull, brick buildings and dreary playground. Many of his childhood friends still lived and worked within a stone throw of where they grew up, content with normal jobs and normal lives, driving to work in the rain with the guarantee of returning home every evening and being left to their own devices every weekend. A safe existence of paying bills and eventually marrying and raising a family.

Hawkins stared across the sun-drenched jungle, one hand resting on the pommel of the sword he had used to kill two human beings the previous morning. If his childhood friends could see him now. Less than a month into the vocation he had chosen – killing for the church – Hawkins found himself wondering how long it would be until he would wish it all away for a simple, dreary existence in the rain of his home town. Safe, secure, predictable.

Hawkins was dragged away from his introspection when Shankar suddenly clicked her fingers to attract Cochrane's attention and pointed to one of her ears. The tall sergeant tapped on his comlog's wrist controls to dial in to whatever conversation Shankar had been interrupted with. Hawkins, like Kapsis, watched them both silently with eager anticipation. His answer came when Shankar opened a communication channel to the entire platoon.

"All units, this is Zero," she announced, concern in her tone. "Surveillance reports enemy units closing from the southeast, less than one kilometer away. Two Section to take position on the perimeter defenses. One Section, assemble at Platoon HQ."

"Boss," Cochrane called across, "another message – potential second group advancing from the west, similar range. Nothing confirmed, but a surveillance drone has a doppler return on scanner."

"The west?" Shankar exclaimed as she slung her Combi Rifle over her shoulder. "How the hell did they loop all the way around there? That must be wrong. Could just be jungle animals."

"I doubt it if a drone scanner has picked it up," Cochrane warned, "and if our surveillance drones are having a hard time picking up their movement through all the vegetation, it could be something a little... stealthier than we've seen so far."

146

Shankar shrugged.

"Then we've got just the person to go take a closer look."

Wordlessly, Hawkins followed Shankar, Cochrane, and Kapsis out of the Platoon HQ room and into the dusty clearing between the control rooms and the northern mining platforms. On the other side of the clearing, Corporal Garcia bellowed at his nine Fusiliers to move them into position, lining defenses where a HMG had been set up atop one of the platforms, with a missile launcher and ammunition on the next platform along. The five survivors of Number One Section quickly gathered in the clearing, along with Major Beckmann and Fusilier Carson of the Platoon HQ.

"Company HQ has reported enemy activity a kilometer from here," Shankar greeted the assembled soldiers. "Surveillance images indicate it's the same Zhanshi platoon we exchanged fire with yesterday morning. Right now, we have little more than thermal imagery showing them at section strength, but we need to be prepared for anything. Two Section has the first line, we'll be in position and ready to respond once we've got a better idea of what we are facing."

Shankar turned to Beckmann.

"Ma'am, there is the potential of a second enemy force to the west. I'm sending you a marker and surveillance imagery now. Company HQ isn't sure, but I think it should be investigated. Are you content to go and take a look?"

Beckmann tapped one finger on her wrist, her eyes flitting from left to right as she scanned through the images transmitted to her lens. Hawkins watched the planning taking place in awkward silence. Beckmann narrowed her eyes.

"There's something there," she said. "I'll go find out what. Do you need the Hospitaller? I'd rather have a second gun with me."

Shankar looked across at Hawkins. Hawkins nodded and looked over at Beckmann. She pointed at his hands.

"You won't need the coffee, Sub Officer," she remarked dryly. "Come with me."

Hawkins looked down at where his hands still clutched the half-full cup of steaming coffee. He placed it down on the window sill of the Platoon HQ room, pulled on his helmet, and unclipped his MULTI Rifle from his back. His perception of his surroundings immediately seemed to increase twofold as the superior lens in his helmet overrode the more basic, functional pieces worn against his own eyes. Shadows in the jungle partially melted away; blurred patches of vegetation sharpened into greater focus. Likewise, the hearing filters in his helmet automatically dampened out the useless background buzzing of insects, leaving a clear audio signal of orders being passed to Fusiliers and the clunk of metal on metal as weapons were made ready.

"Follow me," Beckmann ordered curtly.

The tall woman held her long MULTI Sniper Rifle across her chest and picked up her pace across the clearing, quickly moving to the tree line running along the western edge of the mining site and then moving forward into the jungle. Hawkins watched as the patterns and hues of her clothing morphed and matched their surroundings, fading between different greens and browns as she moved deeper into the jungle. His own suit's sensor array picked up an incoming secure transmission from Beckmann, which he immediately accepted. A vivid blue line instantly appeared to outline her form on his visor, making her easily stand out in his field of view against the greens behind her.

"I'm getting an update from the closest surveillance drone," Beckmann's voice chimed through his helmet's ear pieces as they moved swiftly westward, the slim Hexa operative slipping through small gaps in the foliage whilst Hawkins used his sword to hack his way through. "The automated alert was based off a doppler shift from one of the drone's scanners, so something moving fast enough to be detected. The follow up scan of the area then detected man-made materials, so even without a visual confirmation, that's enough for me to be content that there are enemy forces up ahead."

Hawkins brought his sword hacking down through another thick vine as he struggled to keep pace with the lithe woman as she effortlessly ducked and darted through seemingly invisible gaps in the packed vegetation. He risked a quick look behind them. The path back to the mining site was already gone, seemingly swallowed up whole by the living mass of jungle trees.

"Those drones are good," Beckmann continued, "so whatever is up ahead has some stealth. With the Zhanshi moving in from the east again, everything points to this being reinforcements moving to flank us or at least take advantage of the Fusiliers being distracted to either assess our strength or infiltrate our position. Are you following this, Sub Officer?"

"Yes, ma'am," Hawkins replied quickly.

Hawkins' knowledge of drone surveillance was functional at best; his training was focused around the sword and gun, and faith. Surveillance assets transmitted updates to his suit's sensors. That was as far as his level of knowledge took him.

The two soldiers continued on through the humid jungle, the area ahead growing lighter as rays of sunlight broke through the thinning canopy above them. The vegetation began to spread a little. Patches of bare, sandy earth broke up the trees and colorful bushes, revealing more clearly that the ground was now beginning to slope gently uphill. To the left, a felled tree played colony to a swarming host of large, electric blue insects. To the right, a clear stream gently trickled down through a shallow, narrow chasm of sand-colored rocks.

"Wait here," Beckmann breathed.

She swiftly dropped to one knee behind a small outcrop of sandy rock, jutting from the side of the slope and presenting her with a view down the other side of the sandy ridge line. Instantly her clothing morphed to match its surroundings perfectly, and she disappeared from view completely, save for the outline of her form projected onto Hawkins' eye pieces. He, in turn, moved up to the shallow ridge and dropped down behind a thick tree trunk. Even with the smart fabric dulling the normally vivid red of his Hospitaller surcoat down to almost gray, he felt conspicuous next to the barely visible Hexa sniper.

"This is about as far as I could have moved from that first sensor hit in this time," Beckmann whispered. "If they are heading for the mining facility, they'll be coming this way and they won't be far. Keep a look out and be ready. If you see them first, put a marker on them and send it to me. Don't fire. Understood?"

Hawkins nodded and pulled the butt of his MULTI Rifle against his shoulder, leaning against the side of the light brown tree trunk as he stared ahead. The ground gently sloped down away from them into a shallow valley, along the bottom of which ran a broad, gentle stream of clear, ankle deep water running parallel to the ridge. The stream was completely devoid of trees for a few meters to either side, allowing the fierce sunlight down to sparkle off the gently trickling water and the surrounding white sands. A dozen or so fist-sized creatures with smooth wings of lilac and yellow, not dissimilar to the butterflies of Earth, gently fluttered across the surface of the water.

Hawkins stared up the other side of the valley, into where the trees and bushes thickened and darkened again, and a greater density of yellow rocks jutted out of the slopes. A slow minute passed as his eyes moved from shadow to shadow, occasionally jumping at what he very quickly ascertained was nothing other than a strand of vine swaying from a gentle breeze or a small lizard scampering across a rock or branch. A second minute dragged on and into a third. Birds cawed overhead as a trio of them circled above the long clearing of the stream. Nothing else moved or made a sound in the idyllic setting of the Paradiso jungle as the minutes dragged on.

A marker was suddenly transmitted to Hawkins' comlog. He selected it and brought it up on his lens, highlighting an area of dead ground between two rocky outcrops on the far side of the slope.

"You see them?" Beckmann whispered.

Hawkins stared at the marker, his eyes darting from bush to tree to crevice.

"No," he replied anxiously, "I can't see anything there."

"Look along a bearing of two-five-nine degrees from your position," Beckmann whispered, "about three meters down from the top of the other side of the valley. Do you see the two outcrops, one shaped like an L and the other to the right is lower and smoother?"

Hawkins overlaid a compass onto his lens and stared off in response to the directions. The two outcrops were as clear as crystal, exactly as described.

"I've got the outcrops!" he replied, his voice hushed. "But I... there's nothing there!"

"There's a Fireteam of Tiger Soldiers right there," Beckmann replied, "four... wait... five of them."

Tiger Soldiers? Hawkins let out a long breath. Elite, highly-trained, and deadly medium infantry of the notorious Yujingju Airborne. Hawkins again focused his eyes in the given direction. He utilized his armored suit's sensors to zoom in and refocus. Still he saw nothing.

There – finally. Little more than a slightly angular, natural shape, Hawkins saw part of a figure crouched down behind the larger outcrop of rocks. All he could see was a head, shoulder, and arm but after refocusing, he could just about detect the yellow-orange armor that barely stood out from the paler yellow of the rocks, its alloy plates broken up with wavy black tiger stripes.

"Okay, I see one."

Another marker appeared on Hawkins' tactical map. A pathway, leading from their current position down the shallow valley to their right, across the stream, and then up closer to the waiting enemy Tiger Soldiers. Hawkins' eyes opened wide as he saw the route plotted out in front of him. He turned to face Beckmann.

"You want us to advance on them?"

"Not us. You."

"Me? Alone?"

"Sub Officer," Beckmann whispered, "they've stopped there because they are working out a route across that stream. It's too open for them. They may well fall back and find a better, more covered crossing. We don't have time for that. I need you to move to a better firing position so we can hit them from two sides."

Hawkins swallowed.

"You want me to be bait for a team of five elite enemy soldiers?"

No sooner had the words escaped from his mouth, Hawkins realized how pathetic they sounded. He had volunteered for this. Nobody ever said safety was guaranteed. He spoke again before Beckmann could.

"Alright, I'm on my way," Hawkins said. "Do you want me to..."

"You're not bait," Beckmann said, "just move from cover to cover. Don't let them know you've seen them. I won't let anything happen to you, Kyle."

Hawkins cleared his throat and looked down the slope, the route Beckmann had planned illuminated in blue on his lens. There was no point in any further discussion. Hawkins knew well from experience that the longer he thought difficult things through rather than actually just facing them, the more of an ordeal they became in his mind. With that thought, he stood up and walked downslope toward the start of the path highlighted in his lens.

Both hands clutching his MULTI Rifle as he quickly made his way through the gaps in the trees and foliage, Hawkins hurried down toward the foot of the shallow valley and the gentle stream below. He risked a glance up toward where he last saw the Fireteam of Tiger Soldiers, but already they had faded back into nothingness. His heart thumped in his chest as he edged further downhill, his lens automatically darkening to compensate the sudden intrusion of blinding sunlight as he moved out from beneath the jungle canopy and into direct light. His throat felt parched and the cooling air of his armored suit's environmental control system suddenly turned from comforting to leaving a nauseating taste in his mouth.

"They've seen you," Beckmann's voice whispered through his ear pieces, "they're moving to…"

Hawkins' earpieces faded to nothing. A fraction of a second later, his lens darkened to blackness and his tactical map switched off. Dropping his MULTI Rifle to place both hands on his helmet and tear it off, hot, humid air and the chorus of buzzing insects flooded Hawkins' senses as he dove to the ground. Before he even landed in the sand at his feet, a double crack in the hot, humid air above him sent a small flock of colorful birds rocketing up into the clear sky above the stream as two bullets zipped over his head.

Hawkins scrambled forward to grab his MULTI Rifle before backing quickly away to lay low behind a flat, sandy-colored rock. As instantly as the deadly fire begun, the jungle fell silent again. Realizing he was holding his breath as if the very action of exhaling would somehow give away his position, Hawkins released a slow lungful of air. He brought his left wrist up to run a built-in test on his armored suit, remembering the system shutdown that had prompted his dive for cover. Nothing. His joints were powered by the auxiliary hydraulic reservoir, giving him full mobility, but there was nothing else – for the second time since his arrival on Paradiso, every other system had fallen victim to an unseen enemy hacker.

Bringing his MULTI Rifle up to his chin where he lay behind the sparse cover, belly down in the sand, Hawkins checked the weapon's scope. At least that was fully functioning. He quickly linked the scope to his lens and tilted the weapon up over the cover of the rocks to check his immediate area. There was nothing other than the still paradise of the sunlit jungle stream and the babbling of the clear water.

A low whine suddenly rose in pitch into a shrill howl before stopping abruptly. There was a momentary silence again before a voice yelled out in agony, screaming in a language Hawkins did not understand. The tinny rattle of a submachine gun echoed from the far side of the stream, but Hawkins did not hear any rounds falling near his position. Again, there was silence. Even just a handful of brief exposures to firefights had left Hawkins less apprehensive of confronting the enemy, but he now found his hands shaking and his throat dry as the feeling of helplessness descended upon him in his hiding place. His breathing shallow, sweat dripping from his forehead into his eyes, Hawkins risked a glance over the top of the cover of the rocks.

"Kyle! Stay down!" Beckmann yelled from what sounded like a long way away.

Hawkins ducked back into cover just as the submachine gun let out another burst of fire, followed a second later by the lower thump of a Combi Rifle. Another silence followed, this one seemingly stretching out for long, deadly minutes of inactivity. Nothing. No gunfire, not even the rustle of leaves from movement. Hawkins fought down the rising terror in his chest. For all he knew, Beckmann had been killed by the last exchange of gunfire and the Tiger Soldiers were now moving around to encircle him, helpless without the sensors from his heavy armor. Hawkins glanced across to where he had discarded his helmet. Slowly, carefully, he reached across and retrieved it. He checked his system read outs again. Still dead. Hawkins shook his head. He still had mobility and a fully functioning rifle and sword. He would be damned if it all ended cowering behind a rock.

"Enough of this," Hawkins breathed, jumping up to his feet. He dashed forward toward the stream and the next patch of rocky cover.

The now familiar howl and whine of a high velocity sniper round cut through the dense air, the sound somehow as comforting as church bells. Hawkins dove to cover and brought his MULTI Rifle up to his shoulder, staring through the scope to assess his surroundings. He saw a fallen Tiger Soldier not far from where the enemy Fireteam was first sighted, but nothing else. Then, without a sound, he felt the barely perceptible thrum of his suit's auxiliary power unit rebooting. He quickly dragged on his helmet and felt a blast of fresh air as his eye pieces flared up into life, immediately highlighting Beckmann's position in the high ground on the far side of the stream and a marker showing the position of the enemy unit.

"You online again?" Beckmann whispered.

"Yes."

"Stay down. Stay. Fucking. Down."

Reluctantly, disappointed now that his systems were online and he was fully in the fight again, Hawkins slid back into cover. Perhaps ten seconds, still feeling closer to ten minutes, slowly dragged by until Beckmann spoke again.

"I've hit two of them," she said, her husky voice still hushed, "one seriously. The others have fallen back."

"Can I come out now?" Hawkins asked.

There was another long pause before the answer came.

"Yes. Area's clear. Move to Marker Bravo."

His MULTI Rifle still raised and ready to fire, Hawkins moved quickly forward over the sandy rocks at the foot of the shallow valley, advancing toward the designated marker on his tactical map and lens. He checked to either side as he moved up the opposite slope, still utilizing what cover he could as he neared the crest of the ridge line opposite the initial vantage point over the Tiger Soldiers.

Hawkins stopped. Just at the edge of the shade of the trees, lying on the shallow, sandy incline where he had fallen, was one of the Tiger Soldiers. Even through the soldier's alloy breastplate, Hawkins could see his chest rising and falling, slowly and weakly. A jagged hole had been blown through the man's yellow-orange, tiger striped armor, through the bottom of the ribcage. A pile of glistening, red-pink innards lay in a bloody, sand-covered pile by a large exit wound. Hawkins had no idea how long he stood motionless, staring down at the dying soldier by his feet. The man spoke a word, perhaps two, but Hawkins could not hear him clearly enough to even ascertain whether it was in English.

"He's the first one I hit," Beckmann said, stepping out of the shadows to suddenly appear at Hawkins' side as she removed her hood, the yellows and greens on her clothing solidifying into a clearer pattern. "The other one I think I only clipped. Their hacker. This one is their sergeant, judging by his kit."

Snapped out of his stunned trance, Hawkins dashed forward and dropped to one knee by the wounded enemy soldier. He could hear the words emanating through the grill of the Tiger Soldier sergeant's faceplate now but could not understand them.

"I... I can try to stop the bleeding," Hawkins stammered, reaching up to the small medical pouch on his webbing, "but I'm no medic... I... I can try... Can you understand what he is saying?"

"*Ja,*" Beckmann replied calmly, pacing around the tiny clearing as her eyes scanned the shadows in every direction. "He is saying to fuck you and fuck your god."

Hawkins stopped. He looked down at the subdued white cross on his chest. The Yujingyu sergeant's words did not matter. He could understand the fear and the hatred.

"We can get him back to the mining site," Hawkins said as he pulled a bandage out of his webbing pouch, "maybe call in a Tubarão to get him to a hospital? I don't know, Major, I don't think he has much of a chance, but I'll try."

The Tiger Soldier's shaking, bloodied hand weakly reached up to his hip and closed around the handle of a sheathed knife. Beckmann paced over, unholstered her pistol, cocked the hammer with her thumb, and shot the man twice in the chest, two deafening gunshots echoing across the stream valley. Hawkins let out a choked gasp, the bandage falling from his limp fingers as he stared down at the dead body in the sand before him. Beckmann broke open her heavy MULTI Pistol, smoke wafting up from the two empty chambers in the weapon's cylinder as she paced around, her eyes still tracking across the shadows warily. She calmly loaded two bulky, DA rounds into the empty chambers of the cylinder and snapped the pistol shut again before holstering it.

"We need to move fast," she nodded, "they'll look for another way to the mining site, and they know we're onto them now. Better to cut along the stream rather than go straight after them."

Hawkins sprang to his feet.

"What... what the hell did you just do?" he yelled.

Beckmann stopped and turned to face him, her face twisted in anger and confusion.

"*Vas?*"

"You shot a prisoner!" Hawkins roared. "A wounded man in our care! You... you murdered him!"

Beckmann's jaw set sternly as her fists clenched.

"I don't have time to argue about this with you!" She hissed through gritted teeth. "Now stop being so fucking naive! You seriously think we are going to put the lives of every soldier at the mine in jeopardy by abandoning our position and limping slowly home with an enemy soldier who would have bled to death within ten minutes? Besides, I saw him going for a weapon. Switch on and grow up, you idiot! We've got a job to do!"

Hawkins retrieved his MULTI Rifle and held it purposefully across his chest.

"No," he spat, shaking his head, "no, no. You murdered a prisoner! You knew he posed no threat, even with that knife! You can't just walk away from that! You..."

"Sub Officer! Stop whining and get your shit together!" Beckmann yelled. "We do not have time to debate your fucking morality here! I'll explain it all later, but right now, you need to focus, get your head in the game, and follow my orders!"

Hawkins backed away from the bloodied corpse, brutally at odds with the idyllic, serene setting of his death and the stone-faced, blue-eyed killer stood remorselessly over him.

"No," he shook his head again, "no. I'm not following your orders. I'm not following you anywhere! I'm heading back to the mine. I'm not taking another step with you."

Beckmann stared at him, her brow low, her eyes fixed in concentration, her hands holding her MULTI Sniper Rifle ready. Hawkins had faced down a hundred opponents in sparring rings during martial arts tournaments and training. He had seen the look of total concentration and readiness to fight. He had never before in his life seen a look anything even close to the glare that Beckmann fixed on him. The beautiful, animated, gregarious woman full of heart and soul he had spent an evening with only two nights ago was dead and gone. A cold, inhuman killer stood facing him, not an iota of emotion on her face, her stance displaying the instincts of an apex predator considering whether to move in for the kill. Goose bumps rose up across Hawkins' skin. His breathing grew quicker as he paced back away from her. The realization that she was considering killing him sunk in.

"What are you going to do, boy?" she asked. "Go back to those Fusiliers? Tell them you saw a war crime being committed? You've got no evidence, Sub Officer. It's already gone. Those drones above us, giving us the surveillance feeds, watching us right now – you think they've got a Hospitaller cross painted on them? They're Strategic Security Division. My people are watching our every move. Listening to our every word. Your suit's visual and aural data has already been erased. I told you on the way out here. Leave the nice guy behind. There's no room for nice guys here, Kyle. Just people who get the job done. At any cost."

His chest aching, bile rising in his throat, Hawkins finally gave way to the screaming voices of his conscience and turned his back on Beckmann. He paced quickly eastward and back toward the mining site, hoping and praying with each pace that he would not feel a bullet in his back or a knife across his throat. After only a dozen paces, his nerves gave way and he turned around again to face the little clearing above the stream. Beckmann was gone, leaving the corpse behind.

Chapter Eleven

Warm water from the stream immediately flowed over the top of Shankar's boots to soak her from the knee down as she limped toward the cover of the trees on the far bank. Another rattle of Combi Rifle fire from the foliage behind her made her instinctively duck her head down between her shoulders, as if such an action would somehow protect her from the impact of a 4.5mm bullet. Next to her, one arm wrapped tightly around her shoulders for support, Lance Corporal Abby Reid hissed and groaned in pain as she hopped on her one good leg, blood already seeping through the bandage wrapped tightly around her left thigh.

"Nearly there," Shankar declared, wincing as another bead of salt-laded sweat rolled down between her lips, "just through those trees ahead."

Shankar checked her tactical map. Both of her platoon's sections were falling back from their exchange of fire with the Zhanshi to the southeast of the mining site, with Cochrane taking charge of Number One Section after yet more losses in the opening seconds of the jungle skirmish. Shankar shook her head. Smalls and Byron were now names added to the rapidly lengthening list of dead from her platoon. Pushing the thoughts to the back of her mind, Shankar opened a channel on her comlog.

"Zero-One from Zero."

"Go for Zero-One," Cochrane replied.

"Sitrep."

"Yeah, they're... they're not following us. I'm at Marker November, about three minutes behind you with One Section. Two-One is alerted to your location and has you on IFF, you're cleared to enter the mining site, Safe Gate is Marker Oscar."

After several more minutes of slow limping through the dense trees, Shankar finally saw the rusted, vine-enveloped mining platforms ahead. Anxious of triggering the automated responses from the two perimeter dronbots, she double checked her IFF and that she had Marker Oscar – her agreed entry point through the perimeter – correctly plotted on her tactical map.

As she helped her wounded NCO out of the trees and across the rough, scrub ground running along the eastern perimeter, Shankar looked up and saw Fusilier Armando Ortega tracking their movement from behind a bipod mounted HMG atop one of the platforms. Corporal Garcia was already on his way down the rickety ladder to meet them. He jogged over from the foot of the platform and immediately put an arm around Reid to take the burden off Shankar and help her across to the Platoon HQ building.

"You're alright," he grinned at the red-haired soldier, "let's get that looked at properly."

Garcia opened a channel on his comlog.

"Dani, it's Ang. Abby's got one in the leg. Come here and take a look."

Shankar watched as the burly corporal carefully helped his second-in-command over to the cool air of the Platoon HQ in one of the old control rooms, whilst Mieke, the section medic, rushed over from the south side of
the encampment. Moments later, the remaining four Fusiliers of Number Two
Section's second Fireteam emerged from the jungle.

"Zero-One from Zero," Shankar called. "Two Section's back. Just
your lot to go."

"Yeah, two minutes behind you."

Retreating to the cover of the designated sentry platform, Shankar eyed
the tree line nervously for long minutes in silence, her eyes shifting between
the gaps in the trees, the hunched machine gun armed dronbots patrolling the
perimeter, and the scant pictorial detail being transmitted to her by the unseen
surveillance drones high above. Finally, Cochrane emerged with the survivors
from Number One Section; May, Southee, and Vesilin. He quickly made his
way over to Shankar, grimy and covered in a film of sweat, but his face neutral
and unfazed.

"Jack and Rex have both had it," he greeted grimly, slinging his Combi
Rifle over one broad shoulder. "HMG got them both in one sweep. We couldn't
recover their bodies, their fire was pretty bloody effective. I've marked them
both up so we can hopefully get them back at some point."

"Right," Shankar nodded quietly, the perpetual throbbing pain at her
temples seeming to suddenly escalate a stage.

"How's Abby?" Cochrane asked.

"Took a round in the leg," Shankar replied. "Dani is having a look
now."

"Was there an exit wound?" Cochrane enquired.

"Yes, I think so."

"Ah, she'll be fine, then. Tell her to toughen the fuck up."

Shankar looked up at the tall man and scowled.

"Lance Corporal Reid took a bullet through the leg. She's up to her
eyeballs on painkillers. My plan is to have her medivac'd, not to tell her to
toughen up."

Cochrane rolled his eyes.

"It's a joke, Priya. It's a bloody joke. It's how we keep our shit together when we get stuck in the middle of the woop woop and get shot at."

Shankar found herself unable to meet the older man's stern stare and
took a pace back before removing her beret and running one hand through her
damp, black hair. She quickly toyed with the idea of reminding him who was
the officer and who was in command, but either thought better of it or could
not muster the courage.

"We need rifles back on the perimeter," Shankar declared, "I doubt they'll come close enough after that, but we need to be ready if they do. We should have never gone out to meet them, Jim. We've got dronbots and gun positions with clear fields of fire right here. We should have stayed here."

The veteran sergeant shook his head.

"If they get close enough to take a proper look at this place, they'll realize that we're on the bones of our arses for people. If they know just how few of us are dug in here, they'll come in like a bloody steamroller. No, we did the right thing going out there. I'll get the perimeter set up, I guess you've got to report in to Company HQ."

Shankar let out a long, slow breath and then nodded. She pulled her beret back on and walked off toward the Platoon HQ, still inwardly seething over Cochrane's words and running through a dozen assertive responses she wished she had thought of at the time. She entered the HQ to find Reid motionless on the floor, her eyes closed. Mieke stood as Shankar entered the room.

"She's passed out, ma'am," she said, "but she's perfectly stable for now. There's nothing we can do for that wound here with a medical kit. She needs a medivac."

"Sure," Shankar nodded wearily, "I'm just about to report in to Company, anyway, so I'll get that arranged. Good job, Danielle."

The younger woman turned to leave. Remembering Cochrane's warning over Mieke's apparent relationship with Fusilier May – a soldier who had only moments before staggered back into the encampment having lost half his Fireteam – she thought over whether the complications of that situation were worth discussing. She decided against it, given the display of professionalism from both Fusiliers since the fighting had begun in earnest. Either that or, again, it was a subject she was uncomfortable bringing up and it was easier to just ignore it. After a brief thought on the matter, she told herself it was the former.

Some five minutes after passing her report on to Major Barker at Alpha Four-Four, Shankar was roused from her ruminations as Cochrane entered the Platoon HQ.

"Two Section have got the perimeter," the sergeant said, "I've sent One Section off for some rest. I think we might as well put Ed Carson in with One Section now. We don't really have much of a Platoon HQ, it's just us two, and at least with Ed we can just about muster a third Fireteam."

"Yeah," Shankar surpassed a yawn, "makes sense. They've got no NCO. I'll put Nat Southee in charge."

Cochrane's eyes opened wide.

"Nat? She's not a leader! Rob May's your most experienced digger in that lot."

"Nat's always asking for responsibility and the chance to prove she

159

should be a lance corporal." Shankar shrugged. "So… she can bloody well prove it. I'm putting her in charge."

"Priya!" Cochrane drawled. "Yeah, I get that if we're dicking around back home or on exercise, but out here we can't afford any balls ups. We should…"

"It's my platoon!" Shankar yelled, the volume of her voice surprising even herself. "So why don't you stop arguing and do that whole thing sergeants are supposed to do and offer help and support instead of railroading me every five bloody minutes!"

Cochrane stared down at Shankar, his broad jaw set. He nodded silently and then shrugged.

"Alright."

Shankar sprang to her feet as the sergeant turned to leave.

"Jim! Wait! Look… I'm sorry. That was a shit thing to say after everything you've done. It's just…"

Cochrane turned back again and folded his huge arms across his barrel chest. His features remained stern and impassive. Shankar briefly thought over how much she was willing to divulge.

"I haven't been sleeping," she admitted, "and I'm shattered. But I'm not allowed that luxury because I'm responsible for all of this. Five weeks ago, I was on leave with David, skiing. I'd never been shot at in my life and I'd certainly never killed anybody. Now I'm here, stuck in this nightmare with men and women I'm responsible for, watching them getting picked off like something in a horror movie, and… it's too late for me to realize and admit that I'm in the wrong job and becoming a Fusilier was a terrible idea."

Only then did Shankar witness the big man's features visibly soften.

"That's not you talking," he said quietly, "that's your fiancé."

Shankar raised one hand to her pounding head and looked out of the flickering windows across the parched earth between the abandoned mining platforms.

"No," she said, "no, you always say things like that about him, but you're wrong. You seem to have this picture in your head that David is an overbearing prick, like the villain in some shit romantic comedy. He's a good guy! He spent his first three months after graduating as a volunteer in at the Vedi refugee camps. He's from a rich family and could spend his life as some pampered playboy, but he chose to get out there and become a doctor because he wants to help people! He's a good man!"

Cochrane kept his eyes fixed on Shankar as he gently bit the corner of his lower lip thoughtfully.

"He might be a good man, but he's still trying to control your life. And that's bullshit. You need to get shot of him. And, if you don't mind me being blunt and honest…"

"I've never known you be anything other than that, Jim..."

"...to be blunt and honest, he's fat, balding, and out of shape. In ten years, he'll look like a sack of shit. Ditch him and go get yourself some pretty boy who'll do as he's told and won't give you shit for making your own choices in life."

"Break up my engagement so I can acquire a pliable, obedient pretty boy?" Shankar raised one eyebrow. "Any ideas where I find one of those?"

Cochrane tapped one booted foot against the alloy decking.

"What about Kyle? He seems like a good kid. And Nat and Abby are all over him like a bloody rash."

Shankar's eyes opened in alarm as a wave of cramp-like pain suddenly clawed at her stomach. She quickly opened a comlog channel.

"Broadsword-One from Zero!" she shouted.

She looked across at Cochrane, panic rising.

"I haven't checked in on what was going on to the west of us!"

She returned her attention to the open communication channel as Cochrane paced across to the far side of the small room before leaning over to warily regard the jungle to the west.

"Broadsword-One from Zero, respond!"

"Yeah, Zero, I hear you," she heard Hawkins' voice reply lethargically.

Her chest heaving as she fought to calm her nerves, Shankar dashed across the Platoon HQ to stare out of the window to the west.

"Kyle, where are you? What's going on?"

"I'm on the western perimeter," the Hospitaller replied quietly. "I'm walking the edge of the site with one of the dronbots."

"You're back here?"

"Yes. I got back about five minutes ago."

Almost as quickly as it had flared up with Cochrane only moments before, Shankar felt her temper rising rapidly. She took a moment to subdue her growing anger before she spoke again.

"Kyle, we needed to know. You need to keep us informed."

There was a silence before a terse response was issued over the communication channel.

"You know now."

Shankar narrowed her eyes, confused by the sudden show of petulance. She glanced across at Cochrane but then remembered that he was not dialed in to the conversation on the comlog.

"We need to know as soon as things are happening," she continued, "we need to..."

Cochrane looked across as Shankar's voice trailed off into nothing.

"What? What is it?"

She looked up at him.

"He disconnected on me. He bloody well hung up."

Grabbing her water bottle in the hope that some hydration would ease her aching head, Shankar sank down to sit in the corner of the room, glancing across at where Lance Corporal Reid still lay motionless and unconscious by the doorway. Cochrane looked out of the window above her.

"Here he is. He's coming over."

Moments later, Hawkins barged his way into the Platoon HQ. His MULTI Rifle was slung over one shoulder whilst he carried his helmet in one hand and his still sheathed sword by the middle of the blade in the other. His red surcoat was streaked with green stains, painting untidy and irregular lines almost irreverently across the once immaculate white cross on his chest.

"What?" Hawkins demanded in a tone Shankar did not think the normally calm man was capable of. "What do you want?"

Shankar slowly dragged herself back to her feet and eyed him warily. The young Hospitaller looked down at Reid and the anger in his eyes instantly faded.

"Is she alright?"

"She took a round in the leg. She's been sedated. She'll be medivac'd within the hour. What happened, Kyle?"

Hawkins clipped his sword to his waist and pressed an armored, clenched fist against his lips with his now free hand as he stared down at Shankar, his dark eyes angry again.

"I moved west with Major Beckmann, as ordered," he began, his tone cold, "we encountered a Fireteam of five Tiger Soldiers. Major Beckmann engaged them and killed one of them."

Shankar swore out loud.

"Tiger Soldiers? You saw Yujingyu Airborne? You're sure?"

"Yes, I'm sure!" Hawkins retorted angrily.

Cochrane stepped forward, the normally stoic face of the veteran Fusilier even showing some signs of concern.

"What happened then, sir? Where is Major Beckmann now?"

"The enemy unit fell back. The major pursued them. We were separated. I came back here."

"Separated?" Shankar scoffed in confusion. "How the hell did that happen? You lost her IFF as well as her..."

"We were separated!" Hawkins seethed through gritted teeth. "I don't know how! We got separated! I don't know where she is!"

Faced by the suddenly intimidating stare of the raging religious soldier, Shankar found herself edging away back into the corner of the tiny room. It was the first time she had ever seen a spark of something in the young Hospitaller that supported the dark reputation of the zealous Holy Order knights.

162

Coming from a man she knew to be normally so calm as to almost be timid only made it worse. She took two deep, slow breaths and turned to Cochrane for support.

"You don't need to talk to Lieutenant Shankar that way, sir," Cochrane warned, folding his arms.

Hawkins spun around to face the taller man and glared up at him.

"Or else what?" he demanded, staring at the older soldier without a shred of fear. "What are you going to do about it?"

Cochrane met his stare but said nothing. Hawkins swore under his breath and shook his head.

"Thought so," the Hospitaller spat before barging his way past the Fusilier sergeant and back out of the control room.

Shankar watched the young soldier stomp angrily away back toward the western perimeter with a mixture of abject confusion and no small amount of fear. The sudden outburst reminded her for a second of one of her instructors in basic training; a kindly old captain with a ready smile and an approachable nature whose extremely rare outbursts of anger were so volatile that they were ten times as terrifying as the routinely raging instructors. She had seen Hawkins fight and knew he was dangerous. That was not what she found intimidating. It was the huge contrast between his normal character and what she just unexpectedly found herself on the receiving end of.

"What was that about?" Shankar exhaled, immediately conscious of the irony of her query given her own recent outburst.

"I have an idea," Cochrane replied quietly.

Shankar mused on his words for a brief moment.

"I suppose it was only a matter of time before we saw his true colors," she shrugged regretfully. "I mean, the church's Military Orders do not have a reputation for kindness and charity. They're known for their somewhat explosive and narrow-minded violence. He hid it well, for a while. Even I was convinced."

"No," Cochrane shook his head.

Shankar looked across.

"No?"

"No," he repeated thoughtfully, "it's not *his* true colors. What we've just seen is a conscientious young man, deeply hurt because he has just seen for the first time the way Hexas truly operate. That's what my money is on."

***

"It's nothing," Shankar sighed, closing down the comlog channel from the perimeter Fireteam, "just some big jungle cat coming to take a look at what we're up to here. Go on, ma'am."

163

Outside the Platoon HQ room, one of the machine gun armed dronbots paced slowly past the edge of the mining facility, the whir of its motors faintly audible as its angular, spider-like legs carried its squat, armored body around its programmed route. Up above them, on the tallest of the rickety platforms, the silhouettes of two Fusiliers manning a bipod mounted HMG were visible in the bright moonlight. Shankar checked her comlog. It was nearly midnight. She turned back to where Beckmann stood on the other side of the small room, opposite from Shankar and Cochrane. The tall woman highlighted a route on their shared tactical map.

"We encountered the Tiger Soldiers here, just at the foot of this valley by the small stream. We eliminated one and wounded a second, and they fell back. I gave chase but I couldn't find them again."

The stunningly beautiful woman raised a half-smoked cigarette to her lips and drew in; her deep, blue eyes fixed almost lifelessly on the floor in front of her. Shankar found herself shaking her head at the woman's appearance. Her jumpsuit, now powered down to return from its active camouflage to its natural, leathery black finish, was tied around her waist by the arms to show off her perfect figure beneath her form fitting, cropped vest top. A sheen of sweat and lines of grime from the jungle seemed somehow so complimentary to her curves that it was as if they had been deliberately applied to accentuate her appeal. Even her brown hair looked amazing in its disheveled state, as if make up artists had prepared her for a glamorous action movie rather than real war.

Shankar saw her own reflection in the shimmering window behind the Hexa sniper. In stark contrast, Shankar's combat fatigues were tatty and uncomplimentary in their utilitarian cut. Her red-rimmed eyes seemed sunk deeply above tired bags drooping down to her cheeks. Two white-topped insect bites dominated one cheek; a third had caused one of her ears to swell up. She looked like a wreck, even before standing opposite the sensuous perfection of the Hexa killer.

"Sub Officer Hawkins said you were separated at this point, ma'am?" Cochrane folded his arms.

"*Ja.* Sort of. Hawkins is a good kid. Just out of training; naive view of what warfare is. He thinks honor and chivalry have places in what we do. Obviously, they do not. Certainly not for a sniper. He was upset by what he saw and insisted on returning here."

Shankar exchanged a glance with Cochrane but said nothing before Beckmann continued.

"I tried to track them down for a good couple of hours, but they're good. They disappeared. By the time I doubled back to the start, they had recovered the dead body of the sergeant I shot. I tracked south and then around to where the two of you had reported the earlier firefight with the Zhanshi. I then moved further south toward their base camp and spent a couple of hours probing their perimeter, but there was nothing new to report."

Beckmann paused, her deep blue eyes narrowing and seeming to lose concentration for a brief moment before she resumed her business-like stare and continued.

"Since I was last there, they've bolstered their perimeter. I couldn't get close enough to ascertain anything of value, but there is a clear attempt to keep a pathway maintained to that site. I still think TAGs are a viable threat. After that, I came back to the site of your fight, recovered your two dead Fusiliers, and brought them back here. There is, I'm afraid, every chance that those Tiger Soldiers slipped past me and that they've seen this place. They might know exactly what they are facing here."

Shankar watched the tall woman in silence, mulling over her words. They had to assume the worst – that the Yujingyu force to the south now knew that they were horribly under-gunned and in a poor position to defend the site. But even with that assumption, nothing changed. Their orders were to hold and not allow the enemy through to threaten the flanks of Alpha Four-Four and the research facility.

Beckmann finished her strawberry scented cigarette and tossed the butt to one side before walking to the door.

"Major," Shankar cleared her throat.

Beckmann looked across, her eyes still lacking any tangible emotion.

"Thank you for bringing my soldiers back to be sent home."

Beckmann issued a slight shrug and walked back out into the night. Shankar watched as the tall woman paced slowly over toward the center of the site, her long MULTI Sniper Rifle held in one hand at her side. She walked over to sit alone in the shadows on a stack of old crates before reaching into a belt pouch to recover her cigarettes and lighter. Shankar narrowed her eyes in interest as the tall woman struggled and failed to work her lighter before it slipped through her fingers and into the dust by her feet. Beckmann stared down at her own shaking hands and then pressed them both against her face.

"I don't buy that shit," Cochrane remarked dryly as he appeared by Shankar's side. "She knows we're watching her, defo. I don't believe for a second that somebody like her is… getting affected by all of this."

Shankar tutted thoughtfully. It looked pretty convincing to her. She turned back to Cochrane.

"We need to be ready for them," she declared. "Major Barker is still confident that even with the density of the terrain and foliage, our surveillance cover will give us advance warning of any attack. I don't think we can afford to go out and meet them again. Not like this morning. We lost two good soldiers and we didn't hit a thing in return. What are your thoughts?"

Cochrane leaned back against the pitted alloy wall behind him and crossed one booted ankle over the other. He looked down at Shankar and offered a small smile.

"I think you should get some sleep," he said simply.

"Can't afford that," Shankar countered, "if they..."

"We could be here for a while. You've got a lot going on. You'll do better with it all after some sleep."

Shankar stepped away, throwing her hands out to either side.

"I don't need sleep, Jim, I need to be here and ready for when something happens. Promotion to captain, troubled relationship, all of that shit can wait. I'm compartmentalizing it. It's not on my mind. Keeping this part of the PanOceanian border intact is all that is on my mind."

"Yeah," Cochrane agreed, "but for the sake of two hours, I reckon you can trust me with that. You'd do better when the explosions start up again if you're not exhausted."

Shankar ran a hand wearily across her face, letting out a slight hiss of pain when she irritated the insect bites on her cheek. Two hours. She could be spared for that. Nothing would happen. Probably. Cochrane had a point.

"Two hours," she looked up at him, "not a second more, alright?"

"Not a second more," Cochrane winked with a childish salute, "scout's honor."

***

"Can we talk?"

Hawkins was snapped out of his gloomy introspection with a jolt, his hands instinctively moving toward the MULTI Rifle lying across his lap where he sat at the edge of the mining platform. It was past two o'clock in the morning and a thin film of mist hung in stationary patches at irregular intervals across the darkened jungle below. It was late, he was tired, and he had allowed his concentration to wander. Mentally chastising himself, he turned to face the new arrival at the top of the platform where he kept his solitary, self-appointed vigil over the mining site.

Beckmann dropped to her knees by his side, her eyes on his, slightly narrowed with a hint of what almost appeared to Hawkins to be anxiety.

"I don't think we have anything to talk about, ma'am," Hawkins replied bitterly.

She knew exactly how he felt about what he had seen, of that he was quite convinced.

"Will you give me sixty seconds?" the dark-haired woman continued. "Will you at least hear me out?"

Hawkins turned away to look down over the moonlit encampment again but remained silent. The two dronbots continued their tireless, eternal patrol of the site's perimeter. Two mining platforms were home to bipod mounted HMGs manned by Fusiliers, complete with missile launchers close at hand. Below, Hawkins could just about see Cochrane and Garcia in the dim glow of the Platoon HQ.

"What would you have had me do?" Beckmann asked softly. "With the wounded enemy soldier?"

"As obvious as it sounds, I would not have had you murder a helpless prisoner!" Hawkins spat.

"What should I have done?" Beckmann continued, her tone still calm.

Hawkins let out a frustrated gasp and clenched his jaw.

"You... you should have let me bandage his wounds and get him back here for evacuation and medical treatment."

"They would have shot you," Beckmann said, "staggering back here with a body in tow, if you exposed yourself to enemy fire – regardless of whether you were aiding one of their own – they would have killed you."

"So you murdered him to protect me, that's what you're saying?" Hawkins growled.

"I killed him for a number of reasons. But, accepting that getting that man back here was not a viable option, what would you have had me done instead?"

"At least provide medical aid!" Hawkins answered instantly, the obvious choice of response not even requiring a second's thought. "At least stabilize him!"

"Stabilize a gunshot wound to the torso from a high velocity six point five mil round? Kyle, an operating theater would not have saved that man, let alone your bandage. He was dead. You were just prolonging his pain."

Hawkins span around to face the Hexa sniper, his eyes half-closed and his jaw set in anger.

"You're going to sit there and tell me to my face that I'm supposed to believe that was a mercy killing and not a murder?!"

Beckmann looked away. She swallowed, exhaled slowly, and then turned to face him again. Half of her face remained plunged in darkness, the other half illuminated by the resurrected lighting of the old mining site.

"No. It wasn't a mercy killing. I'm just telling you that you could not have saved him. I shot him so you wouldn't be distracted and would get your mind back on the job of closing with the enemy. I didn't enjoy it, but I also didn't feel a shred of guilt."

Hawkins shook his head in despair, utterly at a loss for words over the hollow feeling inside him as the woman he had up until that morning felt so much for revealed the true depths of her callous nature.

"Two years ago," Beckmann continued, "I was involved in... an operation I'm not supposed to talk about. I was injured, fairly badly. A fragmentation grenade. The field hospital I was being treated in was assaulted, an airborne landing by Tiger Soldiers. Half of the medical staff were civilian volunteers. Next to nobody was armed. The Tiger Soldiers tore through that place like something from the old wars on Earth."

The young woman looked away, pausing for a moment before continuing.

"I saw them beating nurses to death with rifle butts. They slit the throats of patients lying helpless in bed. That wasn't an isolated incident, Kyle. Those bastards are notorious for it. They're not like these Fusiliers, they're not ordinary people spending a quick couple of years in military service before carrying on with normal lives. Fuck... I'd even acknowledge that Zhanshi are just ordinary people doing their job. But Tiger Soldiers. No. They're cold, remorseless, ruthless killers."

For a brief moment, little more than a second, Hawkins felt his feeling thaw as he visualized what Beckmann must have seen in that hospital. To be caught up as a helpless witness in the massacre of innocent people who had dedicated their lives to good. He took several deep breaths before he spoke again.

"But isn't that what you are?" he asked quietly. "A cold, remorseless, ruthless killer?"

"Yes," Beckmann replied with a small nod of the head, "yes, it is. Because even though we are the good guys, we need some people to do bad things. Terrible things. Otherwise our enemies get the edge. As cold as it sounds, sometimes the ends really do justify the means."

"It still doesn't justify murder!" Hawkins urged desperately, wishing in vain that she had not done what he had seen her do. "It still doesn't justify committing a war crime!"

"There was no war crime," Beckmann said softly, "there was no murder. Strategic Security Division Operational Orders. Op Order Five B. 'A Strategic Security Division field operative is permitted to use lethal force against any hostile combatant in the course of carrying out their assigned task, irrespective of conventional laws of armed conflict.' Kyle, if you had killed him it would be a war crime. For me, it's just another day in the office. It's my job."

"And you think that's alright?" Hawkins demanded. "Some loophole means you can't go to prison, and now it's all of a sudden morally acceptable? How the hell can you look yourself in the mirror?"

Again, Beckmann looked away and fell silent. Hawkins turned away from her, wishing more than anything that the events of the past day could somehow be undone and that she would transform back into the beautiful, gregarious woman with the infectious fascination in music and guitars, and the kitten back home. He looked across at her and saw instead a seasoned, amoral killer.

"This," Beckmann whispered, half to herself, "this... isn't me. This is

168

what I've become. It's what they made me. You talk about war crimes, but to me, it's the morality. I shot a dying killer and you're upset. Yet, hours before, I misjudged a shot and I hit a Zhanshi trooper, a girl who looked to be still in her teens, and I blew her arm off at the shoulder. She lay there spraying blood, screaming out the name of a friend. That friend came to help her. He was about her age. He held her hand as he lay next to her. I shot him in the back of the head. Both of those kills were entirely in accordance with the conventional laws of armed conflict. So I guess you're okay with those, huh? Because I'm not. I'm... I'm not okay with that."

Hawkins turned away from her again. He had spent the last few days looking for excuse after excuse to be in her company. Now he wanted for her to leave him alone. The sickening feeling in his gut amplified with each passing minute of the nauseatingly honest conversation. He closed his eyes. As childish and pathetic as it sounded, he wanted more than anything to go home.

"If what I've done is wrong," Beckmann spoke again, "and I am fully willing to accept that it is, will you forgive me?"

"Why do you care?" Hawkins whispered in despair as he stared down at the silent jungle, spreading miles across in every direction below him. "Why do you care about my forgiveness?"

Beckmann darted across the platform to drop to one knee by the other side of Hawkins, back in his field of view and with a look of determination across her face.

"You know why!" she replied forcefully. "You know exactly why I care! You know as well as I do that we've both noticed there's something between us! That's why I care about what you think! About your forgiveness!"

"It's not my forgiveness you need," Hawkins looked down off the edge of the platform at where two Fusiliers paced warily around the edge of the mining clearing.

"Oh, don't give me that bullshit!" Beckmann spat. "You're going to tell me some trite about forgiving myself?! I've got eight years of this weighing on my conscience! Eight years of fucked up things I've been ordered to do that come to haunt me every time I try to sleep! Eight years of slitting throats and blowing people's fucking limbs off, and you're going to tell me I need to forgive myself?"

"No!" Hawkins stared across at her. "No! You think it's that easy? You wear a cross around your neck! You claim you have faith! You need to beg for God's forgiveness, not mine! Not your own! And He knows! If you truly, *truly* repent of what you've done, if you honestly intend to change who you are, then you are forgiven! That's what this is all about! But you can't fool Him! You can't just *say* it and think it's magically all fixed! You need to *mean* it! Really mean it! That's the hard part of faith; there is no deceit. No hiding. If you want forgiveness, you need to ask God. Not me."

"But I'm not asking God. I am asking you."

Hawkins felt his shoulders slump as he looked back across the dimly lit mining site, the patrolling dronbots and Fusiliers and out toward the border and the faceless, invisible Yujingju soldiers in the jungle.

"If that's what you want," he said after a long, pensive pause, "then I forgive you. Not because I want to. Because I have to. I forgive you. But whatever was happening between us, wherever it was going, that's dead. I forgive you, but I don't want anything to do with you anymore."

The platform fell silent. A slight gust of wind cut through the night sky, initiating a gentle, barely audible howl as it whistled through the lattice work frame of the platform's corroded, alloy legs. Hawkins looked across at Beckmann. She stared out across the jungle, her face set in a mask of grim, callous indifference that was completely at odds with the tears rolling down her cheeks. Without a word, she stood up and walked away.

***

Beams of blue-tinged light formed a bright, horizontal line that intruded into Cochrane's mind as he slowly roused from his slumber. He grimaced and blinked away the dawn sunlight as the ceaseless serenade of the jungle swam into his ears. Opening his eyes, it took only a few seconds for him to register exactly where he was and what was going on – dawn, still stuck in that dismal, abandoned mining site in the middle of the Paradiso jungle, sat back against an old, empty, but surprisingly comfortable barrel near the quartet of control rooms. Checking around him to make sure none of his Fusiliers had seen him sleeping, Cochrane rose slowly to his feet and hauled his Combi Rifle over one shoulder whilst he scratched his chin irritably.

"I'm sick of this bloody beard," he grumbled to himself.

He vaguely recalled sitting down at that spot at perhaps four o'clock in the morning for something as mundane as tightening his boots. Here, light-years from Earth and the cradle of humanity, propelled across the void of space to fight over a site containing vastly advanced alien technology, Sergeant James Cochrane fell asleep on duty because he sat down to tighten his boot straps.

Cochrane checked the time. He had dozed off for over an hour. He had gotten away with it. It would probably have done him some good. Scratching again at a relentlessly offensive itch beneath the left side of his chin, Cochrane made his way over to the Platoon HQ room where he set his sights on making one of his awful coffees. As he approached the low, square building, he saw Shankar was still asleep inside. Of course, he never for a moment intended on waking her after only two hours sleep. She had already nearly tripled that. She needed it. He would take the inevitable reprimand later. It was worth it.

Outside the building, Cochrane saw the four remaining soldiers of

Number One Section – Southee, Carson, May, and Vesilin. It was ten minutes until they were due to relieve the support team of Number Two Section on perimeter guard duty. Cochrane cast his eyes over Southee and remembered Shankar's direction regarding command of the section. Swearing under his breath, he shook his head and walked over. On the northern horizon, an uncharacteristic but distinctive smear of blue-gray warned of impending change to the weather. Cochrane swore again as he recalled a five day downpour of torrential rain on one of his previous deployments to Paradiso. He dragged his eyes away from the forbidding weather on the horizon and back to the Fusiliers ahead of him.

"Nat. Come here."

Her Heavy Machine Gun carried down at her side, the young Fusilier obediently walked over to meet her platoon sergeant.

"Morning, Sarn't," she greeted.

"Yeah. Look. The boss doesn't want to dilute Number Two Section to fill in the gaps in Number One Section. It makes more sense to just have three Fireteams. So Number One Section is still you four diggers. The boss has put you in charge."

The young woman's face lit up with an enthusiastic smile.

"I'm in charge? I'm a lance corporal?"

"No, no, no," Cochrane grunted slowly and deliberately, "you are not a lance corporal. The boss doesn't have the authority to start arbitrarily promoting people on the spot. You are still a Fusilier. You get paid the same. You're not getting a little badge to wear. Now look, you can't go lugging that bloody great gun about when you're calling the shots in a firefight, so pick some other digger to carry the HMG. This is your first shot at proper responsibility, so don't balls it up. Don't be a dick about it. If you get any spare time, I expect to see you reading up on section attacks in the Section Commander's Manual. Got it?"

"Got it, Sarn't."

Cochrane looked down at the eager determination in the young Fusilier's excited eyes. He thought for a moment that he would resent her for finding such happiness in an opportunity for professional advancement that came about through the deaths of her comrades, but then thought that she did at least show an eagerness that the others did not. And, more importantly, he had done just the same at her age. For a brief moment, he suddenly and surprisingly found himself feeling a crushing weight of guilt for the two nights he had spent with her some weeks ago. He owed her more than that. His own professional standards should have been far, far higher.

"You'll do alright, mate." He issued a brief smile. "If any of the lads give you shit or try to make it hard for you, send them my way and I'll kick 'em in the balls, alright?"

Southee returned the smile.

"It's alright, Sarn't. I've got this."

She turned and, with a visible spring in her step, paced over to her Fireteam. His thoughts wandering again, Cochrane cut them off by switching his attention to his need for coffee and reaching inside his webbing for a pouch of the foul smelling, brown powder he had acquired. As he grabbed the sachet of powder, his comlog alerted him to an incoming transmission from Company HQ at Alpha Four-Four.

"Three-Zero-One," he responded.

"Jim, it's Captain Waczek," the company second-in-command's familiar voice came through his earpieces, "where's Priya?"

"Indisposed, ma'am," Cochrane replied, keeping his tone casual whilst frantically and silently signaling to the soldiers by the Platoon HQ to go inside and wake up Shankar. "She'll be on the net in seconds few."

"Get her quickly," Waczek replied, "surveillance reports you've got an enemy force heading your way from the south. Platoon strength. With armor support."

Cochrane's jaw dropped.

"Armor support?" He exclaimed. "How the hell do you expect us to stop TAGs?!"

"Dig in and hold your position," Waczek replied, her tone anything but calm. "Reinforcements are on the way."

Chapter Twelve

"Alpha-Zero-One from Three-Zero," Shankar transmitted as she peered anxiously into the jungle ahead, "enemy units now in sight, request update on reinforcements."

Flashes of orange-yellow were now visible through the hundred differing hues of green in the trees to the southeast, announcing the arrival of the lead Yujingyu units. The air was noticeably cooler than it had been for the last few weeks, and the sky was growing darker with gray clouds. From her vantage point atop the central of the six mining platforms, Shankar glanced to either side to check the positioning of her defending force.

Spread out atop the platform with her was the support team of Number Two Section; four Fusiliers manning the HMG and missile launcher, under the command of Cochrane in the absence of their evacuated Fireteam leader. To the left, huddled behind the improvised cover of earth-filled alloy crates atop a lower mining platform, Fusilier Southee and her small Fireteam of four waited behind a HMG and missile launcher of their own, accompanied by the bulky, armored outline of Hawkins. To the right, Corporal Garcia and his Fireteam lay ready in one of the mining control rooms, their Combi Rifles and underslung grenade launchers pointing into the trees ahead. Completely hidden from sight, somewhere off to the west, Beckmann had positioned under her own initiative to provide sniper support from afar. The two HMG-armed dronbots waited on the flanks, deactivated to prevent any electrical signature or transmission giving away their locations, only a single digital command away from full activation and acquiring enemy targets.

All was in place and ready, except the scant intelligence provided to Shankar which still left her all but completely unaware of the size of the force they faced, and the unserviceable communication connection with Alpha Four-Four that left her transmitting updates blindly back to Company HQ with no response, hoping that help was on the way and that their comms had not been hacked already. Shankar watched as the foliage was disturbed at the southern edge of the abandoned site. She looked through her Combi Rifle's scope and zoomed in, briefly detecting the unnatural outline of an armored infantryman crouching below the lip of earth leading up to the site. A second moved stealthily forward, crawling through the low branches and leaves to take position close to the first Yujingyu soldier.

"Come on..." Shankar whispered to herself.

Every second that dragged by without shots being fired was a second closer to reinforcements arriving. Every meter the Zhanshi soldiers edged closer was another meter closer to her catching and isolating their lead elements in a crossfire.

An unfamiliar sound distracted Shankar's attention from surveying the cautiously advancing enemy soldiers. A light, dull ping on the platform a few inches away from her. Then another. She looked across and saw tiny circles of water appear sporadically on the platform and the cover of the crates, and then she felt a rain drop on the back of her neck. The skies above morphed to a deeper, iron gray as the cascading droplets of water increased in volume until within only seconds, a steady shower of rain drifted down in the light winds to darken the ground below them and soak the endless sea of vegetation.

"They're not buying it," Cochrane breathed on a private channel to Shankar. "They're stopping at the perimeter."

"Come on... come on..." Shankar urged, her finger resting against the trigger of her Combi Rifle as she stared down at the edge of the jungle below.

With a dull whoosh, a stream of gray-white smoke shot up from the edge of the trees and darted through the rainy sky before the platform to Shankar's left was lit up with a brief, staccato bang of an explosion.

"Open fire!" Shankar shouted across the comlog channel to all of her units before taking aim at the enemy soldiers at the edge of the jungle and firing.

***

With the tall platform still rocking and tremoring from the impact of the missile, the Heavy Machine Gun blasted into life only inches from Hawkins' head, his helmet's earpieces immediately filtering the noise down to a manageable level without silencing the gunfire completely. Vesilin fired long, sweeping bursts down from the top of the platform into the trees at the edge of the site. Every third round from the weapon – digital tracers, to assist the firer's aim – showed up on friendly soldiers' lenses and visibly darted down through the drizzle-filled air as blue-gray smoke wafted up from the hammering weapon's muzzle. May leaned over Vesilin's shoulder as the older Fusilier fired, directing his aim and standing ready with the next magazine of caseless ammunition.

Hawkins looked down and saw the combined fire from the two platform-mounted HMGs and the similar weapons fitted to the dronbots below sweep through the jungle, blasting apart clumps of earth and chunks of foliage, knocking over trees and scything down bushes as dozens of deadly rounds spat out of each weapon. Below, two separate units of orange armored enemy soldiers attempted to advance on each side of the encampment. The withering fire swept across the ground and through the Yujingyu troopers, knocking back three soldiers in showers of blood. The Zhanshi of the two Fireteams scattered, hurtling for cover as the guns kicked up the wet sand at their feet.

Hawkins raised his MULTI Rifle to a firing position, leaning over the cover of the old crates and lining up his sights on one of the fleeing soldiers. He fired a shot, and then a second, but both flew wide of their target.

"Get down!" Southee yelled from a few paces to Hawkins' right as another missile shot up from the jungle below toward them. A dull crump detonated beneath Hawkins' feet and again the entire platform shook, knocking him off his feet. As if protesting to its violent treatment, the alloy supports of the tall platform groaned and whined, the top surface gently falling a few degrees to one side and leaving the soldiers atop it staggering back to their feet at a diagonal angle.

Hawkins hurried back to his firing position behind the cover of the crates, looking down to see a team of five heavily armored Invincibles advancing steadily to the left whilst on the far right flank he saw a similarly aggressive move by a team of Tiger Soldiers.

"Zero!" Hawkins transmitted to Shankar. "This is Broadsword-One! I'm visual with…"

Hawkins' call to alert the platoon commander was made instantly redundant when, on the platform to the right, a Fusilier leaned over cover and fired a grenade down into the advancing Invincibles, detonating in their midst and showering them with shrapnel, failing to kill any but sending them scattering for cover. A moment later, a sniper rifle cracked from an unseen position behind the Fusiliers, and one of the advancing Tiger Soldiers tensed up and crumpled to the ground as the drizzle suddenly intensified into a down-pouring of heavy rain from the heavens.

***

"Boss!" Cochrane yelled across to Shankar. "I'm marking those missile launchers! We've got to take those bastards out before they bring these platforms down!"

Shankar looked across from the cover of the far side of the platform and issued a thumbs up to Cochrane before returning to her Combi Rifle and firing down into the advancing Yujingyu soldiers. Waiting for a gap in the seemingly endless torrent of incoming fire that smashed and clanged against the improvised crate barricade atop the mining platform, Cochrane quickly leaned over and aimed his Combi Rifle down at the enemy forces below. He saw one of the Zhanshi missile launchers and highlighted the enemy trooper with the targeting designator clipped onto the tactical rail on the side of his rifle's fore grip. The enemy soldier's entire figure was now painted a vivid red on Cochrane's lens; he ducked back into cover and quickly transmitted the priority target's details to every other friendly soldier engaged in the bitter firefight.

"Zero-One to all units!" Cochrane called. "Priority target, missile launcher, designated as Target Alpha-One!"

Fusilier Moulin leaned over the barricade next to Cochrane and was instantly flung back to the ground, a jagged, bloody hole placed dead center in his forehead.

Cochrane swore as he quickly reloaded his Combi Rifle.

"Eagle One from Zero-One!" He transmitted to Beckmann. "We need those missile launchers taken out! Take Target Alpha-One!"

Further down the barricade, Shankar tried to lean over to line up a shot but was instantly met by a hail of fire from below and darted back into cover. She looked across at Cochrane, her face pale, and then opened a channel to Company HQ.

"Alpha-Zero-One! This is Three-Zero! Engaged in firefight with enemy force at my Marker Bravo! Confirm reinforcements are inbound?"

A distinctive howl of a high velocity round cut through the sodden air below.

"Eagle One, Target Alpha-One eliminated," Beckmann reported. "I can't get visual on the other launcher. Relocating."

Cochrane allowed himself a brief gasp of relief with one of the missile launchers now down. As if to disprove him, a missile slammed into the mining platform to the left, engulfing it briefly in smoke and knocking the squealing alloy construct to an even more severe angle. Gritting his teeth, Cochrane hauled himself back up to one knee and brought his Combi Rifle back to his shoulder. He stopped dead, his eyes wide in shock as he saw the line of enemy advance at the southern tree line. There, towering nearly three times the height of an armored soldier, stood the smooth, bulky bipedal outline of a Yujing Tactical Armored Gear. The towering, orange armored figure plunged through the trees and into the open, aimed its MULTI HMG, and opened fire.

***

Shankar tightened her grip around her Combi Rifle as the Yujingyu TAG paced forward, the combined fire from the two dronbots causing sparks to illuminate across its armored surfaces, leaving scorch marks and chipped paint but fully intact armor behind. The lines of the huge, deadly suit – now clearly recognizable as a Gūijiǎ – seemed almost elegant. Long legs led up to a thick, armored torso where the outlines of the human pilot were clearly visible, appearing to be almost bolted on to the front of the mechanized monstrosity with legs tucked into the front of the powered limbs below, and arms left free of the armored pilot's compartment. As the human pilot's arms moved in free air in front of the enormous fighting machine, the TAG's arms moved in perfectly synchronized imitation, mechanical fingers wrapped around a huge, long-barreled MULTI Heavy Machine Gun. She had seen TAGs before, but never an enemy TAG; and she had certainly never faced one in combat.

A missile shot out from the platform to the left, fired by one of Fusilier Southee's soldiers, and hurtled down toward the newly emerged threat. With an almost elegant precision, the TAG swiveled at the hip and dropped one shoulder, dodging the missile attack with seemingly condescending ease. As the missile impacted the ground behind the Yujingyu TAG and briefly silhouetted its distinctive outline in a flash of orange, the huge machine turned on the spot and fired its MULTI HMG. A stream of shells spat out of the weapon, tearing into one of the dronbots and blowing the little machine apart in a cloud of debris.

"All units! Hit the TAG!" Shankar yelled over the comlog. "Fire at the TAG!"

Shankar lined up the sights of her Combi Rifle and fired round after round into the center of the Gūijiǎ, hoping and praying that a lucky shot would somehow find a gap between armored plates or a vulnerable area that might slow the mechanical monster down. Fire from HMGs and Combi Rifles erupted from both sides, sweeping down into the TAG as return fire continued ceaselessly from the Zhanshi, Invincibles, and Tiger Soldiers below. The TAG stepped out with one leg, pivoted on the spot, and gunned down the second dronbot before turning to face the center of the mining site.

Below, Shankar saw Corporal Garcia leading his team in a frantic dash away from the Platoon HQ toward the cover of a set of storage barrels further to the north, falling back from the advancing line of Yujingyu troops. The TAG fired again, sending a deadly line of glowing shells sweeping through the retreating Fusiliers. Shankar let out a cry of anguish as she saw Ortega, King, and Kapsis blown apart by the exploding shells, leaving only Garcia and Mieke to dive for the cover of the storage area. A second later, another missile smashed into the platform to the left, connecting with the access ramp and blowing the metal footpath clean off to twist and tumble through the driving rain to the ground below.

"Boss!" Cochrane yelled across to her. "We need to retreat! We need to fall back!"

***

"Target Bravo!" Hawkins heard Southee yell over the constant din of gunfire. "Three points left of my Marker Delta! Open fire!"

Vesilin fired the HMG down from the precarious position atop the twisted mining platform, sending streams of bullets down into the deadly TAG below as torrential rain smashed down onto the Fusiliers. Hawkins saw a blur of movement further to his left, halfway between the edge of the trees and the open ground leading to the foot of the northern mining platforms. He raised his MULTI Rifle and saw two of the Zuyong Invincible heavy infantrymen rushing forward to resume the advance under the cover of the HMGs of the TAG and Zhanshi. Holding his breath and leading his target, Hawkins fired off three AP rounds. The first two fell short whilst the third caught his target in the midriff, spattering blood up over the Yujingyu soldier's bulky chest plate and sending him falling down into the rain-soaked dirt.

A moment later, the metal walkway connecting the platform to its twinned construct to the right was blasted in half by a missile from below, the explosion sending shards of metal twirling through the air and the walkway itself crashing down to the muddy ground. Hawkins looked across to the next platform and saw Shankar shouting orders to the small team of Fusiliers accompanying her. The pathway between the two was cut off. Hawkins looked down over the edge of their twisted platform. His eyes widened. It was far worse. The falling path had cleaved straight through the ramp leading to the ground, leaving them only with a precarious, exposed ladder as a means of escape.

"Natalie!" Hawkins called across to the Fusilier team's junior leader. "We have to go! The ramp's gone!"

The young woman looked across, her pretty features darkened with an expression that almost seemed excited by the endless gunfire and driving rain.

"We're good, sir!" she called back. "We're hitting them hard! We need to hold our position!"

"There's nothing to hold!" Hawkins yelled. "We need to get off this platform before they knock it down!"

"He's right!" Carson shouted, struggling up to his feet with his Combi Rifle held across his chest. "We need..."

A burst of gunfire erupted from the TAG below and tore into the platform, blowing holes through the thin alloy. A shell caught Carson as he stood, tearing through his back and blowing off his arm and half his chest. The Fusilier medic, killed in an instant, toppled sideways and fell off the platform to tumble through the rain filled sky and smash into the ground below.

Southee looked down at the dead body in the bloodied mud far below, her confidence instantly replaced with fear and sorrow. Vesilin placed a hand on her shoulder.

"Nat. We've got to go."

The young Fusilier nodded. Hawkins moved back to the barricade, his MULTI Rifle to his shoulder.

"Go," he ordered the Fusiliers, "I'll keep their attention on me! Go! Quickly!"

May was the first over the edge of the platform, grabbing onto the bent, rickety ladder and disappearing over the edge as Hawkins fired long bursts down into the enemy, his rounds aimed at the team of Invincibles advancing to the left, the prone line of Zhanshi riflemen taking cover at the edge of the trees, and at the deadly TAG that continued to pour automatic fire into the Fusiliers' position. Southee was next down the ladder; Hawkins had no idea whether she, or May before her, had survived the attempt to reach the ground as he reloaded his MULTI Rifle. He glanced over his shoulder and saw the last man, Vesilin, half slip on the soaked, distorted mining platform before he lowered himself onto the ladder. Rifle fire smashed up into the underside of the platform, Vesilin's eyes opened wide, and then he was gone. Hawkins took up his firing position again, gunning down an exposed Zhanshi trooper before the combined weight of the enemy fire forced him back beneath the barricade. Summoning his courage, he dashed over to the edge of the platform and flung himself over and onto the ladder down to the ground.

***

"Shit!" Cochrane spat as he saw one of his Fusiliers shot off the ladder of the next platform, the soldier tensing up as he was thudded with rifle bullets before he slipped away to fall down to the foot of the lattice work tower.

Hatred burning within him, Cochrane swore again as he brought his Combi Rifle up to search for a target amidst the line of perhaps a dozen Zhanshi troopers at the edge of the jungle clearing and the handful of Invincibles and Tiger Soldiers slowly advancing around their flanks. Only the dreaded Gūijiǎ TAG remained in the open, its outline now hazy through the monsoon downpour that had developed almost from nowhere within the past few minutes, its MULTI HMG pumping shell after shell at the battered platform to Cochrane's left. He looked across to the four Fusiliers cowering behind the cover of the crates atop his own platform. His eyes fell on Fusilier Pine.

"Greg! Gimme the bloody launcher!" Cochrane growled.

The young Fusilier looked across with wide-eyed fear, not hesitating even for a moment in surrendering his missile launcher. One hand pressed against her ear as she shouted over the Company Command comlog channel, Shankar looked up at Cochrane.

"What the hell are you doing with that?" she demanded.

"Boss! We've got to go!" Cochrane urged. "What's left of One Section has already fallen back! That TAG will be shooting us up next! We need to fall back whilst we've still got a route open to us!"

Shankar looked over her shoulder at the ramp leading down to the ground and then across at where the next platform's corresponding ramp had been destroyed, forcing them to use the slow, exposed ladder.

"Alright," she nodded, "we'll regroup the entire platoon at Marker India and reform a defensive line there."

"As soon as we move down that platform, that TAG will swat us like

180

flies!" Cochrane grunted. "I'll keep that bugger busy! You fall back!"

"Jim!" Shankar shouted. "We've lost enough people already! We're not doing heroic last stands! We *all* fall back together!"

"Then I'd best make this little ripper count!" Cochrane grinned, patting the missile launcher over his shoulder. "Cover!"

The four Fusiliers leaned over the barricade and shot down into the enemy positions as a fresh wave of incoming fire clanged and banged off the crates. Taking a breath, Cochrane quickly leaned up over the barricade and aimed the missile launcher at the TAG. The Gūijiǎ was stood still in the open, its MULTI HMG blazing away at a pair of Fusiliers cowering in the cover of a barrel dump to the Northwest of the encampment. The missile's tracker head scrolled through a thousand images from its database of targets in the blink of an eye before sending a simple message to Cochrane's lens: *Gūijiǎ TAG – Target locked.*

"Have this for breakfast, yer bastard," Cochrane grunted and then thumbed the firing button.

Cochrane felt a sudden flare of heat across his soaked back as the missile's first burn shot it clear of the launch tube where it seemed to hover and sink almost comically a few meters in front of him, before the second burn ignited and the deadly projectile shot off through the rain. The missile hurtled down from the platform and straight toward the towering TAG; the Yujingyu colossus's head looked up and it quickly darted to one side with an agility that seemed out of place from a machine of its size. In the split second before impact, Cochrane grunted a laugh. The pilot had evaded too quickly. The missile effortlessly altered course and smashed into the TAG's chest with an ear-splitting explosion.

"Now!" Cochrane yelled. "Leg it!"

The Fusiliers abandoned the platform to sprint down the rickety ramp toward the soaked earth below, the chatter of rifle fire still echoing from behind them as bullets cracked through the air around them and pinged off metal by their feet. Cochrane risked a look over one shoulder as he ran and saw the TAG reeling in the smoke of the explosion but still very much on its feet and operational.

***

Branches whipping at her shoulders as she rushed along the western edge of the mining site, her MULTI Sniper Rifle held in front of her, Beckmann looked to her right at the carnage unfolding. All three of the Fusilier units were now in retreat, leaving the Yujingyu forces to advance from the jungle on the far side of the site and toward the buildings in the center. Beckmann looked up to the mining platforms to the west of the central clearing, selecting one with a clear route up to the lower of its two platforms, where the Fusiliers had dumped a trio of crates for cover in case it was needed for a second line of defense or against an assault from the west. That would have to do.

Beckmann's comlog alerted her to an incoming message on an encrypted channel – the channel she had been exchanging information with her own chain of command in secret since she first arrived on Paradiso under the pretense of supporting the Fusiliers.

"Eagle One, this is Tac Con," a familiar voice, a man she had worked with for years but never once met face-to-face, crackled through her earpiece in her native language of German. "Fusilier casualties at Marker Ida defenses are mounting."

"Yeah, I got that!" Beckmann snapped, dropping to one knee by the edge of the clearing whilst she plotted a route through covered positions to reach the lower mining platform. "I'm moving to Marker Nordpol to get a clear shot at the TAG. Tac Con, send me an armor image overview of a Gūijiǎ TAG, highlighting all areas vulnerable to a six point four A-Plus round."

Up ahead, the combined weight of fire of the TAG's shell-spewing MULTI HMG and the Yujingju soldiers fanned out around it continued to slam into the mining platforms above as the Fusiliers desperately attempted to fall back. As Beckmann darted forward again, her feet slipping through the mud as her suit diagnostics tab warned her of her dwindling power supply, a missile shot out from the central platform to slam straight into the TAG before exploding spectacularly.

"Eagle One," her tactical controller called again as she darted into cover behind a pyramid of barrels, "surveillance reports a missile hit on the enemy TAG."

"I can fucking see that!" Beckmann growled, bringing up her wrist panel to check for any power reductions she could make on her camouflage systems or long range comms. "It'll take more than that to stop that thing!"

Launching herself forward again, Beckmann sprinted through the driving rain toward the narrow ramp leading up to the lower mining platform. She rushed past the upper half of a dead Fusilier, the part-corpse lying motionless in the mud and rain. The dead soldier's head turned smoothly to face her before the eyes flickered open and fixed on hers.

"Not now!" Beckmann hissed through gritted teeth, turning away from the erroneous image she knew was not real, merely an illusion of her wounded mind.

Her booted feet slamming down on the wet metal of the ramp, Beckmann quickly ascended toward the limited cover of the lower mining platform. Dropping to the floor, she quickly unfolded the bipod below the barrel of her rifle and set herself up for a firing position, aligning her body with the weapon to ensure it pointed naturally at the target. She was vaguely aware of the familiar figure sat in the corner to her right, just within her peripheral vision, but knew well from a dozen previous episodes that it was in her mind. She was alone. There was nobody there with her.

"Eagle One, from Tac Con," her earpiece crackled, "enemy forces advancing on both flanks. Damage to TAG is light. Your position is untenable. Recommend you withdraw."

"Eagle One, negative," Beckmann breathed, lining up her sights with the TAG and applying the targeting overlay to her scope.

Her entire view of the jungle and mining site ahead faded into a hundred tones of blue, with only her target vividly painted in red for conspicuity. The armor overlay transmitted by the tactical controller appeared a moment later, highlighting in yellow all of the areas which a 6.4mm round had a chance of penetrating. Her scope reported the exact range of the target, advising her to discount curvature corrections. Wind speed and direction advisory indications appeared alongside her crosshair.

"Eagle One from Tac Con. Message relay from Command. You are authorized to withdraw."

Beckmann hugged the butt of the MULTI Sniper Rifle to her shoulder and adjusted her sights, focusing on the left knee joint of the TAG.

"Tac Con, fuck off," she breathed, "I'm not leaving these guys without support. On glass, contact."

"Eagle One from Tac Con. Message relay from Command. Fusiliers classified as expendable. You are reminded that you are a High Value Unit. You are ordered to withdraw."

Beckmann slowed her breathing. She felt the minuscule rise and fall of the rear of the weapon against her body, pivoting on the stable mount of the bipod. She heard the thrashing rain impacting on the upper mining platform above her. She sensed the presence of the ghostly figure in the corner behind her, still aware that it was merely a product of her mental turmoil and elevated levels of stress rather than a reality. She could smell burning. She spent a few precious seconds monitoring the movements of the TAG, repeating the lifting and lowering of the knee joint in her mind as she pressed gently on the trigger until she felt it at its biting point.

"Tell Command to go to Hell," Beckmann whispered, and then held her breath.

She squeezed the trigger.

The rifle thumped back into her shoulder. The impact seemed to occur at the same time as the brief yellow flash from the muzzle. Sparks danced from the knee of the TAG as the towering construct twisted and staggered, hydraulic fluid spraying from a severed connection of the metallic joint. Beckmann followed up with a second shot but only succeeded in scoring a scorched mark on the TAG's thigh armor due to the rushed nature of her execution and the erratic movements of the damaged war machine. Nonetheless, she allowed herself a brief, grim smile.

The smile was cut short as the TAG's gun swung around to face her and fired. Shells slammed into the mining platform and its supporting legs, exploding violently all around her and filling the space with smoke and shrapnel. Beckmann let out a cry as she felt a sharp burning tear across her back. She quickly backed away from the edge of the platform, pressing herself down against the vine-infested alloy flooring and holding her arms over her head. The thunder of impact was relentless, soon joined by more machine gun fire from the enemy infantry units. A wave of bullets swept across the edge of the platform, and her sniper rifle was cut in half.

"Eagle One, this is Command," she heard the familiar voice of Colonel Berthal, Commanding Officer of Strategic Security Paradiso, growl in her ear. "You have been ordered to withdraw! Fall back to Marker Viktor!"

Curled up in a fetal position, the world exploding around her, coughing from smoke wafting up from something burning beneath her and pain tearing across her back, Beckmann found herself suddenly burst into tears. Whether it was the smoke reminding her of that long, drawn out and agonizing death two years ago or the recollection that she had signed DNRR on her medical records and this was probably the end, she did not know. She heard a child's laugh from the imaginary figure sat on the corner of the platform.

"How are you gonna get out of this one, Razor?" The girl's voice asked.

Her hand shaking, she reached down and unholstered her heavy MULTI Pistol. It somehow brought her some comfort. Her teeth gritted, blinking the tears away, she checked her belt. She still had grenades and knives, as well. This was not over yet.

"Command, Eagle One," she hissed, "is my father with you? Is he watching this?"

Up ahead, the TAG limped toward her position, dragging its broken leg behind it like the antagonist of a macabre horror movie. To either side, Zhanshi and Tiger Soldiers advanced on her position. The lack of response from Berthal told her all she needed to know. Her father had indeed lowered himself from his lofty perch in Combined HQ to visit the Strategic Security operations room and watch his daughter's final moments.

"Tell him to keep watching!" Beckmann growled, tears streaming down her face. "He always said he wanted more damn medals in the family!"

Another salvo of shells swept through the building, and the ramp behind Beckmann was blown apart, cutting off her only avenue of retreat. The smell of burning grew more intense. She fought hard to stop herself from dissolving into panic and tears. Her earpiece crackled again as one last transmission was sent from the coordination cell at Strategic Security.

"Eagle One, Tac Con. All avenues of retreat are now impossible. Strategic Security Command acknowledges your service. Tactical control services terminated."

The line of communication died abruptly.

***

Hawkins slid into cover behind the battered control room, his right pauldron smoking from a HMG round that miraculously failed to penetrate the armor. He was the last soldier at the rendezvous point; the only other survivors of the platoon were already crammed into cover. Cochrane and Garcia leaned around the corner of the building, firing their Combi Rifles into the advancing Invincible heavy infantry to the left. Shankar had one hand pressed against her ear as she frantically shouted on the comlog channel to Company HQ. Only six other Fusiliers remained alongside the lieutenant and two NCOs.

Hawkins glanced back around the corner of the squat building and through the driving rain. Two Fireteams of Zhanshi advanced in the center of the enemy line toward the abandoned, battered mining platforms in the middle of the site. To the left, the final trio of Zuyong Invincibles continued to pelt the Fusiliers with rifle and machine gun fire. The Tiger Soldiers had disappeared completely. Hawkins looked up at the TAG, just as he heard the howl of a sniper rifle's high velocity bullet, and saw a shower of orange-yellow sparks shoot up from the war machine's knee. Purple-pink hydraulic fluid followed in its wake as the wounded war engine staggered back. It turned in place to open fire at a solitary mining platform on the western edge of the site, followed moments later by the guns of the Zhanshi line.

"Guys!" Shankar shouted. "We're still in this! There's three Tubarãos in the air, bringing an entire platoon of reinforcements from C Company! They can't get to us in this weather, so they're fast roping them down a K from here to move in on foot!"

"A kilometer?! In that jungle?" Garcia yelled. "That'll take an age!"

"Gives us longer to kill more of the bastards before those pricks turn up and take the credit, Corporal!" Cochrane grinned bitterly as he tossed an empty magazine aside and slammed a fresh one into his Combi Rifle.

"We still need a defendable position away from that TAG!" Shankar exhaled.

"It's hit!" Hawkins reported, watching the limping leviathan stagger toward the platform to the west. "It's damaged!"

Shankar darted across to stand next to Hawkins, leaning around cover to watch the Gūijiǎ stumble slowly through the mud, its MULTI HMG sending shell after shell thumping into the battered platform. A relieved smile spread across her face.

"It's going after Beckmann," she nodded. "Alright, listen in! Marker November is our next rally point! We fall back north and get in the jungle until we can link up with C Company!"

Hawkins watched the concentration of the entire enemy force's firepower tear apart the mining platform on the other side of the central clearing.

"What about Major Beckmann?" he asked.

"She can take care of herself, she always has so far," Shankar said dismissively as she plotted a route on the platoon's shared tactical map. "One Section on point, let's go."

Hawkins turned to tower over Shankar.

"We're not leaving her," he warned, pointing an armored finger at the bullet-riddled platform, "she doesn't stand a chance!"

"I'm in command here, Sub Officer!" Shankar snarled. "And we are leaving, now, before I lose any more of my Fusiliers! She'd do the same to us! We're leaving!"

Hawkins stared down at the determined Fusilier platoon commander, his fists clenched as rain pelted off his helmet and armor. The snap and whine of bullets was gone, replaced by the thunder of guns aimed at the west.

"You heard the boss!" Cochrane grunted. "Fall back to Marker November! One Section on point!"

Before Hawkins could protest again, his earpiece chimed as a private channel was opened. He looked across at the platform as he heard the anxious voice hailing him.

"Kyle. It's me."

"Ma'am?" Hawkins barged his way past the remaining Fusiliers, looking forlornly at the decimated platform where Beckmann called him from, the TAG only meters away from reaching the building.

"Yeah, I… Kyle, I've got no way out of this, so I've decided to go out with a bang."

"Lisette, no! Wait! My… Marker Juliet, I'm coming across to you now! Hold position, I'm on my way to you!"

Hawkins quickly plotted a route on the map, sending the details across to Beckmann as panic rose steadily up through his body, threatening to engulf him. The guns continued to blast away at the rickety tower.

"Kyle, no," Beckmann replied, the calmness in her voice completely at odds with the mortal danger she faced, "but thank you. Look… I'm sorry for the way it all went. I just wanted to let you know that I made my peace with God, like you said. I know this sounds stupid but… remember me, okay?"

The channel was cut off before Hawkins could reply. He stared across desperately at the tower as the TAG approached it, a huge, metallic hand reaching to its back to unsheathe a blade twice the size of a man. One cold, clinical phrase jumped to the very fore of his mind and dominated his thoughts. *Do Not*

Resuscitate or Resurrect.

"Sir, wait!" Cochrane moved out to stand in Hawkins' path.

Hawkins pushed the Fusilier sergeant aside and sprinted out across the mud toward the tower.

***

The volume of incoming fire had died down significantly, but a semi regular burst of rifle fire rattled against the platform as if to remind Beckmann that she was still the priority target. She sat on the corner of the same, battered lower platform, her back against the twisted lattice work of one of the four alloy legs. Her knees hugged to her chest, blood dribbling from wounds across her cheek and shoulder, Beckmann stared straight ahead into the rainy sky as she heard the thud and scrape of the damaged TAG drawing closer. She pulled her earpiece out and tossed it aside before wiping the tears off her cheeks. She cried too much. She always had.

The smoke from below was gone now, yet still she could smell burning. The last few seconds of relative peace that providence had thrown her way gave her a little time to reflect on her life as her forefinger and thumb pressed against the cross etched into one of her dog tags. She had done terrible things. At least she *was* truly sorry. At least there was hope for redemption.

Forcing herself to her feet, Beckmann checked her MULTI Pistol and then thrust it back into its holster before ensuring she had a grenade to hand. The thudding footsteps in the mud below had stopped. A resounding clang echoed across the entire building and the platform beneath her feet jolted. There was a second bang and another earthquake-like jolt. The TAG was cutting the building down.

Beckmann looked across the platform and took in a breath. She willed her legs into action, but they refused to move, frozen in place with fear.

"Come on," she urged herself, "last push, sprint for the finish! Come on!"

Pushing her fear to one side for the final time, Beckmann ran forward. The edge of the platform bounded nearer with each pace. The fear resurfaced with resounding clarity in her mind. Too late to turn back now. Beckmann looked down over the edge, rapidly planned her descent, and then planted one foot on the rim of the platform to propel herself through the air. Rain drove down into her as the muddy ground rushed up to meet her, two brief seconds seeming like long, agonizing minutes until the impact came.

Beckmann screamed in pain as she slammed down onto the top of the TAG, feeling one side of her ribcage buckle and break on contact with the armored monstrosity. Her fingers gripping desperately onto the edge of a wet, armored plate, the taste of blood in her mouth, she planted her feet on the side of the machine's armored torso and dragged herself up onto the top of the pilot's armored module. She quickly grabbed a grenade and thumbed the activation circuit before jamming the explosive device down in the crevice of the neck.

Tears of pain streaming down her face, Beckmann slid off to one side and cowered down behind the cover of the TAG's back. The grenade exploded with a dull thud, sending a tremor through the machine. Unholstering her pistol, blood dripping out of one side of her mouth, Beckmann clambered back across the top of the TAG as the machine desperately thrashed in place in an attempt to hurl off the deadly interloper.

Beckmann looked down and saw the effects of her grenade – the pilot's armored module was torn open, giving her a clear view of the head of the dark-haired, female pilot inside. The Yujingyu woman looked up and screamed in terror, frantically trying to extricate herself from the war machine's shattered cockpit. Beckmann planted the pistol against the top of the woman's head and pulled the trigger. Blood spattered back against her. The machine tensed up and was still. A second later, Beckmann saw the gray-white streak of a missile hurtling toward her from the Zhanshi firing line. Her entire world changed to black.

***

His armored feet slipping through the mud, Hawkins ran headlong through the rain, heedless of the danger posed to him by the Zhanshi firing line to his left. Ahead of him, he saw three Tiger Soldiers emerge from the trees on the edge of the site, their Combi Rifles aimed up at the bullet-holed platform above them. With a roar, Hawkins tucked his MULTI Rifle into his hip and fired a long burst, his lens mating with the weapon system's own scope to provide corrective advice to his aim as he ran. His bullets slammed and clattered into the trees by the Tiger Soldiers, kicking up branches and leaves before his aim corrected to bring his fire around to cut through one of the Yujingyu Airborne soldiers.

Fire from the Zhanshi platoon whizzed through the air around him as he ran, one shot eventually slamming into his arm and pushing him off course before a second hit him in the leg, forcing him down to one knee. His armor held.

"Sir!" Cochrane yelled from behind him. "Get down! Get in cover!"

The TAG ahead had now reached the platform and was engaged in slamming its long, curve-bladed close combat weapon into one of the building's legs. With another desperate cry, Hawkins forced himself back to his feet and resumed his forlorn sprint across the open ground, spatters of mud dancing up by his feet as the enemy gunfire followed him. Hawkins looked up and saw a lone figure jump off the lower of the two mining platforms, falling down and down until it smashed against the top of the Yujingyu fighting machine. A second later, he heard the thump of a grenade and the machine's torso was briefly hidden in smoke.

He was only a dozen meters away when the smoke cleared. A gunshot sounded and the entire machine locked up in a rigid stance. Panic clawing at his throat, his heart thumping, Hawkins tried to urge his legs into another burst of speed toward the now silent fighting machine. With a whoosh and a stream of smoke, a missile shot out from the Zhanshi line to the left and smashed into the stationary Gūijiă. The Yujingyu TAG was blown apart spectacularly, its long, armored limbs scattered twirling to the four winds as its smoking torso fell to the ground with a thump.

Hawkins screamed out until his lungs were burning, dragging his legs onward to the smoking wreck as shots were exchanged between Fusiliers and Zhanshi behind him. Up ahead, through the billowing smoke, he saw a slim figure stagger up from the wreckage. Hawkins stopped dead in his tracks, only a few yards from the familiar figure.

Her feet spread apart for balance, one hand clinging to a long length of shining control rod from the destroyed TAG that punctured the side of her gut, Beckmann staggered wearily in place. Her muddy, rain-soaked hair was pasted to one side of her face, blood covered the other. Streams of thick, red cascaded from her wounded side and out of one corner of her open jaw. Her blue eyes set in the angry, grim determination of a wounded predator, her free hand still clung to her smoking MULTI Pistol.

Beckmann stopped as her eyes fell on Hawkins. The resolve of the deadly apex predator washed away. Hawkins remained frozen in place, his hands trembling and his hearing seemingly fading away to nothing. For a brief moment, Beckmann's features changed from those of the battlefield killer to a petrified, dying woman. She looked as though she would cry. Hawkins did not hear the gunfire. He saw the trio of shots land; almost graceful blossoms of red erupting on Beckmann's thigh, hip, and then straight in the center of her torso. Her lifeless body slumped to one side.

***

"Cover!" Cochrane screamed over the comlog as he hurtled after Hawkins. "Covering fire!"

The platoon's last HMG from Number Two Section barked away behind him, firing out long bursts of suppressive fire into the Zhanshi positions on the far side of the clearing. In the gray smoke ahead, Cochrane saw Beckmann stagger unsteadily up to her feet, barely an inch of her left uncovered by the blood from her array of terrible wounds. It seemed almost a mercy when a burst of gunfire cut her down again almost immediately.

Hawkins let out a horrified yell, audible through the faceplate of his helmet rather than over the comlog. Cochrane saw the young Hospitaller hurtle forward through the mud, firing long, uncontrolled bursts from his MULTI Rifle until the weapon was empty. Still advancing toward the Tiger Soldiers on the far side of the site, the Hospitaller threw the MULTI Rifle to one side and drew his pistol and sword.

As if their honor was somehow challenged by the drawing of the blade, both remaining Tiger Soldiers produced their own close combat weapons and rushed out from the trees to meet him. Cochrane dropped to kneeling firing position and raised his Combi Rifle to his shoulder, but the charging Hospitaller blocked a clear shot to the Tiger Soldiers. Swearing, Cochrane jumped back up and ran after him.

The first Tiger Soldier met Hawkins with a feral roar, sweeping down with his blade. The Hospitaller caught the attack on his own sword before planting his shoulder into the Yujingyu Airborne warrior, lifting him up off his feet and throwing him over. At some point in the rapid blur of motion that Cochrane's eyes did not fully decipher, Hawkins planted his pistol against the flying enemy's stomach, and with two shots, blew his guts out of his back.

The second Tiger Soldier barged into the Hospitaller and knocked him down to the ground. The two armored warriors rolled over each other in the mud, both trying to overpower their opponent and bring their blades around. The short, bitter struggle was over by the time Cochrane reached them; Hawkins planted a foot against his adversary, kicked him back half a pace, and then cut off the top of the soldier's head from ear to ear with his sword.

"Jim!" Cochrane heard Shankar over the comlog. "Get Kyle and fall back! The platoon from C Company have landed, they're on their way!"

Cochrane planted a hand on Hawkins' shoulder.

"Kyle! We've got to fall back! We've got to go!"

"No!" Hawkins screamed, his raging eyes visible through the lens of his helmet. "No!"

He rushed over to Beckmann's body and dropped down to his knees. Cochrane looked at the bloodied, broken woman in the dirt and the wreckage of the TAG. She had lived by the sword and died by the sword, in the parlance of Hawkins' faith. He did not pity her for that. Holstering his pistol, Hawkins lifted the woman's body up over his shoulder.

"We need to get help!" he urged Cochrane.

"Sir," Cochrane shook his head, "she's had it. She's gone."

"I'm getting help!" Hawkins snarled.

Only now utilizing the cover of the various stacks of crates and barrels did Hawkins return back toward the Fusiliers' firing line. Cochrane followed, his Combi Rifle tucked in to his shoulder and ready. The firing from both sides was now dying down – only nine Fusiliers faced perhaps twice their number across the open scrub land in the center of the old mining base, with both sides occupying cover.

Hawkins reached cover behind one of the control rooms and laid Beckmann's body down. He tore off his helmet and threw it to one side, clenching his fists and letting out a long yell of frustration before he ran both hands through his short, soaking hair. He turned to face Danielle Mieke, Number Two Section's medic.

"Fix her up!" Hawkins yelled. "Get her stabilized!"

Mieke looked down at the battered body in the mud at her feet, her eyes widening as she took in the extent of the wounds.

"Sir, I can't…"

"Fix her up!" Hawkins yelled, taking a pace forward.

The venom in his eyes made Cochrane believe he might actually strike Mieke. He rushed over and planted his hands against Hawkins' chest, holding him back.

"Kyle!" he shouted. "We're still in the bloody fight! We can't do this! Not now! Kyle, listen!"

The HMG set up at the edge of the control room blasted away again, accompanied by the higher pitched snaps of Combi Rifles. Hawkins looked down at the body, then up at Cochrane. His face changed from glowering rage to one of utter despair.

"Jim," he whispered, "help me! I don't know what to do!"

Cochrane looked down at Beckmann. Whether it was to placate the raging Hospitaller or whether it was because she labored under the ludicrous belief that she could make a difference, Mieke hurriedly bandaged Beckmann's wounds. Cochrane looked at the despairing Hospitaller. Of course he knew that most soldiers in the platoon felt something for Beckmann, himself included. But that was purely physical. As he stared at Hawkins, he realized that he had missed the Hospitaller's connection with the deadly sniper grow beyond that and into something far deeper, somehow even transcending the first-hand knowledge of what she was and what she was capable of.

Cochrane could only do what he thought was best. He leaned over, took the black pistol from Beckmann's fingers, and planted it into Hawkins' hand.

"Sir, she's gone," he said evenly. "The only thing left to do now is make those bastards pay. So we do our job. We kill the enemy. We close with 'em, and we bloody kill 'em."

The pain in Hawkins' eyes gave way again. His features hardened as his fingers closed around the handle of the pistol. He issued a single, silent nod. Loading a fresh magazine into her Combi Rifle, Shankar slid back from the muddy slope at the edge of the control room and looked across at her handful of remaining soldiers.

"Two Platoon of C Company are down," she said, "they're on their way here, now. We just need to keep our heads down and hold position until they get here."

Hawkins dropped down by Beckmann's body and took a pouch of pistol DA ammunition from her belt. He broke the weapon open, loaded fresh caseless rounds into the cylinder's empty chambers, and then snapped it shut again before looking down at Shankar.

"Fuck that," the Hospitaller spat before hefting his sword up over one shoulder and walking out to face the enemy again.

Chapter Thirteen

- *All units from Tac Con, report in.*
- *Eagle Two's ready.*
- *Eagle One, in position.*
- *Eagle Three... yeah, all set up.*

...

- *Two has eyes on target. He's moving toward the back door.*
- *One, this is Tac Con, relay from Command. Hold fire, hold fire.*
- *Eagle One copies. Hold fire.*

...

- *Tac Con, this is Three. I've got multiple vehicles moving to the target's address. They're pulling up outside now. Two saloons. Four men are heading to target address, confirm you have my visual feed.*
- *Three, Tac Con, from Command. They're expected.*
- *One, from Two, target is moving to the back garden, you got him visual?*
- *Eagle One, target is visual. He's... wait. There's a kid.*
- *Eagle One, from Tac Con, is there a problem?*
- *Err... stand by... just... This is Eagle One, target has a small child with him. We need to abort.*
- *Razor, are you fucking joking?*
- *Two, from Tac Con, cease transmissions. One, Tac Con, relay from Command. Proceed with the operation. You are authorized to take target.*
- *Tac Con, there's a fucking kid! It's his son! He's taken him into the back garden to show him a present!*
- *Eagle One, from Tac Con. Take target.*
- *No! I'm not shooting! There's a six year old kid down there, and you want me to blow his father's head off when he's showing him his birthday present?*
- *Take the damn shot, Razor! Shit! Tac Con, this is Eagle Two, I'm relocating for a shot myself!*
- *Eagle One, this is Command. You have been ordered to fire. Take target. Now.*
- *Sir, I... there's a child. I can't take the shot.*
- *Lieutenant! Fire your damn weapon!*
- *Eagle One, negative, we'll need to wait for...*
- *Beckmann! Take the target! Fire!*

The memory of the gunshot echoed in Beckmann's mind as she sat bolt upright in the bed, drenched in sweat. A hazy, half-forgotten image of a flock of colorful birds rushing up into the skies in fear momentarily swam into view. Gasping for breath, a hand moving to a tearing pain below her ribs, she

194

stared straight ahead in the dim light of the strange room, the image of the sobbing child covered in the blood of the man she killed still etched vividly in her thoughts. Her mind felt dull, foggy. It was a sensation she was accustomed to – she had been drugged. Her breathing ragged and uneven, Beckmann looked around to take in her surroundings.

She sat atop a thin, narrow bed with wheels on the corners. The impression that she was in a hospital – or, at least, something made to convince her she was in a hospital – was confirmed by her attire; thin, loose fitting trousers of light turquoise and a matching gown top. The room was small and rectangular, with one tall window against the wall to the left, the darkness beyond the cracks in the shutters telling her it was night time.

Fighting through the pain in her side, Beckmann swung her legs off the bed and lowered her bare feet down onto the cold, tiled floor. One step was enough to force her to fling one arm out to grab the bed for balance as the lines of the room swam in and out of focus, twisting gently from side to side. She heard the gentle buzz of an alarm from somewhere. The image of the child covered in his father's blood jumped back to the forefront of her thoughts. Slowly, carefully, she staggered painfully over to a sink on the opposite wall and ran the cold tap, splashing water up across her face.

Pain raging across her abdomen and right thigh, Beckmann took in a deep breath and looked up into the mirror above the sink. An adolescent girl with a shaved head was sat on her bed behind her, three bloody holes torn through her gray combat fatigues, her face deathly pale. Beckmann let out a yell of fear and span around. The bed was empty. From nowhere, a sudden and intense nausea shot up from Beckmann's gut and into her throat. She span around again as a mouthful of bitter bile shot from her mouth and into the sink. The tap continued to run. The soft shrill of the alarm continued to blare away. Her pained right leg buckled beneath her and she fell to one knee, her palms pressed against the wall for support as she struggled to breathe.

The room's solitary door opened to admit a dark-skinned, middle-aged woman whose blue uniform clearly marked her out as a nurse. Beckmann looked up at the woman, her instant feeling of relief rapidly swapped for suspicion as training kicked in. Beckmann did not even remember being injured, let alone where she was and how she arrived there. She remembered being attached to the Fusilier platoon at Alpha Four-Four, with orders to infiltrate the scientific research hub. Seemingly dim and distant memories of the fight against Yujingyu forces at the abandoned mining site in the jungle hazily emerged in her mind. There was little more than that.

"Lisette?" the nurse greeted hesitantly, taking a tentative step toward her. "Are you alright? Can you get back in bed?"

Beckmann looked up groggily at the nurse. She was speaking English flawlessly. But that did not mean this whole setting was not a Yujingyu prisoner handling facility, made to look like a PanOceanian civilian hospital. Beckmann stared up at the nurse but said nothing.

"You're in Rahel Hirsch Memorial Hospital in Klugestein," the nurse said, taking another nervous pace forward, "you were transferred here after sustaining injuries in a training accident. You've been here for a week."

Klugestein? A city on the south coast of Norstralia, built around a starport and a huge industrial harbor. The closest major city to Alpha Four-Four – that much, she remembered. Beckmann saw a flash of movement behind the nurse. She glanced across and saw two tall men staring at her from the doorway. Both had truncheons at the ready.

"Lisette?" The nurse repeated.

"Why are those men armed?" Beckmann demanded, her voice slurred.

She struggled back to her feet. The nurse immediately took two quick steps back away from her, toward the door, nervousness clearly painted across her face. Holding onto the sink for support, Beckmann stared groggily at the three strangers as she pieced together what little information she had from her surroundings, still struggling to push away the memory of the blood-covered child of the drug cartel executive she had assassinated five years before. The drawn weapons and tentative approaches to her told her all she needed to know.

"Who did I hurt?" Beckmann swallowed. "What have I done?"

"It's alright," the nurse forced an unconvincing smile, "everything is okay now. He'll recover. You were delirious. You thought... you tried to escape and hurt one of the guards. He'll recover."

"How badly?" Beckmann closed her eyes, sweat dripping down her brow. "How badly did I hurt him?"

The expressions on the faces of the two hospital guards told her enough. They looked across uneasily, their breathing rapid, their stances betraying their complete lack of confidence in facing her, even though they were armed and she was half-sedated.

"He'll make a full recovery, don't worry," the middle-aged nurse said, risking a step forward again. "Will you please lie down? You've sustained major trauma to the abdomen, severe concussion, three gunshot wounds, broken ribs, several minor injuries... I... they wouldn't give us your rank and official number. Those injuries don't sound like a training accident to me. You've been through something major and you need to rest. You don't need me to tell you how lucky you are to even be alive."

Lucky to be alive. For a woman who had held a gun to her own head twice but failed to pull the trigger, Beckmann begged to differ. Her eyes flitted from the nurse to the two guards. Her vision still swam in and out of focus, but her footing was steady enough. She could take them both. They were good at what they did, all three of them, the whole set up seemed so convincing.

Unless, of course, they actually were telling the truth. But right now, all they had was her name. If this was a Yujingyu ploy to trick her into divulging information, then she would be better placed in attempting an escape after further recovery.

Taking in a breath, she edged over to the bed and sat down again. She remembered falling, a long sickening fall until she slammed against the TAG, her bones breaking on contact. She remembered pressing her pistol against the pilot's head and pulling the trigger. She remembered the smoke of the missile. There was nothing after that.

The nurse sat down next to her and gently took one of her hands.

"Whatever all of this is, rest can only make it better." She offered a genuine smile.

Beckmann stared down at the shorter woman. That simple act, that smile and those compassionate words, were such a rarity in her violent life. Even if it was an act, even if this was a Yujingyu prisoner handling facility, that smile and those words felt like something to cling to, a crutch when she felt as alone as ever. She accepted the help from the nurse in swinging her feet back up onto the bed before carefully lying back down and closing her eyes.

***

Cochrane placed the two whiskey glasses onto the cubicle's circular table and then set about the awkward job of lowering himself onto the semi-circular bench seat and shuffling himself bodily around the far side of the table – all with one bandaged arm still hanging from the sling around his neck. The sports bar in central Klugestein was packed, with patrons lined up around the railings encircling the holographic arena at the far side of the room. The area holographically replicated the Omadon Arena HexaDome, and accepting the five minute delay in transmitting the virtual footage across light-years of deep space, the virtual arena granted the several dozen patrons a view of the action even better than those crammed into the famous venue. An off-season friendly match of *Aristeia!* was the sporting highlight of the month, and fans across the entire Human Sphere packed into venues to witness eight highly trained athletes prepare to shoot, hack, and maim each other in the name of entertainment.

Cochrane tapped through the menus of his wrist-mounted comlog, pairing his lens to both the pre-game commentary and seasonal analysis, but also to a second feed from Oxyd Network's round the clock news channel. A blast of warm air pushed into the sports bar as half a dozen men in their early twenties piled boisterously in from the dark streets outside. Cochrane swore under his breath and shook his head in disgust as he took in their asymmetrical haircuts, tight fitting and slogan-emblazoned clothes, and neon colored footwear.

"Pricks," he mumbled to himself as he dialed in to the settings of his booth to activate the noise reduction field.

Instantly the loud, spirited atmosphere of the sports bar – the main reason most patrons had chosen the place to watch the game, no doubt – was dulled down to a mere background buzz. Dragging his eyes away from the red, neon lights of the surrounding walls and the decor of baseball gloves, cricket bats, and fake *Aristeia!* weapons, Cochrane returned his attention to the Oxyd evening news. Karan Colley – still his favorite news anchor to watch despite her now approaching fifty years of age, was sat between two suit wearing, self-declared defense experts as debate raged over the very conflict he had been med-evac'd from only two days before. An advert for Colley's autobiography flashed up on Cochrane's lens, forcing him to check his security filters for the third time that evening as he listened to the debate on the news.

"...leaves O-12 in a difficult situation. Both sides are claiming rights to the territory, and both sides are accusing the other of being the aggressor. Jensen, where does this leave the PanOceanian government regarding the border dispute in the Glottenberg region of Norstralia?"

"Quite simply, Karan, it leaves us comfortably sat on a legitimate moral pedestal in front of the entire Human Sphere. The Yu Jing StateEmpire's government has every right to question the lines on the map that form the border between their territories and those of PanO, but the simple fact of the matter is that until that border's position is ratified, Yu Jing has to wait! And if there is a valuable commodity close to the border but on our side of it, as has been strongly hinted at by several sources, right now that belongs to PanO – and Yu Jing has no right to simply decide they don't agree with the position of the border so they can claim whatever they want."

"Dylan, any counter argument?"

"Absolutely. The position of that border has been queried and under review for nearly a year now, and the sudden reports of a valuable commodity near the border have only heightened a tension that was already in existence. We're talking about thousands of miles of dense jungle, and if just one positional marker is out of place or missed in a survey, it can have a huge impact in our perception of where that border actually is. The Yujingyu military has every right to patrol their own border, and..."

"Dylan, that's absolute nonsense. The border positional disputes between PanO and Yu Jing are in twelve separate locations on Paradiso, but only now they are interested in whatever has been discovered in Glottenberg. That does not give them the right to send an armed incursion into PanOceanian territory! That is tantamount to an act of war! And that is, of course, assuming that the leaked reports of a Yujingyu SF incursion on a PanO military

site only a day before the initial border clash are untrue, and I don't think such an assumption would be safe to make! Not remotely!"

"Jensen, Yu Jing does not recognize that border. The StateEmpire's government claims that it does not correctly represent what was agreed at the Rilaspur Accord. They have every right to..."

"Invade our territory? They were legitimately challenged..."

"Please! It was hardly an invasion!"

"They were legitimately challenged by a platoon of Fusiliers to see if they were on maneuvers and had accidentally strayed across the border, and their response was to demand our Fusiliers abandoned their position! Even the Yujingyu government does not deny that! They are the aggressors!"

"Yet our military fired the first shots! The Yujingyu government has provided irrefutable evidence to O-12 that the first shots were fired by the PanO military! So in terms of aggressors, that paints us in a very..."

"We're here to debate the politics of the Glottenberg Incursion, not question military decisions we have no comprehension of! That decision to order weapons to be fired was made by a junior military commander with boots on the ground, faced by an aggressive force making unlawful demands on PanOceanian territory! That commander should be given a bloody medal, not criticized by extreme left-wing, apologist defense analysts on the evening news!"

"No, querying that decision is exactly what needs to be done! If our military is responsible for an unlawful killing due to incompetence, then our people need to be held accountable! Irrespective of any lack of military experience from those doing the questioning!"

"The investigation into the initial shooting has already been completed, all evidence presented shows that it was a legitimate shot and a lawful killing! Do you honestly expect our fighting men and women to allow an armed incursion into our territory and then just fall back when a hostile aggressor tells them to? On our soil?"

Cochrane's attention was dragged away from the news debate by a familiar figure appeared at the edge of the booth. Cochrane sprang to his feet and edged awkwardly around the table to wrap his uninjured arm around the shoulders of the newcomer.

"G'day, Dad!" he greeted.

"What happened there?" His father asked after stepping back from what still felt like a slightly awkward and forced single arm embrace. "I got the message that you hurt yourself."

Cochrane sat down again and pushed one of the two glasses across the table to his father. The older man, dressed in a simple collared shirt of beige with smart, dark trousers, sat down opposite him.

"I was a stupid bugger, that's what," he explained to his father. "After that Yujingyu push to take the mining site off us, nothing happened for over a week. Just patrols and swapping between Alpha Four-Four and the mining complex. Nobody fired a shot. Then we were told we were being rotated out for a rest. I had one last patrol and I fell down a bloody ravine. Broke my collar bone."

His father shook his head slowly with a slight grin.

"Do yourself a favor, James, and when you go out later without me, come up with a better story for when the women ask you how you ended up in a sling."

Brian Cochrane was, like his two sons, a career soldier. He had done well to reach the rank of colonel, having stood out from his peers time after time for the first twenty-five years of his career; but once that competition became stiffer, he quickly found that other men and women with a broader span of military experience were the ones promoted to brigadier and beyond. Brian Cochrane had been a colonel for over ten years now, passed over for promotion and forgotten as he saw out the last few years of his military career before retirement. Jim Cochrane had inherited his father's tall, broad physique and brown hair, but perhaps not his patience and maturity.

"You not coming out with me?" Cochrane grinned to his father. "Danny tells me you've finally got back to dating."

As soon as he mentioned it, a message advertising a Maya dating service Cochrane had never heard of flashed onto his lens. He tapped his comlog to save the address link for later. Brian's face fell. He looked down at his glass of whiskey.

"I gave it a go, yeah," he admitted to his younger son, "but... no. It's not right. It's... never mind, hey?"

Cochrane looked away awkwardly. It had been fifteen years since his mother died. Nobody could blame Brian for seeing another woman after fifteen years alone – his two sons certainly did not. But clearly for Brian, fifteen years was still too soon. Cochrane found it hard to even imagine what that must feel like. Losing his mother in his adolescent years had hit him hard, of course, but the years slowly healed the wounds over to the point he could look back fondly on memories of his mother and even laugh with his brother about funnier times in their youth. Their father was still not at that point.

"You back out soon?" Brian asked.

"Yeah," Cochrane said, "this collar bone's nearly sorted now. The rest of my platoon are here in a couple of days. I heard from the boss that they've all been given five days off here, so I'll hopefully get signed off as fit again by the scab lifters and be good to go back out. If it isn't all over by then."

"I've been watching the whole thing from afar, naturally," Brian said, "it looks heavy going. I know the casualties on both sides are far higher than are being declared to the media."

"Yeah," Cochrane agreed, "it's tough, I won't lie. At least it was at the start. It all seems to have died right down now. But yeah, I saw stuff like this in Indigo a fair bit. But never in the Fusiliers. Not these sorts of losses."

"You doing alright?" his father asked, the coolness of his tone at odds with the warmth of his enquiry. A veteran of the NeoColonial Wars, Brian had seen combat as both a platoon and company commander. He knew exactly what was going on at the coal face.

Cochrane nodded.

"All good. I'm fine. It's the kids I'm working with I'm more worried about."

The active noise reduction screen around the booth suddenly buzzed as it surged in power to counter the cheers and roars from the patrons crammed around the holographic arena on the far side of the bar as the two teams jogged out from the dugouts and into the arena. Cochrane nodded with approval as he saw both Gata and Hippolyta pace out – his two favorite *Aristeia!* fighters based purely on them both being attractive women. Brian sampled his whiskey and nodded in approval.

"Simple four versus four game of Assault. Who's your money on?" he asked.

"The Greens. Parvati and Wild Bill are..." Cochrane replied, canceling the tedious advertising message on his lens before it even had time to finish scrolling.

Wild Bill merchandise! Official playing cards! Leisure wear! Animated bumper stickers! Reproduction Colt Peacemakers! Downloads for...

"...Parvati and Wild Bill are both boring as hell, but they're owning this sport at the moment."

"I don't know, James, the Oranges have Maximus and Kozmo. That's a pretty tricky combination to knock down."

Both teams took their positions at their respective ends of the Hexa-Dome, each quartet of warrior-entertainers eyeing their deadly opponents and the temporary scoring zone situated exactly halfway between them.

"You thought about going for that commission?" Brian asked.

Cochrane spluttered on his whiskey, slamming the glass down and hammering a fist into his chest in an effort to stop coughing.

"That came out of nowhere!" he finally managed.

"It's been a while since we've talked about it."

"I didn't think we needed to."

"Oh, come on, James!" Brian leaned forward, his forearms on the table between them. "It's been nine years! It was one rejection! They'd bite your arm off now if you put yourself forward for selection!"

Cochrane looked across at the arena again, draining his tumbler of whiskey as another wave of noise was defeated by the booth's sound shielding as the game began. He surpassed a quiet chuckle as he thought back to his failed attempt at officer selection a month after he graduated from university. Everything was supposed to be working for him – graduate in military history, high achiever in sports, his father was at the time a lieutenant colonel and battalion commander... and then came the fail at the interview board. '*Cochrane failed to demonstrate the requisite levels of confidence and leadership potential...*'

"I'm fine as I am, Dad," Cochrane said, "I'd expect to make staff sergeant out of this job, and that's pretty good going."

"James, your brother was a major by your age. So was I. I'm not... I'm not saying that should put pressure or expectation on you, I'm just saying that it seems to me that you are lashing out at the entire military because of one bad decision you suffered from nearly a decade ago. That board made the wrong decision about you. I told you then and I'm telling you again now."

"Yeah, and I agree."

"So why are you letting that dictate the terms of your entire professional life? You're cutting off your nose to spite your face. Do you really think that any single member of that board is watching your career development and thinking 'Shit! I made the wrong call! Should have let him become an officer back in the day!' They don't know or care!"

"I know that!" Cochrane replied, hearing the anger in his own tone and quickly guarding against it.

He knew what his father was saying made some sense at some level and that it did come from a place of love, even though their relationship strictly avoided the use of that word, and furthermore he owed it to his father above all others to keep his temper in check and show respect.

"So what is it?" Brian continued regardless, ignoring what appeared from the cheers behind him to be an exciting development in the opening rounds of the match displayed in the virtual arena. "You don't want to spoil your image? You don't want the soldiers to know that tough-talking Sergeant Jim is actually from an educated and affluent background? James, the days of linking a commission as an officer to a social background died a long time ago."

"Can we talk about something else, please?" Cochrane urged.

Brian sat back in his seat, exhaled through his thin nostrils, and nodded to himself for a few moments before one hand tapped gently against the table.

"I'm... sorry," the older soldier said after a pause, "that came out all wrong. I'm not trying to steer you toward something you don't want to do."

"It's... fine," Cochrane mustered up a smile, "I'll give it some thought, alright? Deadset. I will. Look, let me get you another drink."

Looks like you want another drink. Do you want to upgrade to booth service plus?

Brian stood up and grabbed the two empty glasses as Cochrane dismissed the offer to upgrade on his comlog.

"No, no. You bought the first round, and I'd rather you weren't trying to barge your way through people with that injury anyway. I'll be right back."

Cochrane watched his father disappear into the small crowd packed around the bar. He switched his attention back to his lens, turning the projection of the game back on. Almost instantly, the bar erupted in cheers and shouts as Maximus slammed his heavy shield into Wild Bill to fling the ageing gunslinger to the ground in a shower of blood, allowing Gata to leap past and into the scoring zone. Cochrane shook his head. His father had been right about the game, it seemed. His father had an annoying habit of being right about most things.

***

"Morning, Lisette," Aanya greeted as she carried a glass jug of water into the room, "how are you doing?"

Half sat up on her bed as rays of sunshine poured into the room from a clear, bright sky, Beckmann turned down the blaring music in her ear piece.

"I'm looking hot and listening to metal," she replied with a grin, holding up one hand and extending her index and little fingers, "so I'm doing good."

The senior nurse connected her medlog to the terminal next to Beckmann's bed and set about checking that her data was correctly recorded. Beckmann looked across her hospital room at the mirror above the sink on the adjacent wall and smiled in contentment. Her face was looking tanned and perfect – the exact skin tone she had ordered in her Lhost before she died and was transferred to the upgraded body – and her loose fitting hospital gown and trousers hid the bandages over her abdomen, hip, and thigh. To the casual onlooker, she could be in hospital for a routine checkup rather than only one week out of Intensive Treatment, where she had spent days fighting for her life in an induced coma.

"Everything looks to be on the mend," the bulky nurse smiled. "The quality of your Lhost has helped a little, there, too. I've got to admit, in twenty years of doing this I've never seen a Lhost like that. They must be paying soldiers a lot more than I thought!"

"They said it would make me five percent sexier, so I paid the money without thinking twice," Beckmann beamed.

Aanya laughed as she continued checking the terminal readouts. Beckmann resumed inspecting herself in the mirror, tilting her face from side to side. Yes, the nurse was entirely correct, the Lhost cost millions, far more than a soldier could ever afford. But when a Hexa assassin lost her mind and went rogue, running away to spend a full year as a mercenary and contract killer, money was not an issue.

Five percent was, indeed, the rough figure quoted to her when she enquired as to how much of an aesthetic improvement the new body would provide. Beckmann recalled what she looked like before the accident that took her life, and to be fair, the most obvious changes were the permanently perfect tan, unnaturally deep blue eyes, and changing her hair color from blonde to brown. The Lhost, as the Akram Biosciences advertisement said, 'doesn't change who you are, they simply create the very best version of what you can be.' Blemishes, even bad hair days, all were made impossible by modern and cripplingly expensive bio-technology. As a naive girl of nineteen when she paid for the Lhost, she had almost looked forward to dying so that she could upgrade. If only she had known then that it would come five years later, burning slowly to death whilst trapped in the wreckage of a crashed sports car rather than heroically on the field of battle as she had imagined.

"Lisette?"

A hand clamped on her shoulder.

Beckmann jumped. She looked up into the concerned eyes of the warm-faced, dark-skinned nurse.

"You alright?"

"Oh, yeah!" Beckmann forced a broad smile, pushing the agonizing memory of the flames, smoke, and searing pain aside. "Feeling good! Which reminds me... I know I'm not allowed to run yet, but is there any chance of getting some small weights in here? Nothing huge, just something to work on my arms or..."

The nurse shook her head and sighed.

"All in time. The notes here are pretty clear, love. Exercise is restricted to walking. You're not ready for anything else. You'll tear open those wounds again if you don't let them heal. And we wouldn't want you to get a scar, now, would we?"

Beckmann's face dropped.

"I'd scar? Seriously? Aanya, are you joking? Seriously? Would I scar?"

A bleep sounded from Aanya's medlog, and she turned to open a communication channel. She looked down at Beckmann and smiled again.

"You've got a visitor downstairs."

Beckmann sat up slowly. Calmly, she looked around her room for anything she could use as a weapon.

"Have they given a name?" she asked.

Aanya tapped a button on her device.

204

"No. It's a man. Tall-ish, dark hair."

Beckmann's eyes opened wide. She looked across at the colorful bouquet of flowers on her bedside table that were delivered the day after she woke up. Her heart jumped.

"You think it's the guy?" Aanya asked. "The one who sent those to you?"

Beckmann caught her reflection again as she slowly turned to sit on the edge of the bed. If it was him... alarm kicked in, a panic more vivid than anything that could be created by even an entire squadron of enemy TAGs. Beckmann grabbed Aanya by the collars of her tunic.

"He can't see me like this! Aanya! Get me some make up. Eyeliner, PerfectSkin spray, anything. Get me make up!"

The severity of her situation clearly not making an impact on the experienced nurse, Aanya burst into a mirthful laughter and pried Beckmann's hands off her collars.

"Lisette, I've got patients to check on. People who need real help."

"This is fucking real!"

"You're fine just the way you are. And I don't carry make up around with me. Now calm down and I'll see you for morning rounds later."

Beckmann watched helplessly as her ally retreated, leaving her alone in her sterile, white-walled hospital room. Again, the idea that the visitor was somebody from her past with ill intent quickly crossed her mind, but then they certainly would not announce their arrival. No, this could be him. Left unarmed without make up, haircare products, or a wardrobe, Beckmann quickly pulled off her turquoise, clinical gown and shoved it beneath her bed before pulling the neckline of her vest top as low as it would go. Letting out a hiss of pain, she then lowered herself to the floor, limped across the room, and assumed a seemingly casual position perched on the window sill, one knee hugged to her chest as she gazed pensively out across the outskirts of Klugestein. It would pass for a posed picture on the back cover of a solo album. It would have to do.

She beat the clock by only a second. There was a light knock at the door, and then it swung open. Her heart hammering anxiously, Beckmann glanced casually across to the doorway. Her high spirits deflated instantly. Anger clawed its way quickly above romance.

"Hello, Razor," Clark smiled.

Beckmann paused, eyeing her visitor with suspicion and rapidly growing unease.

"Why are you here?" Beckmann scowled. "What do you want?"

"It's not what I want. It's what Command wants. You disobeyed a direct order. And we all know what happened last time you did that."

Iain Clark was a tall, lean man with dark hair that was graying at the temples now that he was well into his forties. His thin, pale face perfectly complimented his gray eyes and tan-colored suit. Clark closed the door behind him and walked over to sit on the edge of the hospital bed, tugging up his trousers at the thighs to save wear on the knees as he did so. With a thin smile, he made a number of selections on his comlog.

"Security," he glanced across at Beckmann, "you understand, of course, Razor. I need to set up a blocking field so we won't be eavesdropped on."

"Don't call me Razor," Beckmann warned, "my friends call me that. You are not my friend and never have been."

Clark let out a pleasant, gentle laugh.

"Friends? Do you have any of those left? What is it now: you, Paligutan... all the others are dead."

Beckmann fixed her eyes on his. She brought a knee up to her chin and wrapped her arms around one leg on her perch on the windowsill before smiling venomously at him.

"Except for Matthias Brun, of course. But who knows where he is, right? Complete mystery."

Beckmann knew Brun from the military academy on Svalarheima she attended between the ages of ten and sixteen. Brun had taken to sneaking out at night in his adolescent years. He found a girl. By the age of twenty, even though he was a Garkain killer like the rest of them, he had married her in secret. By twenty-four, he was a father. With years of training and experience in infiltration, he used an assumed identity and persona to take his family and disappear completely. Beckmann and Anna Paligutan helped him to achieve that with spectacular success less than a year ago.

"We'll find Brun, Captain," Clark's smile faded. "Just like we found you when you disappeared."

"Major," Beckmann corrected, "and you found me because I used my real name and left a trail of mayhem and destruction for you to follow. Brun – who knows? But my guess is that he has assumed an entirely new identity and is gone for good. Just like you trained him to do."

Clark's neutral features hardened further still.

"Major?" he choked a short laugh, doubling back to her earlier comment. "Last I checked, you are a Temporary Acting Major for this assignment only. Your substantive rank is captain."

"At this point in time I am a major," Beckmann said as she leaned forward, watching the thin man on the other side of the small hospital room. Even if she wanted to, she doubted she could conceal the hatred she felt for Clark. A man who had spent his entire adult life sending operatives to kill or be killed, often both, when he himself had never fired a weapon in his life. Beckmann let out a quiet, bitter laugh and shook her head in disgust. In that regard, Clark was very much like her own father. But at least her father wore military rank and uniform.

"I can't call you Razor, I can't call you Captain… What do you want?"

"What I want is for you to fuck off and die."

Clark's pursed lips broke into a smile again, followed quickly by a chuckle. He shook his head as if the exchange of words was nothing more than playful banter between old friends.

"Can't do that, Captain. Command has sent me here to talk to you. All of this distraction around the fighting at the mining site has shifted focus from the real objective. You were sent to Alpha Four-Four to infiltrate the MagnaObra research facility and find out everything you could about that Cosmolite."

"Which I have done, successfully," Beckmann sneered, "three times."

"I'd argue that two were successful." Clark folded his arms. "That second time you were in there, you managed to raise the alarm, didn't you?"

"Eagle One, you're cleared to move to Marker Gustav."

Hesitantly advancing, carefully dropping a heel and then lowering her toes in turn, Beckmann crept silently along the main communication corridor of the MagnaObra research facility. It was late, and the research hub was running with half the staff of the daytime shift, giving her the best chance possible of reaching the main data terminal room.

She checked her tactical map as she advanced stealthily through the facility, the material of her active camouflage jumpsuit changing to mimic the cold grays and off-whites of the surrounding walls, floor plates, and ceiling.

"Eagle One, threat inbound from your two o'clock," her tactical controller called in her earpiece, "go static."

Beckmann stepped across to press her back against the wall of the long corridor, staring down toward the threat axis. A researcher appeared from an adjoining corridor to the right, a short man with scraggy, uneven stubble who looked barely out of his teens and certainly not old enough to be entrusted with the research of civilization-changing alien technology. The white lab-coated boy walked straight toward Beckmann. She held her ground, trusting the technology of her suit to make her completely invisible to the human eye just so long as she did not move a muscle.

The researcher walked past her, his attention firmly fixed on a holographic data screen projected in the air above his left arm's comlog. The corridor fell silent again as the young scientist disappeared into another room.

"Threat clear," her Tac Con reported, "advance to Marker Gustav."

Beckmann resumed her slow progress again, patiently moving forward in complete silence whilst her eyes scanned her surroundings and the tactical map projected onto her lens. Hexa technology protected her from the building's state of the art security system; it was the simple act of making noise detectable to the human ear that was her greatest obstacle.

"*Eagle One... err... we've got a problem.*"

Beckmann stopped.

"*What?*" she whispered.

"*You're close enough now that I've got a signal from the main data hub. It's sending an... update, I think, to MagnaObra's Paradiso headquarters. The signal... it's not encrypted the way we expected.*"

Beckmann continued to move forward, only meters now from the door to the data hub and her target.

"*Eagle One, you'll have to hack the system manually.*"

Beckmann stopped.

"*Are you high?*" she whispered. "*I'm not a hacker! I don't know how to...*"

"*I'll talk you through it. Stand by. Hold position.*"

Beckmann paused. She saw red dots move across her tactical map as researchers continued to move about the facility, alone or in small groups. Time ticked by. She checked the power levels of her jumpsuit. A decent amount of charge, still. All was fine.

"*Eagle One, move to the data hub. I'll talk you through the hack.*"

Beckmann stepped forward again. She reached the door of the hub, the target of her entire mission at Alpha Four-Four, and stopped in place.

"*Tac Con, you're sure you've got this?*" she breathed. "*I can just wait for somebody to open the door and slip in with them. If the security system senses a door open with nobody on the cameras...*"

"*Eagle One, you are cleared to proceed. Door security systems are under my control.*"

The door opened. Beckmann saw the bulky data terminal in the center of the room ahead, its access panel illuminated with twinkling status lights as it transmitted its encrypted update off station. She stepped forward. The entire building plunged into darkness. A siren wailed. She jumped back just in time as the door slammed shut again accompanied by red warning lights at regular intervals along the ceiling.

'*Intruder, intruder, intruder! Intruder at the main data hub!*' An automated voice announced mechanically.

Beckmann swore and retreated quickly to the main corridor.

"*Tac Con!*" she gasped. "*What the hell is going on?*"

"*Eagle One, your position is compromised. Abort operation.*"

"*Yeah, I can see that!*"

She looked back down the corridor toward the main entrance and saw figures moving in a hurry, silhouetted by the flashing red warning lights in the darkness. Five, perhaps six were rushing toward the exit. One hurtled right toward her. A dark-skinned man of perhaps thirty years of age, his white coat billowing out behind him, ran purposefully toward the main data hub. The *researcher was instantly highlighted and tagged on her lens.*

  "Eagle One from Tac Con. Threat inbound, highlighted as Target Anton. Take Target Anton."

  "No!" Beckmann whispered. "I'm not killing a civilian!"

  The researcher sprinted past Beckmann and then suddenly stopped. He looked around quizzically as the alarm continued to blare, his face switching from a grim, purposeful expression to one of fear and anxiety.

  "Eagle One, he knows you are there! Take Target Anton!"

  Beckmann stepped nimbly behind the researcher and wrapped an arm around his throat, pressing her other forearm hard against the back of his neck. The researcher spluttered and gasped, thrashing wildly to either side with both arms as Beckmann held him firmly in place, choking the breath out of him. She felt a pang of sympathy for the man as he flailed about pathetically in the flashing red lights, clearly not in possession of even the most basic self-defense training. After a few seconds, he fell limp in her arms, and she allowed him to slip to the floor.

  "Target Anton incapacitated," Beckmann reported.

  A shrill scream wailed from behind Beckmann. She turned and saw a blonde-haired female researcher staring at the prone body of her colleague, yelling in terror.

  "Eagle One," her tactical controller called, "new target, highlighted as Target Berta. Take Target Berta..."

  "...and you didn't kill her, either," Clark shook his head in disappointment. "Although getting your Tac Con to hack her social media account and find something to use against her, that was ingenious, Razor. The poor woman had only just lost her mother, and you creep up on her in the darkness and sing a song that her mother used to sing to her as a child? Good gosh. She'll be having nightmares for the rest of her life."

  "Look, what do you want?" Beckmann exploded, stepping down off the window sill and gritting her teeth as a wave of pain shot up her right leg.

  Clark fidgeted in his seated position at the edge of the bed, backing away from Beckmann just a fraction. It was barely perceptible but enough for her to notice. The very man who taught combat psychology and target manipulation to her and her comrades was scared of her.

  "Command is concerned," he replied, "you've gone into that facility and you've screwed it up. When the shit hit the fan, you disobeyed two orders to take targets. Then there was that debacle with the Yujingyu TAG. You were given clear orders to retreat. You disobeyed them. Captain, do you need reminding of the terms of your commission? You murdered three people! You should be in prison for life! The only thing keeping you out of prison is you returning to Strategic Security and doing your damn job properly!"

"I never murdered anybody, you piece of shit!" Beckmann yelled, limping forward and pointing in accusation. "You *know* that!"

"The court found you guilty of shooting two policemen and that old woman..."

"They shot first! I fired warning shots, but they ignored them! So yes, when those two stupid bastards started firing into a crowd and gunned down some poor old woman in front of her husband, I dropped the fuckers! And I don't regret it! You *know* for a fact that the bullets that killed that woman could not have come from my gun! She was behind me! That evidence was altered! That's what we do, isn't it? But not to our own!"

"Unless your memory has altered the facts," Clark shrugged coldly, "because your mental health track record is not the best. Far from it, in fact. Tell me; do you still think you see the ghost of a thirteen year old girl who was killed in training next to you when you were a child?"

Beckmann stopped in place, her teeth gritted and fists clenched. She stared down at Clark.

"No," she lied, "that's in the past, now. I haven't seen... imagined seeing Praga in years."

"And what were you doing in a crowded shopping mall with a gun, anyway?" Clark demanded.

Beckmann slammed a fist into the wall next to her, cracking the plaster. She turned and scowled down at Clark again.

"We've been through this a thousand times! I needed space! I... cracked! I was eighteen years old and shit was going on! I needed space, and you bastards sent the police after me with orders to shoot to kill!"

"You're a dangerous woman. You know that. You can't just walk away and do what you want to. We've got a history of operatives flipping and losing the plot. It invariably ends violently. We have a moral obligation to stop that from happening."

"Moral obligation?! You?!"

"Yes!" It was Clark's turn to raise his voice. "Every time any of us talk to you about this, you pull the same routine! It's simple, Beckmann! Your life is forfeit for the greater good! We're not cackling evilly as we send you to your doom on every mission! We have spent years training you to an *incredibly* high standard so that you can take lives, and thousands of innocent people will live as a result of your actions! You do some horrible, fucked up shit to a tiny number of twisted, horrible people so that the vast majority of good, innocent people remain safe! Do you honestly think I struggle to go to sleep at night because of what we have done to you? Sacrificing your freedom, your life if necessary, is the tiniest, most minuscule of evils to ensure safety and freedom for everybody else. You've done this for long enough. You need to accept it."

Beckmann stopped. Her head sank and her eyes closed. It almost made sense when he put it in those terms. What sort of monster would she be if she refused to face danger and do the horrible things others did not have the skills to do, knowing it kept countless people safe? Or, was that all bullshit and the professor of psychology who sat before knew her inner workings well enough that the moral guilt line was the best way to force her to comply?

"Command is concerned," Clark continued. "You are being monitored with every shot you take out here. We've got years of data on you, with a resting heart rate when shooting that demonstrates both an incredible level of fitness, but also completely callousness. Your resting heart rate on the shots you've taken on this mission are off the chart! You're panicking!"

Beckmann let out a yell of frustrated anguish and looked around for something to throw. In an instant, the calm acceptance she felt after Clark's previous speech was replaced with a blood-boiling anger and need to do violence. Clark shot to his feet and backed away. Beckmann limped toward him.

"You tell Command to stay out of my head!" Beckmann snarled. "You tell that to my father, too! I can't take this anymore! I… fuck! I've had it! I don't want you controlling my life! I don't want you telling me who to kill! I'll do your missions for you, but I'll do them my way! You tell Command that! The terms of the amnesty were that I work for you for ten years, and I'm doing just that! So the rest… everything else… just back off and stay out of my life, or as God is my witness, you will see me lose my shit!"

Beckmann looked down at Clark. He was by the door now, his face even paler than normal. One of her knees buckled as pain shot across her bandaged abdomen. She stumbled back up to her full, impressive height and eyed her target.

"Clark, you taught me how to lie. You can tell exactly when I'm lying and when I'm telling the truth. So look me in the eyes right now and decide whether I'm bluffing. If you are not out of this room in five seconds, I will rip your throat off your neck with my bare hands."

With one final attempt at a dignified action, Clark adjusted his tie and made his way quickly to the door. He stopped and turned back.

"The instant, the very *instant* these fools sign you off as fully fit for combat duties again, I'm sending you back to that research base to do the job properly and finish what you've started."

Beckmann watched him go before sinking down to the bed again, adrenaline and rage quickly dissipating to leave her feeling exhausted, deflated, and saddened by a dozen memories the conversation with Clark had dredged up from the past. Shaking, she plunged her face into her hands and concentrated on taking long, deep breathes as she fought the urge to burst into tears.

Chapter Fourteen

Dragging his feet wearily across the faded, green carpet, Hawkins was vaguely aware of a group of junior officers watching him from where they sat in the corner of the anteroom. Under the watchful gaze of strangers whilst wearing the uniform of his Order, Hawkins plucked up the energy to stand up straight as he walked.

Earlier, after dropping off his bags in his room at the Kokoda Barracks Officers' Mess, and having realized the delay in his flight had caused him to be too late to take an evening meal, he had wandered down to one of the plush anterooms of the building to indulge in the luxury of a cup of tea. It was there that he was almost immediately disturbed with a summons; a communique issued via his comlog on an Order channel; *'Report to Officers' Mess Briefing Room Two immediately for debriefing.'*

Hawkins sighed as he closed the door to the anteroom behind him. Kokoda Barracks was an oddity of sorts; built not far from the outskirts of the hyper modern and impressive city of Klugestein on the southern coastline of Norstralia, Kokoda Barracks sat just far away enough from the Yujingyu territorial border that it existed with a very low threat state, but close enough that it was a sprawling, major military staging area complete with vast exercise ranges, vehicle maintenance depots, and a staff complex that was home to several officers of general rank.

The Officers' Mess was, like any of the PanOceanian military accommodation buildings Hawkins had visited, an odd attempt to appear grand and traditional combined with obvious cost-cutting measures. Traditional oil paintings of past military actions hung from every wall atop equally traditional, torn, and faded conventional wallpaper; ornately carved wooden armchairs with plush leather cushions regularly punctuated the corners of corridors as if trying to give off the vibe of the exclusive existence military officers once enjoyed some four hundred years ago on Earth. The busy pattern of the carpet similarly exhumed an almost Napoleonic era feeling but was so trampled down by years of combat boots that the lines of the floorboards beneath were clearly visible.

Responding to the message on his comlog that demanded his immediate attendance, Hawkins navigated his way through the winding maze of corridors on the third floor of the Officers' Mess, suppressing a series of yawns from a long succession of near sleepless nights at Alpha Four-Four or on patrol in the jungles around it. In the corridor ahead, he saw a short woman of perhaps forty years of age approaching him, wearing the combat fatigues of a PanOceanian military officer. He leaned forward to inspect the badges on her combat jacket, making out the acronym 'POMC' – PanOceanian Military

Complex – above the right breast pocket and the epaulette of a lieutenant colonel across the front of the chest. The rank badge was lined in red or scarlet or crimson or some color which marked her out as a doctor or dentist or… something. Hawkins, his exhausted mind still working slowly, could barely remember the convoluted and confusing regular military badge system from his years of extensive training.

"Good evening, ma'am," he nodded politely, bracing himself to attention formally as he stood to one side to let the medical officer pass him.

"Hello," the short woman flashed a smile, eyeing his uniform curiously as she passed.

For his part, Hawkins understood how he stood out on an army base. He wore the working uniform of a Hospitaller officer away from front line duties; simple, neat black trousers and a single breasted black jacket that was cut short, falling only to the hip. The military orders did not subscribe to the somewhat confusing and wasteful PR battle that was waged between the army and the navy, necessitating in corporate logos being stitched to uniform sleeves and bold letters spelling out which service the wearer was a part of. Hawkins' jacket merely had his badges of rank on the shoulder epaulettes and a white Maltese cross high on the left sleeve. Nothing more was required.

Following the digital map projected onto his lens, Hawkins weaved along the last length of corridor on the third floor before descending a grubby, poorly-lit staircase in the corner of the building to the ground floor. There, he moved past the mess reception and to one of the building's small briefing rooms where he had been summoned. Outside the door to the room was a brief flash of evidence of higher spending; a holographic data display faded coolly into life at head height, scrolling a personalized greeting message to Hawkins as it mated with his comlog before informing him about the weather and local news close to his parents' home. Hawkins ignored the blue screen and walked over to the dull painting on the wall next to it where a battle was depicted between two sides in slightly differing shades of khaki uniforms, both firing ancient, wooden bolt-action rifles at each other in a violent jungle clash. Hawkins read the painting's accompanying plaque.

"Lieutenant Colonel William Owen leads militiamen of the 39th Battalion, Australian Army, against an attacking force of the Japanese Army 144th Infantry Regiment. Kokoda, New Guinea, 29 July 1942."

Hawkins stared at the blurred, painted image of the violent clash, lost in imagination as he tried to put himself in the moment depicted on the wall in front of him. No armor, no digital maps, no communications other than simply shouting, not even the luxury of a rifle that automatically loaded the next shot. Yet there were parallels, and Hawkins found himself briefly wondering if the barracks being named after the Kokoda campaign was more than mere chance. PanOceania's origins lay mainly, some would argue, with Australian economic and political dominance after the breakup of power of the United States and Europe, and Yu Jing similarly had a huge Japanese cultural influence. And here he now was, the modern descendant of those old clashes on Earth in another age, fighting alongside men and women largely of Australian heritage against the vicious, fanatical attackers descended in part from the Japanese. He suppressed a laugh as he studied the details of the Kokoda painting. He had even been fighting in a remote, isolated outpost in the jungle; but a jungle far more beautiful than the dense, inhospitable nightmare of New Guinea back on Earth.

"Brother Hawkins?"

Hawkins looked up, roused from his fatigued indulgence in historical imagination.

A thin man of a similar age to Hawkins, with a shaved head and long nose, stood by the open door, his Hospitaller's uniform displaying the rank insignia of a Lay Brother – a junior non-combatant of the Order.

"The Father will see you now," the shorter man said with the lack of warmth and humility that Hawkins had grown accustomed to from four years of training as a Hospitaller.

Hawkins was, he confessed to himself, pleasantly surprised to hear the rank mentioned; Father-Officer Valconi was his immediate commander, a veteran soldier perhaps ten years Hawkins' senior who he had met only three times, but on first impressions, seemed approachable enough. Valconi had tried to talk Hawkins out of volunteering for the Paradiso mission, claiming it would be a waste of his time when there were far more important things just on the horizon. He said that patience, as the old cliché went, was indeed a virtue. Hawkins smiled wearily. He wondered how Valconi would react now that the Glottenberg Incursion was headline news all across PanOceania.

The briefing room followed the trend of the rest of the building; a sprawling table of chipped, dark wood surrounded with more of the archaic looking leather chairs, all tilted toward a state of the art briefing terminal and array of virtual screens. More paintings of battles from the Earth's renaissance period up to the NeoColonial wars hung from the walls. A single figure sat on the closest of the chairs, his muscular frame clothed in Hospitaller black in stark contrast to the light skin of his bald head. Hawkins' eyes opened wider in surprise.

"Father De Fersen?" he exclaimed, "I… I wasn't expecting…"

De Fersen looked up at Hawkins, his impassive features seemingly set in stone as he folded his arms across his chest.

"That's all, Rankov," the famed warrior's gravelly voice dismissed the lay brother.

Hawkins watched him depart, closing the door behind him. Hawkins then accepted the senior Order soldier's gestured invitation for him to sit down. Hawkins looked up at De Fersen, tugging uncomfortably on the stiff collar of his black uniform jacket. Father-Officer Gabriele De Fersen was perhaps the most famous, or possibly notorious, soldier within the entire Hospitaller Order. A veteran of two decades of fierce fighting, including the final rounds of the NeoColonial Wars as well as the Ariadnan Commercial Conflicts and facing the EI on Paradiso, De Fersen's dark reputation was gleaned for his violence on the field of battle against the church and humanity's foes. That reputation was further darkened by the fact that he was one of a minuscule number of surviving members of a long dissolved organization that was disgraced in the eyes of the Pope; the Holy Order of the Temple.

"You've been busy, Brother," De Fersen issued a slight smile, eerie in its somehow implied aggression, "all that shit you were taught on Skovorodino… 'facing the heart of darkness' and all that. Well. You've seen it with your own eyes, now."

Hawkins hesitated before replying. His eyes were heavy and his shoulders ached. He just wanted sleep. Being shoved in front of De Fersen in such a state felt like one of the many resistance to interrogation exercises he had faced in training.

"Yes, Father," he replied simply.

De Fersen's brow rose for a moment.

"It's not what you thought it would be like, is it, Kyle?"

Hawkins swallowed and looked away. On the surface, the question could have been construed as one of a sympathetic nature; an expression of avuncular care from the veteran warrior who had personally taken Hawkins under his proverbial wing during training as a protege of sorts. But behind those words, knowing a little of De Fersen's manner as Hawkins did, he knew there was more to it. It was a simple '*I told you so*' from the experienced soldier. Hawkins looked up again.

"I… well… sir. The Yujingyu military sent in an SF team to carry out a clandestine reconnaissance of the MagnaObra research facility at Alpha Four-Four. I was stationed on perimeter security duty when…"

De Fersen held up a hand to silence the young soldier.

"Yes, yes, I know all that. I've read every report you've sent back. I'm not here to find out what's going on at Alpha Four-Four. I'm here to see how you are coping. I'm here to check on you."

Hawkins took in a sharp intake of breath. He again fell silent, carefully and suspiciously guarding his words.

"You're not an initiate now," De Fersen continued, "you're a soldier. I've read your reports. I've seen your post-combat lens footage. You've killed a lot of people, Kyle. A lot."

Hawkins watched warily, confused by the pride in the older man's voice as he verbally praised him for his violence over the past weeks.

"Father Kennedy had his doubts, if you recall," De Fersen said coolly, citing one of Hawkins' most critical instructors in training. "'Kyle Hawkins? He's a nice guy. He'll come home having quit and been unable to pull the trigger, or in a wooden box.' That's what Kennedy said. I disagreed. So did Father Valconi. I told Kennedy that you were a born killer. And you've proved me to be correct."

Hawkins took in another slow breath but forced himself to remain silent. The direction of the one way conversation left him with a building sensation of unease.

"I know why Father Kennedy thought what he thought," De Fersen explained, "most of them did. You're from a loving, stable, and relatively affluent background. You've faced no hardship in your childhood. I share that with you. But as you know, when a man just loses it and goes on a killing spree, that man isn't always from a background of violence and abuse."

"So what, you think I'm a serial killer, now?" Hawkins snapped, leaning forward and staring at the senior soldier defiantly. "You think I'm enjoying this? You think I'm some sort of kill crazed idiot, like a TAG ace painting kill markings on his hand controller? Every life I took out there was legal and necessary, and every one of them has cut through my bloody soul! I hate it! I hate every second of it!"

De Fersen leaned back, his craggy face softening just a little.

"Alright, alright. Now you're talking. We have a dialogue. That's good. Look, this had to happen. I know you feel like shit, but this is the vocation. This is the calling, the way of life we have entered. We do violence to those who would do violence to others. To others who cannot defend themselves. But we've been through this before. There is a time to morally justify violence. There is such a thing as a just killing. Our faith is littered with examples of them. Yes, what we do… cuts through the soul, as you have put it. But it isn't wrong. It is justified. You had to feel this to develop. It's why I sent you here."

Hawkins frowned in confusion.

"You didn't send me here, sir. I volunteered."

De Fersen shook his head.

"This hasn't just blown up out of nowhere. Strategic Security and our own Black Friars were aware that a security leak betrayed the importance of the research site at Alpha Four-Four to the Yu Jing StateEmpire government. Increased activity was an absolute certainty. We knew this was coming weeks ago."

"But… I volunteered," Hawkins repeated.

"You did," De Fersen agreed, "but you were the only member of the Order I informed of the opening I had created at Alpha Four-Four. You were the only one given a chance to volunteer. I wanted you to feel… ownership of your decision. Even though I orchestrated it all. It married up perfectly – Alpha Four-Four needed bolstering, and you had just finished training and needed a first assignment."

Hawkins shot to his feet and turned away. Even though deep down he knew that De Fersen's orchestration was all above board and well in accordance with his authority, he still felt a burning feeling of betrayal. This whole ordeal, his being here and suddenly being plunged into battle, hacking and gunning down soldier after soldier… it was all carefully choreographed. He turned and glared down at the impassive face of his mentor. De Fersen had often been at the monastery during Hawkins' four years of training. Hawkins knew even as a completely novice initiate that he was being singled out for special attention from the notorious warrior with the dark past, but he always assumed it was because he was not making the grade. His 'foolish' and 'naive' interpretations of both scripture and regulations regularly marked him out as lacking the zeal of the rest of his course. But he had his principles. Foolish and naive did not necessarily mean wrong.

"Why me?" he demanded. "Why put me here? I can think of ten names of men and women I graduated with who would have jumped for the opportunity to be here! Who would have led counter attacks straight to the Yujingyu border itself! Why me?"

De Fersen looked up, his face all but impassive yet still not completely without compassion.

"Because you are the only novice who has put me on my arse in a training duel," he replied, "and the day you did that, I knew you were capable of something special within this Order. I'm not pushing you because I want to break you. I'm pushing you because getting the best out of you means getting the best for the Order. And in turn, that means better serving God's will."

Hawkins shook his head and sank back down to his seat. The realization of the realities of this vocation now seemed so different to his childhood aspirations. He thought so much of it would be protecting the weak and needy, a sort of modern day Saint George slaying the dragons of the EI. Resentment building within him turned to anger again. He looked up after a pause.

"I put you on your arse because I worked every day and every night to learn to fight," he growled, "and that yields better results than just paying millions for a combat program to be shoved into your head. Sir."

De Fersen let out a short laugh.

"On the one hand, it's nice to see some spirit in you, boy. On the other, I've now got twenty years of combat experience to consolidate on the foundation that program *shoved in my head* laid out. So I fancy this old dog could still teach you a trick or two."

Hawkins slumped in his seat, the burden of his decision to join the

Order now seeming more cataclysmic than even his darkest days and steepest hurdles in four long, relentless years of training.

"I'm sorry, Father. I should not have spoken to you like that. I owe you more."

"It's alright," De Fersen shrugged nonchalantly, "I expected no less. It's why I'm here. You remember that first day of training in the Order, when you arrived straight from your parents and the comforts of the home you grew up in, only to be stripped of your identity and given a number, then shoved through a succession of horrific training exercises. It's a huge transition, but a necessary one. This is just the same. You've gone from being a theoretical warrior into a real one. It's not a good place to be, I know that. It's why I came to check on you."

Hawkins planted his elbows on his knees as he sat, resting one fist in the open fingers of his other hand and slumping his chin down onto his knuckles.

"What do I do?" he whispered, half to himself. "Because throughout all of this, I've been left wondering if I should be doing this. If I... I should have just become a priest. I'm not meant for war."

"No!" De Fersen said firmly. "No, you are better suited to this than you think. The fact that you are even questioning the moral implications of your actions proves that. I know that right now it doesn't seem that you are doing the right thing. It doesn't seem like you are a part of a force for good. But you are. And you will see it. Bring your Bible up. Let's find you the grace you need, right now. Psalm 69."

Sitting upright in the uncomfortable chair, Hawkins tapped his wrist and brought the Book of Psalms up on his lens, quickly cycling through to where De Fersen had directed him.

It was the better part of an hour before De Fersen finally dismissed him, leaving him feeling at least more content with his decision to take the path of a Holy Order soldier, if still just as thoughtful over the violence that path involved. Hawkins opted to take the outside route back to his room in the adjacent accommodation block, pulling on his black beret as soon as the warm night air greeted him. He looked off to the northwest and saw one side of the tall, coastal hills outside the huge military base painted with lights reflected from the sprawling city hidden behind the high ground. The skies above were clear, granting a hazy view of the sparkling starscape of the heavens above.

Hawkins thrust his hands into his pockets for a few pensive paces before recalling the seniority of some of the officers living at the barracks and then removing his hands again lest he be observed setting poor standards of military bearing. His mind awash with a hundred thoughts, he meandered back to the main doors of his accommodation block, mulling over De Fersen's uncharacteristically introspective and calming teachings from the Old Testament as they wrestled for priority in his head over the darker memories of the past month.

"Kyle?"

Hawkins stopped dead by the doors of his tall accommodation block. He looked up and saw a tall, slim female officer in a military uniform he did not recognize. The woman wore a high collared jacket and skirt of blue-gray, her matching peaked cap worn tilted back and at a stylish angle over her neatly pinned, brown hair. She stepped out of the shadows and into the light of the building's foyer.

"Major?" Hawkins stammered.

Beckmann's peerless and unforgettable beauty seemed to match her smart uniform even more so than the combat attire he remembered her by. A short row of medals for valor lined her jacket above the left breast pocket; the complete absence of any campaign ribbons to accompany them spoke volumes about the legitimacy of the operations that must have led to the awarding of those medals. Prestigious qualifications badges accompanied them, Hawkins immediately recognized her sniper badge and jump wings. A black band ran around her right cuff with silver letters spelling out the words *Strategic Security,* whilst higher on the sleeve was a circular badge with an embroidered screaming skull, around which was the word *Garkain.* The hue of her uniform seemed to straddle the line between PanOceanian blue and the ambiguous gray of the Strategic Security Division's morals.

Beckmann threw a cigarette butt to the floor and stamped it out beneath a gray, high-heeled shoe before walking over. Hawkins snapped out of his trance and quickly brought up his arm in a smart salute. Beckmann offered an apologetic smile and returned the salute with a casual, barely interested raising of her right hand to the peak of her cap.

As if his exhausted walk back to his room had not left his thoughts complicated and conflicted enough, Hawkins' mind raced through a dozen emotions as he recalled the last time he saw Beckmann. He remembered seeing her broken, bloodied body in the rain and the mud as a Fusilier medic fought to stabilize her. He recalled the bitter venom in his heart only hours before when he had seen her kill a helpless enemy soldier. He remembered only too well why it hurt so much, when the plummet to that bitterness was not from an even keel, but from the lofty heights of something he thought could be and probably was love. He tried to look across at her eyes, but his own gaze fell down to the line of medal ribbons on her jacket.

"Are you going to be the first man I've ever spoken to in this uniform who isn't going to attempt a joke about the impressive rack?" Beckmann smirked as she watched the direction of his gaze.

Hawkins looked up at her. Her smile faded. The following silence replaced it with a clear expression of anxiety.

"I… I'm so glad you are well, ma'am. I… I'm sorry for what I said."

"Don't be," Beckmann shook her head, "you were right. I need to change who I am. I can't just look to the past and what I've been made to do as an excuse not to do better in the future. Thank you for having the courage to tell me. I know that whole incident is something we'll have to talk about more at some point. I'm not for a second pretending that it's in the past and dealt with."

Hawkins tried to meet her gaze but failed.

"How are you?" he managed. "You looked… your injuries looked serious."

"They were," Beckmann shrugged with a wince, "they're getting there. I'm still limping and only permitted to carry out light exercise. It'll all heal in time. And I have you to thank for that, from what I heard."

"No," Hawkins shook his head, "I was already next to you. I just carried you to a medic. Fusilier Mieke stabilized your wounds and then Fusilier Southee carried you to an extraction point. Besides, from what I recall, it wasn't us saving you. It was quite the opposite with that TAG."

"But the flowers were from you?"

Hawkins found he had taken a defensive step back before he even realized he was moving.

"Yes. When I heard you were alive but not doing so well. You must get flowers from guys all the time."

"*Ja,* I do. But yours are the only ones I've ever kept."

Their conversation was awkwardly interrupted as a trio of Fusilier officers walked past the two of them, the three men turning to stare at Beckmann before bringing their arms up in salutes. Regardless of whether it was her staggering beauty or the rows of medals for valor that made them stare, Beckmann returned the salute with a sigh of mild irritation.

"Look," she smiled mischievously as soon as they were out of earshot, "at least tell me I looked cool taking down that TAG. I don't remember anything! In my mind, after I was wounded, you were carrying me in front of you, the wind was blowing my hair, I was at that exact perfect mid-point between angelic beauty and sexiness, the sun was setting… Was that how it went down?"

Hawkins saw her impish grin and knew it was an attempt to lighten the mood, but it only brought back the memories of screaming in anguish as he saw her lifeless body, plastered in mud and blood, her blue eyes staring unfocused at the rainclouds above…

"Hey!" Beckmann shot forward and took one of his hands in both of hers. "Hey! It's alright! It's done now! Don't look like that, everything is okay!"

"I'm sorry, ma'am," Hawkins cleared his throat, "it's just a bit too soon for me to joke about? I really couldn't see you… like that. I couldn't cope with that."

Hawkins met her gaze evenly this time, at a loss for words at how the abundance of warmth and compassion in her eyes jarred with the rows of medals on her jacket for killing countless people. Again, Beckmann's response was cut off by a pair of lieutenants walking back to the accommodation block, forcing her to let go of his hand and jump back away from him before returning their salutes.

"Look, I've appeared here out of nowhere, so I should get going," Beckmann said, "but I'm going to do something that people in our position used to do a long time ago, as a normal thing and a matter of course before technology changed it all. I'm going to look you in the eye, and pluck up my courage to ask you out on a date with me."

"Yes." Hawkins was nodding enthusiastically before he even stopped to consider the immense complications in what she was suggesting. "Yes, I'd love to."

"Alright," Beckmann swallowed, "that was scarier than I thought. I guess that's why everybody just meets people online these days, huh? Give me a couple of days to fix this limp, and I'll pick you up here at seven on Tuesday, okay?"

Failing to suppress what he could only assume was a fairly idiotic grin, Hawkins nodded mutely.

"Cool," Beckmann smiled as she stepped back away from him.

Hawkins instinctively saluted.

"Kyle, enough with the fucking saluting! I've asked you out because I want something real between us. Not because I want a junior officer to carry my bags."

"Yes," Hawkins shrugged, "yes, got it. Tomorrow… ah, Tuesday. Seven o'clock."

Beckmann flashed him one last smile before walking off toward the rows of parked cars outside the accommodation block.

***

Five days off. Five days away from bombs and bullets, dangerous fauna, the incessant buzz of damned insects, and a complete lack of modern amenities. It had taken Shankar less than a minute to decide to spend a significant amount of money on five days in an expensive hotel in the center of Klugestein rather than accepting a bland, characterless room in the Officers' Mess of Kokoda Barracks on the eastern outskirts of the city. After dumping her bag on the sprawling, thick bed dominating just one of the four rooms of her hotel suite, Shankar wasted no time in lounging in the equally extravagant bath for the better part of an hour before slipping into the plush, satin black complementary bathrobe and setting about unpacking. Despite the impressive, panoramic display of the sprawling city at dusk offered by the transparent feature wall running behind her bed, Shankar preferred to opt for the more traditional solid setting and cycled through a number of options for wall coverings and carpet colors until settling on a soothing white for both.

Only a couple of minutes into unpacking, the guilt began to gnaw away. Her handful of surviving Fusiliers could not afford the bill for luxurious hotels, so would it be more appropriate for her to spend her few days off at the barracks, a stone throw away from the Junior Ranks accommodation to show some solidarity? Was it even less appropriate, given the surprisingly high loss of life her platoon had suffered in the previous couple of weeks? Shankar pushed the thoughts to the back of her mind. She deserved the time to herself. It was just a few days before the platoon would be dumped unceremoniously back at Alpha Four-Four to continue their part in this small, private war that both sides desperately struggled to keep away from the prying eyes of the Human Sphere's media.

Halfway through unpacking, Shankar decided that her first evening would be well spent with a glass of wine, a good novel, and an early night. She doubted very much whether the Fusiliers of her platoon would be showing the same restraint, given their proximity to the nightlife of Klugestein. Sinking down on the edge of the bed, it was only then that she remembered that her first priority should have been contacting her loved ones and family. She thought of David and his work near Vedi on the continent of Septentria; half a planet away from her but close enough for him to visit her in the five days she had. Sadly, the same could not be said for her parents on Neoterra.

As if operating on the very same wavelength, Shankar knew it could only be her fiancé when the room's communication suite buzzed quietly into life, highlighting an incoming call on the small comlog strapped to her wrist. A smile lighting up her face, she darted off to the suite's living room and quickly pointed the projector at one of the plush, blue armchairs before sitting opposite it on another. With the touch of a virtual button, the familiar shape of David was rapidly painted in green lines on the chair opposite her until his outline was formed and then just as rapidly filled in with color. With only a slight translucence to his form, it was as if he was sitting in the very same room, just as she knew she would be for him in his apartment outside Vedi. Shankar's smile grew even more.

"David! I…"

"What *has* been going on?" David demanded.

"I've got a hotel room in Klugestein," she explained. "I've got five days here. Can you come and visit? I…"

"Yes, perhaps if you'd given me some notice!" Her fiancé shook his head. "But you know how the rota works here! Why are you only telling me this now? You know the hospital can't spare me! But that aside, what on Earth is going on over there?! It's all over the news! I told you something like this would happen!"

Shankar clenched her jaw. She knew, deep down, that the highly accusatory opening statement from her fiancé came from a place of love and concern, but after several weeks in a jungle where the plant-life tried to kill her on a good day and the bombs and bullets of the Yujingyu StateEmpire tried to kill her on a bad day, she found her frayed temper pushed already.

"Nice to see you, too," Shankar raised her brow.

David shook his head. Shankar noticed now more than ever the receding hairline that Cochrane had kindly pointed out to her.

"I'm asking because I'm worried, Priya. We're all worried. Your parents call me twice a day for news. News I don't have. We go days without hearing from you."

"It's busy over here," Shankar sank back into her chair, absent-mindedly reveling in the comfort of the seat after weeks in the jungle, even though the conversation was not going the way she wanted or expected. "There's a lot going on. Come on, you know that! You work twelve hour shifts for six days a week, with shift handover and travel time added on that means I only see you for one day in seven when I'm home! But I support you because I know what you are doing is important!"

Less than a minute. That was how long they managed to hold a conversation before they were arguing. From the few times she had opened up to other junior officers in long-term relationships, this seemed to be the norm for all deployed and away from home, but that did not stop that thought at the back of her mind, worming away no matter how hard she tried to shut it out.

"And we're all supporting you," David countered, the image of him flickering for a moment as if to remind her that it was merely a facsimile, a light-based imitation of the real man thousands of miles away, "no matter how crazy this all is! You said you were injured in a training accident. The Glottenberg Incursion is all over the news, every hour! And, coincidentally, the number of PanOceanian *training accidents* in your part of Paradiso has increased by five hundred percent! Do you think anybody back here is buying this bullshit? You're not popping a few shots off in a little border misunderstanding, you're at war!"

Shankar raised a hand to her head, the seemingly perpetual headache that had finally surrendered upon her arriving in Klugestein now suddenly thundering back forcefully. She let out a long sigh.

"David, did you really call to talk about politics?"

The conversation fell silent. David looked down at his feet and took in a few deep breaths.

"I… look. I'm sorry. I'd like to say that I know it's hard for you, but to be truthful, I don't know anything. None of us do. We have no idea what's going on. We just… go days without hearing from you and then see all over the news that there are political tensions so severe that O-12 are involved, right in the area we know you are. I mean, how many *training accidents* has your platoon suffered? Ten percent?"

"David," Shankar shook her head, disappointed that even her direct plea to divert conversation back away from sensitive subjects was immediately and completely ignored, "I don't go asking for details about your patients. Please repay the courtesy and don't go asking me things you know I can't tell you."

"Priya, I'm freaking out here! We all are! We care for you! What is it then, twenty percent? Thirty?"

For the life of her, in the seconds that followed her reply, Shankar could not comprehend why she said what she said. She was speaking about highly sensitive information over an insecure, easily hacked, civilian communication channel. That was compounded with the fact that the number she quoted, whilst entirely truthful, could do absolutely no good when revealed to her fiancé and, ultimately, the rest of her family.

"Over seventy."

David's jaw dropped. His eyes opened wide. He stared at her silently in abject horror for long seconds before finally repeating the word, the connection between her and the holographic image of her fiancé seeming more real and tangible from the severity of his emotions.

"Seventy?! Seventy percent casualties?!"

"In *my* platoon!" Shankar clarified. "That number is not remotely representative of this entire incident! We were just at the very forefront of it all at exactly the wrong time. Casualties in the rest of the battalion have been far, far lighter."

"Oh, well that's fine, then!" David seethed. "As long as everybody else is alright, we don't need to worry back here at home! Look, I get that people have disagreements, I honestly do. And I'm mature enough, I'd like to think, to realize that it is nearly always a matter of perspective and there are two sides to every disagreement. But this comes back to the same argument we've been having for years now!"

Shankar threw her hands up to both sides and swore.

"This! Again!"

"Yes, this! The simple fact of the matter is that there are no shades of gray in between! It isn't a matter of perspective! It's simple; you were wrong and *everybody* else was right! Joining the infantry was a stupid, stupid idea!"

Shankar sprang to her feet, running her fingers through her wet hair as she paced across the hotel floor in frustration, tightening the belt around her bathrobe.

"Fusiliers!" she corrected. "I'm a platoon commander in the Fusiliers! At least get it right! And I should, no *am* allowed, to do what the hell I want with my life!"

The image of David faded for a moment as the communication channel reception wavered whilst he continued on regardless.

"You keep doing this! You make me sound like some sort of controlling, manipulative bastard with a monstrous... medieval mindset! *Nobody* is telling you not to have a career! Nobody is saying that! All *we* – your parents and I – are saying is that the damned *infantry* is not the job for a business studies graduate! You could do anything! Jeez, I'd be happier if you were a bloody lap dancer – at least I'd know you're safe!"

"Well, that's really mature..." Shankar began, sinking back down to the sofa before she was quickly cut off again.

"Look, at least meet me halfway! If you are absolutely dead set on a career in the military, do something – *anything* – safer! Transfer to logistics or... planning or something else!"

"Logistics!" Shankar exclaimed. "I don't want to be a bloody..."

"Seventy percent!" David cut her off again, "Seventy! Your parents know how stubborn you are, and they're too scared to broach this subject with you! So it's down to me to..."

Shankar grabbed the communication terminal remote and severed the connection. The image faded to nothing in front of her. Sighing, Shankar slumped forward and rested her chin on her hands. The same argument over and over... A stuffy, warm breeze wafted through the open door leading to the hotel room's balcony, overlooking the sea of blazing lights, news screens, and holographic adverts spreading out for miles in every direction. The communication terminal bleeped again to announce an incoming call. Shankar ignored it. She stood again, walking over to the hotel room's small kitchenette to investigate the mini bar.

Retrieving a bottle of champagne, she popped the cork, decided not to bother with a glass, and walked out to the small balcony. The contrast of the warm night air next to the cool, controlled environment of the hotel room hit her like a wave of water as she walked out into the night, taking a long swig from the champagne bottle. She spent several long minutes looking across the spectacular city and the gentle curves of the architecture that formed the glamorous skyline. Lines of twinkling headlights from cars threaded below her through the darkness, following the myriad of curving streets leading through the digital neon jungle of the city. In seconds, she was hit by smart advertising, as her geist's voice, so close to that of a human but with slight robotic undertones, chimed in her ear.

Priya, based on your biometric data, I'm patching through some messages that I think you would be interested in.

Messages in colorful, eye-grabbing fonts scrolled across the corner of her lens.

Too hot in that bathrobe? Komfies guarantees better body heating regulation at half the price! Your body measurements are now uploaded! Your order is one click away...

Monty and Co. knows you have an eye for detail, and as a discerning champagne connoisseur, why not upgrade your taste bud sensation to our summer vintage range...

Behind her, the communication terminal buzzed again. She glanced across and saw that this time it was her parents, no doubt alerted to her difficult attitude by her fiancé. Talking to David was bad enough; facing her parents, particularly with the frustrations of several minutes of delays between each verbal exchange that came with interplanetary communication, was simply not an option. Again, she ignored it and took another long swig from the green, glass bottle.

Leaning over the balcony rail, the breeze tugging at her thin, black bathrobe, she stared down at the busy streets below as cars drifted along the curved grid of roads threading between high-rise residential buildings, offices, warehouses, and commercial blocks. Somehow, isolated on the tiny balcony two dozen floors above ground level, her comlog buzzed as she received an invitation to exchange text messages from a complete stranger.

Priya, you have a conversation request from...
Shankar sighed.
"No."
Conversation request denied.

At least it was a compliment of sorts, if a slightly intrusive one.

After another drain of the bottle, she looked across at it and was surprised to see that in only a couple of minutes it was half empty. Less surprising was the dense, muggy feeling in her head as the alcohol quickly went to work on her well out of practice body. Pushing the frustrations of her argument aside, she tried to recall the last time she had been drunk. She smiled at the memory of nights out as a student in college, in better, more carefree days with a now long dissolved network of friends.

"Screw it," Shankar declared to herself, walking back inside after deciding to get dressed up and find a bar.

***

Checking the time again, Hawkins winced uneasily as he turned his back on the low evening sun. He choice of a smart, short-sleeved black shirt to match his tan-colored, loose fitting trousers seemed all of a sudden too much for a casual first date. This, coupled with the red rose he carried in one hand and the fact that he knew his hair betrayed far too much time and effort in its styling, left him feeling ridiculous. The car park at the back of the barracks accommodation block was half full, with off-duty personnel having headed home or out into the neon metropolis of Klugestein for the evening. Still, a seemingly steady precession of military personnel walked past him to their cars, surpassing smirks as they saw the well-dressed young man with the rose glancing awkwardly at the empty road leading up to the car park. Hawkins checked the time again. She was a full four minutes late. He had, in accordance with the norm for arrangements based on military timings, arrived five minutes early, to the second. Four minutes late actually meant nine minutes late. She was not coming.

Hawkins heard Beckmann even before he saw her. The growl of a high-powered engine accompanied by the thudding of a percussive beat from a car audio system brought his eyes to the horizon a few seconds before a sleek, silver sports car rounded the crest of the hill leading down to the barracks' main entrance. Hawkins watched as the silver convertible rounded the last corner of the road and came to a stop next to him, the eyes of everybody within a few dozen meters tracking its progress. Switching off the engine to silence the thunderous rock music blaring out of the open-topped sports car, Beckmann stepped out.

Dressed in form-hugging, low slung jeans of imitation black leather that tapered out over the top of a pair of black boots with a matching black vest top, her subtle but dark make up complimented her perfect face. Silver charms tangled from a thick, black band on her wrist, the majority of them being musical symbols or guitars, although he noticed a Christian cross in amidst them. She removed her sunglasses and smiled to Hawkins as she walked over, the faintest hint of a limp still apparent.

"I'm sorry I'm late!" she greeted. "I... well, I love making an entrance."

"Yes, I can see!" Hawkins breathed, staring down at her and then across at the car.

He figured that commenting on the car rather than her figure would be more gentlemanly.

"I'm not really a car guy, but is that a Henschel 1200? You do look beautiful, I probably should have led with that..."

"It's a GT70," Beckmann replied, sitting on the long, curvaceous hood of the vehicle and crossing one ankle over the other, "which I'm told is like a 1200 with half the weight and twice the power. Likewise, I'm not a car person. I just picked what I liked the look of. This thing makes me look pretty damn cool, but I don't know the first thing about it."

Hawkins looked back up at her, wide-eyed, and then back down at the GT70. The aggressive wheel arches seemingly melted into the thin body of the vehicle, sweeping up and over the long windscreen and then falling down the back in a graceful curve before drifting up in the car's lip spoiler. Cooling pipes jutted out of the engine compartment, deliberately thick and almost crude in stark contrast to the delicacy of the body, as was the current fashion with Henschel designs. As if mocking him and his meager rate of pay, a message flashed on his comlog offering to download the latest Henschel catalogue whilst directing him to his closest dealership to book a test drive.

Hawkins – like the overwhelming majority of the population of Pan-Oceania – did not even own a car. If he needed to move from A to B, he simply called for an automated vehicle to pick him up at his location. The option then lay with the individual as to whether to travel as a passenger under the safe control of ALEPH, or whether to manually drive the vehicle whilst remaining under the plethora of safety protocols restricting the vehicle's handling. Owning a vehicle was an extravagance – owning a top end sports car was pure decadence.

"These things sell for a quarter of a million! I... that's more than a major earns, right?"

"Right," Beckmann shrugged, "but I... I took a year or so out of the military. I did other things that paid well."

"Oh, was this from your music?" Hawkins asked enthusiastically. "I didn't realize that Strategic Security allowed people to take time off."

"They don't, and no, not music. I was a private contractor. I take it that flower is for me?"

Hawkins stopped. Private contractor. That was a gentle euphemism, given her training and skill set. He looked down at the car again. It was the spoils of her having a brief, unsanctioned career as a hitman. Alarm bells rang again, as they had several times before in their interactions. He knew the right thing to do, the moral thing, would be to stop there and then and demand to know more about her shadowy past. But they were past that now. He knew what she was and had accepted it. It was not his place to cast the first stone, or indeed any. Part of him even wondered if God had put him in her path, to try to help her before it was all too late. Another part of him wanted to jump to the other extreme and make light of it; he had to stop himself joking – *so, you ever killed anybody famous I might have heard of?* Instead, he took a silent pace forward and offered her the flower he was carrying. She accepted it with a warm smile.

"That's very old fashioned of you," Beckmann said in a hushed tone, "I really appreciate that. Thank you."

She leaned over to carefully place the rose on the dashboard of her car, her vest riding up just enough to show that she still had bandaging around her wounded midriff. She looked over at Hawkins again.

"D'you wanna drive?"

"Huh?"

"You can drive."

"Me?" Hawkins took a step back. "I… I've never driven anything this powerful. Or expensive. I'm more than happy to sit in the passenger seat."

"I've had it capped at three hundred break," Beckmann said. "It's not that much of a handful with the limiters on."

"Honestly, I'm fine with you driving," Hawkins offered, realizing he would at best make himself look stupid and at worst cause damage to the vehicle that he could not afford to have repaired.

Beckmann took in a breath that almost made it appear as if she was hesitant to return to the driver's seat, and slid her thin-framed sunglasses back on.

"Right… right."

Hawkins took a seat next to her as she gunned the engine into life.

"Where we going?" he asked.

"I've got a place in mind," Beckmann said. "I've never been, but Maya Places says it has everything we need."

"Is it in Klugestein?" Hawkins asked. "I've never visited."

"You've never visited Klugestein?! Well, that changes things. You've got to experience driving across Alvonia Bridge in a convertible at the very least! My plan can wait! Come on, you haven't done Klugestein unless you've driven over Alvonia Bridge at sunset with the top down, singing power ballads at the top of your voice!"

Hawkins smiled at the thought, finding her enthusiasm infectious even as he noticed with interest just how careful she was in maneuvering the car around the simplest of three point turns, and just how apprehensive she appeared to be in accelerating away toward the base's exit. As the car sped along the coastal road outside the base, Hawkins stared off south at the idyllic, turquoise waves and failed to push the mental images of battle from only days before to one side.

***

The virtual cue ball shot across the simulation of the green felt surface, slamming into the triangle of colored balls with force and scattering them across the table. Two of the holographic balls disappeared into corner pockets in the ensuing chaos; one each of stripes and solid colors. Beckmann stood up from her position at the top of the table, a cigarette dangling from her lips as she surveyed the state of the table.

"Stripes," she nominated, moving around to the side of the table to lean over and line up for another shot.

Leaning on his cue, Hawkins looked around the bar. He was not entirely sure what Beckmann had in mind when she asked him out, but it was not this. It all seemed so... normal. The bar she drove him to a few miles outside the city was part of a popular chain; rather than a dingy dive of a place, the building was clean, homely, and even had a few families sat for evening meals in and around the largely adult clientele. A single MULTI gaming table was hidden away in a corner away from the main seating areas, on a raised platform and next to an imitation historic jukebox, complete with blue neon lighting around its curved wooden top. Beckmann had already selected an extensive playlist of vintage soft rock songs to accompany their game and now, tied after one victory each, she slammed a second striped ball into a top corner pocket to pull ahead in the scoring.

Hawkins took a mouthful of his glass of soda and placed it down on the edge of the table next to Beckmann's tall glass of strawberry milkshake – again, a drink he was surprised to see her order. The surrounding booths were half full with small groups of mainly young adults from a nearby college, the walls of each booth currently set to project an image of wood paneling, fitting the bar's dim lighting and retro, old Earth feel. Even with the low lights, Hawkins could see every pair of eyes watching Beckmann as she moved around the table to gently pot a third ball in a side pocket. Part of him knew that he should feel proud – smug, even – for the masses of attention that followed round the woman who was his date. Yet somehow he felt hollow and uneasy. Perhaps even insecure. As if on cue, he received an invitation to chat on Maya messenger from a young woman in one of the booths. He quickly tapped his comlog to dismiss it and changed his filters to stop any further requests from disturbing him.

"Tell me about your family!" Beckmann flashed a friendly smile. "You've listened to me talk nonsense about music all night. What do your brother and sister do?"

The hollow feeling intensified suddenly.

"How did you know I have a brother and sister?"

Beckmann stood up from the table and fixed him with a sultry stare, pacing toward him until she was just inside his personal space.

"Could be because I invited you out here solely to get close enough to hack your comlog," she narrowed her eyes, "or it could be that I watched a movie with you in your room once, and you had a picture of your family very clearly on display."

Hawkins let out a somewhat embraced sigh of relief as the unease dissipated.

"Yeah. Sorry, I… well, my brother Nathan works part time in retail management, clothing mainly. His wife manages a small project management business, so Nathan does most of the day to day parenting for their children. My sister Sarah recently got engaged to a guy she met in college. They seem really happy. She works in sports therapy. How about you? We've actually spoken about me quite a bit tonight. I feel rather rude that I've been enjoying your company for nearly two hours now, and I haven't learned anything else about you."

"You've learned that I'm good at pool," Beckmann bent over and smashed her cue into the holographic white ball, sending it powering across the table to glance off a striped ball before plummeting into a pocket to grant Hawkins two shots.

"*Scheisse,*" she grimaced and then laughed, "that's really embarrassing."

Hawkins smiled and lined up for his own shot.

"From what I've seen, you're not just good at pool. You're good at… well, everything."

He carefully tapped the white ball and sent a ball rolling smoothly into a corner pocket before chalking his cue – unnecessary, but all part of the retro illusion of the holographic game – and assessing his next shot.

"That's not true at all," Beckmann shrugged, "there's a ton of things I'm terrible at. I just hide them well. I only show people what I want them to see."

"What are you terrible at?" Hawkins ventured, potting another ball.

"Plenty of things!" Beckmann laughed. "Dancing. I'm a terrible dancer. Driving sports cars. You've seen that for yourself!"

"But you are definitely good at pool," Hawkins beamed, attempting another awkwardly angled shot and failing. "When you chose this, I was planning on throwing the game in some sort of chivalrous display, but I'm getting my arse kicked here."

"Yeah, but… I play a lot of pool. I really like it. It plays to my greatest strengths."

Hawkins nodded in agreement as he watched her pull into the lead again.

"Yes, I see what you mean. The whole aiming for the long shots, the physics of projectiles… it kind of is like marksmanship and long range shooting, I suppose."

Beckmann looked up at him and laughed.

"No! What I meant was that I have a really incredible ass and I get to legitimately bend over and show it off! Jeez, Kyle, you need to stop think-ing about military shit and start concentrating on what normal people think about!"

Hawkins shared a laugh with her before taking his turn at the table again and resuming the lead.

"You haven't spoken about your family," he risked.

Beckmann sat on the edge of the table and took a long drag from her cigarette before blowing out a pleasant smelling cloud of pink smoke.

"*Ja*. I don't like to talk about them."

Hawkins lined up for another shot.

"Okay," he shrugged nonchalantly as another ball drifted into a pock-et.

The tall woman shook her head and narrowed her eyes in frustration, tapping her comlog to no doubt dismiss an endless stream of offers to chat on Maya Messenger.

"Alright," she said after a pause, "I'm... the younger of two sisters. My father is a general in military intelligence. My mother is an opera singer. My sister is a concert pianist. I'm... from a wealthy background. There's been serious money in my mother's family for generations. My father has a title. Count Ludwig von Beckmann, if you believe somebody could have a name like that in this day and age. That's an overview of my family in twenty sec-onds or less."

Hawkins looked up.

"Lisette *von* Beckmann?"

"I don't use the 'von' part. Makes me sound like the bad guy from an old war movie."

"I see where you get the musical aptitude from, though," Hawkins offered.

His last ball sunk, he lined up on the black to win the game. Taking his time, concentrating on perfecting the angle, he took his shot. The black ball sailed into the pocket, immediately followed by the white.

"Damn," he grimaced as he stood, "buggered that up. You win the decider."

The tall woman narrowed her eyes suspiciously and shook her head, locks of dark hair falling over one blue eye.

"You threw the game on purpose. You didn't have to do that. But it was very gentlemanly of you. It was a nice gesture."

Hawkins finished his soda.

"Who says I threw the game?" He grinned. "I'm out of practice."

"And a terrible liar. It's sweet."

Hawkins caught himself staring at her, realizing that the duration of the pause in their conversation was now unnatural. He opened his mouth to ask her more about her family but remembered her reluctance to talk about it and thought better. She rescued him from the silence by speaking again.

"You want to get out of here? I've got a place on the beach I'm renting for a few days. It's pretty awesome. We'll go watch a movie or I'll teach you to play the guitar. Just a couple of hours before we call it a night. I'm not trying to seduce you or trick you into anything. I… well, it's not me. I'm not like that."

Hawkins placed his glass down and looked across the table at her. He believed her, even before she carried on.

"I know… how I come across. You watch any shitty teen movie on Maya, and there's always some ridiculously hot but bitchy head cheerleader type. She's the villain, but the one the guys watching are really going to be staring at for the whole movie. That's me, I know. The hot, bitchy villain. But at school and in training? My friends called me Razor…"

Hawkins frowned, instantly uncomfortable with where the story was going.

"You don't need to look like that, this isn't some horrific story about bladed weapons and me cutting people up!" Beckmann laughed. "About ten or fifteen years ago, there was a resurgence in this… youth sub-culture group. Straight edge. Straight edge was about being strong in faith and morality. No alcohol, no drugs, no sex before marriage. Pure living, working hard, worshipping whatever God you believe in."

Beckmann looked down and fiddled uncomfortably with her charm bracelet for a moment before continuing.

"Whilst all my friends were using the skills we learned in espionage training – lying, basically – to screw whoever they wanted and con their way into amazing nights out, I was staying in my dorm and working on my masters in psychology. They all drank hard and partied hard. I sang in the local church choir on Sundays. They called me Razor because straight edge wasn't enough for me – they said I was *so* boring, I was razor edged. I wish I was the hot, bitchy head cheerleader. But that's not true."

Hawkins found himself staring yet again. He had never been comfortable with heartfelt words, always stumbling over stupid things to say when his very best intentions were clumsily verbalized. Regardless, he decided that honesty, as always, was the best policy.

"I really appreciate you being so open with me," he began hesitantly. "And I can honestly say that tonight, this… you're the best company I ever remember sharing, and I'd be honored if you taught me how to shred a guitar."

Beckmann let out a breath and looked down at her feet. She looked up again, smiling broadly, and then took his hand in hers and walked out of the bar. The warm night air was still outside the bar. A two lane road ran to their right, punctuated only by a handful of vehicles running toward the curved, almost artistic spires of the skyscrapers of Klugestein ahead. To the left was the inky blackness of the sea, the gentle rush of the waves across the sand seeming to meld into the hum of traffic from the road and the thrumming of insects hidden in the dense sea of bushes on the other side of the highway. Hawkins looked ahead to where Beckmann's car was parked, reveling in the moment of holding her hand, the jungles of Glottenberg and the guns at Alpha Four-Four finally seeming to be light-years away from the present moment, if just for a few short hours.

"I feel kind of stupid saying some of these things to you," Beckmann admitted as they walked toward the line of parked cars, "but it's also like a weight being lifted. There's one thing I told you once that isn't true. It's been hanging over me. I've never liked lying. I told you once that I wasn't some lost cause. That I have a life outside the Division. That's not true. I did something a long time ago, and I'm still suffering for it now. I'm always being watched. Always. They think I'm unstable. Dangerous."

Hawkins looked across at her.

"It can't be easy. Living with what they've made out of you."

"I don't know anything else. But I didn't want that lie hanging over us. I made it out like I have freedom. Like being a Hexa killer is cool and exciting, like in Maya movies. When I was given the job of coming to Alpha Four-Four, you know what I was doing? The movies would tell you that I was in the middle of a spectacular shoot out or cruising sexily through a casino. The reality was that I was sat on my kitchen floor, holding my pet kitten, and crying my fucking eyes out. I don't even remember what I was upset about. I just remember getting the call and the mission. *Scheisse*, I cry a lot when I stop and think about it. Even the sentimental bits in kids' movies set me off!"

Hawkins stopped and turned to face her. In the space of a few minutes, the laughter and the flirting of the past two hours had suddenly been replaced with something seemingly more real. A real truth that felt like a cry for help. Beckmann half turned away from him, her face screwed up as if in embarrassment at what she had just admitted. Again, he searched for the right words.

A scream of fright dragged his attention ahead. Two men of about his age were stood by Beckmann's car where the driver's door was open. Both wore rugged, grimy clothes in dark colors; one man had a sleeve tattoo covering one arm whilst the other had a shaved head and closely cropped, red beard. A third man, well-dressed in a suit, backed away from them with blood streaming from his face. Clinging desperately to the bleeding man's leg was a screaming girl in a blue dress. A warning message flashed on his lens as his geist detected an injury in the stranger a few paces ahead, asking if he wished to alert emergency medical services.

It did not take much to work out what had happened – the third man, walking to his car with his daughter, had caught the other two men attempting to steal Beckmann's GT70 and tried to challenge them. His broken nose was all the evidence Hawkins needed of the thieves' willingness to do violence. He paced out and stood in front of the father and daughter protectively, holding up one palm to the two thieves.

"Back off!" Hawkins warned. "Get away from the child, right now."

"You want a fucking slap in the face, too, pretty boy?" The shaven-headed man spat, stepping forward.

Hawkins glanced over his shoulder and saw the bleeding man retreating away, clutching his crying daughter's hand. He looked forward at the threat.

"Stay away from the child," he warned again, sizing up both men to assess them, rapidly thinking through the quickest and least damaging ways of incapacitating them if it came to it.

Beckmann strode past Hawkins and out to the red-bearded aggressor, her eyes fixed in concentration, devoid of even a hint of the emotion he had seen in them only seconds before. The man looked down at her and smiled broadly.

"You serious, hun? Get back on the fucking catwalk, you dumb c..."

Beckmann lashed out with a slow, almost clumsy right hook that Hawkins recognized as a deliberate attempt to telegraph a move. Her opponent easily and predictably blocked the attack. Moving her hand around in a small circle to lock his wrist, Beckmann pulled the man's arm aside and smashed her free palm up into his elbow. Broken bone was driven bloodily up through the split skin of his forearm before she smashed a fist into his nose, snapping it audibly in a shower of blood as his head was thrown back.

With lightning speed, she followed up with a knee to his gut, bending him over double before slamming a fist into his bloodied face to knock him back upright. As the shaven-headed man staggered back, Beckmann span around and swung out an expertly timed hook kick, the heel of her boot ripping the man's cheek open before he fell to the ground, bleeding and sobbing. Hawkins lens flashed up with warnings of violent unrest in his proximity and asked him to confirm this so that the police would be notified. A fraction of a second later, they were automatically cancelled, declaring that the incident was a false alarm based on erroneous data.

The second aggressor, the taller man with the sleeve tattoo, flung a jab at Beckmann's face. She deftly swung to one side to avoid the blow and countered immediately with a punch to the man's throat. Choking, the tattooed man staggered back. Beckmann smashed a side kick into his gut to double him over before grabbing the back of his head and slamming his face into the windscreen of her car, cracking the glass.

"Lisette!" Hawkins finally snapped out of his trance, darting forward.

Beckmann smashed the man's head into the car windscreen a second time, the cracks instantly spreading out to form a spider web of damage across the glass. For a third time she flung his face into the glass. Blood spattered across the battered windscreen. Hawkins' eyes opened in alarm as he saw a knife in Beckmann's hand. He grabbed her by the wrist to stop her from stabbing the bleeding man crumpled over the hood of the car and slipped his other arm beneath her arm pit and across her neck to restrain her.

Only years of martial arts training allowed him to feel the slight shift in her weight as Beckmann first attempted to throw him over her shoulder, reverse head butt him in the face, and drive a heel down into his foot. Hawkins smoothly, but with difficulty, countered all of her attempts to attack him.

"Go!" He shouted at the two broken, bleeding car thieves. "Get out of here!"

Hawkins pressed a thumb into a pressure point on Beckmann's wrist, but watched astounded as she completely ignored the pain that he knew was surging along her entire arm and still held firmly onto the knife. Looking over his shoulder, he saw the two thieves staggering and limping off toward the main road. He pushed Beckmann away from him and raised his fists to defend himself.

The Hexa assassin turned and stared at him with narrowed eyes, her teeth gritted and her feet spread in a fighting stance.

"What the hell are you doing?" Hawkins demanded.

"Defending the girl and her father," Beckmann spat venomously, her husky voice low and dangerous, "and you."

"You pulled a knife on two men who were already beaten and helpless!"

"I *took* the knife from some dumbshit criminal who pulled it on me."

The voice of conscience, that nagging in the back of his mind that persisted through all of times where he convinced himself that forgiveness was divine, finally burst through.

"Oh, bullshit!" Hawkins shouted. "Again with the lies! Look around you, we're surrounded with surveillance devices! You can't keep lying! Or let me guess, have *your people* already corrupted and changed the surveillance data? I saw the police warning was cancelled quickly! Was that *your people,* too?"

The anger faded from the Hexa operative's blue eyes, replaced by something between hurt and disappointment as she took in a few deep breaths. She took a pace forward and then half fell to one knee, pain wracking her features as one hand shot up to her wounded side.

"I didn't come out armed, Kyle. Why would I? Even if I did, I wouldn't bring a cheap, shitty little blade like this, I…"

"I don't want to hear it!" Hawkins snapped. "I'm sick of hearing it! Your answer to everything is to just… kill everybody! Do you not think there is more to life than that? Do you not think you could have just talked those two men down, or restrained them without breaking them into bloody pieces?!"

"No!" Beckmann snapped, throwing the knife down into the gravel between their feet. "No! Those two pieces of shit chose to break the law! This is on them! I don't need to show them Christian compassion! I *need* to do my job and defend innocent civilians who were in danger! And I did just that! What would you have me do? Invite them for a fucking beer and then preach scripture to them to show them the error of their ways? No! I put them down! And you should have done the same! You should have had my back, not tried to fight me!"

Hawkins watched as Beckmann staggered over to her car and planted a hand against the open door for support, her breathing labored and her other hand still pressed against her bandaged midriff. He shook his head, wondering if that, too, was just lies and all for show. Anger at the endless succession of dishonesty coursed up through him as he met her glare evenly.

"My job here wasn't to have your back," Hawkins folded his arms, "my job was to stop you from murdering two men in cold blood. Like I should have done if I was quick enough with that Tiger Soldier. All the rumors about you and your lot are true, aren't they? Just… lies and murder. Have you spoken a single true word tonight? Because the woman I've spent the evening with is not the same as the killer I'm looking at right now. And I think I've finally worked out which one is the lie and which one is the real you."

Beckmann held an arm across her abdomen, her breathing slowing, her dark stare still driving into his.

"I was wrong about you. You really are a sanctimonious prick, aren't you?" she whispered. "I was an idiot to think you could be any different from those bastards who brainwashed you."

Beckmann reached into her car and retrieved the red rose from the dashboard. Hawkins watched, expecting her to tear it up or throw it away, but instead she limped across to him and carefully offered it to him. He took it.

"This would never work out between us," she said quietly, "it never could."

Emergency service sirens wailed from the far end of the highway as police vehicles sped toward the bar's car park, and Hawkins watched Beckmann slump into her vehicle and speed away in the opposite direction.

Chapter Fifteen

Yawning as he wandered across the dusty scrub ground between the accommodation blocks and the Platoon HQ, Cochrane looked up at the sun-soaked, clear blue skies above Alpha Four-Four and grinned. Yes, one could argue that being stuck in an isolated outpost with hundreds of miles of jungle, infested with vegetation that could literally kill and eat a man, was sub-optimal – but Cochrane did at least love the weather. His last job before being transferred to the 12th Fusilier Regiment was at Kaldstrom, freezing his balls off in a temporary administrative role, so the nearly endless sunshine was something he still had not grown tired of.

The base itself had changed in a dozen patently obvious ways since Cochrane was flown out of Alpha Four-Four with a broken collar bone and decimated pride just over two weeks before. The perimeter had expanded again, with long, clear fields of fire for HMGs and missile launchers mounted in their armored bunkers, as well as line after line of cutting foam to slow any unarmored assaulting force. The number of rectangular accommodation blocks had doubled, now stacked three high and clumped together with metal stairs leading up to grated walkways running around them. Still dominating the center of the base was the smooth, white-walled MagnaObra research hub. Cochrane paused by the doors of the Platoon HQ, staring at the mysterious building for a few moments as he remembered the night he had rushed through the darkened building in an attempt to stop the faceless intruder, and how close he then stood to a real Cosmolite.

"Hey! The big guy's back!" Angelo Garcia greeted as Cochrane entered the room, his olive-skinned face lit up with something between a friendly smile and a jeer. Two other corporals - neither of whom Cochrane had seen in some time, turned from their conversation to face him.

"G'day, war heroes!" Cochrane beamed as he paced over to greet the three soldiers. "How's it all going? Lucia, good to see you back on your feet!"

Lucia Rossi flashed a half-smile to accompany her nonchalant shrug, the mirthful expression seeming out of place on the normally doleful, short-haired woman. Cochrane remembered the extent of the head injury she sustained in the opening exchange of fire with the Zhanshi platoon at the beginning of the conflict and found himself surprised to see her returned to front line duties so quickly. He looked across at the third corporal.

"Bloody hell! Sahal Kotal! We must be getting desperate if some-body's given you a second stripe!"

"Hello, Jim!" The slim, brown-skinned soldier stepped forward to shake his hand. "Haven't seen you since Utar Shivir! Yes, it all seems to be getting desperate with you as Platoon 2IC and me as a section leader! They brought me in to take over Number One Section. I heard about Jonny Lanne. So sorry, mate, so sorry."

"Likewise, I heard old Angus bought the farm with your lot in the 17th," Cochrane winced sympathetically. "Glad you're okay, but I guess that dickhead had to run out of luck one day."

The younger soldier's face lit up.

"Oh, didn't you hear? Angus is fine! Got resurrected."

"What, *again?!* Well, bugger me with a barbecue fork! Have you met the rest of your guys?"

"Only a couple of them," Kotal replied, "most are still coming back in drips and drabs from leave. I've met my 2IC, Lance Corporal Dubois."

"Oh, Erin's fit for fighting again?" Cochrane nodded in approval. "She's a good kid, mate, great team leader. You'll do well with her. How about you, Lucia, who've you got as your lance jack?"

Corporal Rossi folded her pale, tattooed arms and narrowed one eye.

"The newly promoted Lance Corporal Natalie Southee," she sneered. "Lieutenant Shankar wrote a letter of recommendation to the colonel, and he bought it."

Cochrane's smile faded.

"Well... shit."

"Yeah, my thoughts too," Rossi grumbled, pulling her blue beret out of her trouser pocket and pulling it over her head. "I'm off to see her now and see if I can convince her to spend less time on her hair and more worrying about how to properly position a support team's HMG and launcher in a fire-fight. See you all later."

Cochrane watched the stern corporal disappear into the blistering heat outside, shutting the door behind her. He turned back to the other two NCOs.

"How was your leave, Jim?" Garcia asked, taking a swig from his water bottle. "Any success playing the wounded soldier routine for a root?"

"Of course, mate!" Cochrane grinned. "Six nights on the town, only three girls. I'm getting slow in my old age. One of them won't stop calling me, but that's understandable, her eyes aren't painted on, eh?"

Kotal joined Cochrane in laughing, whilst Garcia issued a thin, insincere seeming smile. Of course, Cochrane's account was a slight exaggeration – a white lie. He had attempted his moves on perhaps a dozen women and succeeded in spending the night with one at a hotel. He had tried to call her several times over the next week but received no replies. But he had a reputation to uphold, and his version of events was far more appropriate to tell his subordinates.

"That researcher girl you liked has gone home," Garcia said. "I mean, they've thinned out about half of the MagnaObra personnel now that the Yujingyu have got a foothold at the mine. Apparently she was going home any-

---

way; something that happened to her on that night you and Sub Officer Hawkins went charging through the research hub. Really messed her up."

Cochrane vaguely remembered Marcia Gamble telling him something about hearing her dead mother singing a song in the darkness... but it was the mention of the mine that caught his attention.

"Wait, wait, wait... We've lost the mine? When did that happen?"

"Number Two Platoon was holding it for about a week after you busted your shoulder. Second Lieutenant Howe took a round to the arm and got sent home, so Dev Bakshi was running the show there. They were ordered to pull back. The Zhanshi just walked in and took it, unopposed. I'm sure there was a reason for that. I bloody hope there was."

Cochrane sat down on the cheap, plastic chair by the HQ's briefing table. What a waste. He thought of that desperate fight, of the Tubarão hot drop into the combat zone, and the frantic advance to push the Yujingyu forces out. He remembered Jonny Lanne and his team being blown apart by the missile, and then the scything fire of the Yujingyu TAG in the counter attack cutting down so many of his men and woman. All for a tactical retreat days later and an unopposed advance by their enemy. All for nothing.

"Come grab a coffee with us, Jim," Kotal slapped a hand on Cochrane's shoulder, "there's not much going on right now. D'you still like really shit coffee?"

Sighing, Cochrane raised himself to his feet and forced a smile.

"Yeah. Yeah, I do."

***

Shankar let out a descending whistle as she paced around the dormant war machine stood rigidly to attention in the hangar. The vibrant, blue armored skin of the towering Cutter TAG stood out in contrast to the dull alloy flooring and walls around it, the ceiling mounted lights reflecting off the machine's smoothly angled armor and the four meter long machine gun on the ground by its feet. Shankar had seen, and even faced, Cutters in simulated combat before but had never seen one up close for real. She turned to Colonel Talau, the small hangar's only other occupant.

"If we'd had this thing back at the mining site, it all would have gone rather differently, sir."

The Cutter TAG stood at roughly a similar height to the Yujingyu Gūijiǎ she faced some two weeks before, but it possessed a suite of environment-adaptive technology that placed it an entire generation ahead of the cumbersome enemy machine. Perhaps of greatest note, the PanOceanian TAG was remotely piloted from miles – sometimes even continents – away from the battlefield.

"Nice of the Navy to help us out with this beast," Colonel Talau remarked, his hands clasped at the small of his back as he wandered slowly around the fighting machine. "These things were actually devised with amphibious operations in mind, but I'm informed that the environment-adaptive surfaces and sound suppression kit are just as home in the jungle. Anyhow, as we had a few minutes before the meeting, I thought seeing this might put a smile on your face."

Shankar continued to walk slowly around the TAG, taking in the flared armor at the ankles and knees, the powerful impression of its bulging chest and shoulders, and the compact control module in the comparatively small head.

"How did we even get this thing here, sir?" she asked the regimental commander. "I thought the O-12 embargo stopped any further reinforcements from entering this area, for either side."

The older soldier turned and flashed a wicked smile.

"It takes some time for O-12 to actually be in a position to realistically enforce an embargo, even after they have decreed that it is mandatory. That's a window of opportunity that we have taken advantage of, just as I'm sure those Yujingyu bastards have. Come on, I'll explain it all. Let's go catch up with the others."

Shankar stole a last look at the awesome war machine as she followed the colonel out of the hangar, pulling on her beret before stepping out into the blistering heat of Alpha Four-Four in mid-morning. An Uro utility vehicle drove along the dusty road weaving in between the TAG hangar and the base's new power generator as Shankar closed the hangar door behind them. Two Fusiliers from Number One Platoon carried tanks of water from the supply depot to the guard positions at the perimeter defenses whilst a Tubarão lifted from the landing strip and nosed forward gently to transition away into the cloudless blue sky. Shankar stared across for a moment at the landing strip. When they first arrived, a lot of her Fusiliers used to play cricket on the flat, scrub ground that was there before. She shook her head. They were simpler times.

Shankar walked alongside the colonel toward the Company HQ building, pushing aside a momentary invasion in her mind as bitter memories of her conduct during her five days' leave in Klugestein threatened to distract her from her core business. After only a short walk, the two arrived at Company HQ. Major Barker jumped to his feet as he saw the colonel enter the room; Talau held up a hand to stop him.

"Don't worry about the formalities," he greeted, his tone oddly formal for such a declaration, "gather around, everybody."

The assembled Fusiliers moved across to stand around the room's central briefing table. Major Barker and Captain Waczek stood next to Talau as the command team of A Company; Lieutenant Hunar Juthani and Sergeant Jane Fletcher stood for Number One Platoon, whilst with Rory Howe being wounded, Number Two Platoon was represented only by Sergeant Dev Bakshi. Cochrane moved across to stand next to Shankar.

"I'll keep this quick," Talau said, leaning over the table, "Captain Waczek will ensure your briefing files are sent onto you. Before I begin, I'll inform you formally that the information I am here to discuss with you is classified as secret. You are all to confirm that your comlogs and geists are off. Not a word of this briefing is to be discussed outside these walls. O-12 has mandated a ceasefire across the Glottenberg region, which both parties have agreed to. Naturally, we still have the high ground in that we were attacked, but inside information indicates that O-12 is leaning more toward believing the border dispute will fall on the Yujingyu side."

Shankar raised one fist to her lips. An 'indication' that the border was indeed in the favor of the Yujingyu argument was as good as saying that at that very moment, they were all stood in a briefing room that was as good as trespassing on ground belonging to the StateEmpire. In turn, that meant that Alpha Four-Four and the Cosmolite did not rightfully belong to PanOceania. Shankar mused on that further, wondering how long the PanOceanian government were aware of this, and if that was the reason for the Fusiliers holding the line – to extract as much scientific data as possible before being ordered to withdraw.

"After Number Three Platoon suffered such heavy casualties at the mining site," Talau continued, nodding toward Shankar and Cochrane, "you will, no doubt, want to know why we have withdrawn and surrendered the location to the enemy. The fact is that now O-12's embargo is firmly in place and measures have been established to ensure neither side receives any further reinforcement of soldiers or equipment, it is now a game of attrition. The reinforcements you have recently received have been brought here under the official line that the men and women who have recently arrived were already assigned to this unit as a natural rotation of personnel. Read into that what you will."

Shankar smiled grimly. Her platoon was now back up to ninety percent strength thanks to a massive influx of reinforcements from the regiment's Second Battalion. Anybody with even the most basic knowledge of military organization could look at that rate of change and know it was to replace combat losses, not as part of the natural progression of personnel churn.

"We need to know what they are fielding against us," Talau said. "They know precisely what we have, to an extent, because we've destroyed the entire jungle around Alpha Four-Four, and now this is an easy site to assess with surveillance drones. Abandoning the mining site gives us a similar advantage, to a lesser extent. We can see what is going on there far better than under dense jungle."

"It does bring them a lot closer, sir," Lieutenant Juthani of Number One Platoon offered. "We do have less advance warning if they do make a move on us here."

"I know, Hunar," Talau nodded, "that's why we are re-instigating patrols. At any one time from now on, around the clock, I want an entire platoon in the field, scouring the area between here and the mining site."

Concerned looks were exchanged between the Fusilier officers and sergeants. Shankar decided to speak.

"How does that work with the O-12 sanctions, sir? Surely the conditions of the ceasefire also mean that conducting offensive patrols would be considered a sign of aggression? As far as the rest of the Human Sphere is concerned, any moral high ground we have here will be lost."

"With respect, ma'am, I get that," Sergeant Bakshi countered, "but by the same logic, if we don't get out there and show we're not to be fucked about with, we are telling the entire Human Sphere that we accept a hostile incursion into our territory without a fight."

"I lost seventy percent of my men and women in two weeks, Sergeant," Shankar snapped. "I don't need you to tell me that we aren't putting up a fight."

"Alright, alright," Talau intervened, "look, you're both entirely correct. We cannot be seen as the aggressor, but we cannot be seen to be a soft touch either. That is why the decision has been taken to conduct overt patrols, and to be seen doing so. Remember, this border is still not ratified, so at this moment in time, this is our land and we have every right to patrol it."

"And if we bump into any of those buggers, sir?" Cochrane asked. "Can we shoot the bastards?"

"No," Talau shook his head, "not first. If you see them, you form a defensive line and you don't let them through. If they approach, you deliver the normal series of escalating warnings in accordance with standard Rules of Engagement. If they are not adhered to, you fire. If those pricks fire first, you fire. Are we all clear on that?"

A series of affirmations sounded from the assembled soldiers, ranging in enthusiasm from bold declarations to cautious mumbles.

"Finally," Talau said, "I wanted to at least give you some idea of what exactly it is you and your soldiers are risking your lives for. You all know this is about the research hub a stone throw from here. You all know MagnaObra's ethical reputation, but the company consistently honored its contractual obligations with the PanOceanian government, and progress is ahead of schedule. Naturally, we won't hear anything until there is a public release of information. All I'll tell you – and I'll remind you that this information is classified as secret – is that it has been confirmed that the Cosmolite here is in the best physical condition of any Cosmolite yet discovered and holds new information on the alien civilization that was once prevalent on this planet. That's how important this site is."

Mark Barber

Shankar glanced across at Cochrane, knowing well how intrigued the big man was with all that was going on in the research hub. She saw his eyes twinkle, his mouth all but salivating at that tiny but cataclysmically important detail. The site was a key to unlocking the secrets of the past, possibly holding information vital to defeating the EI invasion on the very same planet that PanOceania and Yu Jing now squabbled over, despite the deadly, foreign incursion.

"That's all for now," the colonel concluded, "I'll get around and see you all individually before I leave this evening. Get to a secure location and read your briefing packs. Any questions, wait until you can see me face to face. That's all."

Shankar grabbed her beret from her leg pocket, exchanging a brief nod with Captain Waczek as the taller woman walked to the exit with Major Barker.

"Priya, Jim, a moment please."

Shankar and Cochrane turned to see Colonel Talau walk across to them. He folded his arms across his chest and waited in silence until the others had departed, leaving the three soldiers alone in the Company HQ briefing room.

"How's the platoon holding out, Priya?" Talau asked. "By God, your lot soaked up some hits for the team out there."

Shankar winced at the choice of words. Her soldiers had not soaked up hits in a team game. They had been gunned down and killed.

"The NCO cadre are relatively well-placed, sir," she replied with an effort to keep her tone even and professional. "I've got two out of my original three section leaders and 2ICs, and my third corporal who has just arrived from Number Two Battalion comes with a solid reputation and a lot of experience. As for the troops... I've got a handful of young men and women who have survived being thrown into the deep end and are now understandably tired, cautious, and pretty miserable, and I've got a ton of fresh faces who are scared shitless about what they've heard from the few survivors."

"We'll kick 'em into shape, sir," Cochrane smiled grimly. "We're on the defensive now. Far easier job in this terrain. No worries."

Talau's cool eyes moved back to Shankar.

"Do you share your sergeant's optimism, Lieutenant?"

Shankar paused.

"Yes, sir," she lied curtly.

"Well, your work out here hasn't gone unnoticed, either of you," Talau said, "it's a tough job. That's acknowledged at the highest levels. You did well holding the mining site. Which reminds me. Major Barker suggested we recommend Major Beckmann for a bar to her Military Cross for her actions in destroying the TAG. Obviously we are going off lens footage which is blurred

245

and confused at best, but having spoken to three of your men who were at the battle, they all agreed that Major Beckmann took out the enemy TAG practically single-handed. Apparently she shot out its knee and then suffered life threatening injuries whilst destroying it with explosives at close range. Would you be willing to confirm that in writing, Priya?"

Shankar cleared her throat irritably, tugging on the neckline of her combat shirt. She felt a knot in her stomach as she remembered Beckmann's words on one of their first meetings. Something about kicking her teeth out and leaving her crying in the dirt. She remembered Beckmann pushing her and shouting at her at the mining site, accusing her of a lack of care until she was blinking tears out of her eyes. The knot in Shankar's stomach began to physically hurt.

"No, I wouldn't agree with that at all," Shankar folded her arms. "In fact, I'd go as far as to say the prospect of it is disingenuous to the men and woman of my platoon. That TAG was caught in a crossfire by the HMGs of my Fusiliers, under my orders and direction. I didn't see anything that could confirm the leg shot came from Major Beckmann. Likewise, all I saw was her falling on the thing when it got close. I distinctly remember the shot that destroyed the TAG was actually a stray missile from its own lines. So no, sir, I am not willing to support any suggestion that Major Beckmann should be awarded a medal."

Talau's eyes narrowed, almost suspiciously. He took in a breath.

"That's a shame, Priya. A real shame. Politically, a recommendation from a Fusilier unit to award a medal to an operative of the Strategic Security Division would potentially build some very much needed bridges. Jim, what do you think?"

Cochrane looked across at Shankar and then back at the colonel, his mouth opening and closing twice before he spoke.

"I mean... well... it's exactly as the lieutenant says, sir. Team effort taking that TAG down. I didn't see that Hexa major do anything remarkable. With respect to the diggers you spoke to, sir, these are lads in their late teens who don't care about the bigger picture here. If you ask 'em if the hot girl should get a medal, they're gonna say yes. Doesn't mean it's true."

"Shame," Talau repeated. "Still, it is what it is."

"It's only a bar, sir," Cochrane shrugged, "it's not like she needs the medal anyway. Besides, we're never going to see her again."

"Second bar," Talau corrected, "I hear she has already been awarded the Military Cross twice. And you will be seeing her. As soon as she is fit for combat duties, in accordance with the O-12 sanctions, she is authorized to return here. Any day now, in fact. More importantly, you two need to read those briefing folders. Have a chat through the details and get back to me before I leave at nineteen hundred. Oh, and arrange a time for me to have a chat with your Fusiliers before I leave later. Face to face. I want to tell them what a fine job they've done so far."

Talau paced to the door and walked out into the sun, leaving Shankar alone with Cochrane. The tall sergeant scratched his beard thoughtfully and looked down at Shankar. She recognized his expression; she had done something he did not approve of, and he was struggling with the words of how to phrase it without upsetting her. Was she that easy to offend?

"Go on," she grumbled, "what is it?"

"You've sent Rob May home," Cochrane raised his hands to either side. "Why would you do that? He is, or was, the most experienced Fusilier we had other than the NCOs. He was perfect for Lance Corporal. Instead, you sent him home and told the colonel to make Natalie Southee a lance jack instead!"

"What is everybody's problem with Nat Southee?" Shankar exclaimed. "I put her in charge of a Fireteam at the mining site, and she did a bloody good job! And as for Rob May, I told you, it wasn't a casual fling between him and Dani Mieke. It was serious. So I did the right thing and told them that one of them had to go. I know you told them to just 'keep it in their daks' – brilliant advice, Jim – but the funny thing is, if you get a load of young, single men and women and then drop a load of rockets and bombs on them to make them emotional, you can't be bloody surprised when romantic entanglements ensue!"

"I'm not surprised, Priya! I'm just saying they should get it out of their system and move on!"

"Well, call me soft as shit for having a heart, but I don't see it that way," Shankar planted her fists on her hips. "I say best of luck to them. And there are rules in place because this does happen from time to time, so we follow the rules and one of them goes. I am short on good combat medics, so I elected to keep Dani Mieke here. I know what you all think of Natalie Southee, and I know her reputation from earlier in her career. I know she didn't shower herself in glory."

"Well, she sure seemed happy to shower herself in…"

"Jim! I don't want to hear it! For heaven's sake, know your audience! I don't think jokes like that are funny or appropriate! She's trying hard to turn things around, everybody deserves another chance, and I think she is criminally underrated as a soldier by you and your NCO mafia. So, I recommended her for an acting promotion until she is officially selected for advancement."

Cochrane's mouth again opened and closed a few times before he spoke.

"I would have appreciated it if you'd at least spoken to me. Asked my advice. *Pretended* you gave a shit about my opinion. Before all of this kicked off, you used to."

Shankar sighed, shook her head, and walked toward the door. Her frustration and unease doubled in an instant as that memory from her leave in Klugestein again raised its ugly head. She stopped and looked back at Cochrane.

"I already knew your opinion. On both matters. You told me, in explicit terms. Besides, you were in the hospital. This is my platoon, and I can run it without calling you when you are undergoing surgery, Jim! You're like every sergeant I've ever met! Do you honestly think that they select the wrong people to be platoon commanders and then the year's training to earn a commission is all spent at cocktail parties and playing polo? I know what I'm doing. I'm going to be a captain in less than a year! I've done this whole lieutenant thing for a good few years now."

Cochrane walked across to catch up with Shankar as she carried on toward the door.

"And I've worked with a lot more lieutenants than you have sergeants. And you're actually nothing like any of them. You're stubborn and think you know best all the time. I do actually have some experience, you know. I do actually know what I'm doing. I'm not just here to look amazingly handsome and be eye candy for you."

Shankar burst out laughing as the smirking soldier held the door open for her.

"Alright," she confessed, "alright. I would do better for consulting your advice more often than I do. Fine. All joking aside, give me your honest opinion. Did I do the right thing by saying Beckmann shouldn't have got a medal?"

Cochrane followed Shankar out into the open air outside. A team of naval maintainers struggled shifting two large boxes out of the back of an Uro toward the TAG hangar. Three new Fusiliers from Shankar's platoon wandered across toward the dining hall. Shankar turned to Cochrane and looked to him for an answer.

"Yeah," he said, "you did the right thing."

"You sure?"

"Yeah. Seeing that girl take down that TAG was one of the bravest things I've ever seen. The action deserved that medal ten times over. But the individual did not. You made the right call. Now, will you answer a question for me?"

Shankar looked across at the tall, bearded soldier as they walked.

"Go on."

"You were in a foul mood before I left for the hospital. Since you've got back from leave at Klugestein, you've been even more irritable. What happened?"

Shankar instinctively turned away and shook her head. She considered talking through her issues, voicing her concerns over her domestic upheaval and the guilt of her thoughts and actions. But only for a moment before firmly clamping a lid on her emotions again.

"Not now, Jim. Not now."

***

The holographic recording transmitted directly onto the lens, occasionally flickering as the figures on the recording stepped across the few items of furniture in the sparse accommodation room. The recording clipped and cut, but the message came though clearly.

"...sorry we didn't get a chance to catch up properly, and sorry you didn't really get any time off. Little Maria here got the birthday message you sent, and the present..."
"Hi, Uncle Kyle!"
"...yeah, the present went down well."

Hawkins pulled on his gauntlets, dragging the alloy gloves down to connect to the forearm plates of his armor, clenching and unclenching his fingers to check he had full mobility. The projection of his older brother's message just caught a flurry of snow through the window behind the homely living room where he sat with his two daughters, the clarity of the image almost making Hawkins feel the familiar chill of the frost.

"Maria says as soon as you get home, you can take her to the zoo again. So get back home here soon, okay? These little monsters miss you..."

Hawkins finished the final connections and initiated the suit's built-in test function. It came back as functional, with only a slight degradation in his tertiary communication transmitter which he had been carrying and unable to repair since before leave. He pulled on his red surcoat over his head.

"...mum and dad say you claim you were going on a date, which I find hard to believe. Seriously, what's it been, four years? Anyhow, hope it goes well and I hope the girl is as sweet as mum says you've told her. Just... you know I'm not great with the sentimental stuff so I'll keep it quick. Take care of yourself. Seriously. We'll see you soon. God bless."

Hawkins watched Nathan's image fade from his lens as he buckled his pistol belt around his waist and pushed his heavy, Huntley Mk.VIII MULTI Pistol into its coarse, canvas holster, all six chambers loaded with heavy AP rounds even though the cylinder was designed to provide the function of multiple ammunition choices. As much as he appreciated the message from his older brother, it was not the time to dwell on it. Standing in the center of the room, he dropped to one knee and closed his eyes, bowing his head in prayer.

"Hail Mary, full of grace, the Lord is with thee…"

He thought on each and every word as he spoke it aloud, looking for new meaning in the familiar lines of the prayer he had said thousands of times, far too often mechanically and without really contemplating the meaning.

"…pray for us sinners, now, and at the hour of our death. Amen."

Hawkins opened his eyes. He checked his comlog. It was time to go. Time to push the nice guy aside, as he was once told, and go out to do his job. Clinical; efficient; focused. He clipped his MULTI Rifle to his back and grabbed his sword and helmet. Outside his room, the night was barely illuminated by one new moon and one waxing crescent that had not even deigned to rise into the bleak, black sky. The nocturnal insects of the jungle hissed and rattled from all sides around the Alpha Four-Four encampment. Klugestein, leave, and his mental turmoil already seemed so far away. On the horizon, a thin line of purple announced the coming of the dawn sun.

Hawkins made his way across the silent camp, past the research hub, and to the scrub ground outside the Platoon HQ block. In the dim light, he saw some thirty Fusiliers gathering together in groups, conversation hushed and silent. To the left, a tall, dusky skinned corporal he had not met before ushered Number One Section together. Ahead, the ever dependable Corporal Garcia exchanged words with his second-in-command, Lance Corporal Reid. To the right, Corporal Rossi walked along her line of Fusiliers, checking their weapons and equipment as Acting Lance Corporal Southee followed close at her heels.

"G'day, mate!" Cochrane greeted, a broad grin just about visible beneath his bushy beard, his Combi Rifle held casually over one shoulder.

"Good morning, digger," Hawkins grinned.

"Sounds faintly ridiculous when you say it with that accent, mate. You ready? All set?"

Hawkins looked across as Lieutenant Shankar walked toward them from the Company HQ Block, no doubt with the final instructions for their patrol into the jungle. Hawkins hauled on his helmet and activated his environmental controls to send a blast of cooling air through the heavily armored suit.

"All set," he confirmed.

Chapter Sixteen

The warm water of the broad stream flowed gently by as Cochrane waded across to the far side, his Combi Rifle held just above waist height to keep the weapon dry. The jungle opened out spectacularly to either side, plunging down to the north into a valley where the vegetation spread out to showcase picturesque clearings and idyllic ponds, whilst to the south the trees closed together as if seemingly becoming one solid, homogenous block of wood and drooping, lime-green leaves. It was mid-morning now, only a few hours into the patrol as the three sections advanced along their route in an arrowhead formation, Number Three Section taking the point of the advance whilst Cochrane and the rest of the Platoon HQ followed not far behind.

An obnoxious sounding bird suddenly let out a long warble of increasing volume from the trees ahead as Cochrane waded out of the stream and onto the sand on the other side of the water. He looked back at the rest of his team as they negotiated the clear, gentle waters before the stream narrowed and picked up pace closer to a short waterfall.

"All sections from Zero-One, report in," Cochrane called over the comlog as Fusilier Mieke made her way out of the stream and stopped to grab her water canteen from her webbing belt.

"Zero-One from One-One," Corporal Kotal called from where his ten Fusiliers advanced a few dozen yards to the north, his normally jovial tone now utterly professional, "advancing along Route Echo, nothing to report."

Cochrane surpassed a smile as he saw Shankar struggling to cross the stream, the water reaching up practically to the short woman's neck where it had barely reached Cochrane's ribs. Her Combi Rifle held over her head, she tentatively moved forward inch by inch whilst behind her, acting as the team's rearguard, Hawkins plunged effortlessly through the water with his high quality, resilient, and reliable MULTI Rifle held below the water line, safe in the knowledge that soaking the weapon would not stop it from functioning.

"Zero-One, Two-One," Corporal Garcia responded, "on track, Route Golf. Ops normal."

Cochrane pulled off his beret and ran one hand through his sweat-soaked hair. His beard itched. Every day spent in the jungle, he promised himself he would shave it off as soon as he had a chance at Alpha Four-Four. Every time he returned to his room and spend a few minutes flexing his biceps and smiling into his mirror, he changed his mind.

"Three-One, we're all good," Corporal Rossi called in last from only a minute or so ahead of the Platoon HQ team, her doleful tone telling Cochrane that she was less than enthused to be back in the Paradiso jungle after recovering from her wounds.

"Zero-One to all units," Cochrane replied, pasting his Indigo beret back on over his soaked hair, "ops normal copied. Proceed to..."

A thud shook the ground as an explosion blasted through the jungle to the north, echoing through the trees as a flock of vibrant, red and blue birds shot up into the air. Cochrane flung himself to the ground, followed a moment later by Mieke, just as Shankar was wading ashore. A Combi Rifle crackled from off to the left, followed a moment later by the deep, guttural thudding of a Heavy Machine Gun. They abruptly stopped a second later as Cochrane heard a shout, yelled out loud rather than over the comlog, from the direction of the rising gray pillar of smoke in the trees.

"Cease fire! Cease fire!"

The jungle fell silent, save for the endless clicking of insects and a few panicked cries of alarm from larger creatures hidden amidst the foliage on all sides. Cochrane's tactical map scrolled with a casualty report.

- Fusilier Gerhard Drecker – dead
- Fusilier Valeria Silva – severe abdominal wound

"Sarn't?" Mieke called across from where she lay prone a few feet away, her soaked uniform and body armor plastered in sand.

"Wait, wait, wait," Cochrane replied rapidly, holding up a hand to silence her as his eyes scanned the jungle around.

He heard a long scream of pain as he checked his tactical map. Nobody had highlighted an enemy unit.

"One-One, this is Zero," Shankar called as she tentatively raised herself back up to one knee, "sitrep."

"Boss, this is One-One!" Kotal replied, his voice shaken. "We're in a fucking minefield! I've got one dead and one wounded! I... we can't get to her and she's in a bad way!"

Cochrane swore. He doubted very much that Kotal's section had stumbled into an entire minefield in the middle of thousands of miles of jungle; given his experience of facing Yujingyu forces previously, it was more likely to be an isolated explosive device at an obvious choke point on the route.

"Alpha-Zero from Three-Zero," Shankar called on the Company Command frequency, "multiple casualties at my position, suspect explosive device, wait out."

Shankar quickly changed channels back to her own platoon.

"One-One from Zero," she called Kotal, "how bad is your wounded soldier?"

"I... I can't get to her! I can see her and she's bleeding everywhere! I..."

"One-One, calm down," Shankar said, rising to her feet, "hold your position, I'm on my way to you."

Cochrane looked up.

"Boss, you can control it from here! If that mine was just to draw us out, there could be a sniper or a team of those bastards watching us right now! We need to stay in cover!"

"Kotal's lost it, and that wounded soldier is going to die unless we grip this, now," Shankar answered. "I'm going across."

"I can come with you, ma'am," Mieke offered, clambering back up to her feet.

"No, you wait here. That section already has a medic. I just need to get the casualty to him. The three of you stay here. Sergeant, send sit reps to Company HQ and see about getting us an explosive clearance team and a medivac."

Cochrane remained in the cover of the stream bank with Mieke and Hawkins as Shankar jogged quickly toward the sound of screaming and the pillar of gray smoke that was dissipating above the trees to the north.

***

Her eyes scanning the surrounding trees warily, Shankar's feet thudded softly into the sand along the stream bank. She reached a steep slope by the side of the waterfall at the end of the stream and slid down before rushing along the outside of a small, picturesque pond of turquoise water, wild flowers of purples and reds surrounding it. The heavenly scene was at complete odds with the screams of pain not far ahead and the smell of burnt charge from the recent explosion.

The line of trees up ahead was sparse, thinner than most in this region of Glottenberg, allowing Shankar to see the site of the detonation from a good twenty meters away as she approached. A blackened crater was blown in the sand ahead, around the lip of which were various body parts from an unfortunate Fusilier who was so new in her platoon that Shankar had never even spoken to him. A few feet away, a young woman of perhaps twenty years of age lay on her back, her hands clutching at a smoking piece of metal jutting out of a vicious wound torn across her belly. The woman screamed in pain, tears rolling down her grimy cheeks and the sand around her red with blood. Shankar looked across to her left and saw the remainder of Number One Section had taken to ground, lying behind whatever cover they could exploit in the folds and dips of the terrain.

"Boss," Cochrane called on a private channel, "I've got through to Company. Medivac is airborne and on the way, only minutes out. No luck with engineering support."

"What about drone surveillance?" Shankar breathed, dropping down by a copse of trees overlooking the bloody site of the detonation. "Can we get a ground scan to see if there're any more devices here? Or even a look for enemy units?"

"Nothing," Cochrane replied, "drone surveillance out here is in violation of the O-12 ceasefire. Can you go old school and manually clear the ground ahead?"

Shankar swallowed as she surveyed the terrain. Her hackers could use their devices to scan the ground ahead for explosive devices, but it took time and most modern explosive devices were clever enough to mask their signal. That left the proper old fashioned way. Belly down, crawl forward, and combat knives out to carefully stab the ground ahead – if you felt stiff resistance in the sand, mark it up and move around it.

"She's bleeding out, Jim, there isn't time!" Shankar breathed, looking the handful of meters ahead at her wounded Fusilier as the woman's screams became quieter. "Look, I've... I'll just have to hope that there's only one device out there."

"Priya! Stop!" Cochrane called. "Don't be a bloody idiot! You run out there and set another mine off, and our problems are doubled!"

"Jim, get the area secured," Shankar commanded, placing her Combi Rifle down and removing her pack, "find a decent site for casualty extraction and get the area covered."

Switching off her ear piece to prevent any further objections from Cochrane, Shankar sprang to her feet and made her way quickly down the shallow slope toward the site of the explosion. Sweat dripping down her back, she edged forward cautiously, aware that the eyes of every Fusilier in Number One Section were following her. The wounded Fusilier had stopped screaming. Her breathing looked shallow, even from that distance. Shankar looked ahead at the sandy ground between her and the crater. Nothing on the planet could help her identify whether there were any further explosive devices now, and if there were, where they would be. Edging forward or running, it really made no difference. It was all down to providence and providence alone.

"Screw it," Shankar breathed.

Staring straight ahead at the wounded soldier, she sprinted forward. It was only ten steps. Each time her foot planted down in the soft sand, it seemed to take a lifetime. Halfway across, she felt a solid object beneath her left foot. Her heart hammering, she looked down. Only a jagged rock was visible poking through the sand. Shankar swallowed and dashed forward for the final few steps. The wounded Fusilier looked up at her weakly, her face spattered in blood.

"Let's get you out of here," Shankar smiled, crouching down and reaching across to grab the woman by her arm and heft her up over her shoulders. "The Tubarão will be here for you any second now."

Shankar retraced her steps back across to where she had left her Combi Rifle and pack. Evans, the new section medic, was already waiting for her.

"Let's take a look, Boss," the bearded Fusilier said as he helped the wounded soldier down to the ground and immediately set about stabilizing her wound.

Her breathing labored, her hands shaking, Shankar walked away from the medic and his patient as the men and women of her platoon took up defensive positions around a small clearing to the south. Shankar slumped down to sit on a smooth rock by the pool at the foot of the waterfall and took in a few breaths in an unsuccessful attempt to control her nerves. She replaced her ear piece and heard Cochrane barking out orders to her platoon. Within a minute, she heard the far off thrumming of the inbound Tubarão's engines. A shadow fell across her. She turned to look over her shoulder and saw the armored bulk of the Hospitaller blocking out the low sun.

"You took a bit of a chance there, didn't you?" Hawkins asked, a vaguely sinister, metallic tone to his voice as it emitted from within his helmet. "Are you alright?"

"Fine," Shankar replied, "I'm... fine."

"You know," Hawkins continued, "an old hand at this soldiering game once told me that if you rely on luck out here, you flip a coin. Heads, you're a hero. Tails, you look stupid and then you die."

Shankar placed a shaking hand on the water canteen at her side and unclipped it before taking a long swig.

"Sounds like the sort of thing Sergeant Cochrane would say," she replied, without looking up again, "except with a lot more swearing."

"It was," Hawkins replied.

Shankar looked up at the Order warrior and forced a smile.

"Well, you can ignore most of what he tells you. He can be a real dick sometimes."

***

The digital map of the Sandtal region of Glottenberg projected onto Shankar's lens, appearing as a series of green lines to illustrate the topography of the ground as it hovered over the briefing table of the Company HQ building. The 3D map turned in place as Captain Waczek manipulated it, zooming in on the exact site of the opening hours of Number Three Platoon's patrol and the explosion that killed Fusilier Drecker.

"It's not the most obvious route," Major Barker scratched his graying moustache, "but it's logical enough, unfortunately, when one examines it with the benefit of hindsight. Given enough time, the Yujingyu forces in the area could feasibly have mined dozens of paths like this. So let me start with the good news."

Shankar and Cochrane looked across the table from where they stood opposite Barker and Waczek, both showered and fed after the uneventful completion of the patrol, but still weary.

"Fusilier Silva is stable," Barker said, "she's in the medical bay at Kokoda Barracks. There's no concerns about her making anything but a full recovery."

"And the bad news, sir?" Cochrane asked.

"Well, according to the intelligence cell, judging by the blast pattern, that mine was an Armadilha. One of ours."

Shankar's eyes opened wide.

"You mean... we planted that thing there and then stumbled right over it? Its IFF failed to recognize a friendly soldier?"

"No," Barker shook his head, "we don't just plant explosive devices at random and keep our fingers crossed. Deployment of ordnance is tightly controlled. We know exactly where all of our mines are in this region. No, this is a captured weapon planted by Yujingyu forces. They've done that because they know when we scan an area for disturbances, our engineers don't routinely look for the signatures of our own weapons. Disabling a mine's original IFF is easy enough, apparently. Suffice to say, we will be looking from here on in. My guess is that this has been put here recently and is one of a significant number."

Shankar narrowed her eyes. Two months ago, she would have warily shared a drink with her opposite number in a Zhanshi regiment. Now, having seen the extent of their efforts to find new and devious ways to kill PanOceanian soldiers, she wondered if she would even accept a surrender from a Yujingyu soldier.

"Priya?"

Shankar snapped out of her thoughts and looked across the table at Barker.

"Sorry, sir."

"No, no. Don't worry about that. Look, I know your platoon has been like a shit magnet out here. First shots on the first night this all kicked off, first firefight with the enemy, the highest casualties at the mine, and now this. But, at the risk of giving you even more to think about... Priya, the analysis from our engineers came back. That mine was one of three. When you walked across to recover your wounded soldier, you were about half a meter from stepping on a second device and being killed yourself."

Shankar raised her left hand to rub her eye, which developed a sudden itch. Her stomach ached. She looked at the map projection on her lens, at the site of the blast, and at the two mines that she avoided by luck and a hair's breadth. It certainly put her problems from leave in Klugestein into perspective, but that was not much of a silver lining.

"You undoubtedly saved that soldier's life," Barker leaned forward, "but one step to the left and you'd be dead. You took a gamble and it paid off. I'm sure your soldiers appreciate your bravery. But don't do that again, Priya. We rely on training, experience, tactics, technology… but not luck."

"Yes, sir."

The company commander's features softened a little.

"Alright, you two go get some rest. Two Platoon are already out there and Number One has guard duty. I'm standing you down for a day."

"Awesome!" Cochrane beamed. "Let's go out and get pissed! Oh, hang on…"

"Funny, Jim, funny," Barker smirked. "Now piss off out of my briefing room and go get some sleep."

Shankar walked out of the briefing room, silently accepting Cochrane's polite gesture of accelerating ahead to hold the door open for her. Outside, a line of blue-gray clouds had gathered along the western horizon, threatening to bring one of the region's infrequent but torrential downpours of rain. She glanced across to Alpha Four-Four's landing site to assess the wind from the orange windsock atop its pole – coincidentally, just as a Tubarão appeared over the horizon – and noted that the wind's direction did, at least, ensure the clouds were coming nowhere near them.

Shankar exhaled as she thought of the communication she would need to record for her dead soldier's next of kin. That was becoming a full time job in itself and was not getting any easier. It at least distracted her from leave and from David. She surpassed a short chuckle as she looked up at the cloth windsock hanging from the tall white pole. Surely in this day and age, there was better technology available for a pilot to assess the direction and strength of the wind? Then again, she remembered the same counter argument from an instructor in basic training when she had dared to query the technology behind the basic function of a Combi Rifle.

"D'you know how many centuries armies used the simple bow and arrow for, Officer Cadet Shankar?"

"Yes, Sergeant. But the bolt action rifle was made obsolete as a standard infantry weapon in only decades."

"What about your knife, Shankar?"

"Sergeant?"

"You've got roughly the same knife that was issued to soldiers of the Roman legions. Perhaps you think we should all have progressed to turbo-ultra-mega-thermo-knives? No. Because sometimes things are fine the way they are, and cheap and reliable can be better than hyper modern shit that breaks all the time."

Cochrane grumbled as he scratched his beard, watching the Tubarão draw nearer and distracting her from her memories.

"Y'know," he drawled, "I bloody hope that thing is carrying cheese. We were promised fondue night last Friday, and then it got shit-canned because we're all out of cheese. What kind of primitive bloody war is this when a digger can't even get a wedge of cheddar?"

Ignoring the pointless attempt at humor, Shankar walked briskly over to where she noticed a gathering of eight of the Fusiliers from her platoon by a pair of benches laid out next to the stream running through the base. Evidence of more simple times when only a single platoon was necessary to keep an eye on the perimeter of the sleepy, secluded MagnaObra facility. The men and women still wore their body armor and had weapons close to hand; some had clearly not even washed since returning from patrol.

"Hello, Boss," Garcia greeted cheerily, standing up respectfully.

The other soldiers followed with a series of greetings, the more experienced following Garcia's lead whilst the junior Fusiliers opted for the more formal '*ma'am.*' She detected a note more enthusiasm in their responses, no doubt garnered from her display of enduring danger to rescue the wounded Fusilier from the site of the explosion the morning before. The simple action lifted her spirits significantly.

"Major Barker has stood us down for the day, so you're all free to go into town and get pissed," Shankar greeted.

A series of laughs ensued from the Fusiliers, some perhaps a little forced and over enthusiastic.

"Yeah, that was my joke, Boss," Cochrane said from her side.

"Sounded funnier when I said it," Shankar remarked dryly. "So… what's your plan for the afternoon?"

Any response was cut off as the Tubarão came in to land, its engines swiveling in place to divert their thrust from forward flight to the hover position, directly opposing the aggressive looking aircraft's weight. Responding to the hand signals from the marshaller stood at the edge of the landing pad, the Tubarão dropped down and sank a little on its landing oleos before its engines died down from a growl to a low whine after being powered down to their ground idle setting.

Shankar watched as the aircraft's rear ramp was lowered, and two naval maintainers were cleared to approach the Tubarão. They set about manually shifting a heavy looking box, no doubt filled with parts for the maintenance-heavy Cutter TAG that waited in its hangar. A single figure then walked down the ramp and away from the whining Tubarão. Anger surged up through Shankar as she clenched her jaw.

Beckmann practically strutted away from the landing pad, clad in fashionable ankle boots, a black t-shirt emblazoned with a heavy metal band's title and crude artwork, and denim shorts that showcased every inch of her perfect legs. She carried a long, camouflaged kit bag over one shoulder. Garcia shot to his feet and let out a cheer, followed by three other Fusiliers who accompanied him with claps and whistles. Beckmann glanced over, smiled, and threw a cocky wink before sliding on her sunglasses.

"Cut that out!" Shankar bellowed at her soldiers. "What the hell do you think this is? A strip club?"

"Sorry, ma'am," Garcia's faced dropped as he turned to regard his platoon commander. "I was cheering the major for coming back out here in one piece after getting shot to shit saving us all from that TAG. I wasn't cheering the way she looks."

The assembled Fusiliers stared up at Shankar in an uncomfortable silence. She opened her mouth to remind them about her own bravery, of taking risks to rush across the ground by the exploded mine to save a wounded soldier, but thankfully she thought better of it before speaking. She could practically feel the unpleasantness of the atmosphere, all good will she had garnered seemingly destroyed with one comment. And it was not their fault. It was not Shankar's, either.

"Boss, wait! Boss!" Cochrane urged as Shankar strode away from the benches and out to meet Beckmann.

"What the hell are you wearing?" Shankar yelled as she paced out to meet the taller woman.

"Ten seconds," Beckmann sighed, "ten fucking seconds back here and I'm already having to put up with your shit."

"We're in the middle of a war!" Shankar snapped, struggling to keep pace with the tall woman as she stomped angrily alongside her, "I've spoken to you before about maintaining even the lowest levels of standards and military bearing! You come strutting in here, dressed like a…"

"And I told you," the Hexa operative cut her off, her tone calm, "that I'm a major and you're just a shitty little lieutenant, so you don't get a vote. Furthermore, these are my travel clothes. I get to strut in here wearing them because I'm Special Forces. You don't get that privilege because you are a Fusilier. The dregs of the entire military. The lowest common denominator. So why don't you fuck off before…"

"Before what?" Shankar snarled, jumping out in front of Beckmann to stop her in her tracks. "Before you kick the shit out of me? Knock my teeth out? Bullshit! You're all talk! You're tough when you're skulking behind a rifle, a mile away from your target, but I haven't seen a shred of evidence to prove you know how to throw a punch!"

Shankar stopped and took in a breath. She had no idea, absolutely no idea, where the sudden and enormous outpouring of aggression came from. Stress? Fear? Guilt? A thousand things nagging at her very core, all weakly capped and held in place by the knowledge that any day in Glottenberg could be her last? Beckmann threw down her kitbag and removed her sunglasses. She folded her arms, the utter perfection of her figure driving Shankar to an even greater level of anger and hatred.

"What is your problem with me?" Beckmann demanded.

"It's not me! It's everyone!" Shankar growled. "Everybody here hates you! We all know who you are and what you are! We're all here to do a job to the best of our ability, even if we are the dregs and the lowest common denominator! Even if our dumb, blue beret doesn't meet your lofty standards! You cruise around here like you own the place, cutting people down without a second thought from your cowardly hiding positions with your rifle, and then shoot your mouth off, thinking how you deserve more medals for it! I'm not giving you any marks of respect! I don't see you as a major in the military! You're just a psychopath, nothing more!"

The two women stood facing each other, halfway between the landing pad and the accommodation blocks. Shankar knew that, even out of earshot of her soldiers, they were all watching the confrontation. She glared up at Beckmann, unflinching. For a moment, just a fraction of a second, she thought she saw hurt in the beautiful killer's blue eyes. It was instantly replaced with a mask of arrogant indifference.

"Medals," she repeated, "you think I want medals? When I was six or seven, I collected pony stickers. I got the whole set. When you filled your sticker book, you took your spares into school, and at play time, you threw them up in the air so the other kids could get them, because you didn't need them anymore. That's what medals are to me. You see, I've collected the whole set. I've got them all already. If I get any more, I'll just throw them up in the air at play time. D'you follow me, you stupid, bitter, jealous bitch?"

"Is there a problem here?"

Shankar stopped. She turned her head to look at the conversation's new arrival. Stood a few paces away to form a triangle between the three women was Captain Waczek. The short-haired, blonde woman looked across at Beckmann. The Hexa killer turned slowly in place to regard the new arrival, still managing to loom menacingly over Waczek, herself well above average height. Beckmann reached a hand into the pocket of her minuscule shorts and produced a pack of cigarettes and a lighter.

"What d'you want?" she demanded as she lit a cigarette.

"Major Barker requests you see him at Company HQ, as soon as you have changed into uniform," Waczek replied.

"Fine. Understood. That's it then, fuck off."

Waczek glanced across and issued a slight smile of solidarity to Shankar and then walked back away toward the Company HQ block. Beckmann took in a long drag from her cigarette and then exhaled a cloud of blood red smoke, the pleasing smell of cherries at complete odds with the almost vampiric-looking gesture. She picked up her kit bag and slung it over her shoulder again.

"Maybe you're right," she sighed to Shankar, "maybe I'm not so good in a fist fight. But then again, maybe I am. Either way, we're not doing this here. I think your sudden burst of bravery is reliant on the fact that you know even I will get in trouble for beating you to death in broad daylight. But fortunately for me, that's not always the Garkain way anyway. We can be horrifically subtle up until that last moment of explosive, nightmarish violence is required. As you'll find out in the next few days. So... I'd tell you to watch your back, but even that won't stop me."

Beckmann leaned over, flashed a patronizing smile, and slapped Shankar playfully on one shoulder.

"Nothing will stop me now," she issued a last threat, and walked off toward her accommodation block.

***

Beckmann pulled a blue-gray vest on over her head, looking into the mirror of her sparse accommodation room as she tied her hair back in a ponytail, and then spent a few minutes pulling strands down to fall stylishly down over one eye. She tentatively eyed the corners of her room through the mirror. Nothing. Nothing abnormal, at least. Just a bed, a chest of draws with a solitary framed picture and a paper copy of the Bible, a wardrobe of clothing, and a secure crate of weapons and equipment. She looped her pistol belt around her combat trousers and took her replacement sidearm – a TauruSW Marreta 0.50 caliber pistol – and secured it in her drop-leg thigh holster. Opening her wardrobe, her eyes came to rest on the de-badged blue beret she wore last time she was at Alpha Four-Four. Her argument with Shankar still resonated.

"...just a psychopath. Nothing more."

How in the whole Sphere could the words of such an idiot cause so much hurt to a cold, hardened expert in combat psychology? Beckmann picked up the beret, tossed it into the bin by her door, and grabbed a blue-gray field cap. She removed the officer's cap badge from the hat – very unlikely that the Yujingyu would have snipers positioned around Alpha Four-Four but better to play safe, and she was sure that everybody on base knew exactly who she was anyway – and made her way across to Company HQ.

Major Barker was waiting for her outside, which caused her to raise a curious eyebrow. The lean man walked out to meet her as she paced across.

"Thanks for coming across so quickly, Major," Barker greeted. "Flight across okay?"

"Ja," Beckmann folded her arms, "what's the job?"

"Straight to the point," Barker said, gesturing for Beckmann to walk with him as he stepped across to the dusty path leading away from the HQ and toward the stream that bisected the base.

Beckmann followed him silently, the sun beating down on the back of her neck and shoulders.

"You fit for combat?" Barker asked.

"Yeah," Beckmann replied, "I took a Combat Fitness Test yesterday. I scored above average. I normally get graded as exceptional, so I've still got a bit of recovery to go, but the doctors signed me off as fully fit for combat duties."

The Fusilier major reached into his pocket to produce a pristine pack of stubby, PanO cigars.

"You smoke?" he offered.

"Yeah," Beckmann replied. Fishing her own crumpled cigarettes out of a pocket, "but not that shit. Do you have any idea what those do to your breath?"

She pulled a cherry flavored, Haqqislamite cigarette out of her own pack. She thought a change from her normal strawberry cigarettes would be interesting but already regretted it only halfway through the pack.

"I'm not too bothered about my breath out here," Barker grinned as he lit his cigar, "I'm not planning on kissing anybody."

Beckmann ignored his offer to light from the chemo-lighter from his cigar box and flipped open her Ariadnan Zippo lighter.

"So, you and Lieutenant Shankar not seeing eye to eye? My 2IC mentioned stumbling into something of an argument."

Beckmann took a step back away from the noxious cloud of bitter smoke emanating from Barker's cigar and drew on her own cigarette. The sugary fumes sent a mild tingle through her. She only smoked Haqqislam brands – the only manufacturers who had perfected cigarettes with absolutely no negative effects. She considered her next words carefully. Shankar was one of Barker's own. He would not be neutral. In all likelihood, this entire conversation was probably heading toward a request for Beckmann to lay off the aggression. Screw that. But, to make things transition along as easy as possible, a professional approach might be better.

"No, we don't see eye to eye," Beckmann agreed. "I'm sure your lieutenant is a good woman. A nice person, if you like. But she's not cut out for combat. Our job is to kill, or facilitate killing, plain and simple. Your lieutenant isn't very good at that and so is lashing out at me because I am."

"Lieutenant Shankar is highly regarded in this regiment," Barker folded his arms, his noxious cigar still smoking away, "very highly regarded. She's been selected for promotion to captain and has a bright future ahead of her. She proved a remarkable level of courage to us all only yesterday."

Beckmann fell silent. She bit on the butt of her cigarette and stared at

Barker for a long moment before speaking again.

"So, what's your fucking point, Major?"

The veteran Fusilier narrowed his eyes. It was obvious to her that Barker was not used to being spoken in such a manner. She met his stare effortlessly.

"Colonel Talau has asked me to talk to you," he continued finally, "a… favor, if you like. In the last few weeks out here, we have lost a far higher number of men and women than we were expecting. The colonel, well… he's a lot more sentimental than he would have anybody know. Doesn't show it. But these were *his* people, you understand? *His* men and women."

"War stinks," Beckmann shrugged. "The Black Widows did a song about it, and everything."

The classic rock reference clearly being lost on Barker, he continued regardless.

"We lost another soldier yesterday morning. Gerhard Drecker. Eighteen years old, five weeks out of training. His father, Colonel Drecker, commands the Fifth Regiment and is a close personal friend of Colonel Talau."

Beckmann looked down at her feet, where her suede combat boots left imprints in the soft sand. She nodded slowly. A name and an age made that one life infinitely more real. More tragic.

"I'm sorry for Colonel Drecker," she said honestly, "eighteen is no age to die. I'm sorry."

She wondered for a moment if Major General von Beckmann would give even a second's thought if his younger daughter was ever killed in combat. Barker looked across at her with cool eyes.

"Colonel Talau was wondering if you, with your extensive experience in these matters, could think of a way of… conveying that message to the Yujingyu forces shored up at the mining site."

Beckmann took another drag from her cigarette. Again, she considered her words carefully.

"That's why you've brought me out here, away from the briefing room and the tech? This one off the books?"

Barker stared at her in silence.

"You all went revenge? Is that it?" Beckmann asked.

The question sounded like an accusation, but in truth, it was an emotion she fully understood. Of course there were rules to war. But sometimes they just got in the way.

"If you want to prove a point, this needs to be done quickly," Beckmann continued, "if you want that message to be loud and clear. And it needs to scare the shit out of them. Right within their perimeter. Anybody can shoot someone. If you want to send a message, what you want is two or three of them killed right in the heart of their defensive position. And with a knife. To show them that they have no defenses and when it comes, it'll be eye to eye."

There was an element of truth to her claim that the sooner the job was done, the better. Overriding that was her desire to leave Alpha Four-Four as soon as humanly possible. There was still one confrontation she wanted more than anything to avoid.

"Whatever you think is best, I'll leave that up to you," Barker blew out another cloud of smoke. "So... you're thinking of leaving as early as tonight."

Beckmann shook her head and tossed away the butt of her cigarette.

"I'll be on my way in ten minutes."

***

Tossing her pistol belt and vest on her bunk, Beckmann pulled her re-active camouflage coveralls from their hangar and dragged the black suit over her legs and arms before zipping it up to the sternum. She pulled on the suit's combat boots and webbing belt before activating the system and linking the components. As she turned away from her wardrobe, her eyes fell on the paper Bible by her bed. Beckmann let out a long breath. She walked over, rested a hand on the sacred book, and closed her eyes.

"Don't watch what I'm about to go and do," she whispered.

The feeling – that normal charge of confidence and aggression – faded away. Beckmann sank down to sit on the edge of her bed and rested her face in her hands. Was there any point in this? Could it be justified? This whole thing would blow over within a week. Did anybody else need to die? Life was so much easier when the targets were drug cartels or the brutal aliens of the EI. As much as she vehemently opposed the ethics and morals of the Yujingyu military, they were still... people. Men and women, doing their jobs. Beckmann swore. Why was she thinking like this? Why, all of a sudden, was there a huge reluctance to grab her weaponry and stride out into the jungle to do what she was trained to do?

"*Scheisse*," Beckmann breathed again.

She raised herself to her feet and walked over to her sink. Resting her hands on the edge of the sink, she stared at herself in the mirror.

"Maya Music," she called to the room's terminal, "play 'Dogs of War' by Megaton."

The familiar opening of a screeching guitar leading into a perfect cacophony of sound seemed to focus her mind. Staring into her own eyes, listening to the thundering beat, she took a few breaths and pushed aside the weak, pacifistic sentiments invading her thoughts.

"Maya – louder."

The doleful lyrics drowning out her world, Beckmann buckled on her pistol belt and Marreta 0.50 caliber. Her eyes fell on the holographic picture on her dresser. Four figures in neatly pressed blue-gray dress uniforms by an original, 19th Century Krupp field cannon, a picturesque panorama of a blue water bay behind them. The day of their graduation and commissioning as officers in the Strategic Security Division. Her eyes fell on the lead figure. Anna Paligutan, Second Lieutenant. Raven-black hair, pretty, highly intelligent, confident, and charismatic. The natural leader of the group and predicted to go far. Seven years after the photograph was taken, Paligutan was now a major in Strategic Planning and the only one still in contact with Beckmann.

Beckmann pulled on her shoulder holster and slotted in the lighter, 8.5mm TauruSW Ferro; a weapon that handled a suppressor far better than the heavy Marreta. She placed three magazines in the pouches on the opposite side of her shoulder holster as her eyes fell on the second figure on the photograph.

Matthias Brun. A brash risk-taker, jumping between reprimands and accolades on an almost daily basis. Disappeared just under a year ago, rumored to have used his skills and experience to begin a new life with his wife and child. Brun was the only winner in the Hexa game.

Reaching into her secure crate, Beckmann looked through the knife shelf for weapons appropriate to her task. She took out a long, curved blade and attached it to her back. Akalis Commando fighting knife, Mod 2, E/M capable, Kirpan style forty centimeter blade. Her second knife would be her primary choice, as long as she remained undetected. Switech Penna fighting knife. Nineteen centimeter, twin-edged, matte black stiletto blade. Practically ancient in its origins but still un-bested for silent, close-quarter killing. Beckmann slotted the knife into its pouch behind her left thigh pocket.

Beckmann shook her head sorrowfully as her eyes fell on the photograph's third figure. Karl Schrader. Pale, calm, unassuming, calculating, ideally suited to infiltration. Killed in Action during the raid on the Caledonian warship *Glasgow*. Stayed behind with the bomb. Posthumously awarded the PanOceanian Star of Valor in a secret ceremony. Only son of a widowed mother who never found out about his final moments, or the medal.

"Maya, stop."

The music ceased abruptly. Beckmann hauled her light pack onto her back and secured the straps, ensuring her Akalis Commando knife was easily accessible. She picked up her MULTI Sniper Rifle. Nothing more was needed now. She looked at the final figure on the photograph, stood rigidly to attention, cap perfectly straight.

Lisette Beckmann. Second Lieutenant. Nineteen years old. The quiet, studious academic. Graduated top of class, theoretically the perfect trainee operative but attracting doubts from instructional staff over her lack of killer instinct. Went crazy only a few months later and shot up a shopping mall, killing two policemen and allegedly a civilian bystander. Convicted and sentenced to life imprisonment; killed another prisoner within six hours of beginning her sentence. Moved to a maximum security psychiatric hospital. Escaped six months later and spent a year at large as a mercenary and contract killer. Returned to the Strategic Security Division in exchange for a pardon. Murder convictions still under review.

Beckmann turned away from the photo. It was time to go. Her rifle slung over her shoulder, her eyes set in grim determination as all thoughts of anything other than the job in hand were successfully banished, she walked over to the room's exit and flung open the door.

Hawkins stood by the opening, one hand raised and ready to knock on the door that was closed a second before. Clad in the darker shade of Hospitaller combat trousers and a black t-shirt, the same clothing as the day she met him, he looked down at Beckmann. His expression was anxious and uncomfortable as he quickly dragged his black beret off his head. Like a bottle being tipped upside-down, Beckmann felt every last iota of purpose and aggression pour away and disappear. A pain flared up in her solar plexus as if she had been punched. She swallowed and looked down.

"What do you want?" she managed uncomfortably.

"I... I heard you were back, and... well... I thought I should give this back to you."

The aggression would not come back. It was normally so easy to switch on. The thoughtful, idealistic academic that once was barely ever broke through the stifling cocoon of the cold killer that came to be, but now when she needed the hatred and fire, it refused to come. She looked up. Hawkins offered her a pistol in its holster. She recognized it as the one she lost during the fight with the TAG.

"That's it?" she asked quietly. "That's honestly what you've come here to talk about?"

The Hospitaller looked helplessly across at her but said nothing.

"Did you look at the knife, in the car park, like I told you?" Beckmann asked.

"Yes."

"And you saw that it wasn't mine?"

Hawkins nodded slowly.

"Yes."

"And you didn't stop to think that maybe you could come and apologize, instead of offering me a gun?" Beckmann demanded, her voice wavering.

The Hospitaller fell silent again. So many thoughts raced through Beckmann's head. She remembered driving away from him, the tears and the anger, the car skidding to a halt on the edge of the road running around the cliff, and then standing in the beams of light from the headlamps as she heard the engine purring at idle, staring down at the rocks below and contemplating that one last step.

"But you're not sorry, are you?" she whispered.

"Lisette, I... I'm truly, honestly sorry about the way things ended up. It was never what I wanted."

Beckmann ran a hand across her face and nodded. That was not an apology. Not really. That was just saying sorry for how things ended up, not a personal acknowledgement of any sort.

"Right. Right."

She barged her way past and out into the midday sun, the jungle ahead seeming almost inviting in its invitation to swallow her up and exchange the current, heartbreaking awkwardness for the well-known and understood threat of battle. Still the aggression would not come. She turned around again to look up at him, one hand gripping and re-gripping the strap of her sniper rifle.

When she drove away, in the minutes that followed that fight in the car park, she thought of so many things she should have said. Articulate, well-for-mulated things that would have explained how she felt and why she did the right thing in jumping forward to protect the little girl and her father. And Hawkins. She could, of course, say them all now, but what would be the point? The moment was gone. There was no point in trying to describe just how much it took for her to open up as much as she did when they walked toward the car. Just how huge it was to say the things she said about her past.

Beckmann looked down at the holstered pistol again. She felt a tear on her cheek. Now the anger came, at herself, embarrassed for such a display of weakness.

"I didn't want the gun back," she choked, "I wanted the rose."

She took only five paces forward toward the jungle, her blurred eyes set dead ahead, before she stopped again. It was done. That was it, confron-tation dealt with. There was nothing left to say, just a few days of awkward avoidances in the dining hall queue and standing on the other side of Platoon HQ during patrol briefs. Then she would be gone, whisked away to her next fight. She could not let her last words to him be so pathetic as to be about a flower. She turned again.

"The Huntley Mark Eight kicks like a bitch," she nodded at the pistol. "You won't get stoppages, it'll work in any conditions, but it's crude and it kicks. Keep the back of your hand low on the grip."

Already mentally chastising herself for giving advice on handling re-coil to a man who fought in servo-powered armor, but satisfied that this was the best amount of control she could expect from a situation she had never before found herself in, Beckmann turned to face the jungle, stood up straight, and walked away to face the task ahead of her.

Chapter Seventeen

A shrill alarm sounded in Cochrane's earpiece, accompanied by the word 'ALERT' in red in the upper corner of his lens. A second later, the site's attack alarms sounded – a long, drawn out wail. By that point, Cochrane had already sprang to his feet and shot away from the poker table to grab his body armor and Combi Rifle from the corner of the recreation room. Cochrane dialed in to the platoon comlog channel as he hurriedly buckled on his armor. He heard the dull thudding of a HMG from somewhere outside.

"Correct fire! Correct fire! One point left!" Cochrane heard Lance Corporal Reid's voice yell over the comlog channel, the thumping of the HMG more clearly audible in the background from her own microphone.

Hawkins, Cochrane's poker opponent, was also already up on his feet.

"I'm going to go get booted and spurred!" he shouted to the Fusilier sergeant, pointing in the vague direction of the armory where his armored suit waited. "Don't look at my bloody cards while I'm gone!"

Cochrane brought up his tactical map whilst he finished fastening his armor; Numbers Two and Three Sections had perimeter guard duty with Shankar coordinating from the PSC, and Number One Section on standby. The shooting was highlighted red on the northern edge of the map, only a stone throw from the recreation block where he now stood.

"One Section from Zero," Shankar called, "you are activated. Relocate to Marker Alpha."

Cochrane grabbed his Combi Rifle and backed out of the door, bringing up a live feed from Reid's lens. The afternoon was unnaturally windy, with a high layer of cloud denying the normally dependable blue skies and hot sun. Reid, located in one of the defensive bunkers on the northern perimeter, looked out over the long slope of bare scrub land ahead and across the lengths of foam wire as a HMG next to her spat out bursts of fire into the trees some two hundred meters away.

"Correct fire! One point right!" Reid shouted to the gunner. "No, *right*! Bloody hell! Gimme the gun!"

"Zero from Zero-One," Cochrane transmitted to Shankar as he looked across to the bunker on the northern perimeter, "I'm right by Marker Alpha. Confirm you're content for me to move to Alpha rather than meet you at the PSC?"

"Zero-One, move to Marker Alpha and take charge," Shankar replied immediately.

Cochrane sprinted up past the second line of defense, watching as streams of fire spat out of the bunker and obliterated the vegetation at the far end of the cleared ground. He rushed past the shallow trench spanning out to the side of the hastily constructed position and into the cramped bunker. He saw Abby Reid hunched over the bipod mounted HMG, her left hand grabbing the top of the buttstock as she poured fire out of the smoke-filled bunker whilst Greg Pine and a newly arrived Fusilier named Khan stared out of the firing slit. Cochrane rushed over and pushed his way between the two Fusiliers, zooming the weapon sight of his Combi Rifle in to focus sharply on the devastated foliage downrange.

"Greg, grab a missile launcher!" he commanded. "Abby! Mark your target! I can't see what you're firing at!"

"He was right there!" Reid growled between bursts. "I saw the bastard!"

On the tactical map, five blue dots moved alongside the bunker as Lance Corporal Dubois led her own Fireteam from Number One Section up to take position in the trench. The HMG clicked empty.

"Magazine!" Reid yelled, ejecting the empty ammunition container from the underside of the smoking weapon.

"Zero-One from Zero," Shankar called, "sitrep. What are you firing on?"

Cochrane scanned his weapon sight through the debris of the jungle. Broken trees, snapped branches, dust and smoke…

"Abby, hold on a second," he said.

Reid slammed a fresh magazine into the machine gun and cocked the handle to move the first round into position.

"I saw something there!" she snarled, her teeth gritted as she leaned into the weapon and lined her right eye up over the gun sight.

"Lance Corporal! Check your fucking fire!" Cochrane boomed.

"Zero-One from Zero, sitrep," Shankar repeated.

"Just checking, Boss," Cochrane replied over the comlog channel, "holding fire."

"Zero to all units, hold fire, hold fire," Shankar ordered.

A new channel crackled into life in Cochrane's earpiece as he stared into the smoky jungle.

"What have you got, Jim?" Major Barker's gravelly voice asked.

Cochrane zoomed out again. He slowly scanned around the area of destruction and then to either side. Still nothing. He quickly paired his communication channels with Barker and Shankar.

"Alpha-Zero, Three-Zero, from Three-Zero-One," he sighed. "I'm not visual with anything. We've received no enemy fire. I cannot confirm enemy contact. Recommend perimeter sweep."

Reid turned to face Cochrane, her angry determination immediately replaced with despair.

"Sarn't! I saw a…"

"Get back on the gun, digger," Cochrane commanded, "I believe you. Now keep that thing pointing downrange and be ready to fire."

The white-hued smoke slowly dissipated from the stuffy bunker. Reid hugged the HMG into her shoulder and swung the weapon slowly from left to right on its bipod, staring intently to the north. Pine held a missile launcher ready. Khan swallowed uncomfortably and peered around the edge of the firing slit, his face shinny with sweat. Minutes rolled by.

"Jim, it's me," Corporal Garcia called over the comlog, "one of the navy boys has just grabbed me. He wants to know if they should fire up the TAG."

"Bloody hell!" Cochrane growled. "No! That thing's supposed to be secret! Tell those stupid bastards to go back to rum and sodomy, or whatever they were doing five minutes ago…"

"All units, stand down to Alert State Two," Shankar called over the comlog. "Three Platoon to maintain primary perimeter defense. Two Platoon to conduct perimeter sweep."

Cochrane took a step back and nodded.

"Greg, take the gun for a minute," he ordered.

Pine carefully laid the launcher down and took position at the HMG whilst Reid responded to Cochrane's gesture and followed him outside. After the confines of the cramped, smoke-filled bunker, even the muggy, stifling heat of the Paradiso jungle on an overcast day seemed to provide some cool respite. Erin DuBois and her Fireteam knelt in the shallow trench to the left of the bunker, their weapons pointing north. To the west, Cochrane saw a section from Dev Bakshi's platoon advancing cautiously forward toward the northern tree line at the end of the cleared scrubland. He turned to face Reid.

"What did you see?" he asked.

"One guy, I think. Could have been two. I definitely saw movement, and it was the size of a soldier. I zoomed in. The shape I saw, it looked armored. Medium, maybe? I don't know, Sarn't, not for sure."

Cochrane watched as the section from Number Two Platoon reached the outer perimeter and divided into two Fireteams before disappearing into the undergrowth. A second section moved up behind them.

"Well, we'll see, won't we, mate?" He flashed a smile to Reid. "Although I don't think they'll find anything."

The red-haired lance corporal's face dropped.

"You think I imagined it? You think I'm shooting at shadows like a Nod?"

"Dunno, mate," Cochrane answered honestly, "we're all tired. We're all jumpy. Could be that. Or it could be that this has all died down and there's an enemy team out there right now, wanting to know more about how many of us are here and what we're up to. Either way, those diggers out there won't find anything."

Reid tutted and shook her head. Cochrane watched the second team from Two Platoon break off to the left and sweep through to the northwest.

"Who'd you take the gun from?" he asked Reid.

"Khan," she replied, "he's one of the new guys. He can't shoot for shit."

"Why was he on the gun, then?"

"He's done the course," Reid shrugged, "he's qualified. Some of the others aren't."

"Greg's done the HMG course. Get him on the gun until we can get home and get this new guy up to scratch," Cochrane said.

"Shall I run that by the boss?" Reid asked.

"You don't need to run it by the boss," Cochrane replied a little tersely, "I'm telling you."

He brought up Two Platoon's progress on his tactical map as their Fusiliers swept around the base perimeter. Whether Reid was jumpy or there was an enemy team out there, he was still not sure. However, given the number of times he had been in the team scouting an enemy position, he was confident that they would by now be long gone. At best, some evidence of their presence might be stumbled upon, as had happened on the very first day of the Glottenberg Incursion conflict.

Cochrane's thoughts were interrupted as Hawkins strode boldly across toward him. Devoid of his armor, the Hospitaller wore his dark combat trousers with a black t-shirt and beret, and carried a mug of tea.

"Right!" he called across with a merry grin. "I've got an over-sized pistol and a cup of tea. I'm ready for war! What's happening?"

"Mate! Get your bloody head down," Cochrane called across urgently, "we're at Alert State Two!"

"I think you'll find it's Alert State Three," Hawkins smiled and nodded, taking a quiet sip from his mug. "Lieutenant Shankar called that quite a few minutes ago."

"She called State Two!" Cochrane exclaimed.

"Shit!" Hawkins gasped, wide-eyed, dashing over to the cover of the bunker with one hand protectively across the top of his mug.

It was the better part of three hours before the alert state was stood down and off duty personnel were permitted to leave the perimeter. Cochrane walked back toward the recreation block with Hawkins, scratching his beard irritably.

"You think there was anything out there?" Hawkins asked.

"It's not beyond the realms of possibility," Cochrane mused. "Everybody seems pretty fired up about all of this. I'm still bloody dying to know what's in that hub and what this is all about."

"Can't help you there," Hawkins shrugged, inspecting his empty mug with disapproval. "Are we finishing this game?"

"Can't be arsed, mate, if I'm honest," Cochrane remarked. "I might go and do the rounds. See how everybody is. Lots of upside-down smiles around here at the moment."

"Really?" Hawkins put one hand in his pocket and looked pensively down at his mug, as if willing it to re-fill. "I hadn't really picked up on anything."

Cochrane stopped by the bench seats near the stream. The thin layer of cloud high above was breaking up in the late afternoon sun as the first of the perimeter patrols from Number Two Platoon wandered back up toward the inner defenses.

"Come on, mate, you're the worst of the lot," Cochrane said quietly.

"Me?" Hawkins' face contorted in confusion. "What have I done?"

"Simple," Cochrane replied as he took a seat on the closer of the two benches, placing his Combi Rifle down next to him with a clatter, "you stopped moping. It's not about wandering around with a long face and crying all the time. It's about changes in character. You're naturally... mopey. You've been full of life and jokes since you got back from leave. It's like you're trying too hard, mate. So something's up."

Hawkins placed his empty mug down on the bench. He removed his beret, scratched the back of his head, and took a couple of steps away. Cochrane resisted his natural urge to keep talking and watched the pensive younger soldier expectantly.

"I know this must be a terrible cliché," Hawkins said, "but the opening rounds of this... well, the killing quite simply got me down. We were trained for war for four years, and we discussed the morality of taking a life over and over and over again. I found that once I'd done it... well... it's bloody awful. It's all I thought about for days, weeks. You know... moping."

"What changed?" Cochrane asked.

"Leave," Hawkins replied. "I was visited by a senior member of my Order. We discussed things and put them in perspective. Nobody is supposed to like killing, after all. It's just treading that line between knowing you have to react and apply lethal force instantly on one day, and the next day, a different situation might mean that you have to do everything in your power to leave lethal force as the absolute last resort. Nobody ever said I have to like it. I've just got to do it. I mean, it's all died down now anyway. I haven't fired a single shot since we came back. There's only been that poor fellow who trod on the mine. Nothing else has really happened."

Cochrane let out a long, slow breath and stared up at the rapidly growing holes in the clouds above.

"I don't get it," he finally admitted, "you're telling me that you've come to terms with the killing, or at least accepted it, but you're also admitting that you're feeling worse now? Me, I can't say it ever bothered me that much. It started off as just me or the other guy. Now I look up years later and I'm even more desensitized than that. Doesn't bother me, really. Most of 'em... well, some of 'em, get resurrected anyway, so bugger it. Moral dilemma over. Anyway, I'm going on about me again. If the fighting isn't getting you down so much anymore, what is?"

Hawkins folded his arms and rocked back and forth on his heels for a few moments before answering.

"There's this girl..."

"Ah!" Cochrane interjected, suddenly more interested in the conversation than talking about war. "There's always a girl."

"So you've got one in your life?"

"No," Cochrane admitted, "but I did when I was your age. Dozens of 'em. Why d'you think I had to grow this rancid beard? I needed to cover my gorgeous face because even these arms were so stuffed from holding all the women back. Anyway, go on."

Hawkins shrugged again.

"No. That's it, really. There's a girl and the whole thing has got me thinking. About a lot of things."

"Have you apologized?" Cochrane offered.

Hawkins looked across.

"How do you even know if I've done anything wrong?" he demanded.

"I don't, and it doesn't matter. You're a bloke. She's a woman. You need to apologize."

Hawkins nodded slowly.

"I know. I know I do. I was... well, she called me a sanctimonious prick."

"Well, she's got you there, mate!" Cochrane beamed. "I mean, Holy Order knight... sanctimonious prick is what you guys do best."

Cochrane paused for a moment. A few clues seemed to add up. To slot into place. A few admissions, recollections, exchanged glances, explosions of emotion under fire...

"You known her a long time?" Cochrane asked his testing question, keeping his tone easy going and neutral.

"Oh no, not long. Just a few weeks."

Just a few weeks. Just the few weeks he had been attached to Number Three Platoon. The final piece in the puzzle slotted into place. Cochrane looked across at Hawkins, dead in the eye.

"Kyle," he said seriously, pointing a finger into the jungle toward where he knew the Yujingyu forces lay in wait, "are you sure that that woman – keeping in mind everything she has done and is capable of doing – is *the* one you want to fill in that form for your Order and ask for their blessing in pursuing something long term and real?"

Hawkins nodded slowly but with determination.

"Yes. A hundred percent."

Cochrane hopped down from the bench and picked up his Combi Rifle.

"Bloody hell, mate," he shook his head, "then you're as bad as she is. Come on, I've changed my mind. Let's finish that game of poker."

***

"*...and whilst the PanOceanian government claim to be fully open and transparent to O-12 investigations, it is also thought that a thorough and accurate confirmation of the missing border marker in the Glottenberg region may take months. Yujingyu officials continue to accuse the PanOceanian government of dishonesty and stalling for time, claiming that there is clear evidence of procrastination in a thinly veiled attempt to ensure the recently declared MagnaObra research facility, designated 'Alpha Four-Four,' does in fact lie on Yujingyu territory and that all research materials must be surrendered to...*"

Cochrane sat on the bench by the stream and looked up at the crescent moon hanging high in the blue-black sky, the news report quietly droning on in his left ear. The clouds had cleared, and the night was hot and still; even the once irritating chorus of insects hidden in the trees seemed faintly melodic. Number One Platoon now had perimeter duty, allowing his Fusiliers what would hopefully be an uninterrupted night's sleep. Cochrane brought up the timer on his lens. 10:36pm. He regretted that last coffee almost as much as growing the beard.

"Hey."

Cochrane looked over his shoulder and saw Shankar walk over to the benches. She sank down next to him and stared off numbly in the same direction.

"Can't sleep either?" he offered.

She shook her head.

"You're looking awfully thoughtful for a Neanderthal-esque buffoon with no inner monologue or meaningful thoughts," Shankar offered after a few moments.

Cochrane laughed.

"I've got meaningful thoughts, I'll have you know." He grinned. "I just keep 'em to myself."

Shankar reached into her left leg pocket and produced a small, rectangular hip flask neatly wrapped in brown leather. She took a swig and then offered it to Cochrane.

"What is it?"

"Cherry brandy."

"Bloody hell, Priya!" Cochrane whispered. "You're drinking! Out here!"

"One mouthful a night," Shankar shrugged, "just one. Never more. I know people are depending on me and I need to be focused. It's not fair or legal to be anything else. But one mouthful helps."

Cochrane shrugged and grabbed the flask.

"Yeah. Fair enough. Just the one."

He took a swig from the sweet, fiery liquid and handed it back, feeling the pleasant warmth it left in his chest.

"Kyle said you had a long chat with him today," Shankar continued, hiding her hip flask away again.

"Yeah. He's alright. Shame about all the religious bollocks, but I'm a great guy, so I can look past that."

Shankar sighed, shook her head, and planted one elbow on her knee before pressing a palm against her face.

"Religious bollocks? D'you ever stop to wonder why, in an era where we can traverse the stars and resurrect the dead, that the *majority* of people still have a faith?"

Cochrane narrowed his eyes and turned to face her.

"Not you as well. I get enough of this shit from Kyle. I didn't have you down as one of his lot."

"I'm not," Shankar shrugged, "I'm agnostic. It means I'm open to the possibility of a higher power, I'm just not convinced by any one particular faith."

"I know what agnostic means, Priya, I'm an educated man," Cochrane grumbled.

"Define educated?" Shankar smirked.

Cochrane stood up slowly and thrust his hands into his pockets. His taste buds craved another of his trademark, terrible coffees.

"University degree in Military History," he replied, "I passed with a distinction. But I never needed that to work out that there isn't some guy with a white beard watching me from the clouds, and that dinosaurs *did* exist on Earth, even if they weren't written into some book."

Shankar sat on her hands and looked up at him.

"I never knew you had a degree."

"It's been on my service record all the time I've been your platoon sergeant," Cochrane replied seriously, wondering why he had finally admitted to his little known, academic past. "Maybe as your deputy, you should have read my service record at some point in the last year."

He sat back down on the bench again and extended his legs out in front of him, crossing them at the ankles. The talk of his degree reminded him of his last meeting with his father and the resumed pressure to consider applying for a commission as an officer.

"I don't think Kyle is one of those guys, Jim," Shankar said. "I'm pretty sure he believes in dinosaurs and evolution. And even if he doesn't, so what? We've got an alien invasion landed on this very planet and we spend our time fighting each other over politics and belief. Still, in this day and age! Maybe we should all just live and let live a whole lot more... I... look, anyway, Kyle certainly speaks highly of you. Even said you were helping him out with some advice with his disastrous love life. It's why I came to talk to you, actually. I was hoping Jim Cochrane, Romance Consultant, was still open for the day."

Cochrane let out a long, booming laugh. He turned around to face Shankar again. Her lips shared his smile, but her eyes did not.

"Why the bleedin' hell is everybody so serious all of a sudden?" Cochrane chuckled. "Did I miss something?"

Shankar's face became serious again, half shadowed by the moonlight.

"I think everybody is so serious because the end is coming," she said gently, "because of everything we hear. The Yujingyu forces just over the horizon will come here soon. Maybe even tomorrow, I don't know. This will all explode spectacularly any minute now, and we all know it. I think that's why everybody is heightened and on edge at the moment."

Cochrane fidgeted uncomfortably on the bench seat, leaning his folded arms down onto his lap.

"Alright," he said, "what's on your mind?"

Shankar stood up slowly. Her hands clasped loosely at the small of her back, she paced along the edge of the stream for several long moments.

"I think I'm done with this," she finally said.

Cochrane sat bolt upright.

"No, mate, no! We've been through this before! You can't jack it in now! After all you've worked for! This is David talking!"

Shankar shook her head and sighed.

"Him, too, I think," she said quietly, "all of it. I want to start again. I've ended up with a life I didn't want. And I need to change it all before it's too late."

"Priya!" Cochrane jumped up. "C'mon! You're saying that about David because of... I dunno... pre-wedding day nerves. You're saying you want to leave this because, exactly as you've just said, something big is coming! It's just nerves! We've all got them! Well, I don't, but everyone else..."

"I made a mistake on leave," Shankar suddenly declared, cutting him off. "Nothing huge, but it was nearly catastrophic. I haven't told anybody else. I… I can't. On my first night of leave, I talked with David. We had an argument. The same tired argument we have every time. I had a bit to drink and I went out into the city. I… met a guy. We talked a lot. We danced. I saw where it was all going and I stopped things before I did something really stupid. But… it's hard to explain."

Cochrane watched the young woman struggle over her words, suddenly finding himself well out of his depth.

"On the one hand, I danced with the guy," Shankar said, "and I did so without David knowing. I know it won't seem like much to you, but as far as I'm concerned, I did something behind my fiancé's back and I haven't told him. That is disloyal. I'd almost call it cheating."

"Priya!" Cochrane shrugged. "C'mon!"

"But on top of that," she continued, "the real problem is that I was fairly content to go a lot further. I stopped because it was morally wrong. But the very fact that it seemed like a perfectly good way to spend my evening makes me really, truly reconsider my feelings for David. I think that night was a shot across my bows. A warning that I need to stop this whole thing with David before it is too late."

Cochrane stared at her in silence. Shankar nodded to him expectantly, inviting him to speak.

"Oh," Cochrane managed to stammer, "erm… shit."

"That doesn't help me."

Cochrane considered asking for Shankar's hip flask again. He doubted that would help either. Scratching his beard in that same spot just to the left of his chin, he took a few thoughtful paces.

"Priya, we all balls things up from time to time," he started pensively, still with no idea where he was going with the whole speech he found himself making up on the spot, "so, if I were you, I'd just put it behind me. Put it down to stress. Nerves. Whatever. Don't ever tell him it happened. He doesn't need to know. No good will come from him knowing what happened. It was just dancing with a guy. Jeez, I get drunk and make a complete dickhead out of myself on the dance floor with worryingly regularity…"

"But you're not engaged to be married."

Shankar turned her back on him. Even though she stood bolt upright, shoulders straight and stable, he could tell from a mile away how distressed she was. He toyed with the idea of hugging her but figured his noble intentions to be a friend would probably backfire spectacularly.

"Mate," he tried again, "there's two options I see. You either pretend it never happen and move on, or… like you say, you see this as a sign that this isn't gonna work and you call the whole thing off. He doesn't need to know exactly what prompted it. I mean, it's not like you rooted this guy…"

"I can't just lie!"

"Lying and withholding the truth aren't exactly the same. Sometimes it's better to shit-can the boy scout sense of honor and nobility and keep quiet. And as for leaving the Fusiliers? C'mon! What would you do? Have you given it any thought? You're good at this! Can you see yourself working in property management or some shit like that? Priya, they don't make bleedin' action movies about property management! Stay here where you can travel the whole bloody Human Sphere and blow shit up!"

Cochrane looked across and saw Shankar's shoulders tremoring in the combined light of the moons and the security lights of the surrounding buildings. He watched her, saddened and concerned for several seconds, until it dawned on him that she was not crying. She was laughing. The short lieutenant turned back around.

"Of all the people I know, I didn't think it would be you who would manage to make me laugh!" she said before her mirth melted away and she continued. "But I wonder if it is because I've come to you knowing that you will tell me what I want to hear. Not necessarily what is right."

Cochrane shrugged. A speck of rain from an unseen cloud somewhere above dabbed onto the back of his neck. A moment later, another hit his wrist.

"Bugger what other people think, mate," he offered as his final sage words of wisdom, "you've got to go get some sleep. And when you're rested, you've just got to ask yourself whether you carry on with David, or whether this is actually some big warning sign that it's time to pull the pin and throw it away. Only you can make that decision, but do it after a good night's sleep. And for heaven's sake, don't leave the army."

Another droplet of rain landed on Cochrane's face before the rate began to pick up to the gentlest of showers. Shankar walked across to him and patted him on the forearm.

"Thanks, Jim," she nodded, her face a picture of sincerity and appreciation, "you go get some sleep, too. I'll see you in the morning."

***

Tapping on his wrist comlog, Hawkins changed the setting of his room for the third time in as many minutes. Fading the color of the thin carpet into a white sand to accompany the upbeat, tropical blue-green walls of his first selection did nothing. Snow whites to remind him of winter at home was no better. His most recent selection as he lay in his bed, aware that the clock was ticking closer to midnight, was a desert orange-pink floor and sunset red walls in a final attempt to sooth his senses into ignoring the hammering rain than pelted against the roof of his rectangular accommodation block.

Hawkins let out a moan of despair. He sat bolt upright and switched on his bedside light. The orange sand floor and red walls just seemed at odds with the rain more than anything else, confusing his senses rather than easing them into rest. Hawkins stumbled up to his feet and pulled on his combat trousers and t-shirt. After resetting his room's colors to a neutral beige, he spent several minutes pacing the floor as he thought of the best remedy to try to calm himself into a second attempt at sleep. Read a book? Watch a movie? Record a message to send to his family?

The door to his room sprung open. A figure, silhouetted in the darkness of the night outside, stepped in and slammed the door shut behind to muffle the pounding of the rain once more. Hawkins looked across, unable to hide how startled the apparition made him. Beckmann stepped into the center of the room, her face set in a scowl. Her soaked hair dripped down across her reactive overalls, which now powered down and reset to their natural, glossy black material. Faded lines of green streaked across her soaking face, chest, and hands from her trek through the jungle. She lowered her MULTI Sniper Rifle down on the low table in the middle of the room and then peeled her backpack off before dropping it down next to the rifle.

Hawkins, now startled out of his half-asleep state, stared at the soaked, grimy, and armed to the teeth woman warily. He opened his mouth to speak, to say something that he had thought of in his moments alone in the last twenty-four hours, and began to mumble an apology.

"Shut up," Beckmann snapped curtly.

Hawkins complied.

The tall, lithe Hexa operative walked across the floor in front of him, back and forth, her eyes fixed on him like a tiger sizing up its prey. She finally spoke.

"I'm going to do a lot of talking now," she said, her tone as aggressive as her half-closed eyes, "and all you are going to do is listen. Do you understand?"

Hawkins nodded.

"Your answer is 'yes, ma'am'."

"Yes, ma'am," Hawkins replied.

Beckmann folded her arms, her eyes never leaving him for a second.

"I've just come back from a debrief with my tasking authority," she began. "I was sent to do something. Doesn't matter what. It's all the same. Go somewhere and kill some people. Sometimes make it loud, sometimes keep it quiet. I've just told my tasking authority that I killed four enemy soldiers. That was a lie. I haven't killed anybody. I infiltrated an enemy position and I was there, knife in hand, ready to become somebody's fucking nightmare. But I didn't do it."

Beckmann finally broke eye contact, turning to continue pacing as she ran one hand through her dark, rain-soaked hair.

"I was close enough to hear them talking. The Zhanshi, the Tiger Soldiers, all of them. Close enough to hear them talk about boredom, family back home, being afraid of us, all the things normal people talk about. And I stopped and thought... 'why bother? This will all be over in a few days. Do these people really have to die?' So I left something there to make sure they knew that an enemy soldier had infiltrated their position, and I left without hurting anybody."

Hawkins cleared his throat.

"Lisette, I owe you an..."

"Kyle, shut up. I won't tell you again. You see, I wasn't concentrating on my mission. That happens sometimes, things cause distractions. But not like this. I've just had a conversation in my head over and over and over for all the time I was out there. A conversation with you. This conversation. And you are going to listen to everything I have to say, because I will not accept how that last conversation between us ended."

The veteran soldier again paced the floor, leaving the carpet soaked and stained green beneath her booted feet. Her eyes wild with anger and a thousand thoughts, she again ran a hand through her hair and succeeded in smearing streaks of green across one cheek. On anybody else it would look dirty and unkempt. She somehow managed to make it look beautiful.

"You told me about God's forgiveness," she started again, her eyes darting from side to side intensely, "you said that I just needed to ask for it and mean it. And I meant it! I... fuck! I had this planned out! I knew what I was going to say! I... look, I'm sick of being the bad guy! I'm not the fucking bad guy! I am what they made me, I didn't want to be this, and I'm trying to change! And you, you judgmental bastard, you're supposed to forgive me! And you didn't! You didn't!"

Hawkins looked at her pain and anguish with nothing but sorrow and sympathy. Everything she said was true. He had come to that realization himself. He opened his mouth in an attempt to apologize to her again, sincerely and wholeheartedly, but a warning hand came up to stop him.

"You call yourself a Christian," she sneered with contempt, "but... you're one of the zealots. The extremists. You, like me, are what they made you. You don't forgive! You judge! You judge and judge and then judge again! And you shouldn't! You don't have the right! You're barely out of your fucking teens, Kyle! You're twenty-two years old, you've done a few weeks in a war zone, and *you* think you get to judge *me!*"

The last point was emphasized with a clenched fist slamming into the room's tall wardrobe. Beckmann again began pacing. Hawkins watched silently, her anger and frustration remaining firmly in control. She turned to stare at him.

"Ask me something," she suddenly demanded, "ask me something you know I don't want to answer. Ask me something you don't think I should tell you."

"Major, I…"

"Ask me!" Beckmann yelled.

Hawkins watched her cautiously, utterly at a loss of how to deal with the random, incoherent scatter shot of thoughts and emotions that escaped her snarling lips as her wild eyes bored into his. All he wanted to do was apologize. Apologize for not listening to her. For calling her a liar when she had opened up to him. But at that moment all he could do was adhere to her demands.

"How did you die?" he asked quietly.

"Car crash," Beckmann replied, "Henschel GT120. Eight hundred horsepower. They told me at the dealership that I needed to go on a specialized driving course to manually handle a car that powerful without ALEPH traffic control. I told them to go fuck themselves and I signed their safety waiver. Because I knew better. I always know better. To compound things, I even used a Strategic Security operational code on the car to stop any police involvement when I decided to break the speed limit. I lost control and rolled the car over only two miles from the dealership and broke both my legs in the crash. There was an electrical fire from the engine. The filtration still just about worked, so most of the smoke was dealt with. That meant I was conscious for about five minutes while I hung upside-down with two broken legs and burned to death. It's been nearly two years since then, but when I'm scared, *really* scared, I still smell burning."

Hawkins raised both his hands to his mouth.

"Lisette, I'm so sorry."

For a second, a brief moment, those few words seemed to placate her. There was a slight calm. Then the pacing and the staring came back. And then the anger.

"I opened up to you!" Beckmann pointed a finger of accusation. "Just then! I didn't want to, but I did it! Just like I did in that car park when I held your hand! How many dates do you think I go on? Really, how many? Can you even comprehend how important that night was to me? I didn't get to buy pretty dresses and get taken to the movies when I was sixteen! I was learning to slit people's throats and make bombs! My sweet sixteen date night had a ten year delay! It was with you, on that one date! You think… you think I get the chance to do that often?"

Hawkins took an instinctive pace backward as she advanced on him, noting she was still armed with two pistols and a pair of fighting knives. Her blazing rant continued.

"*'Hi Lisette, my name's Bob! I'm a primary school teacher and I help cute kids with finger painting! I like long walks on beaches! What about you?*

283

Well, Bob, funny you should fucking ask! I'm an assassin in a deniable Special Forces unit! Do you know what a V-Op is? It's a Vengeance Operation! When terrorists do messed up, twisted shit, I get sent in to "send a message!" I find terrorists, gut them like a fish whilst they're still breathing, and then hang them by their own innards and leave them for their friends to find so that they get the message: don't fuck with the PanOceanian government! What can I get you to drink, Bob? 'You think that's how it goes down? No! I don't open up to people, Kyle! My head is a wreck! I haven't got much of a heart, but you fucking broke it!"

Hawkins took a step toward her. This time, Beckmann backed away. Again, the finger of accusation came up to point directly at him.

"You knew this," she said quietly, shaking her head in despair, "you knew enough about me. You knew what I was. You shouldn't have let me down like you did. And it hurts more than anybody else has hurt me. And that's because I'm in love with you. And I have to be the one to say it out loud, because even though I know you feel the same, you don't have the fucking spine to say..."

Hawkins grabbed her by both shoulders, pulled her in, and kissed her. Beckmann wrapped both of her arms around his neck and reciprocated. His mind a blur, he held on to her, happy in the knowledge that it was clearly what she wanted and that her hands were well away from her fighting knives. After a long minute, Beckmann finally backed away. She took a few breaths, looked back up at him with angry eyes, and grabbed him by the back of the neck before slamming him painfully into the wall behind him and kissing him again aggressively.

After another long moment, her head slumped down on his shoulder. Hawkins stood back against the wall, holding her as she finally fell silent, her soaking, grimy form pressed against his and her various implements of killing digging into his ribs. The rain eased off. Midnight passed. It was perhaps a quarter of an hour before she finally spoke again.

"I'm not the bad guy," she whispered calmly. "After I drove away, I... I could have gone out in a rage, I could have had any man I wanted. Easily. I didn't. It's not me. Instead, I went to church and I prayed. I asked for God's forgiveness. I'm not the bad guy."

Hawkins held her tightly, his mind whirring as he struggled to process the mass of information she had smashed into him with her explosive, agitated rantings. But honestly was always the best policy. He spoke his mind.

"God will always forgive you. Will you forgive me?"

"Of course I will, you idiot," Beckmann whispered.

Still holding her, still jumping over a thousand mental obstacles as he tried to order his thoughts, Hawkins stared straight ahead. All logic told him that he needed to let go. To push her away, to end anything before it started.

But he had absolutely no interest in logic. There was not even a clash or contest within him. Common sense be damned. He felt the same way she did. After another long silence, she finally stepped back.

"Just tell me," she said quietly, "that we're done with all this confusion, messing around teenaged bullshit. That we're both being honest and that we... the two of us, we're a thing now. We're somehow going to make this work."

Hawkins nodded. After another moment of thoughtful silence, Beckmann paced across the room to recover her pack. She slung it across her shoulder and grabbed her MULTI Sniper Rifle. She looked back at him and smiled.

"This is going to be... difficult," she smirked.

Hawkins finally allowed himself to smile. His only worry was why, after the strangest confrontation in his entire life, he did not feel worried. Her face suddenly devoid of anger and frustration, the negativity now replaced with a serenity mixed with an almost mischievous, slightly embarrassed grin, Beckmann walked back out into the night, carefully shutting the door behind her.

Chapter Eighteen

"I know, I know," Waczek held up her hands defensively and took a step back, "this isn't our fault, Sergeant. But it is our problem. Can you make this problem go away?"

Cochrane grumbled into his terrible coffee, turning his back on the blazing, mid-morning sun as he stared down at the four crates of curved, Combi Rifle magazines and the stacks of boxes of loose 4.5mm ammunition left dumped outside the door of the Platoon HQ block.

"Leave it with me, ma'am," he grunted as the bitter liquid flowed down his parched throat. "I'll get this shit sorted out."

"Thanks, Jim."

"No worries."

Cochrane watched the Company 2IC walk away, finding he suddenly appreciated the figure of the rather masculine-looking woman more than he had ever noticed before.

"Bloody hell, Jim," he shook his head, "you've been out here too long, mate."

Within five minutes of the call he transmitted on the platoon's comlog channel, six Fusiliers stood beneath the canvas sunshade outside the Platoon HQ.

"Ammunition resupply arrived at dawn, so that's good news, isn't it, heroes?" he started with a grin. "Bad news is, those lazy bastards at Battalion HQ couldn't be arsed to put the bloody bullets into the magazines, so we've got to do it. With all of them. The resupply for the entire Company. And they didn't send any speed loaders, so we're doing it manually. So grab a box of bullets and start thumbin' in those hard ones. Don't roll your eyes at me, Nat! Get to work!"

Each of the soldiers sank down to sit or kneel on the plastic grate flooring, grumbling in protest as paper boxes of cuboid, caseless ammunition and bundles of Combi Rifle magazines were handed out. Sitting on one of the supply crates to ensure he sat higher up than any of his subordinates, Cochrane peeled open a box of rounds and set about clicking them into place as the air around him was filled with the dull clunking of loading the magazines.

"Sarn't?" piped up Ty Rand, one of the new replacements who barely looked old enough to have graduated from high school. "The rumor is that patrols are kicking off again. Are we going out again soon?"

"'Fraid not, digger," Cochrane drawled as he finished loading his first magazine – quicker than any of the others, he noticed with satisfaction. "From the command brief this morning, it was made very clear that we are to remain on the defensive. My guess is that if the colonel had his way, we'd be out there now charging headlong at those tricky little bastards, but politically it doesn't look so good back home when the body bags get filmed coming off the ships."

"So we just wait here?" Southee asked glumly. "It's been days."

"Yeah, Nat, we just wait here," Cochrane mimicked a sad voice to mock her. "C'mon, a steely-eyed veteran lance corporal such as yourself should know by now that the light infantry is only one percent bayonet and grenade charges for medals and action movie scripts! The rest of it is thumbin' the hard ones into magazines because some lazy bugger at battalion needed to get home earlier on a Friday and couldn't be arsed."

"It was probably Angus," Greg Pine muttered, "he's a right twat."

"Whatcha doing?" a feminine voice asked from behind Cochrane.

He turned to look over his shoulder and saw Beckmann stood a few paces away, her beautiful features hidden behind sunglasses and a blue-gray field cap. Cochrane's soldiers immediately mumbled a series of greetings to her, varying in enthusiasm from wariness to hero-worship.

"We're bombing up magazines from this morning's supply run, ma'am," Cochrane replied.

"Bombing up magazines manually?" The stunning woman removed her sunglasses and raised one eyebrow. "What is this, World War Two? Do you want some help?"

"If it was World War Two, ma'am, given our respective heritages," Cochrane grinned bitterly, "I wouldn't be accepting your help. I'd be emptying the rest of my Owen gun into your corpse."

Cochrane's smile broadened as he was encouraged by sniggers of laughter from his troops. Beckmann walked over and, planting her hands on her knees, bent down to bring her eyes on a level with his. Cochrane's own eyes were instantly drawn to the plunging neckline of her vest and refused to move.

"Sergeant, my ancestry is German," Beckmann said, "according to what I'm reading on Maya right now, the Owen gun was designed for use in the Pacific Theater against the Japanese. And you're supposed to have a degree in military history?"

Tutting theatrically, Beckmann accepted the laughter from the assembled Fusiliers and stepped past him to grab a handful of magazines and bullet boxes. Halfway between embarrassed, insulted, and aroused, Cochrane watched her sit down cross-legged at the back of the assembled soldiers and set about rapidly clipping bullets into a rifle magazine. The assembly fell quiet again, the silence broken only by the clicking and clunking of round pressed against round within their magazines. Cochrane wondered if any of his soldiers had picked up on the sparkling revelation that he was a college graduate. Or cared.

"Any of you smoke?" Beckmann offered, reaching into the pockets of her combat trousers for her cigarettes.

Cochrane jumped in before any of his soldiers could respond.

"Not around live ammunition, no, Major," he replied coolly.

"Oh," Beckmann shrugged, putting her pack of cigarettes back, "well, I guess we all have a couple of vices here and there."

"Oh?" Cochrane leaned forward. "And aside from smoking, what vices do you have?"

Beckmann stopped and slowly lowered her magazine and handful of bullets. She looked down at her feet, her eyes half-closed in sorrow before then swallowing uncomfortably and looking across to the far horizon.

"There is something," she whispered, her eyes focused far away, "there is one vice."

The assembly fell silent. The clicking and clunking of reloading stopped. All eyes turned to face the veteran Hexa killer.

"It's about the same time every year," she continued quietly, "normally in the middle of spring. You see... well... I should just come out and say it. I watch the PanOvision Song Contest. Every year. I'm a hard rock girl, truly I am, but I just can't help myself. I have this soft spot for retro disco and terrible pop music. I think it's a German thing. I even join in with the voting..."

The rest of Beckmann's exaggeratedly theatrical, hazy-eyed faux-confession was cut off by a chorus of laughter from the assembled Fusiliers. Cochrane shook his head in disappointment at his subordinates as they sycophantically supported the attempt at humor from Beckmann as she shot a sarcastic smile up to him. He could not blame them. Physically, she was utter perfection, down to the last detail. But one had to look past that, at the bigger picture.

The thought reminded Cochrane of an event that happened to him or, more specifically, his older brother Danny, some years ago. The details were not so important, but it culminated in the two brothers being stood in silence just after midnight, looking down at the blazing wreck of Danny's car. The car that Danny had lovingly restored for two years. The car his now ex-girlfriend had set fire to after their break up.

"Jim-boy," Cochrane remembered his older brother saying to him philosophically as they watched the burning wreck, *"there's a lesson here for you. And that lesson is – never put your dick in crazy."*

Cochrane looked back down at his magazine and resumed loading.

"On the subject of music," Beckmann smiled pleasantly, "none of you thought to put anything on whilst you're stuck here, doing this?"

"I've got something on already, ma'am," Pine replied.

"No, I meant socially!" Beckmann shrugged. "You're not creating a geist group so you can all listen to the same thing?"

"I mean, I can..."

"If you're listening to rap, Fusilier, I'll strangle you with my bare hands," Beckmann narrowed her eyes playfully.

"It's alright! I've got this!" Southee beamed. "Here, I've sent you all an invite."

Cochrane's geist alerted him to the invitation, technically against regulations in an operational theater as it was an unmonitored and insecure transmission that could alert an enemy unit. The reality was that the range of the invitation was limited to about ten meters, so Cochrane was happy to let it go. He accepted the invite and immediately winced as the monotonous beat and tinny treble of mindlessly upbeat, retro disco tunes flooded from his earpieces. He immediately turned the volume down by half a step.

"Nat! This is shit!" Pine complained.

"Well, I like it."

"As a point for the future," Beckmann smiled sweetly, "when a Hexa operative asks you to open an insecure channel to your geist and invite her in, don't do it. It's fine now, but when you're a general one day, well, that's how people like me find shit out."

Cochrane frowned as again Beckmann was rewarded with a chorus of laughter from his soldiers. She sat cross-legged, almost exhibiting an air of innocence in her pose in stark contrast to her normal style of aggressive postures, glares, and clenched fists. Why was she so happy all of a sudden? Cochrane did not really care. He was, however, pissed off that she could just waltz into his arena and immediately hold court, captivating all with her every word. Still, he doubted charisma had anything to do with that. Life was probably very, very easy when you had huge tits, a supermodel's face, and were surrounded by testosterone-filled men every day. A few seconds later, he wondered if that was why he found himself turning his proverbial guns around on Southee.

"Nat?! A bloody general?!" Cochrane scoffed. "Pull the other one! She's lucky enough that we trust her with her own gun!"

This time it was Cochrane's turn to be rewarded with a volley of laughter that drowned out the disco classics from three decades before. The humor was shared with him by all but two. Southee glared across, her jaw open and her head tilted to one side. Beckmann's uncharacteristic friendliness and jovial nature was immediately transformed into the more familiar brooding menace as she stared across.

"I don't think that's fair, Jim!" Southee protested as the laughter from her peers died away. "I've done pretty well out here, I'll have you know, and…"

Cochrane, having slept with her twice, felt more than a morsel of sympathy for Southee. However, the combination of the encouragement he felt from the laughter from his soldiers and the challenge to his status he perceived from her using his first name in front of junior Fusiliers pushed him on to continue.

"It's 'Sergeant,' mate!" he boomed with a grin. "And as for you doing 'pretty well,' I guess you've already forgotten about the time you put a round through the company commander's Uro when you dropped your bloody rifle!"

Southee's face flushed red as she turned away, falling silent as the hollers of laughter from the other Fusiliers grew louder. Satisfied that he had defended his position as alpha male of the pack and put down the challenge from his subordinate in its infancy, Cochrane clicked the last round into his magazine and grabbed another.

"Yeah! You all bloody listen in, ya bunch o'pricks! I'm the fackin' big dog here! Look at the color of my hat, digger! Look at the Indigo bloody hat! Yeah?"

Cochrane's head shot up as an explosion of laughter greeted the booming impersonation of him. His teeth gritted, he stared around angrily to suppress this new, more insulting display of insubordination. Her chest puffed out patronizingly as her head wobbled from side to side as if impersonating an imbecile, Beckmann let fly with another round of insults.

"Check out the arms, ladies! Check out those fackin' guns, yeah! I'm not a gym queen, digger! Who told ya I'm a bloody gym queen?! Look at the Indigo hat, yeah? I've done... count 'em now... *five* real missions, yeah? This one time, some bugger actually shot at me, like, for real, so you respect the Indigo hat!"

Cochrane glared at Beckmann, watching her exaggerated parody of his accent, his diction, even the way he carried himself physically. His soldiers stared between Cochrane and Beckmann, bellowing in laughter.

"You think you're pretty funny, do..." Cochrane growled.

"You think you're pretty funny, do ya, yer kraut bitch!" Beckmann interrupted loudly, still imitating his accent perfectly. "Bugger off, ya bloody dill! I'd come over there and whack that smile off yer face right now, but I can't stop checkin' ya out, and I don't know what I wanna bang first! Yer big tits or yer little arse!"

Cochrane knew he was defeated. Even he could tell the impersonation of him was perfect which, coupled with Beckmann's rank and the automatic popularity that came with five young men desperate to impress her, resulted in him being outgunned on every level. Any response he gave would at best be seen as bitter and petty; at worst could easily be turned into a charge of insubordination with plenty of witnesses to back it up. Conversely, accusing her of rank-bullying would make him a laughing stock.

The sly, predatory grin Beckmann flashed at him confirmed that she knew all of this, too. That was when the penny dropped for Cochrane – that was the whole point. That was exactly what he had done to Southee only minutes before. Bravo, Hexa psychopath, you have proved your point.

Cochrane looked around in bitter disappointment as his soldiers demanded more impersonations from her merrily. They, of course, did not have the experience to realize that she was not an expert at adopting accents and different personas as a humorous party trick for laughs. It was all there to become a different person to enable infiltration and killing. Ignoring the continuing laughter and jovial conversation, Cochrane silently turned away and set about silently loading a new magazine.

***

From the small, raised knoll a few meters away from the Platoon HQ block, Shankar looked across the scrub ground at where Lieutenant Hunar Juthani and his sergeant, Jane Fletcher, set about inspecting the weapons and equipment of Number One Platoon. The thirty-five Fusiliers stood informally in their Fireteams as their commanders walked amidst them, checking the weapons and webbing of the newer soldiers whilst pausing quickly to exchange a few words with the more experienced. The late afternoon sun hung low in the clear sky, casting long shadows over the yellow-orange dust of the scrub ground. The heat seemed no less bearable than when the sun was at its zenith at midday.

"You okay?"

Shankar turned and saw her company commander, Major Barker, walking across to her from the Platoon HQ building. The short, wiry soldier scratched at his graying moustache and stopped next to Shankar, looking across at where one of his three platoons finalized its preparations for their patrol.

"You think they'll actually go, sir?" Shankar asked. "Will we get the order?"

The latest update at the midday command brief had been vague at best. Intelligence reports indicated that there was a viable possibility of a full scale Yujingyu assault on Alpha Four-Four. Number One Platoon had been stood up, ready to move out into the jungle to act as a first line of defense whilst Numbers Two and Three Platoons would remain behind to protect the site itself. It was not the first time this threat had been relayed on to them by the battalion intelligence officer. However, judging by the atmosphere in the brief, this time it appeared that Barker was taking it significantly more seriously.

"I think we'll find out very shortly," he replied, his eyes still fixed on his soldiers as they prepared to depart.

Shankar wiped a bead of sweat off her temple. As she had vocalized to Cochrane only the day before, fighting between the various squabbling factions of the Human Sphere – ridiculous thought it seemed, given the threat to humanity's very existence posed by the EI – was relatively common. Yet, for whatever reasons, the 12th Fusilier Regiment never found itself in the fighting.

For years, Shankar had watched with envy as friends of hers from her initial training at the Aquila Officers' Academy on Neoterra had been whisked away to see real combat, sporadic though it most often was. At the same time Shankar took part in training exercises, ceremonial guard duties or, at best, disaster relief operations. Now, with the Glottenberg Incursion reaching its climax, she found herself realizing how lucky she had been to be safe for so long.

"You look thoughtful," Barker observed.

Shankar felt a pang of guilt flare up suddenly, as if her commanding officer somehow knew about her inner turmoil over her engagement and her career in the Fusiliers. She quickly dismissed the irrational thought.

"I think they're coming here," she admitted, "the Yujingyu. I know that sounds a bit... alarmist, but I can't see how they can stand by any longer. They know we're stripping this Cosmolite of all its worth with every day that passes. They know O-12 is limited in its power. I think they're on their way."

Barker nodded slowly.

"You and I both, Priya."

"A funny thing occurs to me," Shankar found herself blurting out, surprising herself with her uncharacteristic display of verbalizing her inner thoughts, "well, not funny. That's not the word. This will all be over soon. It's been... hectic. Full on. I've just realized that in all of the fighting that my platoon has been involved in, I've only actually shot one enemy soldier."

Barker glanced across at her, one eyebrow raised.

"How many should you have shot by now?" he queried, his tone disapproving.

"No, sir, that's not what I meant! I mean..."

"Remember the basics, Priya. Your job is the same as it has been since the likes of you and I stood in line with a saber instead of a Combi Rifle. Lead the platoon. Direct their fire onto the enemy accurately and efficiently. Your weapon is for self-defense."

Shankar closed her eyes and exhaled through her nose. Her jumble of words had come out all wrong. That was not what she meant at all. It was not the number of enemy soldiers she had killed, or lack of. It was the absence of... feeling. The void of remorse or pensiveness. She knew of the more gung-ho types – the Cochranes of the company – who seemed to believe that killing another human being only proved that you were stronger. She also knew of many who dwelled uncomfortably on the thought. But for her? In her mind, they were all volunteers. Not a single conscript among them. They knew what they signed up for. Killing was unpleasant but necessary. No need to ruminate on it, it was their job. She just found herself questioning her own morality that it did not have any effect. It did not move her one bit.

"You'll miss this, when it's over," Barker said, rescuing her from her self-doubt.

"Sir?" she queried.

The older man flashed a friendly grin.

"Platoon command. You'll be a captain soon enough. After this whole incursion debacle, I wouldn't be surprised if they make you an acting captain until your substantive rank comes through. You'll be a company second in command, and then onward and upward, and you'll never have your own platoon again."

Shankar stopped. She had not thought of that either. She spent a few moments to examine that thought. Did it really matter?

"Platoon commander was the most rewarding job I ever had," Barker continued, "you're there, full of enthusiasm and in the prime of your life, only half an idea of what the hell to do and with thirty pairs of eyes looking at you to make decisions. When you move up to company level, thirty becomes about a hundred, and all of a sudden there aren't enough hours in the day to get to know everybody. Not properly. Not the way they deserve. It's not the same. It's not the same as trudging through the snow to check on your lads and lasses, making sure they're all hanging in there, knowing each and every one of them and the right thing to say to them. You'll miss platoon command, Priya. I know I do."

Shankar looked down, deep in thought. She looked around at the gently sweeping hills hidden beneath the endless, ever-present canopy of dense vegetation. The hot, thick air, the persistent dust and insects, the trickle of the beautiful streams cutting through the jungle. Was this really a moment she would remember forever? A stamp in time she would look back on as an old woman, showing her grandchildren some ageing footage of her as a young, energetic and brave leader of soldiers in some long forgotten war? Was the Glottenberg Incursion a defining moment she would cling to from here on, those handful of weeks of terrible violence in the idyllic paradise of Norstralia, where she found her courage and faith in herself?

Barker's face suddenly hardened. He pressed a hand against one earpiece. He nodded several times before speaking.

"Alpha-Zero, copied."

Barker turned to Shankar, his drawn face grim.

"Lieutenant, get your platoon closed up and on the perimeter. The Yujingyu advance has started. I'm ordering the evacuation of all civilian and-non essential personnel."

***

The jungle sky looked like it did on most other nights. Clear with a blanket of twinkling stars scattered across the purple-blue, punctuated in only a few places by thin, wispy clouds above the undulating spread of green tree-tops. Hawkins leaned against the wall of his accommodation room, staring at the clear image projected onto the alloy in front of him from one of the perimeter cameras, as clear as if the wall of the block was actually a long window. His sword, pistol, and MULTI Rifle lay on the low table in the middle of the room. The chest plate of his armor lay by the door. Number Three Platoon had been stood down some six hours after assuming perimeter guard duty along-side Number Two Platoon, once news came through that the Yujingyu advance through the jungle was painfully slow. Flights had come and gone for hours, ferrying out all of the research staff and their possessions. Hawkins let out a breath and shook his head. Number Three Platoon had been sent to 'get some sleep' before the attack. He doubted whether anybody would manage even a minute of that.

Looking back up at the stars, Hawkins quickly found himself lost in thought again. He remembered something his older brother, Nathan, once said to him as a child:

'Light takes so long to reach us, you know, Kyle? Even though it is so fast! You see all those stars? They're not there. They're dead. Gone. The light leaves those stars and takes thousands and thousands of years to reach us. By the time you see it, entire planets all the way up there have seen evolution, the rise and fall of a thousand civilizations, and then death. Everything up there, it's all gone now. You're just seeing a ghost of what once was.'

Hawkins remembered how angry their parents were when he told them what Nathan said. A clear attempt to upset his younger brother, knowing full well how thoughtful and overly sensitive he was. Nathan came back later, having been forced to apologize.

'Two guys were arguing at school today. One said that science has proven everything about the birth of stars, even the birth of the universe. We know how it all started. So there can be no God. It's just some outdated belief that idiots cling to, even though we've got science now. Anyhow, the other guy says that we know what started the universe and we know it didn't come out of nowhere. It needed something to cause the bang. And somebody must have put the exact amount of what was needed in the right place to make that happen. And that's how he knows there is a God. Anyway, Kyle, I thought it was cool. Thought it might cheer you up. Sorry for what I said.'

Hawkins looked over his shoulder as he heard the door to his room open. Beckmann took a step inside, offered him a warm smile, and then shut the door before tossing her field cap onto the table and walking over to him. She stood behind him and wrapped one arm around his waist, resting her chin on his shoulder.

"You lost in thought?" she asked quietly.

Hawkins smiled and placed a hand on top of hers. Twenty-four hours ago she was pacing this very floor whilst shouting at him in a confused, seething rant. Then he kissed her, and then a whole day passed by without them crossing paths. Yet now here she was, an arm around him as if they had been together for years.

"I'm just overthinking things," he admitted.

"By way of a change."

"Yes, by way of a change."

The two looked out in silence at the stars above the eastern horizon where, somewhere amidst the dark trees, the Fusiliers of Number One Platoon were dug in lying in wait as the first line of defense against the Yujingyu attack.

"Those bastards," Beckmann whispered, "attacking tonight. I had plans for tonight."

"What plans?" Hawkins asked.

Beckmann walked over and sat on the edge of his bed, her folded arms resting across her lap.

"Well," she smiled uneasily, "you know that Shankar and I don't get on so well?"

"Everybody knows that, I think," Hawkins leaned back against the wall.

"Yeah… I've got a smoke grenade in my room. I took a copy of her biometric data so it's signed out in her name. You see, every night at about the same time, she goes for a walk around the perimeter. Lost in thought whilst she plans how she will become a colonel before she is thirty, I guess. Anyhow, there's a small, blind spot in the surveillance devices about halfway along the western perimeter line…"

Hawkins' eyes widened.

"Lisette! What are you telling me exactly?"

"Just… I was going to slap a smoke grenade on her belt, activate it, and then push her in a trench."

"Lisette! You can't do that!"

"Stop worrying! I've checked the spot, there's no way I could be seen. The grenade is signed out to her. There's no way I would be caught."

"That's not the point!" Hawkins exclaimed. "This isn't some teen movie hilarious prank! In that moment she looks down and sees a grenade flashing on her belt, about to detonate, she won't know it's only smoke! In that moment, she will actually think she is about to die!"

Beckmann's face lit up with a dark grin as she nodded enthusiastically.

"*Ja!* That's the whole point! She'll *know* I could have killed her if I wanted to. And gotten away with it, because it looks like she tripped. She'll know I can do whatever the fuck I want and that she needs to back right off giving me a hard time."

Hawkins swore under his breath and pressed one hand against his face. He took a breath and walked over to sit next to her. He had had days to think about this. Just as she said, he knew exactly what she was. There was no point in losing his temper.

"Lisette, you can't do shit like that. You're not getting one up on a rival. You're risking serious psychological harm to her."

"Like I care," Beckmann shrugged. "I was a good kid before I got shoved in the military preparatory school from hell. A friend of mine killed herself next to me when we were thirteen. It fucked me up. I still see her sometimes, like a ghost. I hear her talking to me in my head. Since then, I've lost count of how many head injuries I've had and how many traumatic experiences have left me as a complete psychological disaster. So, if life threw that at me when I was a pretty good, sweet kid, tell me why I shouldn't give a nightmare or two to some bitch who lacks even a single redeeming feature? Who said life is fair?"

"Because you told me you weren't the bad guy," Hawkins replied slowly, carefully planning his words, "and just because life isn't fair doesn't mean we can't try to make it as fair as possible for others. But as for those things you mentioned... maybe we should be spending more time talking about what help we need to get for you. You can't carry on with all of this weighing you down. It's alright to ask for help."

Beckmann glared across at him, hugging one leg and resting her chin on her knee.

"I can't decide if you're being a sanctimonious prick again, or if you're right. I think it's both."

Hawkins offered a passive smile and shrug.

"So... you're not going to frag Lieutenant Shankar with a smoke grenade? And you'll think about getting somebody to help you with these things going around your head when we get out of here? You're not the bad guy, remember?"

Beckmann narrowed her eyes and smiled mischievously. She slid over to straddle his lap, wrapping her arms around the back of his neck.

"I never said I was good, either," she shrugged, "and I never told you what else I had planned with these next few days."

Hawkins noticed her lack of a response to both of his questions. However, his willingness to lecture from his lofty moral pedestal melted away with his resolve and he returned Beckmann's kiss as she leaned in against him. Unanswered questions and outstanding issues of real importance raised in their conversation over the last few minutes still failed to push him into stopping her and saying something. They melted away into insignificance. Perhaps as long as ten seconds of his perfect moment were allowed to transpire before fate intervened and she backed away.

"I've got to go," she whispered, tapping her wrist mounted comlog. "I've… just been activated. I've got to go."

Beckmann stood up and grabbed her field cap from the table.

"You're… you're going out there?" Hawkins exclaimed as he snapped out of his trance, pointing out to the jungle as he shot to his feet.

Beckmann shook her head.

"Then what is it? You've been sent away from here? You're leaving Paradiso?"

"No, I'm not going anywhere," Beckmann replied quietly.

Hawkins froze in place. Pieces slotted slowly together. If she was not going anywhere, the operation she had been activated for had to be right here. At Alpha Four-Four. The timing… the distraction of the fighting in the jungle would drag all attention outside the perimeter. Leaving her free to do something inside for Strategic Security. Hawkins felt his pulse racing as he mentally mapped out a dozen questions from the last few weeks and one potential answer. He looked across at her.

"The night I went into the research hub with Jim Cochrane," he asked, "was it you in there? Were you the intruder?"

The Hexa assassin looked across at him coolly. An uneasiness broke through her normally stoic veneer.

"I'm going to make you a deal, right now," Beckmann folded her arms, "and here's my part. From this second onward, I will never lie to you. Ever. Under any circumstances. But I want something in return."

Hawkins watched her warily, the unease that seemed to rise up within him in every encounter with her now rearing its ugly head once more.

"You want the truth from me?" he asked hesitantly.

Beckmann burst into laughter.

"Don't be an idiot! I knew within about ten seconds of meeting you that you are completely and utterly incapable of lying. That's one of the main things that attracted me to you. No, I know I've already got the truth from you. What I want is your trust. I don't have the luxury of fighting with God's cross on my uniform. I do dark and dishonest things. So I want you to trust me that if you ask me a question and I tell you that you might not want to know the answer, it's because I don't think you need to know and I think knowing some things will put you in a difficult position. A position where you might have to report things to your Order that you shouldn't know. Is that a deal?"

Hawkins met her stare, watching her as she held her hands out to either side. He ran back through what she had told him. He thought on her words and the implied threat behind them.

"Was it you in the research hub that night?" he repeated. "Were you the intruder I went in to stop?"

"Yes," Beckmann replied simply, "I had orders to infiltrate the installation and copy the research data. There were suspicions that MagnaObra were withholding information from the government. I was sent to transmit information from their main data drive."

Hawkins winced and let out a breath. Now he knew. She was entirely correct. That truth did put him in an awkward situation. Did he have to report this to his chain of command at the Order? Was he duty-bound to raise the alarm? He stopped and thought on the wording of his mission. Assist the Fusiliers in defending Alpha Four-Four. So surely his loyalty was to the PanOceanian Military Complex and not to MagnaObra? Surely, if anything, he should be supporting the Strategic Security Division with his silence? Yet the idea of that did not sit well. Not at all.

"Why did you hurt that scientist?" Hawkins demanded. "Why was that man unconscious?"

"Because he was in my way and my tactical controller directed me to kill him," Beckmann answered, taking a tentative step forward, "and I wouldn't do that. I never would. In all the time I've been doing this, I've only ever killed two types of people. One: those who present a threat to me or the people I'm sworn to protect. Two: people who fucking deserve it. Those scientists in there are neither, so I would never kill them."

Hawkins inhaled deeply and then let out a long, slow breath. He nodded.

"Alright. I… jeez. I'm getting less and less shocked by these conversations. Like you said, I know what you are. It's not my place to judge. So, do you know what they've got in there? Do you know what this, the Yujingyu interest, the PanOceanian delaying, O-12's intervention… do you know what this whole mess is all about?"

Beckmann tilted her head to one side.

"A little. Enough, yes. I don't do the whole information technology thing. I'm no hacker. I do infiltration and I do killing. They have to talk me through the data transfer. But yes, I've seen enough during that. I know roughly what this is all about. Kyle, I don't think it would do you any good to know. I don't think you should ask me."

Hawkins nodded again. He had pressed the metaphorical test button on her deal to see if she would tell the truth, and it certainly seemed as though she was. It felt as though trusting her as she had asked was the right thing to repay her honesty. On the surveillance image projected onto the wall to their side, the eastern horizon flashed white, accompanied by a brief rumbling like thunder. Hawkins and Beckmann both turned to watch as another flicker of white danced along the horizon. It looked somehow beautiful, like distant fireworks in celebration or the simple majesty of nature in a thunderstorm.

But from the location, it could only be one thing. The detonation of munitions as the Fusiliers of Number One Platoon came into contact with the advancing Yujingyu forces in the jungle. Those beautiful flashes were all that could be seen of the explosions miles away that signified death and destruction in the fight that was edging closer to them.

"I've got to go," Beckmann said again, "they'll activate you any moment now. Get what rest you can because when the fight gets here... look, just hold your position and do your job. No hero shit. Just get through this in one piece."

Beckmann kissed him again and walked over to open the door. So that was it. She was off to do something in the research hub that he knew he should not ask about whilst the war marched inevitably toward him. And he had no idea when he would see her again. Hawkins suddenly found himself taking an instinctive step after her, desperately blurting out the first words that jumped to mind.

"Lisette! Look... last night. You told me you loved me and I didn't say it back."

Beckmann let out a laugh and shook her head.

"Kyle, I've known you've been in love with me for a long time now. You didn't need to say it. But when you look this hot, you make a man work for it. Now keep your head down, no action movie heroics, and get through this in one piece. If you die out there, I'll fucking kill you."

Hawkins' comlog transmitted a message to him as the door to his room closed. He checked his lens. Number Three Platoon had been activated and ordered to return to the perimeter defenses.

Chapter Nineteen

"Hold your fire! Three-Zero! Tell your shooters to hold your fire!" Shankar heard Sergeant Fletcher's hoarse, breathless voice yell over the comlog channel. "I'm inbound to your position! I've got wounded and we've got three soldiers with no IFF! Hold your damn fire!"

"One-Zero-One from Three-Zero," Shankar acknowledged as she stared out of the bunker's narrow firing slit toward the eastern edge of Alpha Four-Four's firing lanes, gunfire still echoing through the trees ahead, "acknowledged, we're holding fire and you are clear to approach through my Marker Delta. Get your platoon through the safe gate and into..."

"Three-Zero, I'm not bunching up my entire platoon into one area!" Fletcher yelled, the booming of gunfire and explosions audible through the sergeant's own microphone. "I need you to hold fire along the entire line until we're in!"

Shankar glanced across the cramped bunker interior, past the two soldiers from Number One Section to Cochrane. The veteran soldier issued a simple shake of the head.

"One-Zero-One, negative," Shankar ordered calmly, "we've got inbound enemy units on all sides, and I'm not compromising an entire line of defense. Do not allow your soldiers to run back here in a disordered panic. You are to regroup your platoon and conduct an organized withdrawal via the safe gate at Marker Delta. If you have soldiers with no IFF who attempt to run at my defensive line outside the safe gate, they may be fired upon. Confirm you understand my instructions?"

A loud explosion thudded from the dense jungle ahead, followed moments later by plumes of gray smoke wafting up into the morning sky through the canopy of green.

"One-Zero-One, copied," Fletcher replied.

Shankar brought up her tactical map again to update her markers. Against Cochrane's advice to coordinate her half of the base's defensive perimeter from the safety of the centrally located PSC, she had taken her command team to one of the support weapon bunkers. She stood with Cochrane behind two soldiers from Sahal Kotal's Number One Section – Fusiliers Weber and Brooks – whilst Hawkins and Mieke crouched in the cover of the trench outside with the remainder of the section.

"All units from Zero," Shankar spoke over her own platoon's channel, "we've got friendly forces inbound to our position, in contact with the enemy. Multiple IFFs are US. Safe gate is Marker Delta. Do not fire upon any unidentified target in Marker Delta. Any other targets outside safe gate may only be fired upon once you have visual confirmation."

302

"Bloody hell!" Cochrane grumbled. "Jane Fletcher should know better than asking to charge headlong over the perimeter in a blind panic, with enemy soldiers snapping at her heels!"

Shankar peered through the bunker's firing slit again as two figures appeared at the edge of the jungle, highlighting in blue on her lens as their friendly IFF transmissions were detected. She heard a soft click in her earpiece as she was hailed on a separate channel.

"Three-Zero from Alpha-Zero," Major Barker called, "I've monitored your exchange with Number One Platoon. Bring them back in through the safe gate and keep your people switched on to anything else along the perimeter. Also, be advised that battalion intelligence reports that our location has been hit by an orbital targeting beam. We may be getting measured up for an artillery bombardment. How copied?"

Shankar shook her head as she watched the first two Fusiliers from Number One Platoon sprinting through the safe gate she had designated and across the open ground in front of the base's firing lanes, between the lines of cutting foam and toward safety. An artillery bombardment was something she had never experienced before, but academy training had instilled a deep fear backed up by multiple combat simulations. She looked across at Cochrane.

"It's the boss," she tapped her earpiece, "says we've been hit by an orbital targeter. Possible artillery strike coming our way."

The tall sergeant recoiled in confusion and shook his head.

"No, I don't think so. They want this place intact, it doesn't make sense. I think it's far more likely to be setting up a..."

Cochrane's opinion was cut off when simultaneously a red warning flashed in the section status bar on the side of Shankar's lens, and the distinctive thud of a HMG sounded from outside the bunker. Her eyes wide with alarm, Shankar quickly identified the offending section and opened a channel to their leader.

"Two-One from Zero!" she snapped at Corporal Garcia. "Cease fire! Cease fire! We've got friendly units coming in through the safe gate!"

"Zero from Two-One!" Garcia responded. "I have visual confirmation of enemy heavy infantry probing our position! My support team is firing on Marker..."

Number Two Section's leader's words were cut off by the unmistakable blast-hiss of a missile launcher being fired in close proximity of Garcia's microphone. A second later, Shankar saw a white trail dart out from the trenches to her right and shoot across the open ground before thumping into the edge of the jungle and exploding. A second HMG opened fire from the left, glowing tracer rounds sweeping across the cleared firing lane. Shankar quickly directed a feed from Garcia's lens and overlaid it onto her own. She watched as the stocky corporal turned to boom out a series of orders to his two teams before then turning back to stare across the firing lane, zooming in at the jungle edge beyond it.

Darting out from the edge of the trees, Shankar saw two figures in the bulky, orange-yellow armor of Yujingyu Invincibles. As if proving a need to live up to their name, two HMG rounds slammed into the second of the two soldiers and knocked him to the ground. The heavy infantryman was back on his feet a moment later, recovering his Boarding Shotgun and dashing forward with only two smoking smears of black on his armor to show for the experience. A second pair of Invincibles appeared at the jungle edge behind him. Shankar checked the markers set up by her two section leaders and, content with the accuracy of their positions, opened a channel to all of her units.

"All units from Zero, enemy units confirmed at Markers Echo and Foxtrot. At those markers, you are weapons free, weapons free."

The bunkers and trenches spanning out to either side of Shankar opened up in a deafening roar of Combi Rifle and machine gun fire.

***

Supporting his left forearm on the edge of the trench, Hawkins pulled the butt of his MULTI Rifle into his shoulder and lined up his shot. Zooming in with his scope, he saw another Fireteam of Terracotta Invincibles advancing quickly from the tree line toward the base's perimeter. He led his target by a pace and fired. His first shot missed altogether whilst the second succeeded only in winging the Yujingyu soldier's hip. A moment later, rounds from Fusilier Pine's HMG blasted into the Invincible, gunning him down bloodily.

The first two Fusiliers from Number One Platoon were over halfway to the comparative safety of the inner perimeter now whilst another group of their comrades appeared at the safe gate ahead of Shankar's bunker. Spread out to either side of Hawkins in the shallow trench were the Fusiliers of Number One Section, the two teams of soldiers continuously firing at the advancing enemy forces as they appeared from the dense jungle. Hawkins lined up his sights for another shot on a new target, holding his breath and waiting patiently for the soldier to leave the cover of an immense tree trunk whilst the overwhelming display of firepower from the PanOceanian defensive line continued to hammer away. The Invincible shot forward out of cover, and Hawkins fired a burst of armor penetrating bullets into the enemy soldier's gut, sending him crumpling to the ground.

Another missile whooshed out from the bunker to Hawkins' left, the thin smoke trail rapidly spewing out in the wake of the deadly projectile before it impacted the ground in the midst of the Yujingyu positions. A loud explosion sounded even above the din of gunfire and dark gray smoke blossomed up from the impact point. Hawkins switched his helmet visor's visual filter to infrared and saw another pair of Invincibles moving up through the smoke, hunkered down low over their Combi Rifles. Hawkins fired a single shot and then heard the MULTI Rifle's bolt lock back to signify his magazine was empty. He dropped down beneath the lip of the trench and pulled the empty, curved magazine out of its housing ahead of the pistol grip and tossed it aside before grabbing a replacement from his webbing belt. Sporadic exchanges continued across the platoon's comlog channel as he reloaded his rifle.

"One Section! Targets front, Marker Echo!"

"Deac! Get a missile on Foxtrot! They're bunching up!"

"Shit! Shit! Those bastards have got a HMG!"

The dull crump of an explosion sounded from only a few yards ahead, shaking the ground and showering Hawkins with dry clumps of earth and sand. Even without the clarity provided by his helmet's augmented hearing, Hawkins recognized the now familiar cracks of bullets flying over his head as they broke the sound barrier. He fed the fresh magazine into his MULTI Rifle, checked it was secure, and then released the working parts forward to chamber the first round before clambering back up to peer over the edge of the trench.

***

"Three-Five from Zero-One," Cochrane opened a private channel with Lance Corporal Southee of Number Three Section's support team. "Nat, watch your HMG. Your man is burning through ammunition at twice the rate of our other gunners. You need to grip him, mate."

"Three-Five, copied," the simple response filtered through Cochrane's earpieces above the constant backdrop of gunfire.

He zoomed out on his tactical map, his back pressed against the wall of the bunker to one side of the firing slit, checking the situation faced by Number Two Platoon defending Alpha Four-Four's western perimeter. They, too, were now in contact with the enemy, their own HMGs firing into the edge of the jungle as teams of Zhanshi advanced toward the base to complete a full encirclement.

"Stoppage!" Henning Weber, Number One Section's HMG gunner, shouted out as he removed a magazine from the smoking, bipod mounted weapon. Shankar crouched at the back of the bunker, fighting through the requirement for a constant flow of communication with both her own platoon and Company HQ, whilst Fusilier Brooks lined up her missile launcher through the firing slit. That left only Cochrane to keep a flow of fire on the enemy whilst Weber fought through clearing the jam in his HMG.

Cochrane pushed past Weber to squeeze himself against the firing slit, pushing his Combi Rifle through and quickly picking out one of the heavily armored Terracotta Invincibles to the northeast, at the edge of the outer perimeter. There were perhaps a dozen of the Yujingyu heavy infantry in plain view now, using what scant cover there was at the edge of the base to fire across at the Fusiliers in the trenches or down into the cleared firing lane where the survivors of Number One Platoon struggled to reach the safety of the base's inner perimeter.

Cochrane picked out a target – an Invincible whose position was already being pelted by at least two other Combi Rifles from the firing line – and fired a short, controlled burst. His firing was accurate, but at this range he saw only puffs of dust kicking up around the enemy soldier; whether he was hit or not, Cochrane could not tell, but certainly nothing was penetrating the thick armor of the Invincible.

A second later, Cochrane's entire world was lit up in a brief flash of yellow, and he felt a familiar blast of heat against his face. A missile streaked out from ahead of the bunker and shot into the Invincibles, exploding in the enemy positions and throwing one of the heavy infantrymen through the air as if he were a rag doll. Cochrane turned to look across at Jan Brooks.

"Good shot, digger, but remember to bloody well tell me when you're firing, alright?" He grinned briefly before returning to his Combi Rifle.

"Yes, Sarn't!" The young soldier stammered as she quickly loaded another clip of micro-missiles into the launcher. "Sorry, Sarn't!"

"How's that stoppage coming along?" Cochrane shouted back to Weber as he fired off another burst toward yet another team of Invincibles emerging from the jungle.

Any response was interrupted by a colossal bang above Cochrane's head, the force of the explosion jolting the ground itself and forcing him to fling out one hand against the wall of the bunker to stop himself from falling. Cochrane's hearing faded to nothingness the briefest of moments after the impact as the active noise cancellation of his earpieces filtered out the harmful noises around him. Dust fell down in plumes from the bunker's low ceiling above. The sounds of battle fading back into life just as quickly as they had faded away, Cochrane heard Shankar's voice shouting orders over the comlog channel as he leaned into his Combi Rifle and fired another burst at the advancing enemy infantry.

"These deployable bunkers won't stand up to missiles for long!" Cochrane warned Shankar across a private channel. "They're not like the proper ones. Another hit like that and we should be getting the hell out of here!"

From the back of the bunker, Shankar issued Cochrane a thumbs up to signify she registered his concern as she pressed one hand against her ear and continued with her conversation on another channel.

"Stoppage clear!" Fusilier Weber finally reported, dragging back the HMG's cocking handle and letting it fly forward with a loud clunk of metal.

Cochrane stood back from the bunker's firing slit to give Weber room to pivot the weapon. The HMG chattered into life again, spewing a volley of bullets westward to join the platoon's other two machine guns in laying down sustained fire against the slowly advancing enemy infantry. A few paces away from the bunker, the first two Fusiliers from the ill-fated Number One Platoon finally staggered along the last few meters of open ground leading up to the safety of the trench line. Hands from soldiers of Shankar's Number Three Platoon reached up to drag the exhausted Fusiliers down into cover.

Cochrane dashed out of the thin opening in the back of the deployable bunker and out to the trench to the right. The first soldier from Number One Platoon, a tall man barely out of his teens, slid down into the cover of the trench. Gasping for air, his dark skin gleaming with sweat, the young Fusilier looked up wide-eyed at Cochrane as the second soldier of Number One Platoon fell down into cover after him.

"What's going on out there?" Cochrane demanded, dropping to one knee by the two soldiers and leaning in to shout above the din of gunfire. "What happened to your platoon commander?"

"We were ambushed!" the first Fusilier to jump into the trench shouted. "They hit us from both sides! There's an entire platoon of Invincibles out there! And the TAGs! I didn't see what happened to Lieutenant Juthani!"

Cochrane swore aloud, hunkering down as another explosion detonated only a dozen yards away, showering the trench with falling sand.

"They've got another TAG? You're sure what you saw, digger?"

The dark-skinned soldier shook his head frantically.

"No, Sarn't, no! They've got three of them!"

Cochrane let out a breath, physically winded by the news from the young soldier. *Three TAGs?* How the hell had those bastards smuggled that amount of firepower right beneath O-12's nose? Just one of those was enough to threaten their perimeter, let alone three supported by a full platoon of heavy infantry.

"Alright," Cochrane nodded, pulling himself together, "you two get to Company HQ, quickly! You find Major Barker and you tell him face to face exactly what you saw! Got it?"

The two soldiers did not need telling twice. Both Fusiliers scrambled out of the other side of the trench and darted off toward the center of the base as a third survivor slid down into cover. Cochrane dashed back to the rear entrance to the bunker, opening a channel to Major Barker and Lieutenant Shankar simultaneously so that he could deliver the bad news. He stopped by the bunker's doorway. If Cochrane believed even remotely for the briefest second in anything supernatural or that could not be explained by science, he would have said it was a sixth sense. A gut feeling that something was not right. Hairs on the back of his neck standing. He remembered Shankar asking him for his opinion on the orbital satellite hit on Alpha Four-Four and being cut off before he could respond. He looked up warily at the scattered clouds above for a moment before squeezing back inside the bunker.

"Alpha-Zero, Three-Zero," he called over the comlog to Barker and Shankar, "this is Three-Zero-One. I've just sent two survivors from One Platoon to the Company HQ. They say they saw three TAGs out there. Three. My gut feeling is that they're setting up a coordinated attack, and that the orbital targeter is cueing in an airborne assault from an orbital platform on our position."

***

The lip of the trench was ripped apart in a rapid series of small eruptions of sand. Accurate fire from an enemy HMG set up at the edge of the outer perimeter forced Hawkins to duck beneath cover into the shallow trench; one of the new Fusiliers was not so quick and was thrown back down, blood spraying up from a wound in her shoulder. Mieke was instantly over by her side and pulling off the young woman's smoking armor to access the injury. Hawkins dragged himself back up to his feet and brought his MULTI Rifle up to a firing position. Ahead, on the far side of the firing lane in front of Shankar's bunker, another handful of survivors from the jungle staggered toward the safety of the line. To the left, plumes of dense, white smoke wafted up to envelop the open ground as the Yujingyu soldiers lobbed smoke grenades to cover their advance through the lines of cutting foam.

Hawkins stared through his MULTI Rifle's scope, but as soon as he attempted to look into the smoke screen, his view flickered and was obscured by lines dancing across the eye piece. He looked over the top of his rifle, through the crude iron sight, but the eye pieces of his helmet were likewise disturbed with interference from the electronic effects of the smoke screen. Through his flickering lens, he just about made out the shadowy figures of three Yujingyu Invincibles moving toward the edge of the smoke.

Just ahead of the heavily armored Terracotta Soldiers, Hawkins saw a haggard, filthy Fusilier staggering toward cover, weighed down by a wounded comrade draped across his shoulders. Two of the Yujingyu heavy infantrymen dropped down at the edge of the smoke screen and raised their Combi Rifles, taking aim as calmly as if on a firing range before gunning the helpless Fusilier down. Return fire from the Fusilier line tore into the two Yujingyu soldiers, but the Combi Rifle bullets failed to penetrate their heavy armor. The wounded Fusilier in front of them staggered up to his knees, struggling over to position himself protectively between the Invincibles and his injured comrade, his hands held up in surrender. The two Terracotta Soldiers fired again, executing both wounded Fusiliers.

"The bastards!" Hawkins spat. "The murdering bastards!"

Before he even knew what he was doing, Hawkins angrily slung his
MULTI Rifle onto his back and unsheathed his sword. He was halfway up the
trench when a hand fell down on his shoulder.

"Sir!" Lance Corporal Dubois yelled up at him. "You need to stay in
cover! We need to get our soldiers into the perimeter, not let more out!"

The advice made no sense. Hawkins was alone in that trench in the
protection provided by his state of the art armor and four years of intensive
training. It fell on him to act. And to act was not about being an instrument of
God's will; right now, it was about punishing those responsible for what he had
just witnessed. It was about vengeance. His thoughts enveloped in a red cloud
of anger, Hawkins shrugged off Dubois' hand and looked across to her section
leader to deliver the first combat command of his life.

"Corporal Kotal!" Hawkins yelled. "Lay down a smoke screen between here and my Marker India! Now!"

Hawkins quickly marked up the edge of the existing smoke screen,
giving Kotal's section a target to lay down smoke to cover his own advance.

"One Section! Smoke! Marker India!" Kotal obediently relayed the
command to his soldiers.

His lens continuing to flicker and shut out as Kotal's Fusiliers' grenades spat out plumes of white smoke, Hawkins pulled off his helmet and
threw it into the bottom of the trench. Immediately the sheer, undiluted din of
the battle smashed through his senses – the deafening roar of gunfire, the thick
heat of the jungle air, and the stench of expended ammunition.

"Covering fire!" Hawkins yelled, unholstering his heavy pistol and
clambering up out of the trench.

His eyes now hindered only by the natural effects of the smoke and not
the electronically interference mixed within, Hawkins sprinted forward into
the cloud. The foul tasting, acrid fumes immediately swam up through his nostrils as he blundered forward blindly, bullets zipping aimlessly to either side
of him from both ahead and behind. Hawkins hacked his way through the first
line of cutting foam with ease before reaching the second and vaulting across,
his thick armor leaving him impervious to any damage from the sharp spikes.

"Broadsword-One!" Cochrane yelled, his voice tinny and artificial
now that it was transmitted to Hawkins' ear pieces rather than through his
helmet. "Back in the trench! Fall back!"

His eyes narrowed, his teeth gritted, Hawkins continued his mad, blind
dash through the smoke screen, his fingers tight around the handle of his sword
in one hand, his thumb cocking the hammer of his MULTI Pistol in the other.
Darker patches of smoke seemed to momentarily form into the silhouettes of
the distinctive, bulky outline of Terracotta Invincibles as Hawkins hurtled on,
the lack of information from his confused, flickering tactical map leaving him
unsure even as to what direction he was moving in. His anger and tempestuous

drive slowly receded along with his pace, leaving him edging forward in the smoke with a growing feeling of anxiety as he cut his way through the lines of defensive foam.

A shadow up ahead formed into the unmistakable shape of a soldier in heavy armor, rifle held at the ready. Hawkins brought his pistol up, extended his arm to line the bulky weapon's sight with the targeter in his lens, and squeezed the trigger. The pistol boomed and jumped in his hand, the yellow muzzle flash seeming brighter and more vivid in the white smoke screen. Hawkins heard a clang of metal on metal and saw the shape ahead stagger back a pace but remain upright. Hawkins pulled back on the trigger to snatch off a second shot, this time resulting in the figure dropping to its knees and crumpling over to one side.

Almost instantly, another two figures were hurtling through the smoke toward Hawkins. He raised his MULTI Pistol and fired a third shot into the closer of the two bulky figures but was rewarded only with another dull clang as the soldier twisted from the impact of the shot and carried on running. A moment later, the figure was on Hawkins, now close enough to clearly be identified as an Invincible by the smoothly formed, yellow-orange heavy armor. The veteran soldier lashed out with a long, curved blade, but Hawkins was quicker, raising his sword to block the attack.

Then the second Invincible was on him, firing off two shots from a pistol that thudded into Hawkins' chest but failed to penetrate his armor. The Hospitaller Knight stood his ground, dropping his pistol to place both hands on his sword to parry and deflect the flurry of blows that were issued from his two adversaries. Hawkins quickly stepped to his left to place both of his opponents in a line and deny them the chance to surround him; another flash of the curved blade forced him back a step as he moved his body out of the way of the blow. A follow up strike was even quicker; Hawkins parried it to one side and immediately struck out with his own blade, catching the Yujingyu soldier across the gut and tearing a neat line through the alloy armor plates.

With a rage-filled yell, Hawkins followed up by stepping in closer and bringing an armored knee up into his opponent's gut, bending the Yujingyu warrior over double with the force of the blow. Before he could capitalize on the opportunity he had created, he felt the impact of another bullet to the chest from the second Invincible's pistol, but again his stout armor shrugged off the attack. The first warrior forced himself upright and brought his blade up again. Again, Hawkins was faster. He charged his opponent down, slamming his shoulder into the man's torso and forcing him back a step, arms thrown to either side. The Yujingyu warrior fell back into a line of cutting foam, and with two neat sword strikes, Hawkins took one of the Invincible's arms off at the elbow and then reversed the strike to lop off his head.

Unfazed by his comrade's bloody demise, the remaining Invincible flung a heavy kick up at Hawkins' gut, slamming an armored foot into him with astounding force. Hawkins let out a gasp that was quickly followed up with a grunt of pain as the Invincible whipped his pistol butt around to slam into the Hospitaller's temple. The Yujingyu soldier flipped his pistol around and aimed it at Hawkins' face; Hawkins rapidly reached up to grab the barrel of the pistol and push it aside, just in time to hear the gun blast out as a bullet whizzed past his cheek.

Holding the pistol at bay with one hand, Hawkins flung the cross guard of his sword forward to smash through his opponent's faceplate, shattering the helmet's lens and sending the soldier staggering back a step. He quickly followed, plunging his sword straight through the Invincible's gut, twisting it in place and then withdrawing the blood-soaked blade to hack the defeated warrior's chest open and send him crashing to the ground in a fountain of blood. Quickly snatching his pistol from the ground, Hawkins paced forward with his weapons held up and ready. Leaving behind the corpses of the three men he had killed, remembering the hatred for his foes he felt from their actions only minutes before, Hawkins let out a yell of rage to challenge any other Yujingyu soldiers waiting for him in the slowly dispersing fog.

For a second, a brief moment of clarity in amidst the rage and bloodshed, Hawkins realized that he had just become everything he always said he would never be. His face twisted in anger, the blood of his dead foes spattered across his bullet-holed, cross-emblazoned surcoat, and God's love and mercy as far from his mind as could be, Hawkins was now everything that his compatriots in training had always wanted to be but he had wanted to avoid; a figure of frenzied, raging hatred to spread terror into the enemies of the Church. Pacing purposefully forward, his ears ringing from the painful strike to the side of his head, Hawkins quickly broke open his pistol and loaded three rounds into the empty chambers left vacant in the cylinder.

He saw silhouetted figures up ahead in the smoke again and raised his weapons.

"Come on!" he roared. "Come and fight!"

"Wait!" a voice yelled back. "Don't shoot! Fusiliers! Don't shoot!"

Hawkins continued to advance warily, his pistol tracking the two figures advancing toward him. Their forms took shape; slimmer than the Invincibles with lighter armor and the distinctive slant of berets on their heads.

"Over here!" Hawkins called.

Two young Fusiliers, bleeding from hastily bandaged wounds, staggered over to him.

"You need to get back to the perimeter!" Hawkins urged, pointing over his shoulder. "You need to get in cover! How many more of you are there out here?"

"Just one, sir!" one of the exhausted Fusiliers replied hoarsely. "Sergeant Fletcher! She stayed back to cover us all! She's the last one!"

"Right," Hawkins nodded grimly, "I'll find her! Keep moving, don't stop! You're outside the safe gate so keep shouting out to our line, your IFF is offline! Go!"

The two Fusiliers disappeared into the mist as Hawkins carried on, a few beams of sunlight now penetrating the field of white as the smoke continued to disperse. He saw unobscured daylight and the edge of the jungle up ahead as the din of battle continued to either side. A neat row of felled trees lay in his path, dumped by the engineers at the edge of the cleared firing lanes weeks before. Hawkins picked up his pace again and dashed out of the mist, dropping to one knee behind the felled trees and returning his pistol and sword to his side before recovering his MULTI Rifle from his back. To his left, he saw a Terracotta Soldier at the edge of the trees, orange-yellow standing out in stark contrast against the bright green foliage behind. Hawkins fired off a long burst from his MULTI Rifle but succeeded only in forcing the enemy soldier to fall back and out of sight.

Now clear of what little remained of the smoke, Hawkins' tactical map responded as soon as he tapped his wrist, projecting onto his lens. As anticipated, he was now at Alpha Four-Four's overrun outer perimeter, in the midst of the enemy advance, isolated and alone. What did come as something of a surprise was how far left of his line of advance he had veered when disorientated in the smoke screen. He quickly opened a channel to Number One Platoon.

"One-Zero-One from Broadsword-One," Hawkins breathed desperately, "are you on comms? Can you hear me?"

There was a brief silence, accompanied by a momentary lull in the battle before Hawkins heard a female voice in his earpiece.

"Broadsword-One, I hear you."

Hawkins quickly entered a waypoint into the tactical map at his location.

"Sergeant, I'm at Waypoint Juliet. How far away are you?"

"I... just a couple of dozen meters! I'm just northeast of you. I'll be with you in a few seconds!"

Hawkins winced warily, glancing quickly to either side. His last shots would have no doubt revealed his position, but he needed to link up with Sergeant Fletcher quickly and get back to the PanOceanian line. He moved around the edge of the log pile and raised his MULTI Rifle to a firing position. A blue outline in the jungle ahead showed Fletcher's movements as his lens detected her IFF. The tall sergeant dashed quickly out of the foliage. She looked up and breathed a sigh of relief as her eyes met his. Then the howling whine of a sniper rifle rang out, and Fletcher's eyes opened wide in surprise as a patch of red appeared in the center of her chest. The light of life was gone from her startled eyes before she even hit the ground. An instant later, a second shot sounded,

Mark Barber

and Hawkins was flung down onto his back.

His breathing caught in his chest, warning messages flashing across his lens to alert him of his armor's damaged systems, Hawkins looked down and saw a neat, smoking hole in his chest only an inch to the left of the center of his surcoat's white, blood-stained cross. He grabbed his MULTI Rifle and rolled quickly into cover, looking back at the seemingly impossible stretch of open ground separating him from the Fusilier trench line he had left minutes before. He checked his diagnostics again. Primary power at peak efficiency; secondary cooling system offline; tertiary rerouted. Breastplate fractured, protection compromised.

Gasping in pain from the heavy bruising across his chest, Hawkins lowered himself to the ground in the long grass by the log pile. A HMG continued to thud away from the right whilst he heard voices in a language he could not understand and running feet to his left. The smoke screen had completely disappeared, and Hawkins could see the yellow flashes and twinkling of gunfire from the Fusilier positions along the trenches and bunkers of the inner perimeter. He tapped his comlog.

"Zero, this is Broadsword-One," he gasped, "I'm... I'm cut off at my Marker Juliet."

A few seconds transpired before Shankar's voice calmly responded.

"Kyle, lay low and wait. We've got a lot going on. Just keep your head down and don't move. I'll contact you as soon as I can."

Hawkins swallowed and took in a deep breath.

"Copied," he replied, "I... Sergeant Fletcher is dead. She was the last of Number One Platoon. It's just me out here now. You can close the safe gate. They've got a sniper out here. That's who killed Sergeant Fletcher."

Again, a pause punctuated by rifle fire in all directions followed before Shankar responded.

"Copied. Enemy sniper operating in vicinity of Marker Juliet. Wait out, Kyle. Keep your head down."

Hawkins wiped an armored hand across his sweat-soaked brow. His breathing slowed. His thoughts cleared. In only a handful of moments, he decided he would be damned if he was going to sit the fight out and await rescue. He was not a Fusilier. He was a knight of the NeoVatican, an elite warrior of the Order of the Hospital. He did not skulk on the sidelines. Hawkins dragged himself back up to one knee, his back pressed against the log pile as he struggled to pick out the voices of enemy soldiers above the crackling of rifle and machine gun fire. He checked his tactical map. East; they were east of his position. Hawkins glanced across to the tree line a few paces away and planned his move.

At that moment, the earth tremored. Not the dull thump of a nearby explosion, but something rhythmic and repetitive. The foliage rustled noisily

313

and thick branches squealed in protest as they were bent and snapped. The thudding grew louder. Hawkins risked a glance around the log pile. There, only paces away, stood the towering form of a Gūijiǎ TAG. The pilot, almost clumsily bolted onto the front of the towering orange war machine, directed the colossus to stand at the edge of the forest, a shimmering sword of blue alloy clamped in one hand. The blade, some two meters in length and viciously hooked at the tip, was held out ready as the mechanical biped's small head turned from side to side as if trying to sniff out the enemy.

His heart pounding in his chest, terror rising and threatening to overwhelm him, Hawkins staggered back away from the deadly war engine. The TAG's head pivoted around and stared down at him with inhuman eyes; the sensors that had no doubt detected him and sent a signal directly to the human pilot attached to the machine's front. The Gūijiǎ stomped almost gracefully forward and kicked the log pile to one side as Hawkins leapt to his feet. He dropped his MULTI Rifle and unsheathed his sword, standing his ground alone and staring up at the giant TAG as its shadow fell down across him. There was nowhere to run now.

The trees behind the Gūijiǎ seemed to shimmer. Clearly defined lines of green in the foliage suddenly seemed to warp together, melding into a blurred and confused sequence of irregular shapes. Another towering figure emerged, just a little shorter than the Gūijiǎ but stockier; more angular, standing at nearly four meters with its communication antennas. Green faded into two-tone camouflage of deep blue and smoky white. The lines solidified into a familiar shape. A rectangular pauldron sported the blue and white globe symbol of PanOceania. The word 'NAVY' was emblazoned across the new arrival's armored torso. Hawkins' jaw fell open as he exhaled in relief. The PanOceanian Cutter TAG sprinted out of the trees.

The Gūijiǎ turned smoothly in place, one hand reaching up to grab the MULTI HMG on its back. The remotely piloted, stealthy Cutter was faster. Its outline still half-blurred and hidden by its environment-adaptive skin, the PanOceanian TAG raised its long, four-barreled machine gun. The colossal weapon opened fire with a deafening roar, the multiple barrels whirring around until they merged into a blur of death-spouting destruction. The Gūijiǎ was knocked back as shells slammed into its body, tearing off huge chunks of armor and sending them spiraling up into the air in all directions.

The Yujingyu Gūijiǎ TAG brought its own MULTI HMG up but managed only a half second burst of fire before the ceaseless stream of destruction from the Cutter swept across its legs, knocking the huge machine down to the ground. With an almost human display of agility, the immense war engine rolled over and up to one knee, its sword arm detaching just below the shoulder and falling away in a shower of electrical sparks as it did. The Cutter sprinted forward, planting a foot onto the chest of its heavily damaged adversary and booting it back down to the ground. Again, the Cutter's long gun came up and its motors whined and whirred to bring the barrels up to speed before the thunderous blast issued again. The Gūijiǎ shook apart violently as it was held in place underfoot by the Cutter, blown apart by the ferocity of the huge gun. The Yujingyu TAG's head detached entirely and the pilot's armored housing was blasted into shreds as the human component of the TAG was torn bloodily limb from limb.

With the Yujingyu TAG completely destroyed, the Cutter carried on firing for a good two to three seconds afterward, twisting and tearing the wreckage of the war machine apart. Fire from Yujingyu infantry in the jungle pelted into the PanOceanian TAG. The remotely operated machine turned in place, fired a brief sweep of its gun into the trees in response, and then melted almost impossibly into thin air as quickly as it had appeared, its state-of-the-art adaptive skin and signature masking technology turning it effectively invisible in the blink of an eye.

Muttering a brief prayer under his breath to thank the Lord for his unlikely and explosively violent savior, Hawkins grabbed his MULTI Rifle and looked around for cover. His ear piece crackled into life.

"All units, from Alpha-Zero," Major Barker called, "enemy airborne units inbound."

Hawkins looked up to the clear sky above. Tiger Soldiers, on their way. They would be going straight for the research hub. Cognizant of the deadly enemy guns right behind him, but also of his mission to defend the research site at all costs, Hawkins put his faith in God and the gigantic armored Cutter hidden in the trees behind him, and he sprinted headlong back toward the PanOceanian trenches and bunkers of the inner perimeter.

Chapter Twenty

"Eagle One from Tac Con. Three airborne teams descending on your position, no friendly IFF."

A speck appeared in the sky above Alpha Four-Four; at first little more than a black dot moving at such a linear rate that it stood out to both the human eye and the range finding and targeting prediction software of the rifle scope. From where she lay prone on top of one of the accommodation blocks toward the center of the base, Beckmann tracked the dot's movement with her MULTI Sniper Rifle, gently manipulating the controls on the side of her scope. Her arms aching from the full weight of the rifle due to her unnatural firing position of pointing almost straight up at the heavens, Beckmann patiently watched the falling target.

"Tac Con, Eagle One, on glass, contact," Beckmann informed her tactical controller.

A second dot appeared next to the first, both slowly growing in size until they took on bipedal forms. A red bracket appeared on the scope around the first target, together with a white crosshair highlighting the falling man's predicted path of movement. Beckmann transmitted the data to the Fusilier Company HQ, ignoring the constant chatter of communication across the channel between their major and the two platoon commanders. After another few seconds, a third target was visible and the scope's software accrued enough data to calculate the falling man's velocity – some two hundred miles per hour. An OLLD jump – Orbital Launch, Low Deceleration – a technique Beckmann herself had used on several operations but only ever once under enemy fire.

Four targets were visible on her scope now as she lowered the barrel of her rifle toward the horizon. No point in shooting at this range at a target moving so fast – all of the training, expertise, and technology in the world would not make the shot remotely possible. Five targets now, a full Fireteam, close enough to make out the orange-yellow of the armor of the airborne troopers and the white jet packs on their backs. Beckmann zoomed in for a quick, futile attempt to visually identify anything that might confirm the ranks and roles of the diving enemy soldiers. Nothing – no amateur display of status or ludicrous ceremonial sword at the hip. She would have to rely on doctrine; the Yujingyu military invariably insisted upon its leaders diving into action first and leading from the front, no matter how ill-advised and dangerous it was for those individuals in key positions. Beckmann settled down behind her rifle and tracked the lead jumper.

One thousand feet and they had barely decelerated. The sudden deceleration to the hover in a matter moments would be lethal without the compensators built into their armored flight suits, but it still required peerless physical fitness and insane courage to pull off. And the Yujingyu Tiger Soldiers were possibly the best in the entire Human Sphere at doing it.

A phrase jumped out of the background chatter of communications between the Fusilier units, grabbing her attention.

"Alpha-Zero from Two-Zero-One, I'm visual with a second team of jumpers, descending on your position!"

"Zero from Three-One, I've got a third team! Just south of the perimeter!"

Beckmann swore quietly under her breath. Not the time to get distracted. She had her target now. The orange armored figure in her sights swung his legs down to dangle beneath him, blasts of air shooting from his jet pack to violently bring a halt to his meteor-like descent. The Yujingyu Tiger Soldier visibly tensed in her crosshairs as she tracked his movement toward the surface, slowing suddenly until for the briefest of moments he hovered only a few feet from the dusty ground.

Beckmann squeezed the trigger. The Tiger Soldier's body jerked as a cloud of red mist appeared in front of his chest before he dropped from the sky to lie still at the end of his courageous, skillful descent from orbit. Beckmann brought her rifle to the right for a second shot, but her opponents were too quick. They had already reached the ground and scattered, dashing off toward the cover of the empty TAG hangar. Beckmann fired, winging the last of the four airborne troopers but failing to penetrate the soldier's armor.

An explosion thudded only a few meters away, quickly followed by a pillar of black smoke and the chatter of automatic gunfire. A second explosion detonated and more dark, noxious fumes wafted up from the Company HQ block, only a few dozen yards from Beckmann's position.

"Eagle One, Tac Con," Beckmann heard the dreary voice in her ear piece. "Tactical support assets are being jammed. I have no surveillance feed. Tactical control service is terminated. I am monitoring this frequency."

"Yeah, thanks, Tac Con," Beckmann spat, "enjoy your extended fucking lunch break."

The Hexa operative folded the bipod up underneath the barrel of her rifle and then scrambled down from her firing position atop the accommodation block. Slinging her MULTI Sniper rifle onto her back, unholstering her heavy pistol, and changing the setting on her reactive camouflage to save the battery now she was on the move, Beckmann quickly darted along the side of the accommodation blocks toward Company HQ, her heavy pistol held at the ready in both hands.

The sound of gunfire was loud and clear from around the last corner of the accommodation blocks; Beckmann recognized an exchange of fire from the distinctive sounds of both the PanOceanian Dayak Combi Rifle and the deeper rattle of Yujingyu Yungang rifles, as well as the rapid screech of a Xing 6.7 Spitfire. Pausing at the corner of the block, her back to the wall and her pistol raised, Beckmann quickly patched in to the lens of the Fusilier Company HQ soldiers – two were in contact with a Fireteam of Tiger Soldiers at the main entrance to the building, one of whom already lay dead a few paces inside.

Content that she knew roughly what she was facing, Beckmann leaned around the edge of the accommodation block corner, quickly took in the positions of the four Tiger Soldiers, and shot the nearest of them twice in the chest before ducking back into cover. Immediately the corner of the building was chewed up by a rapid volley of bullets as the tell-tale screech of a Spitfire echoed from the far side of the scrub ground separating the accommodation area and the Company HQ building.

Holstering her pistol, Beckmann grabbed at the rim of the first accommodation block's roof and hauled herself quickly up, climbing nimbly up the side of the rectangular blocks as enemy fire continued to pelt her previous position. Her teeth gritted, weighed down by the cumbersome sniper rifle on her back, Beckmann dragged herself up onto the roof of the third building and unholstered her heavy pistol again. Springing up to one knee, she looked down on the trio of enemy airborne soldiers and lined up her red fiber-optic sight on the Spitfire-wielding Yujingyu soldier.

Beckmann's pistol thumped in her hand as she fired, the first shot catching the Tiger Soldier in the hip and spinning her in place, almost directly into the path of the next two shots which caught the woman square in the chest. The airborne warrior crumpled back to slide down against the wall of the Company HQ building, ending in a rigid, seated position below smears of scarlet blood on the wall behind. The last two Yujingyu elite soldiers fell back, spraying Beckmann's position with automatic fire, and forcing her to throw herself prone.

Dropping back down to the ground, Beckmann advanced quickly and cautiously toward the two soldiers she had killed, her pistol trained on them and ready in case of any signs of movement.

"Alpha-Zero, Eagle One," she called on the Company HQ channel, "I'm at your location, moving in through the main entrance. Hold fire."

Beckmann moved quickly through the main entrance, her pistol pointed down at the first of the three dead enemy soldiers. The Tiger Soldier's torso was torn apart by rifle caliber rounds, his striped body armor punctured in half a dozen places. Up ahead, Beckmann saw Captain Waczek hunkered down behind the makeshift cover of a toppled Maya terminal, accompanied by two Fusiliers. Two bodies lay prone only meters from them. One was Major Barker. Beckmann holstered her pistol and grabbed a Combi Rifle and underslung grenade launcher from one of the felled Fusiliers, the weapon's firing circuit showing green as soon as its software recognized her PanOceanian IFF. One of the Fusiliers dashed over to kneel by Major Barker and set about bandaging a tear in the side of his head as Beckmann shoved two rifle magazines into her webbing.

"You," Beckmann pointed to the other Fusilier, "get on the door, quickly!"

Waczek hurriedly loaded a fresh magazine into her Combi Rifle as she moved out to meet Beckmann.

"They were in here in seconds!" she gasped. "I... I know they're supposed to be good, but..."

"Three teams have landed," Beckmann interrupted, "and there's still two TAGs left out there, as well as a full platoon of heavy infantry and Zhanshi. You need to call in air support."

Waczek looked down at Barker, swallowed, and then looked back up at Beckmann.

"You're the ranking officer at this site now, Major," she said, "confirm that you are taking command of the defenses?"

Beckmann narrowed her eyes and took a step back.

"Captain, I'm Special Forces, not line infantry! The largest team I've ever led in combat is ten soldiers! My job is to infiltrate enemy lines and cause fucking mayhem. *You* are the company second-in-command! It is literally your primary role to replace the company commander in case he becomes a casualty! It is your job to coordinate the defenses!"

"I... I've never..."

Beckmann paced forward, her eyes ablaze with rage, and pointed a finger of accusation in Waczek's face.

"Step up to the plate and do your job, right now, or I *will* take command here! What's it gonna be? Are you doing this, or am I?"

Waczek looked down at Barker again. The Fusilier medic knelt over him was finishing securing a pad and bandage to his head, but the veteran officer remained completely motionless.

"I... I have tactical control," Waczek nodded, "I've got things here."

"Good," Beckmann growled, pacing toward the door and the din of gunfire outside, "get air support here, right now."

"Air support?!" Waczek exclaimed. "That's against the accord we've agreed to with O-12! We can't get any more reinforcements in!"

"Are you fucking serious?!" Beckmann snapped, turning back to face the blonde captain. "These bastards have turned up with a full platoon of heavy infantry, three TAGs, and an orbital airborne drop, and you still think now is the time to go for the moral high ground and stick to O-12's rules?! Get communications established with your Regimental HQ and get support here, fast! Or we're all dead!"

Casting aside a series of nagging doubts at the back of her mind – mental alarm bells telling her that it was *her* responsibility to assume command, that Waczek was not up to the job and that she was walking away because she was scared of the responsibility of assuming command of a completely unwinable situation – Beckmann paced quickly over to the Company Command HQ exit to rejoin the fight.

***

Shankar dropped to her knees in the bowels of the cramped bunker, closing her eyes and instinctively shrugging her shoulders up around her head. Another volley of shells slammed into the bunker, thumping loudly against the armored alloy shell and filling the interior with dust. Shankar waited until the firing stopped and then jumped back up, staring out of the firing slit as the HMG next to her thundered into life again. The enemy TAG to the southeast paced forward across the battlefield, its smoking MULTI HMG now aimed at the Fusilier trenches as it spat out another destructive salvo of shells. A dronbot from further down the defensive line fired a long burst into the advancing TAG but to no avail.

"All units, Alpha-Zero-One now has tactical control," Shankar heard Waczek's voice over the command channel.

She turned and looked across at Cochrane. The burly sergeant shook his head.

"Major Barker?" Shankar asked. "He's dead?"

She allowed herself the briefest moment of relief after checking her comlog's company casualty roster and seeing Barker listed as wounded.

"Worry about it later, Boss," Cochrane said, "Number Two Platoon is holding well against the Zhanshi to the west. We're taking a bloody pelting here with two TAGs and Invincibles to deal with. We've now got Tiger Soldiers air dropped behind us and only the remnants of One Platoon to keep 'em busy."

"Then what do you suggest?" Shankar asked, bringing up her tactical map and marking one of the two enemy TAGs as a priority target.

Cochrane's response was cut off as a bulky figure in blue-gray armor, wrapped in a holed surcoat of red, sprinted across the last few feet of open ground and slid down into the trench to the right of the bunker. Cochrane shoved his head out of the back of the bunker and yelled over the hammering of guns to the new arrival.

"Kyle! Simple 'yes' or 'no' answer: was running into the enemy line all on your own a good idea? Yeah, that's what I bloody thought!"

A colossal explosion sounded above Shankar's head, knocking her down to her knees. Her ears ringing, she looked up and was momentarily blinded by the blazing sunshine and blue sky, now that a full third of the bunker's roof had been blown off. She accepted Cochrane's hand as he helped her back to her feet, her senses still numb and her hearing half replaced by a high pitched whining. She groggily brought up her tactical map again.

"Jim, we can't stay here!" she shouted as Fusilier Brooks fired another missile out of the crumpled bunker. "We've got two TAGs facing our Cutter, and we're barely slowing those Invincibles! Look… there's a path through the site generator complex here… We can set up a support team and try to get a HMG and launcher on their flank."

Cochrane's eyes flickered from side to side as he took in Shankar's plan on his own lens' tactical map. He looked across at her.

"Priya, that's bleedin' aggressive! We're outnumbered, outgunned, and at least here we've got cover!"

Shankar shook her head.

"Jim, we're running out of time! We're surrounded on all sides and within our own perimeter, and we will be overrun! We've got to keep them on their toes! I want to attack them!"

Cochrane quickly examined the map again.

"Alright, but if you want to do this, go all in. Send a section up by the generator, but also another section southeast by the armory. Hit them on both sides."

Shankar checked her map and quickly added markers to her two objectives.

"Right," she said, "I'm taking One Section up to Marker Romeo by the generator. Two Section can position at Marker Sierra by the armory."

"Priya, you can coordinate that from here!" Cochrane urged. "Sahal Kotal can set up a support team by himself!"

"No," Shankar checked her Combi Rifle, "you stay here with Three Section. I'll get the HMG and launcher in position. Kyle can take charge of Two Section."

"Kyle?" Cochrane exclaimed. "He's a brave kid, but he's never led anybody in a fight before!"

Shankar winced and hunkered down again as a burst of rifle fire ricocheted across the crumpled bunker's roof.

"I don't need a tactical genius, I just need aggression and firepower. Kyle can do that. Keep that closer TAG suppressed as best you can whilst I'm gone. I'll be back as soon as I can."

Shankar pushed her way out of the bunker, pausing behind the cover of the squat fortification to quickly gather her thoughts before opening a channel to her platoon.

"One Section, on me!" she called. "Advance to Marker Romeo! Two Section, under the command of Broadsword-One, advance to Marker Sierra!"

"One Section! Smoke! Marker Tango! One-Seven – covering fire!" Corporal Kotal shouted.

Grenade launchers sounded with their distinctive, hollow thuds as smoke grenades were fired off in the open ground separating the PanOceanian defensive line and the Yujingyu advance. The platoon's three HMGs continued to blast away as the first Fusiliers from One and Two Sections left the trenches, quickly forming up into their Fireteams and ready to advance. Shankar rushed across to Kotal and dropped to one knee next to him, her Combi Rifle tucked in to her shoulder.

"Advance your Section to Marker Romeo!" She confirmed her orders, pointing in the direction of advance with the outstretched fingers of her right hand. "Set up your support team for flanking fire on the main enemy advance!"

Kotal tapped his wrist and a series of interim waypoints appeared on the platoon tactical map between their present position behind the trench and their objective at the generator building.

"One-Two! One-Four! Advance!" Kotal yelled.

Fusiliers Evans and Perez sprinted forward, bent over nearly double as the smoke from the grenades wafted back over the trenches. The remainder of Kotal's Section fired into the direction of the advancing Invincible heavy infantry; a well-drilled and standard Section maneuver to keep the enemy suppressed whilst soldiers advanced rapidly in pairs. Evans and Perez reached the cover of a perimeter checkpoint and took up firing positions, pointing their weapons into the smoke ahead. Kotal looked across at Shankar.

"Boss?"

Not the norm for a corporal to give orders to his platoon commander, but Shankar was not going to waste valuable seconds debating who should be coordinating the section's advance. Clenching her fingers around her Combi Rifle, Shankar nodded.

"Zero! One-Three! Advance!" Kotal commanded.

Shankar leapt up and rushed over the open ground behind the trench line toward her first marker, the smoke to her right obscuring any vision of the enemy to the east. Willing her legs to propel her faster, she saw Fusilier Ricci pull ahead of her. The telltale crack of a bullet sounded over her head, forcing her to duck down lower as she ran. Her heart pounding, her lungs burning, Shankar reached the cover of the checkpoint and dove behind the shallow, alloy shelter. She quickly raised herself to a firing position and brought her right eye to her scope.

There – just to the left edge of the smoke screen – she saw the armored bulk of four Yujingyu Invincibles lying prone in the open firing lane leading from the edge of the site to the inner firing line of the trenches and bunkers. Muzzles twinkled from the enemy soldiers' weapons, and Shankar saw a flash of impact as one of her Fusiliers hit their target, the round punching through the thick armor of the heavy infantryman. Numbly aware that Kotal was now sprinting up to join them, Shankar took aim at the closest of the four enemy soldiers and held her breath. She felt the thump of the rifle in her shoulder and smelled the burn of expended ammunition, but her shot flew high. She quickly corrected her aim and fired again but saw no impact.

To Shankar's left, Perez suddenly let out a scream and collapsed down to the ground. Shankar looked down and saw the young woman lying in the dusty sand, writhing in pain as blood fountained up from her neck.

- Fusilier Isabella Perez – severe wound, airway...

Perez was in cover. She could reach her own bandage. Shankar knew that her priority was to fire her weapon. She settled down behind her scope again, found her target, and fired. This time her shot was perfect, striking one of the four Invincibles in the chest. She saw the enemy soldier lurch from the impact, but enemy fire forced her to duck beneath cover before she could confirm whether her target was down. Kotal dove down from his frantic dash to skid through the dust and stop next to Shankar. He immediately opened a webbing pouch and grabbed a bandage.

"No time for that!" Shankar yelled. "We need to keep going! We've got to get the support team up here! One-Two! One-Three! Advance!"

Evans and Ricci jumped up and charged ahead to the next marker. Kotal pressed his bandage against Perez's neck and moved her hand to hold it in place. The wounded soldier looked up at the two commanders weakly, fear in her dark eyes.

"We'll be right back for you!" Kotal smiled. "Just keep your head down and keep pressure on this!"

"Zero, One-One! Advance!" Shankar ordered, jumping to her feet again and rushing forward toward the generator.

***

Leading from the front, his situational awareness increased seemingly tenfold now he had recovered his helmet, Hawkins hurtled away from the trench line and toward the armory. Corporal Garcia and his rifle team followed close behind whilst Lance Corporal Reid's support team laid down covering fire, falling back slowly behind them. To the east, the PanOceanian Cutter TAG was caught between the two Gūijiǎ TAGs, the three immense war machines stomping through the edge of the jungle as they ducked and darted in almost human looking attempts to avoid fire. The closest of the two enemy TAGs was only seconds away from the armory, its armored feet kicking through the trees and bushes as it rushed toward the trench line.

"Rifle team! Take cover at the armory!" Hawkins shouted, only a few paces now between him and his objective. "Take position to lay down covering..."

The entire armory exploded. The small building was blown open from within, an immense fireball enveloped in billowing, black smoke rising instantly up into the blue sky. Hawkins felt the heat of the blast even through his armor, the force of the explosion stopping him dead in his tracks and knocking him back a pace. Before he could respond, four Tiger Soldiers leapt out from behind the flames with their weapons blazing.

Hawkins felt a double strike against his legs, sending pain flaring up his thighs. Deadly fire whooshed out from one Tiger Soldier's light flamethrower, enveloping two Fusiliers and sending them writhing to the ground, their high-pitched screams of agony accompanying the stench of burning flesh. With an angry yell, Hawkins swung his MULTI Rifle around and fired a long burst from the hip, catching the Tiger Soldier and blasting his innards out of his back.

Rage tearing through his core, Hawkins dropped his MULTI Rifle and sprinted forward to engage the Yujingyu airborne soldiers, grabbing his sword from his waist. His first strike sliced neatly through a Spitfire-wielding Tiger Soldier, cutting the warrior in two from shoulder to waist. A tall, powerfully build Yujingyu trooper barged into him a moment later, slashing out with a long fighting knife. Hawkins deftly avoided the blow but then let out a gasp of pain as an armored foot swung around into his stomach. He batted aside a follow up kick with one forearm and stepped in to drive home an attack of his own, half-severing his opponent's wrist.

Blood shooting from the vicious, open wound, the Tiger Soldier nonetheless attempted to continue his attack with a slice at Hawkins' neck. The Hospitaller Knight ducked beneath the blow and lanced his sword through the Tiger Soldier's gut. The Yujingyu airborne veteran sagged forward on Hawkins' blade, his knife dropping from his hand. Hawkins unholstered his pistol, pressed it against the Tiger Soldier's forehead and blew his cranium apart before kicking his corpse off his blade.

The last Tiger Soldier was already motionless on the ground, gunned down by Garcia, Rand, and the team's medic. The medic was on his knees by one of the victims of the flamethrower, frantically trying to administer aid to the scorched, whimpering wretch. The second Fusilier was already dead.

"Support team," Garcia gasped, one hand clutching a bleeding wound on his bicep, "get the gun and the launcher in position and set up! Quickly!"

Lance Corporal Reid and her Fusiliers rushed over to find what cover they could a few meters away from the blazing wreckage of the armory. Hawkins turned to survey the battle behind him. The epic clash between the TAGs continued, with the Cutter firing a long burst from its gun into the further of the two Gūijiǎs, the four barrels spinning rapidly as they spewed out shell after shell. Finally, battered by dozens of attacks from machine guns, rifles, and missiles, the frontal armor of the Gūijiǎ gave way and its gun arm fell limply down by its side. The huge war machine slunk away, one leg dragging awkwardly behind it as sparks showered from a severed power connection in its hip joint.

A second later, the world erupted into gunfire again as the final Gūijiǎ TAG, now stood only meters away from the blazing armory and the Fusiliers, fired its own MULTI HMG into the Cutter's back. Ragged pieces of blue debris flew off the PanOceanian TAG, ripping through its armor and into the vulnerable systems inside its core. One long, blue-white leg paced to the left as the Cutter attempted to turn to face its attacker, but another salvo of shells smashed into it and suddenly, without ceremony, the Cutter stopped dead in place. Its adaptive skin failing and leaving its brutal outline now clearly visible for all, the defeated, disabled machine froze where it stood, its power system destroyed and leaving it locked in place as a grim statue of what nearly turned the tide of battle in PanOceania's favor.

The Yujingyu TAG turned slowly in place, its smoking gun swiveling to line up with the battered, wounded Fusiliers only paces away. Without a second thought, Hawkins raised his sword and charged at the Gūijiǎ.

***

"On the marker!" Shankar shouted, pointing to the corner of the curved generator building at the point where her tactical map marker was now highlighted on her lens. "Get the HMG in position!"

Back to the south, Number Three Section still held the defensive line at the original trenches and battered bunker, their weapons firing continuously into the Yujingyu forces advancing through the lines of cutting foam from the east. White smoke dissipated across the open ground between the defenses and the jungle edge, but thick clouds of black now blossomed up from the burning armory building further south, where one of the Gūijiǎ TAGs was now locked in direct combat with Number Two Section. The last, heavily damaged TAG limped over toward Shankar and her Fusiliers, dragging a crippled leg slowly behind it as it closed the gap with murderous intent. The bulk of the Invincibles platoon continued to advance directly toward the main defensive line, but now a full section of heavy infantry had diverted and was firing at Shankar and Number One Section.

From her prone position near the generator building, Shankar raised her Combi Rifle to her shoulder again. She counted seven enemy soldiers clad in their bulbous, heavy armor as they skirted around the edge of the tree line to the northeast, firing in pairs as they steadily advanced. Shankar tracked the movement of one enemy soldier as a pair darted from cover to cover, led her target by half a pace, and fired. The Terracotta Invincible span a quarter of a turn at the waist but continued to stumble forward before collapsing behind the cover of another thick tree.

Weber dove down to his marked position by the generator building, quickly unfolding the bipod of his HMG before firing a long burst into the jungle edge ahead. Almost simultaneously, the long chatter of a Yujingyu Type 6.1 heavy machine gun sounded from the tree line, and rounds zipped over the top of Shankar's Fusiliers.

"One-Eight, get the gun!" Shankar shouted to Fusilier Brooks on the support team's missile launcher. "Take out that HMG!"

Shankar heard the howl-whistle of a high velocity shot, and her Section's HMG fell silent.

- Fusilier Henning Weber – dead

"Sniper!" Corporal Kotal yelled. "Get to cover!"

Her eyes wide with fear, Shankar leapt to her feet and sprinted desperately for the cover of the generator building. She heard another shot ring out as her two teams charged for the safety of the blocky building. Another casualty report scrolled across the top of her lens.

- Fusilier Carlo Ricci – dead

"Smoke!" Kotal screamed, throwing a grenade out from where he crouched at the edge of the building.

Her heart thumping, bile rising in her throat, Shankar counted her soldiers in as they rushed over to her position behind the generator. Two dead and Perez left behind, wounded. Seven Fusiliers, including herself.

"Smoke!" Shankar repeated Kotal's command. "Both sides! They know we're here, so we need to move! Smoke out the whole area!"

Lined up with their backs to the thrumming generator building, the Fusiliers at both ends of the section quickly tossed smoke grenades out to either side. White smoke sprayed up and spread out to cover the area. Content that they had the best chance possible of evading the deadly gaze of the hidden enemy sniper, Shankar rapidly checked her map for an alternative position to bring the fight to the enemy. There – further north still. There was one of the original site barricades set up before the defenses were bolstered.

"One Section, on me!" Shankar yelled as she sprinted out through the smoke.

Gunfire continued to blast away from the right; the earth thudded with the heavy steps of the damaged TAG limping closer. Shankar highlighted the barricade on her lens, now appearing as a new marker only meters ahead. The smoke quickly thinned. Another pace and Shankar found herself running in the open, facing two huge, orange armored Terracotta Invincibles rushing toward her unit from the jungle edge. She stopped dead in her tracks, instinctively raised her Combi Rifle, quickly took aim, and fired.

Her shot, aimed at the center of mass of her target, smashed through the Yujingyu soldier's faceplate, and blew the contents of his head out of the back of his skull. Kotal appeared at Shankar's side, firing an automatic burst from his Combi Rifle at the hip, his rounds slamming into the second Yujingyu soldier and knocking him down. Breathing heavily in relief, Shankar stared at the two dead bodies and then past them at the relative safety of the gray, alloy barricade. She turned to look back into the smoke.

"Jan," she yelled, "get the launcher up here! Get the launcher…"

A burst of heavy machine gun fire spat out from the jungle edge and cut Shankar down where she stood.

***

Drenched in sweat, almost relieved by the mild respite provided by the hole in the roof of the bunker, Cochrane stared out of the firing slit at the advancing enemy soldiers. The smoking HMG continued to thump away from next to him, its barrel now just starting to glow red at the tip. To the southeast, Hawkins and Number Two Section were locked in a fight against a small group of Tiger Soldiers next to the blazing armory as one of the Gūijiă TAGs advanced toward them. To the northeast, Shankar led her soldiers up toward her designated flanking position. Another casualty notification scrolled through.

- Fusilier Henning Weber – dead

A second later there was another.

- Fusilier Carlo Ricci – dead

Swearing out loud, Cochrane dropped down to take cover below the half-destroyed bunker's firing slit and quickly surveyed his tactical map. He dialed in his comlog frequency to monitor Shankar and Number One Section. He heard the panicked scream to alert the unit of an enemy sniper. Cochrane leapt to his feet.

"Lucia," he yelled out of the back of the bunker to Corporal Rossi, "you have command here! Hold the fucking line!"

Rossi turned from her firing position in the trench and gave Cochrane a brief thumbs up as he scrambled out behind the defensive line. He sprinted north, tracing the steps and markers of Shankar and her section only moments before. To his right, the heavily damaged TAG continued to limp slowly toward Shankar and her soldiers. Machine guns blasted away. Smoke wafted out up ahead to envelop the generator building. Cochrane closed the gap, sweat pouring down his face as he sprinted up the slight incline toward the smoke. Then came another casualty notification.

- Lieutenant Priya Shankar – severe wound, abdominal

Letting out a cry of anguish, Cochrane patched in to Shankar's lens in a desperate attempt to work out exactly where she was and what danger she faced. He heard her choked breathing and saw the world through her eyes; a shaking hand reaching weakly up in front of her, covered in blood, moving across to her comlog to program in another marker for her team.

"One Section from Zero…" Shankar whispered hoarsely. "Set up… launcher… at Marker Uniform… can still get around their flank…"
"Priya!" Cochrane yelled. "Get in cover! Get in cover!"
On his tactical map, Cochrane saw Number One Section's medic rush out to position for a ranged shot with his medikit's needle gun.
The rattle of an enemy HMG sounded again as Cochrane sprinted headlong through the zipping and cracking of flying rounds.

- Lieutenant Priya Shankar – severe wound, chest

"Priya!"
"Marker Uniform…" Shankar whispered weakly. "Don't let the attack stall…"
Cochrane heard the quick, moaning wail of a sniper rifle from up ahead.

- Lieutenant Priya Shankar – dead

Cochrane stopped in place, slumping down to both his knees, his hands desperately gripping his Combi Rifle. Gunfire continued to hammer away from every direction. Vomit threatened to rise up from his gut. The air was hot, close, and stank of expended ammunition and burning. She was gone. If he did not act now, more would follow. Cochrane stumbled back up to his feet.
"All units from Zero-One. I have tactical control of the platoon. One Section, fall back to my position."

Flinging himself to one side, Hawkins just managed to avoid a killing blow as the Gūijiǎ brought its arm down in an overhead strike, its long blade slashing toward the Hospitaller's head. With near clinical precision, the arm and blade stopped as one to avoid digging into the dusty earth. The TAG pivoted in place and rapidly lashed out with the blue-hued blade again in an attempt to decapitate its comparatively tiny opponent. Hawkins ducked beneath the blade, feeling the disturbed air rush across the back of his neck as he avoided death again by only inches. He brought his pistol up and fired three shots into the pilot's compartment on the front of the TAG; all three succeeded only in causing minor dents in the thick armor. Smoke continued to billow out from the blazing armory behind the TAG, the flames reflecting off its smooth, orange armor. Garcia and his Fusiliers remained in cover behind the Hospitaller, firing into the flanks of the main Yujingyu attack on the eastern perimeter whilst Hawkins frantically struggled to keep the TAG busy.

The Gūijiǎ TAG swung in to attack again, forcing Hawkins back with another sword swipe and then sweeping a huge foot up and into the Hospitaller. Hawkins let out a cry as the giant war machine connected the blow, slamming into his chest and propelling him back through the air. He landed with a thud in the dust, skidding several feet before coming to a halt with arcing lines of electricity snaking over the cracks in his fractured armor. The Gūijiǎ TAG hurtled forward to finish him but was stopped in its tracks as a missile slammed straight into its chest, exploding with a dull crump and splitting open the war engine's armored neck.

Fusilier Rand attempted to capitalize on the moment created by his comrades and darted out toward the TAG, a grenade primed and ready to cram into a vulnerable joint on the deadly machine. The TAG jerked forward into life again, smoothly swiping its long close combat blade down to hack open Rand's chest with a rapid, killing strike. Given a few feet to maneuver with, the TAG immediately followed up by grabbing its MULTI HMG from its back and firing at short range into the PanOceanian soldiers, blasting Fusilier Khan apart where he stood and scattering the others in every direction.

Fighting off the pain from his bruised body and the exhaustion from fighting head to head with the towering TAG, Hawkins dragged himself to his feet, brought up his blade, and rushed in to attack again. The Gūijiǎ swept its MULTI HMG around like a man-sized club aimed at his head; Hawkins jumped back and then saw the blue blade hurtling down at him again. He instinctively brought his own blade up to parry, but the inhuman force of the blow drove him down to his knees, his own sword wrenched from his grip. Hawkins rolled to one side, picked up his blade, and lunged in to attack. Remembering the only time he had seen a TAG fought and destroyed, he lanced the tip of his blade into a connecting cable at the Gūijiǎ's knee. The Hospitaller Knight's blade ripped the cable open with a steaming stream of hot, purple-hued hydraulic fluid. Seemingly unaffected, the TAG brought its long sword up again for another attack.

Chapter Twenty-One

Rapid, light footsteps and muffled voices were clear now, even above the relentless crackling and thumping of gunfire and explosions. From where she stood motionless, back pressed against a blue storage container, Beckmann waited patiently. She quickly checked the Fusiliers' casualty report to ensure Hawkins' name was not on it and then expelled the thought from her mind to concentrate on the job in hand. The high angle of the sun lit most of the alleyway running between the long lines of storage containers, just to the west of Alpha Four-Four's center. Number Two Platoon had succeeded in beating back most of the Zhanshi attack, but one of their sections had been eliminated entirely; and now two Fireteams of Zhanshi were rushing toward the vital research hub.

Beckmann's reactive camouflage coveralls and hood were powered up fully, leaving her colored a dull, dusty blue from head to toe and effectively invisible as she lurked in the shadows of the storage container alleyway. The footsteps drew closer. At the far end of the alleyway, a Zhanshi soldier took cover at the corner of the first container and brought his Combi Rifle up to a firing position, covering the advance of a second trooper. A third soldier moved past, rifle at the ready, before the trio quickly and silently made their way down the alley toward her. Beckmann remained still, silent, calm, and unfazed. This was a scenario she had played out a hundred times before.

The three Zhanshi moved toward Beckmann, weapons ready and covering the shadows, one Combi Rifle pointed straight at her. The three soldiers – two men and a woman – were all young, possibly not even out of their teens, clad in black body gloves and attachments of orange-colored light armor. Beckmann recognized one of the men from when she had infiltrated the Yujingyu base at the mining facility only days before. She had lurked in the darkness, stalking her prey, hearing them talk to each other about life, love, hopes, and fears… and she had let them go. Now this enemy soldier, a man she showed mercy to, had no doubt killed PanOceanian Fusiliers. That was on her. That was her fault for displaying a misguided sense of compassion and fair play. That was something she needed to remedy, now.

The trio of Zhanshi moved past Beckmann, one-by-one, close enough to touch. Silently she unsheathed her slim, black fighting knife from its sheath on her left thigh. The enemy soldiers moved on. Beckmann singled out the young trooper she had spared days before and quietly moved out of cover. Three paces and she caught up. She wrapped a hand around her target's mouth and slid the knife tip up against the very bottom rim of the torso armor, through the back of the ribcage and into the vital organs. The dying man let out a muffled yell of surprise and agony into her hand, struggling against her as she held him tightly in place and slid the blade around to open the wound and increase the internal trauma. The Zhanshi dropped his rifle with a clatter.

The two other Yujingyu soldiers turned in place and brought their weapons up. Beckmann dropped the body of her victim and darted out to one side, stabbing her dagger into to the eye of the second trooper. The man dropped his weapon and screamed in pain, both hands grabbing at the black knife protruding from his eye socket. Beckmann unholstered her pistol and brought the weapon smoothly up in one arm, shot the man twice in the chest, and then continued the fluid motion to bring the weapon around into a two-handed grip to point at the last Zhanshi.

The young Yujingyu woman had already thrown her weapon aside and raised both hands in surrender. Her pale, smooth features were twisted in abject terror as she stared ahead at the flickering blur of the camouflaged monster that had brutally killed her two friends in seconds. She shouted out a word twice. It took a moment to register to Beckmann; Mandarin was her third language after German and English, and one she was out of practice with.

"Stop! Stop!"

The girl's eyes stared desperately up at Beckmann. Her hands, held out to either side, were shaking in fear. She managed a single word in heavily-accented English.

"Please... please..."

Her face twisted in a snarl, both hands calmly gripping her heavy pistol, Beckmann aimed the weapon at the woman's face. Her finger tightened on the trigger. The trigger bit the firing mechanism just a little, enough to begin the movement of the hammer at the back of the weapon. The blurred outline of a small, blood-soaked teenaged girl appeared at the periphery of Beckmann's vision.

"Go on," a familiar voice whispered, "do it. Kill her, Razor. Fucking waste her..."

"Eagle One, from Alpha-Zero-One..."

"Kill her! What's wrong with you? Pull the fucking trigger!"

"Eagle One, come in?"

Her teeth gritted, Beckmann took a pace forward. The girl was just a Zhanshi. Not one of the fanatically committed and disciplined warriors of the Terracotta Invincibles; not one of the ferocious and merciless veterans of the elite, airborne Tiger Soldiers. The Zhanshi were professional and highly trained soldiers, but they were the backbone of the StateEmpire's military. Ordinary men and women.

"Eagle One, respond," Captain Waczek called again.

The Zhanshi soldier dropped to her knees and hung her head in silent acceptance. She whispered a single word quietly.

"Daddy..."

Beckmann eased her finger off the trigger.

"Alpha-Zero-One, Eagle One," Beckmann replied, "I've got a prisoner I need to have secured."

The communication channel fell silent for a few seconds before Waczek spoke again.

"Eagle One, we have no facilities to secure prisoners. It isn't an option. Request you... free yourself up and are ready to accept tasking."

Beckmann heard the voice in her head again, the voice she knew was nothing more than a ghost conjured up by her damaged mind.

"Kill her."

The young Zhanshi woman looked up at her. Ten seconds was all it was. Ten seconds ago, this Yujingyu soldier would have gunned her down without a thought. Beckmann tightened her finger around the trigger again.

"Eagle One, confirm you are ready for tasking?"

No. Things had to change. Things could not keep going on like this. Beckmann took her finger off the trigger and shoved the muzzle of her pistol into the Zhanshi's face.

"Turn around!" she yelled in Mandarin. "Get down! Get down on the ground, or I'll put a bullet in your fucking head!"

The terrified woman obliged, her arms still out to either side as she slowly turned around and lowered herself to a prone position.

"Lens!" Beckmann shouted. "Lens and ear piece! Now!"

The woman slowly removed her contact lens and ear piece as Beckmann warily checked around her for any further threats. Once the lens and ear piece were placed down, Beckmann crushed them under a booted foot to effectively sever the enemy soldier's connection to her unit. She then dropped down to hold the woman in place with a knee on her back before grabbing a set of tie-wraps from her webbing belt and binding the woman's ankles and wrists.

"You keep your head down!" Beckmann growled. "You stay here and you don't move! Not until this is all over! If you move, I will find you! You understand me? I will fucking find you!"

The young woman nodded, terrified. Beckmann backed away slowly from her, her pistol still trained on the bound enemy soldier lying prone between her two dead comrades. The blurred apparition on the edge of Beckmann's sight was gone.

"Eagle One, ready for tasking," Beckmann breathed.

"Eagle One, Alpha-Zero-One," Waczek called. "Reaper, Reaper loose in vicinity of Marker Zulu. You are activated in role Guardian."

Beckmann swore under her breath as she cautiously rounded the corner and left the alleyway between the storage containers behind her. Partially at the thought of the new task ahead, but also at the pointless and pretentious use of Brevity Codewords. Reaper – enemy sniper. Guardian – counter sniper role. She checked her map for Marker Zulu. There, to the northeast of the site perimeter, where Shankar was leading a section of Fusiliers moments before. Beckmann checked the company tactical update for locations of suspected casualties inflicted by the enemy sniper. Five of them already; four dead.

One was Shankar. Beckmann swallowed and muttered a brief prayer. Of course she hated Shankar, but they were on the same side, and she never wanted this to be the outcome. Plotting a route across the center of the base to find a firing position to the northeast, Beckmann holstered her pistol and took her Combi Rifle and grenade launcher from her back, where it was slung next to her MULTI Sniper Rifle. Eliminating an enemy sniper required patience and a cool head. The reality was that there would be no face off, no knife fight, no quick draw or shooting the enemy through their scope. None of the movie bullshit. It was simply a case of whoever was better at the job would get to live.

"Eagle One, activated in role Guardian," Beckmann confirmed.

***

Hawkins was not quite fast enough. The barrel of the gigantic, MULTI HMG swept around in a wide arc and clipped the side of his head as he attempted to dive back out of the way. He heard a crack and squeal of torn alloy and felt a sudden outrush of air sweep past his face as the cool interior of his armor gushed through the broken lens of his helmet's faceplate. The impact of the blow span him around and lifted him off his feet, leaving him with the sickening sensation of weightlessness for a long second before he slammed down into the dust near the towering TAG's feet.

Quickly rolling to one side, Hawkins felt the thud of an armored foot descend into the ground where he lay only a moment before. The Hospitaller dragged himself groggily to his feet, the side of his head pounding, and staggered back away from the deadly war machine. Exhausted, he tore his shattered helmet off and threw it aside before placing both hands on his sword and forcing himself back forward to attack. Sparks danced along the Gūijiǎ's thick, curved shoulder armor as a Combi Rifle rattled from somewhere behind him in a desperate attempt to find a lucky kink in the seemingly impervious armor. A second later, a missile whooshed out toward the TAG, but the Yujingyu war engine deftly bent one knee and dropped a shoulder, nimbly avoiding the deadly projectile.

Hawkins saw his chance. The TAG's bent knee, lowered close to the ground, was the same joint he had attacked earlier and severed a hydraulic line. Summoning on every last reserve of energy, Hawkins sprinted forward and brought his heavy sword up over one shoulder with both hands, hacking out at the same knee joint with all of his might as he passed. His blade caught the second hydraulic line, severing the silver piping and sending steaming purple fluid spraying out.

Almost immediately, the TAG's left leg dropped with a jolt. The knee struck the ground, sending up plumes of thick dust as the torso was flung forward. Its movements echoing the human motion of its pilot, the TAG dropped its gun and flung out a hand to steady itself against the ground, struggling to push itself back up to its feet. His eyes set in grim determination, Hawkins rushed back over to the front of the deadly war machine, dodging past the long, struggling limbs as he crossed around its flank to the very front. The pilot's compartment was now down at ground level and exposed. Hawkins hefted his sword up and hacked down again to lop off one of the pilot's arms.

Blood gushed out of the severed limb, the TAG jolted upright in response to the pilot's agonized spasms; the wail of pain from within was clearly audible even outside the war machine. With no signal leading from the pilot's missing limb, the Gūijiǎ TAG's sword arm fell limply to one side, the lethal close combat weapon falling to the ground with a loud thunk. Exhausted, Hawkins collapsed down to one knee in front of the defeated enemy war machine. Within seconds, two Fusiliers rushed past him to clamber up onto the TAG's frame, planting their Combi Rifles down through the top of the mutilated pilot's armored compartment and emptying magazines into the core to execute him.

Hawkins felt a tug on his arm and wearily obliged as he was ushered away from the battle, the tip of his bloodied sword dragging through the dust behind him. The five remaining Fusiliers of Corporal Garcia's Section took cover behind a large hunk of debris from the blazing armory whilst Mieke crouched next to Hawkins, pulling off a tattered hunk of armor from his upper arm and applying a pad to a wound before wrapping a bandage around it.

"Thank you…" Hawkins stammered to the assembled Fusiliers. "I'm sorry we couldn't drop that thing sooner… thank you…"

"There's still one more of them, sir," Lance Corporal Reid smirked, nodding her head toward the north, "if you fancy another go."

Garcia, a hand pressed against a bandaged wound of his own, grunted and shook his head.

"We're not doing jokes right now, then?" Reid grimaced.

Garcia raised his arm and tapped his comlog.

"Zero from Two-One," he called Shankar, "Marker Sierra secured, positioning HMG and launcher."

There was a brief lull before a reply was issued.

"Ang, it's Jim," Cochrane said. "The boss is gone. I've got tactical control. We can't hold the line, mate. We've got to fall back."

Garcia's eyes opened wider.

"Zero-One, say again? The boss is down?"

"Ang," Cochrane said, "you're out on a bloody limb, mate. You're exposed out there. You've got to fall back. We're rallying at Company HQ. Fall back."

Garcia swallowed and nodded.

"Two-One, understood," he said hoarsely, "falling back to Marker Alpha."

Sheathing his sword and taking his MULTI Rifle from his back, Hawkins followed the Fusiliers as they retreated quickly toward the center of the site.

***

The neatly set tables of the dining hall seemed ludicrously out of place as Cochrane rushed past the long windows of the familiar building. Seats were positioned ready by long tables, with places already set for meals that would never be served as a grenade detonated somewhere close, jarring the earth beneath his feet. Ahead of him, Lance Corporal Southee led her support team toward the Company HQ, all five Fusiliers somehow unscratched despite the bitter fighting. Cochrane turned to look behind him and saw Corporal Rossi leading her rifle team to catch up, minus one casualty left behind in the trenches.

"One-Zero-One from Alpha-Zero."

Cochrane slowed, placing one hand to cover his earpiece as his face screwed up in confusion.

"One-Zero-One," he responded. "Sir? That you?"

"Yes, it's me, Jim," Barker replied, his tone worryingly groggy. "I'm up and running again, I have tactical control. Jim, they've broken through to the west. Half of Number Two Platoon are casualties, the other half are cut off and surrounded. The survivors from Number One Platoon are defending Company HQ and the research hub. The Zhanshi have an almost clear run to the hub. Can you get there first and reinforce One Platoon?"

Cochrane did not need to check his map – the research hub was only a stone throw away. But, if Dev Bakshi's platoon had fallen, the enemy was just as close to it.

"Alpha-Zero, we're on it," Cochrane reported, setting a new marker on the research hub before opening a channel to the entire platoon.

"All units from Zero-One," Cochrane announced, "new objective is the research hub. The western defensive line is gone. One Platoon is defending the research hub and we have to reinforce them. Fall back by sections."

Pausing momentarily behind the cover of the dining hall, Cochrane took in a few long breaths as sweat continued to pour down his face in the stifling jungle heat. He could still hear the footsteps of the final, damaged TAG not far away. There were longer gaps between the blasts of gunfire now as the pace of the fighting began to slow. Cochrane could practically taste defeat in

338

the humid air. He thought of Shankar's body lying not far away. He had let her down, of that he was sure.

"Pull yourself together, dickhead," Cochrane growled quietly to himself, looking back again to check on Corporal Rossi's team's progress.

The five Fusiliers jogged steadily toward him, crossing a dusty patch of undulating earth between the dining hall and the recreational rooms. Rossi half turned to face her soldiers, holding up one hand and bringing it down in chopping motions in the direction of the research hub.

"Hurry it up, you slack bastards!" the short woman yelled. "Pick up the pace, or…"

The low howl of a sniper shot rang out. Rossi span half around from the impact of the shot, remained upright for a brief moment, and then slumped to one side.

"Sniper!" Cochrane yelled. "Get in cover! Move!"

The four Fusiliers scattered in different directions, instantly transformed from a cohesive fighting unit into four panicked and isolated individuals. Cochrane turned to look westward, where Southee was leading the Section's support team. Content that their journey was largely covered from the direction of enemy fire, he opened a private comm channel to her.

"Nat! It's Jim! That sniper is back on us, and Lucia's dead. Look, mate, it's down to you to get to the research hub. Get your team there and dig in with One Platoon. Dig in and hold for as long as you can, alright?"

"Got it, Jim," Southee replied, determination in her tone.

***

From her position on top of the deserted platoon HQ block, Beckmann possessed a commanding view of the battlefield. To the west, half a platoon of Zhanshi still exchanged fire with the isolated remnants of Number Two Platoon. In the center, not far from her current location, the survivors of Number One Platoon had taken up firing positions around the research hub, where they had swiftly managed to gun down a Fireteam of Zhanshi who had broken through the line. To the east, Number Three Platoon was scattered. The six remaining Fusiliers of Number One Section were advancing cautiously back toward the center of the site from the northwest; Cochrane led Number Three Section from the western trenches whilst Hawkins and Number Two Section sprinted back from their fight to the southeast by the furiously blazing armory.

As for the enemy, the main threat still remained to the east. The platoon of heavily armored Terracotta Invincibles had their steady progress visibly punctuated by their own fallen, clearly visible in their orange armor. But, even with significant casualties, they still outnumbered the Fusiliers and, for all the bravery displayed by the PanOceanian light infantry, a Fusilier was no match for an Invincible even if the numbers were more equal. And then there was the final remaining TAG, even without its gun. Finally, there was Beckmann's primary problem. The enemy sniper.

Beckmann remained prone, motionless, hidden to the world by the technology of her active camouflaged coveralls and hood. Her MULTI Sniper Rifle resting against its bipod and tucked in to her shoulder, one leg bent high at the knee to form a comfortable, stable firing position, she slowly scanned her scope across the edge of the jungle behind the Yujingyu heavy infantry. She briefly wondered about the shooter she was facing. Haidao Special Support Group? That would make sense supporting Zuyong Invincibles. No. This shooter knew camouflage and the art of remaining hidden. Hundun Ambush Unit? Even for a unit based out of Svalarheima, that was more likely.

The Invincibles had stopped momentarily, dashing for cover after she had blown the head off one of their NCOs. A risky move – she dare not give away her location – but for the sake of one shot and one kill, she had caused enough terror to grind the enemy advance to a halt and buy some much needed time and space for the Fusiliers.

Then Beckmann heard the shot. The howl of the high velocity round. The panicked cries and yelled orders across the Fusiliers' comlog channels. She checked the casualty reports. Corporal Lucia Rossi – dead. She placed a marker on Number Three Section's location and opened her own communication channel.

"Tac Con, Eagle One, friendly down at Marker X-Ray. Analyze lens footage."

"Tac Con, analyzing," the reply was issued instantly.

Beckmann resisted the urge to bring up the lens footage herself. She knew she needed to trust the stranger on the other end of her communication network; the nameless, faceless partner who assisted her from the safety of an environmentally controlled office, thousands of miles away in another time zone, watching her war onscreen as if it were a Maya movie. Beckmann's job was to stay sharp and be ready to fire in an instant. Between her and the jungle's edge, Cochrane took cover behind the dining hall and yelled out orders to what remained of his platoon. Beckmann waited patiently on her tactical controller's analysis. He would be rapidly bringing up the lens footage of every soldier in proximity of Corporal Rossi, looking for any clear view that showed the impact of the round that killed her and the angle of the impact. With that footage and the wonders of modern technology, Beckmann would soon have what she needed. Her answer came quickly.

"Eagle One, Tac Con. Friendly killed by six point four mil, high velocity round. Bearing... zero eight three. Elevation... eleven degrees. Range... estimated six hundred meters. Your target box accuracy... ten meters cubed."

Beckmann swung her rifle around to the cubed area highlighted on her lens by her tac con. The ten meter cubed box was lined in red; the base of a clump of trees, like any other for thousands of miles, sprouting out of the top of a small verge. Beckmann slowly scanned her scope across the bases of the trees, switching visual settings in an attempt to find her target.

"Eagle One, how copied?" her tac con asked.

"Yeah, I got it," Beckmann whispered, "wait out."

Nothing. She could see nothing. She opened her mouth to query the tac con's confidence in the information he provided but decided against it. It was a simple job. They knew what they were doing. Her problem was not the information; it was the skills and technology of the enemy sniper. However, she had a ten meter box now. As soon as the bastard moved, she would have him.

***

From where he crouched below the long windows of the dining hall, Cochrane glanced back to the scattered soldiers of Rossi's Fireteam. The footsteps of the half-crippled, relentless Gūijiǎ TAG drew ever closer. The only gunfire he could hear was off on the western perimeter, where Sergeant Bakshi's Platoon continued the fight against the surrounding Zhanshi. On his map, Cochrane saw Southee quickly leading her own team in the direction of the research hub. That was something. However, as it stood, the survivors from Number Three Platoon's other five Fireteams were separated at best, cut off at worst, and pinned in place by a sniper hidden in the jungle to the east. A light appeared to the right of Cochrane's lens, alerting him to the Platoon HQ communication channel being opened.

"Cochrane, it's Beckmann," the Hexa operative's voice whispered in his ear.

"Yeah," Cochrane replied tersely, "I hear you."

"I'm in overwatch, looking over your position," Beckmann said. "I've got the enemy sniper's position narrowed down. You've got six Fusiliers of your Number One Section, northeast, they're clear of the enemy sniper's field of fire. You can move them to the research hub. The rest of you need to stay put."

His breathing labored under the stifling sun, Cochrane looked over his map. He opened his mouth to reply but then stopped as a wild thought entered his mind. What if Beckmann *was* the enemy sniper? No. That made no sense.

"How sure are you?" Cochrane demanded.

"I've been doing this shit for about as long as you have, Sergeant," Beckmann whispered, "so either take my advice or leave it. You don't have long."

Cochrane changed channels quickly to speak with Corporal Kotal.

"One-One from Zero-One, intel update on the position of the Reaper. You're safe to proceed to the research hub. Hurry it up!"

"Got it," Kotal replied warily.

Cochrane saw the six IFF signatures on his map from Kotal's section move quickly toward the center of the base. He nodded and let out a long breath. Barker had ordered him to move the platoon to the research hub to support the defense. With Kotal's entire section and Southee's Fireteam on the way, that was half his job achieved. It just left him with the leaderless remnants of Rossi's Fireteam, and Hawkins isolated off to the south with Garcia and his Section. As if on cue, Hawkins joined in on the Platoon HQ channel.

"Jim, it's Kyle. Any idea what's going on with that sniper?"

"Hold position, mate. You and Ang are well in his firing line."

"Broadsword-One from Eagle One," Beckmann cut in, "I have the enemy sniper narrowed down to a ten meter box. As Zero-One says, you and your section are well in his firing arc."

"Could I draw him out?" Hawkins offered.

"Stay put, Broadsword-One," Beckmann breathed. "Don't do anything stupid. Not now."

"Could we smoke ourselves out?" Hawkins offered.

"Area's too large, mate," Cochrane said, "and my lot here have used so much of the stuff we've only got a couple left."

Again, the blazing jungle world fell silent save for the dragging steps of the Gūijiǎ to the east and the sporadic crackle of gunfire to the west.

"Cochrane," Beckmann said, "I need you to draw his fire."

Cochrane's head jerked upright in surprise. For the first time since his earliest days of soldiering, he felt a sharp stab of helplessness and fear in his chest.

"Are you bloody kidding me?" he snapped.

"I can do it," Hawkins said, "I can…"

"Kyle, if you move a fucking muscle out of cover, I'll shoot you in the legs myself!" Beckmann yelled. "Stay put! That's an order! Cochrane is doing it."

"Why me?" Cochrane growled, looking around helplessly. "Why the bloody hell should…"

"Because you insist on wearing that Indigo beret!" Beckmann breathed. "So you might as well have painted a crosshair on your head yourself! That bastard out there won't reveal himself for any target of opportunity, but if I was him, I would damn well take the shot on the only soldier in the entire enemy force wearing an SF beret! That TAG is close now, there isn't time for this shit! I'm sending you a marker. On my signal, you run at it. Simple as that."

And probably die. Simple as that. The plan did not appeal to Cochrane. Not one part of it. He was more than content to go to war and accept risk. But only when he could fight back. He would be targeted for his Indigo beret? What about the religious zealot in the heavy armor and red surcoat, complete with convenient aiming point marked in a white cross over his heart? Shit. She would not let Hawkins draw the sniper out. She felt the same way about him. And now Cochrane was going to die because he was picked as the bait to save some twisted, Bonnie and Clyde-like romance between two psychopaths. He looked at the marker on his lens, a simple waypoint on the far side of the open ground in front of the dining hall, near the cover of the TAG hangar.

"What are the chances?" he asked.

"Fair bit better than fifty-fifty," Beckmann replied.

Cochrane took in a deep breath and stared ahead at the marker highlighted on his lens. A fair bit better than fifty-fifty in his favor seemed as good as it would get, and he knew that the longer he thought about it, the harder it would be. He decided that if this was it, he would at least have one final say in the outcome, one tiny element of personal control over his destiny. He would choose when to run.

"On my mark..." he said to Beckmann, "...now."

Cochrane propelled himself up and straight into a sprint, bent over low as he dashed forward out of cover. His heart pounding, every step slamming down into the dusty earth seeming to take an aeon, he hurtled across the exposed ground toward the hangar. Three steps. Four steps. He darted off to the left, changing the direction of his mad dash. Six steps. Nothing was happening. He changed direction again.

Cochrane felt something on the front of his neck. His breath caught in his throat. Only a moment afterward did he hear the howl of the sniper rifle's bullet. Somehow he was still running, still alive, his mind frantically trying to pick apart the events of the previous two seconds to calculate how he was not dead. It was the disturbed air from the bullet – a narrow miss, right near his throat. The sniper had missed. Then Cochrane heard the second shot.

***

Beckmann saw Cochrane leap forward and straight into a run, his Combi Rifle held across his chest. He had not even waited for her command. For her to be ready. She had told him clearly enough that the enemy sniper's chance of hitting Cochrane was a fair bit better than fifty-fifty.

"Fucking idiot!" she scowled, quickly returning her watchful gaze to her rifle scope and the highlighted box at the jungle's edge. She took in a lungful of air, slowly let half of it out, and then held her breath. Her finger took up the pressure of the trigger, just the smallest amount of force now required to fire. Nothing stirred in the jungle ahead. No point in looking at Cochrane now, just the branches and the leaves. Any indication of the enemy shooter that might give him away. She heard the shot. She saw nothing.

"Eagle One, Tac Con, three meter cube."

The box to focus her attention narrowed significantly due to the updated information from the last shot. She still saw nothing. Then a bush seemed to move. The bastard was relocating. Beckmann saw a blur, a shimmer of green as a hunched figure in a reactive camouflage cloak half stood up and backed away. It was not even a difficult shot.

Beckmann fired. The MULTI Sniper Rifle kicked back, the padded butt digging back into her shoulder. Almost instantly, Beckmann saw something fly up and twirl away from her target. She recognized it as an arm. She opened the comm channel again.

"Got him. He's down."

A HMG opened up from somewhere along the Invincible line of advance. The TAG reached the outskirts of the inner perimeter.

"All units from Zero-One," Cochrane gasped, "enemy sniper neutralized, fall back to the research hub."

Beckmann knew that she needed to relocate – the same technology that had identified her target to her could just as easily be used against her. But, the chances of a second enemy sniper stalking her were slim, and those Fusiliers below her needed every extra second she could buy for them. Beckmann swung her rifle around on its bipod and took aim. She quickly fired a shot into the dirt by one of the Invincible Fireteams hidden behind cover – just enough to stop their advance for another minute or two – and then fired a second shot straight into the center of the damaged TAG's torso.

The TAG continued on regardless. Beckmann smoothly eased back from her firing position, well aware that this was the exact maneuver that had revealed her opposite number to her only seconds before, and then dropped down from the roof of the platoon HQ to make her own way over to the research hub.

"Tac Con, Eagle One," Beckmann called, "what's going on with our reinforcements? Where's the air cover?"

"Eagle One, Tac Con. Standby for update..."

Chapter Twenty-Two

The defensive line around the research hub consisted of nothing more than crates, containers, and battlefield debris dragged into a circle around the building, resembling something akin to an ancient wild west holo movie rather than a viable military position. Cochrane jogged over with the four remaining Fusiliers of Number Three Section's rifle team, ignoring a hand offered by a Fusilier from another platoon as he clambered over the small barricade. Cochrane dropped into cover and looked around at the other defenders. Fourteen Fusiliers from his own platoon – with another six on the way with Hawkins – was all he had to bolster the dozen survivors from Numbers One and Two Platoons, as well as the two surviving ORC heavy infantry soldiers from the unit who had been attached to Number Two Platoon. About a platoon's worth. All that was left of A Company, save the handful of soldiers at the Company HQ.

"Who's in command here?" Cochrane grunted.

"I was, until you got here, Sarn't," Corporal Kotal crawled across from the far end of the research hub wall. "What's the plan?"

A valid question. Ensuring the position was defendable was the first priority. Cochrane created a channel for all friendly IFF codes within a twenty meter radius, covering the Fusiliers from the three different platoons and the two ORC soldiers.

"All units, this is Three-Zero-One," Cochrane said, "I have tactical control of the research hub defenses. Form up into Fireteams. Three Platoon has defenses north and west; everybody else, position yourself south and east. Check weapons and ammunition, and report any problems in via your team leaders. Hold fire until I give the order or you are fired upon."

Cochrane opened a channel to Company HQ.

"Alpha-Zero, from Three-Alpha-One, I'm at the research hub. Ready for instructions."

Cochrane's query was greeted with nothing but silence. He tapped his wrist-mounted comlog to bring up his communications page on his lens, only to see that the Company HQ channel was inactive. Nothing.

"You won't get a response."

Cochrane span around and saw nothing but an empty space behind him where the voice came from. A dust covered Sinag MULTI Sniper Rifle lay propped up against the slanted side of the research hub building. Then, after the briefest moment of a blurred, hazy outline against the cream-colored wall, Beckmann appeared as her coveralls returned to their natural, glossy black state and she folded her hood back into her collar. The Hexa operative took a pack of cigarettes and a chrome lighter from one of her webbing pouches.

"They're gone," she said coolly, "Company HQ, Two Platoon… all of them. We're all that's left. Us here, and them."

Beckmann nodded in the direction that Cochrane's back was facing. He turned to see Hawkins, Mieke, and the five survivors of Number Two Section rushing over to the sparse cover of the barricade surrounding the research hub. Even the gunfire had stopped. The jungle was silent again, save the normal, droning orchestra of insects and warbling chirps of exotic birds. Cochrane grabbed his water canteen from his belt and emptied the last drops into his mouth as Hawkins and Garcia made their way across. He looked down at Garcia, noting with concern the severity of his old friend's wounds.

"You holding up alright, mate?" he asked quietly.

The short corporal nodded, but his pale face said otherwise. Cochrane clapped a hand against the younger NCO's shoulder and looked across to Hawkins.

"Bloody hell, sir, your lot did alright. Taking a TAG down by yourself."

"We didn't do it," Garcia winced, one hand pressed against his side. "Sub Officer Hawkins did. All but single-handed, pretty much."

"That's not true," Hawkins said uncomfortably, "I just kept the thing busy whilst these fellows did all of the…"

Beckmann shot to her feet and paced over, her face twisted in anger. "You did *what?*"

Hawkins looked across at her uncomfortably. The beautiful woman held out a finger and beckoned, her blue eyes still blazing in rage.

"Sub Officer. Come with me. Now."

Hawkins complied, following the tall woman to the relative privacy of the hub's doorway. Cochrane sank down next to Garcia, signaling for Mieke to come over and check his wounds. The platoon's other surviving NCOs – Kotal, Reid, Southee, and Dubois all made their way over to crouch by Cochrane.

"What now?" Garcia asked.

Cochrane looked over toward the Company HQ block. Two Fireteams of Zhanshi jogged out to either side of the building and took up covered firing positions in the surrounding wreckage. Cochrane did not have an answer.

"I heard something about support," Kotal offered. "Weren't we holding the line until air support arrived?"

"There is no air support," Beckmann said, appearing at the edge of the gathering with Hawkins and dropping to her knees. "There's no support of any kind. This is it."

"How would you know that?" Cochrane grunted. "The line to Company HQ is down. We don't know that for sure."

Beckmann tapped her ear.

"I've got my own chain of command and my own comms, Sergeant.

347

Mine are down, too, now. We're being hacked. But I had an intelligence update about three minutes ago and this is it. Just us. And there's a fresh platoon of Zhanshi moving across from the border as we speak."

"Then we don't have any choices, do we?" Kotal said, his shoulders slumped. "We're screwed."

"We do have one more card to play," Beckmann said, nodding to the research hub. "This entire place is rigged with explosives. We could fight our way out and blow the whole thing up. That way these bastards don't get anything."

"What, and lose even more diggers just to spite some ragbag pollies in the StateEmpire's capital?" Cochrane exclaimed. "Not a bloody chance, ma'am. And how would you know this place is rigged to blow up, anyway?"

Beckmann shook her head and took a long drag from her cigarette.

"Well," she narrowed her eyes dangerously, "for starters, because I planted the explosives myself, last night. I have my orders, too. I have all along. My orders are that if the defenses of this base are compromised, I am to destroy this research hub and everything in it. And last time I looked, a sergeant doesn't even come close to outranking a major, so you – all of you – will do exactly what I tell you to."

Cochrane stared across at the cool-eyed sniper crouched opposite to him. He had been right all along. It was her breaking into the hub. She was the intruder. She was what they had all been fighting to keep the entire site safe from. The beautiful killer met his gaze without flinching, the strawberry-scented cigarette dangling from her perfect lips wafting up pink-tinged strands of smoke.

"Sarn't," Lance Corporal Reid said, her tone anxious, "they're moving into position to surround us."

Cochrane checked over his shoulder. True enough, a Fireteam of Invincibles moved swiftly around to take up firing positions near the Platoon HQ block.

"Nat, Erin," Cochrane nodded to two of his three Lance Corporals, "get around this perimeter and make sure we've got a HMG and a launcher at the very least on each corner. Go on. Ang, Sahal, Abby, you stay here."

The two lance corporals moved away quickly to carry out Cochrane's orders. Cochrane looked back at Beckmann.

"You blowing this place up," he smiled grimly, "that's not how it's going to play out, Major."

"No?"

"No. Y'see, I've got tactical control. I could give that to you, but I won't. And I know you'll come straight back with your rank, but that doesn't mean much. You could be a naval dental officer wielding a commander's rank, but you'd still be a bloody dentist, unqualified to take charge of this situation.

What matters is your role. And the wording of your attachment to A Company is as an 'advisor.' So I'll listen to your advice. But I'm in command here."

Beckmann's head cocked slightly to one side. Her eyes flitted from Cochrane's as another Fireteam of enemy soldiers approached from the west. The thud of the final, damaged TAG's footsteps started again.

"We don't have time for this!" Beckmann snapped. "You can talk shit about the nuances of tactical control all you want! But what is inside this building is strategic! It's another level of command entirely! What's inside there is what everybody has been fighting and dying for since this whole thing began! This is bigger than your ego! My orders are to destroy it, and my orders are your orders! You will do what I fucking tell you to do!"

Cochrane tapped his comlog. He brought up a targeting menu. Another two taps, and Beckmann appeared bracketed in orange on his lens. He transmitted the new data to his soldiers.

Eagle One – possible hostile.

Kotal and Dubois turned in place to face Beckmann, their Combi Rifles held ready. Garcia unholstered his pistol.

"Sergeant," Hawkins said, his tone betraying his nervousness, "that's a step too far. We're all on the same side here."

Beckmann looked back over her shoulder at the Hospitaller Knight. She turned slowly back to face Cochrane, a smirk playing on her lips as she tossed the butt of her cigarette into the dust by her feet.

"What role is Sub Officer Hawkins listed as in A Company?" The Hexa operative demanded.

Cochrane's grim smile instantly faded away.

"It's not advisor, is it?" Beckmann leaned forward. "He's fully attached to this company in a combative role. So, in accordance with the rules you've just quoted at me... Sub Officer Hawkins is in command here. Not you. He outranks you and has a combat role. So it's over to him. And let me warn you, Sergeant. You highlighting me in orange is on the lens footage now. You'll get away with it because Strategic Security are the bad guys and we sometimes go rogue. But if you dare to highlight Sub Officer Hawkins as a hostile, as God above is my witness, you will fucking see what I am capable of. You understand me?"

Deflated, defeated by the rules of his own game, Cochrane looked across at the bewildered Hospitaller.

"She's right, sir. You're in command."

"Wait... wait!" Hawkins exclaimed. "I... I'm not a Fusilier. I take my orders from the NeoVatican. I'm just here for combat experience."

"The forces of the NeoVatican are signed up as a fully integrated part of the PanOceanian Military Complex," Cochrane sighed, "and you are fully attached to A Company in a combative role. You're in command."

Wide-eyed, Hawkins looked across at Cochrane, over to Beckmann, and then back to Cochrane again. At the northeast corner of the small, defensive perimeter around the building, Cochrane heard the tell-tale clunk-clunk of a HMG being cocked.

"Give… give me options," Hawkins stammered.

"Your best option is quite simple, Sub Officer," Beckmann said, "we fall back west into the jungle and we keep going west. They won't follow us because they only care about this site. Once we clear, we detonate it. Simple as that. Hell, I don't even know why we've stopped shooting! There are enemy units within visual range and we've still got ammunition!"

"We've stopped shooting because it plays into our hands!" Cochrane growled. "We're surrounded, completely outnumbered, outgunned, and cut off from our chain of command! Every minute we wait is another minute closer to reinforcements arriving! So I'm not in any hurry to start shooting again and have more of my men and women killed!"

"Reinforcements?!" Beckmann yelled. "What reinforcements? There's nothing coming! We need to take care of ourselves instead of sitting here and waiting to be rescued!"

"They won't leave us out here! This is PanOceanian soil! They won't just bloody well abandon us!" Cochrane roared. "And I've seen nothing from you that would ever convince me that you are capable of the truth! I don't believe for a second that you have had any intelligence update! You're just manipulating us all to get your job done for you!"

Hawkins moved over to crouch down between Beckmann and Cochrane, his hands held up passively. He looked across at the Hexa sniper.

"Ma'am," he asked gently, "did you receive an intelligence update? Are we cut off and surrounded?"

"Yes," Beckmann nodded, "but the second wave of Yujingyu forces isn't here yet. We still have time to fight our way out west."

Hawkins nodded slowly, his eyes fixed on the dusty ground by his feet. Cochrane opened his mouth to protest, bitterly disappointed in Hawkins for believing the lies of the professional liar. The pious, holy warrior, so easily manipulated by nothing more complex than a plunging neckline and fluttering eyelids.

"Did you transmit any data from here last night?" Hawkins continued. "Is there any new data inside that building that has not been sent out to PanOceanian intelligence?"

Beckmann tapped her comlog.

"There's your answer," she shrugged, "I'll tell you. But I'm not saying it out loud. I'm not telling anybody else."

Hawkins' eyes flickered as he read a message across his lens. Again, he fell silent and nodded. Long seconds passed as Yujingyu forces advanced toward their position. Hawkins turned to Cochrane.

"Sergeant, we're staying put," he declared. "Carry on exactly as you were. Keep this defensive line intact and don't provoke a firefight unless you have to. You know how this works ten times better than I do, so I'll trust you with it."

Cochrane's bearded jaw twisted back into a grin. That was not expected at all. The boy was listening to him.

"You got it, Boss," Cochrane grinned.

"Major," Hawkins turned back to Beckmann, "would you please open the door? I'd like you to show me what's going on inside there."

Beckmann slung her MULTI Sniper Rifle over one shoulder and shrugged.

"If that's what you want," she said simply, "follow me."

Staying low behind the makeshift barricade, Beckmann moved across to the hub's door and pressed her hand against the lock. Without even a challenge for a secondary means of identification, the doors slid open. Cochrane stared at the opening, wishing for all he was worth that there was a reason, an opportunity for him to go inside and finally find out what this whole mess was all about. Hawkins looked across to him.

"Jim, I'm going to transmit every last iota of data in there. And then I'm going to blow this place up. I need you to buy as much time as you can. If reinforcements arrive, fantastic. If they don't… you fight your way out or you surrender. As you see fit."

Cochrane let out a long breath and nodded.

"And you?"

Hawkins grinned, his handsome features almost inane, clueless.

"I'll think of something." The smile faded almost instantly. "And… I'm sorry about Priya."

Cochrane forced a smile. He offered his hand. Hawkins shook it firmly.

"Good luck, mate," Cochrane said genuinely, "you're as good a digger as I've ever worked with."

"Best of luck, old chap," Hawkins forced a final smile before he followed Beckmann inside the research hub.

***

The research hub's interior was illuminated in red, a warning alarm blaring away from speakers in the corners of the reception lobby and the main corridors. Although hurriedly evacuated only the day before, the entrance hall gave the impression of being long abandoned. Power terminals in the walls lay dormant with faded patches on the floor and furniture showing where computers and interfaces had been removed, whilst the once sterile, tiled floors were now covered with dust and clumps of plaster shaken from the ceiling after near misses from explosions in the last few hours.

"Are you alright?" Beckmann shot over to Hawkins and placed a hand on his cheek as soon as the doors shut behind them, looking down over his cracked armor and bullet-holed surcoat. "You look shot to shit!"

"It doesn't matter about that now," Hawkins said, pushing past her, "we've got to get this place transmitting again."

"It matters to me!" Beckmann countered. "I care! Getting this mission done is secondary! I told you to keep your head down and stay out of trouble, not go picking fights with TAGs! Look how that turned out for me last time I tried!"

Hawkins rushed over to the incessantly blaring siren and tapped through interfaces on his comlog in a futile attempt to shut off the noise.

"Why is it doing that? Why can't I turn it off?"

Beckmann tapped her own wrist and the siren stopped abruptly.

"This building is powered by the site's main generator, and that's offline," Beckmann said. "The siren is warning of the main power failure. This place has its own backup generator but it will only last for a few days. So what's your plan? What now?"

Relying on his vague memories of his one visit to the hub's interior, Hawkins clipped his MULTI Rifle to his back and made his way quickly toward where he thought he remembered the main terminal room was located.

"Your message to me, just outside a moment ago," Hawkins said as the two hurried through red-lit, abandoned corridors, "you said that all you did here last night was plant explosives, as you were ordered to. So you didn't transmit any data? That means that there is still valuable information here we need to send to the correct authorities before we blow this place up."

Beckmann tapped Hawkins on the shoulder as he attempted to turn right at a junction in the corridors.

"No. This way. It's worse than that, Kyle. The data I've been transmitting... it's minuscule in scope. For me to get in here undetected and allow my controller to hack the system – we can transmit data for less than a second. The daily update the research staff have been sending to MagnaObra's HQ? It's up to an hour long. Every artifact, every measurement, every 3D scan – everything is catalogued and transmitted to Neoterra. All I had time to do was transmit the CEO's update file with the most important points. That's it."

The two soldiers reached the main terminal room. Beckmann again tapped her comlog and the door opened, but the alarm instantly blared back into life.

"We never did get the hack entirely right for this room," she explained, darting across to the hub's main data terminal.

Hawkins glanced back down the corridor toward the main entrance. Still silent, still no gunfire. But time was short. Beckmann looked at him.

"What do you want me to do?"

Hawkins swallowed.

"Set up a link with the correct authority and start transmitting as much data as you can."

"The correct authority?" Beckmann's eyes widened. "You mean the Yu Jing StateEmpire?"

"What?" Hawkins demanded. "What do you mean?"

"We're on Yujingyu soil," Beckmann said, "we always have been. This Cosmolite is legally theirs. A mapping team stumbled on it nearly two years ago. With it being so close to the border, that's why Strategic Security removed all of those border posts around the planet. To cast doubt on the survey. It was really all about this one post not far from here. Remove that, and this Cosmolite appears to suddenly be on our side of the border."

Hawkins took a step back, his mind racing. The siren continued to blare, hammering away at his head as he struggled to assemble his thoughts.

"You mean... we lied about the position of the border? This whole border dispute, we caused it? Just to put this Cosmolite in our hands? We've been lying this whole time and we've known about it?"

Beckmann's eyes narrowed sympathetically.

"It's how it works, Kyle. We don't all get to be white knights. This is reality. Our government saw an opportunity, and we took it."

Hawkins turned away. He looked around the small, cramped room as if inspiration or answers would lie somewhere behind the dust-covered terminal or between the smooth, white tiles.

"Why?" he found himself demanding. "What's so damned important about this place?"

Beckmann took a pace after him.

"I... I don't know much about this place," she said, "I'm no hacker. I don't know computers. I certainly don't have a brain for science so I can't understand more than half of what I read here. All they trained me to do is infiltrate and kill. It's all I know."

"But you must know something!" Hawkins insisted. "You must have seen the headlines in those files you sent to Strategic Security!"

"Yes," Beckmann nodded, nervously eying the corridor back to the main entrance, "yes, I saw enough. These Cosmolites, they're what's left of a previous alien civilization, we knew that already. What was here before our human settlers arrived in the *Aurora*. But they've all been damaged by nano-technology. A virus. But not this place, where we are right now. At least, not as much as any of the others. A few artifacts survived here relatively intact. That's what this whole thing is about."

"Artifacts?" Hawkins shouted over the din of the alarm. "We're fighting over some bloody museum pieces?!"

Beckmann shook her head, her eyes dark.

"No. Not any artifacts. They've survived intact enough to have their origins identified. They're Tohaa. This whole thing, whatever happened here to the Aurora settlers, whatever the Ur-Probe was… the Tohaa were part of all of it. That's what's so important. Whoever has the confirmation of this information has a really, really big bargaining chip with the Tohaa. And MagnaObra were accepting PanOceanian government funding to run this place, but they weren't sharing the information about the Tohaa. They were keeping this to themselves! That's why I was sent here. To find out what was really happening. And that's why we *have* to destroy this place before the Yujingyu get in here!"

Hawkins took another step back and then sank down slowly onto an empty crate in the corner of the room. The siren continued to blare. The flashing red lights carried on painting Beckmann and the terminal room in shades of scarlet. Hawkins blinked and tried to control his breathing. This was huge. This could alter the political balance across the entire Human Sphere and beyond. The Tohaa, the advanced alien civilization locked in bitter conflict with the EI, sharing a hatred of humanity's greatest foe… but the Tohaa themselves were part of the complete annihilation of the Aurora colony?

"Why do we do this?" Hawkins whispered. "We're here, threatened with extinction, and we shoot and stab each other because of ideology. Because of lines on maps. Why do we do this when we should be coming together to face real evil?"

Beckmann looked down at the floor.

"It's the way we've always been," she said quietly, her voice all but lost behind the alarm, "it is humanity. It is our downfall."

A HMG thumped away from outside the research hub. Combi Rifles began to chatter. Grenades exploded.

"Kyle!" Beckmann shouted above the alarm. "We need to act! What do you want us to do?"

Throwing aside the gravity of the situation created by Beckmann's revelation, Hawkins leapt to his feet.

"Power up the data terminal," he said to Beckmann, "you know how to do that, right? You know enough to get that thing going?"

Beckmann darted over to the terminal, the MULTI Sniper Rifle and Combi Rifle on her back clattering against each other as she bent over to boot the system up.

"We need to transmit as much data as we can," Hawkins said, leaning out of the doorway to look warily back down the main corridor, toward the thump of explosions and hammering of guns. "I don't know what information is on that thing, but every second it is transmitting, somebody with the knowledge to decipher it has a chance of finding out something more vital to use against the EI. And the Tohaa, it now appears. We need to get this thing transmitting."

Beckmann looked up at him as the main screen flickered into holographic life just above the hard keypad.

"It's ready," she said, the blue-white of the screen lighting up her face in contrast to the surrounding red of the alarms, "but like I said, I don't know how to use this! All I can do is put every single file on this terminal in one, huge data stream and then hit 'send'. That's all I can do. So who do you want me to send it to?"

Hawkins looked down at her, his eyes narrowed.

"You need to choose!" Beckmann urged. "My orders were to send information to the Strategic Security Division. But if you are still going to tell me that morality outranks all and we should do the right thing, the honest thing, then this information belongs to Yu Jing. So what's it going to be?"

Hawkins met her stare evenly, but with his confidence fast draining away. They both stumbled as an explosion shook the building and dust fell from the ceiling. Hawkins tapped his comlog and sent a small file to Beckmann.

"Neither," he said, "don't send it to either of them. Send the file to this address."

Beckmann's focus shifted to her lens. She leaned back over the terminal and rapidly pressed a series of soft keys hovering amidst the holographic display screen.

"Done," she replied, "the files are transmitting. Every second we buy now is a second they'll receive more information. Now what?"

"Jim, it's Kyle," Hawkins turned to call Cochrane over the comlog, "we're transmitting data. We're up and running. Every second we can buy now might make a difference. But when we detonate this place, we need to be well, well clear."

"Got it," the simple answer came.

Hawkins turned back to Beckmann.

"We need to head back outside," he breathed, rushing toward the data room door, "we need to go help Cochrane and the others and buy as much time as we can."

A hand shot out and grabbed Hawkins by the shoulder as he rushed past Beckmann. He stopped and turned to face her. Her features darkened again.

"Kyle," she said, her voice low, "those Fusiliers out there, they can surrender when they've had enough. They're just soldiers in the PanOceanian army. The Yujingyu have little interest in them. But you and I? A warrior of the NeoVatican and a Major in Strategic Security? We don't have that option, I'm afraid. And now we've just done what we've done, we both know too much. And they *will* get that information out of us if they get hold of us. We can't surrender. We can't go back out there."

***

His Combi Rifle pulled against his shoulder, Cochrane squeezed the trigger and let out another short burst of fire. His rounds caught a Zhanshi rifleman across the top of the chest, blowing the enemy soldier back to disappear beneath the cover of the edge of the Platoon HQ. His weapon clicking empty, Cochrane dropped down beneath the barricade and ejected his magazine before grabbing a fresh one from his webbing. He looked down. After this one, only one magazine left. And from the reports sent up to him from his team leaders, nobody else was faring any better. They did not have long left.

"HMG!" Abby Reid shouted from further along the barricade. "Five points left of Marker X-Ray!"

The newly set up HMG chattered into life, spewing bullets into the barricade with an echoing series of thumps and thuds. A Fusilier from Number One Section fell back, a bloody bullet hole in his forehead. From the northeast corner, one of the heavily armored ORC Troopers quickly stood up and fired a burst from his MULTI Rifle, gunning the Zhanshi HMG operator down.

"Three-Zero-One from Alpha-Zero."

Cochrane's eyes widened in alarm.

"Three-Zero-One from Alpha-Zero," the voice repeated.

"Sir?" Cochrane queried hesitantly.

"Jim, it's the boss," Major Barker's voice crackled through his ear. "Sergeant, it's over now. It's time to stand down."

To his right, Cochrane saw another of his Fusiliers manning a HMG crumple forward and lie still, slumped over his gun. Lance Corporal Southee quickly hauled the body clear and took position on the gun herself, firing long bursts up at the advancing TAG. Suspicion suddenly set into Cochrane's mind. HQ had been offline for a good while now, and now Barker was apparently back on comms, his very first order was to surrender? Impersonating an enemy unit over a hacked communication network was easy enough to do.

"Alpha-Zero from Three-Zero-One," Cochrane asked hesitantly, bringing up his cryptographic coding screen on his lens, "authenticate."

"From Alpha-Zero," Barker replied, "I authenticate – Four Mike."

Cochrane checked his codepage for the correct response on the very second he made the demand. The response was correct.

356

"You're right to check, Jim," Barker said, "I'd be wary, too. They've got us now. All of us. You're all that's left. I'm here with their commanding officer. They're treating us well. They're tending to all of our wounded. Jim, I didn't get any more orders from Regimental HQ before they hacked our comm system. We're on our own. They're asking me to get you to surrender."

Cochrane took his position back at the barricade, raising his rifle to his shoulder again. A Zhanshi appeared around the edge of the accommodation blocks with a missile launcher. Cochrane quickly highlighted the target as a priority and fired three single, aimed shots off at the enemy trooper, enough to force him back into cover.

"Sergeant," Barker continued, "we're out of options. You're losing soldiers pointlessly. You need to stand down."

Cochrane knelt down again to take cover, running his limited options through in his mind. Taking a breath, he made a decision.

"Boss, is the enemy CO there with you?" he asked.

"Yes."

"Are you ready to take down my message to him?"

"Yes, ready," Barker replied.

"Okay. Tell him to bugger himself sideways with a bloody bonsai tree. Or whatever else he has to hand. I'm not fussy."

***

"So... what do we do?" Hawkins asked incredulously. "You're saying we can't go out there, and we need to blow this whole building up and most of what's underneath it? You're not honestly suggesting that we..."

Beckmann held a hand up to silence the Hospitaller. Unslinging her Combi Rifle and grenade launcher, she walked out into the corridor leading back to the main entrance. The siren continued to wail incessantly as the red lights of alert lit the entire building interior.

"Down that way," Beckmann pointed to the right, "second right turn. At the end of that corridor is a hatch. That's the only way out now."

Hawkins looked down both ends of the corridor; one leading to the fight outside and where his sense of duty told him he ought to be.

"Where does the hatch lead?" Hawkins asked.

"To the Cosmolite itself," Beckmann replied, "to what's left of the entire Tohaa settlement, or installation, or whatever was once down there before the nanobots ripped it to shreds."

"And there's a way out through there?" Hawkins asked.

Beckmann shrugged. Her features lacked any of their normal drive and determination.

"I don't know. I've never been down there, not very far at least. All

357

of the artifacts in good condition that weren't evacuated are in the first two rooms. That's where I've planted the bulk of the explosives. Once they're destroyed along with the main terminal, this place is just another Cosmolite. But it stands to reason that there should be more than one way out. This entrance right here can't be the only one."

Hawkins took a few paces toward the corridor, his fingers gripping tightly to his MULTI Rifle. He half turned to face her. Beckmann still stood by the corridor junction.

"But… we're just leaving the others behind?"

"Kyle, this place has to be destroyed. If you go out there, you will die fighting or you will surrender. They will interrogate you and then kill you. If you stay here, you will go up with the explosion. Your only chance is to get down into those tunnels and hope you can find a way out. It might take you an hour. It might take you a week. I don't know. But it's your only chance. You need to go."

Hawkins' jaw dropped. His Multi Rifle fell down to one side in his loose grip. Only now did he pick up on the meaning behind her words.

"What… why… why just me? What are you doing?"

Beckmann looked across at him and smiled. The smile did nothing to lighten her features or cast away the despondence and despair in her eyes.

"Kyle," she said softly, "you never really thought we would have some fairy tale ending, did you? You know how important this place is. You know the severity of what is at stake here. Every second I can buy is a second of data that could change the entire course of human relations with the Tohaa. I'm staying here. You need to go."

"Don't talk nonsense!" Hawkins snapped, pacing forward. "This isn't worth dying for! Any of it!"

"And those Fusiliers outside?" Beckmann said. "The ones dying to keep this building from falling into enemy hands long enough to transmit the data – should we tell them to surrender now? It doesn't work that way."

"But you can't stay here! They have a chance out there, a decent chance! If you stay, you're dead! No questions! Come with me! This is ludicrous!"

Beckmann stepped forward and took one of his hands in both of hers, exactly the same way she had when she had met him outside his block at Kokoda Barracks after she was released from hospital.

"It's alright," she said, "it's honestly alright. Let me go out on my terms. Let me go out on a high. This… between us. It can't work if we make it back to the real world. It could never work. I don't want to go back to being what I was. What they made me into. I can't do it again. I've had enough, Kyle. I've tried to end it before but I never could. Let me go."

Hawkins looked down at her, his own despair sinking deeper as he desperately tried to think of another option, a way to convince her to leave with him. As the din of battle continued outside, he thought of what it would be like even if he did escape, knowing that he left her behind. Knowing that his decisions forced her into that hub and to her doom. He shook his head.

"No. No. If you are staying, then so am I. No. I'm staying here with you."

Beckmann placed her hands on his neck and leaned up to kiss him. She forced another unconvincing smile.

"Go," she urged quietly.

Hawkins stared at her impassively, his jaw set in determination.

"No. I'm not leaving."

Beckmann's smile faded. She took two steps back away from him. Her chin dropped until she was looking at the floor, locks of her dark hair falling to cover her eyes. The Hexa operative took in two deep breaths and then looked up. When she swept her hair back out of her face, Hawkins felt as though he was looking into the eyes of a complete stranger. The spark and energy from her features was gone. Her eyes seemed dull and lifeless. Even her stance seemed completely different.

"Alright, Sub Officer," she said, "enough is enough. Let's end the charade."

A sickening claw grasped Hawkins' heart as he listened to the words. The German accent was gone, replaced with a soft, non-rhotic, Australian twang.

"Lisette," Hawkins said, "what do you…"

"Major Lisette Beckmann doesn't exist," the woman said nonchalantly, "she never did. Just a cover identity to get this job done. Come on, Sub Officer, were you never suspicious? Insanely beautiful woman drops into your world, with the same religious values as you, same taste in music and movies… and somehow needing you to put her life on track? Almost as if… I don't know, you were profiled by Strategic Security the moment you set foot on Paradiso, identified as an easy way to get a foot in the door of this place, and a character was fabricated to achieve that in case it was needed as a secondary method of infiltrating this hub?"

Hawkins let his MULTI Rifle fall down by his side and dangle off its sling. He raised both armored hands to his face and stared at the stranger through the gaps between his fingers. His heart hammered and his chest physically ached painfully.

"Now I've still got a mission to achieve," the woman said, "and it involves you leaving me alone with this data terminal. I have my own exit plan, and it doesn't involve you. So, as a professional courtesy to your Order, I've given you a lifeline. A way out. I suggest you take it. Or, as the old saying goes, there is the other way."

The tall woman's hand moved to her side. Hawkins heard the soft double click of a pistol being cocked. He looked into her eyes. The woman with the dull stare and the dead features looked back at him emotionlessly, a blank canvas without a shred of evidence of feeling. A complete stranger. Hawkins took a step back. The weight of his decisions – decisions with massive implications across the entire Human Sphere – weighed more heavily on him than he thought possible. His lost love, the betrayal of his heart and soul caught his breath in his throat. Completely at a loss for words, Hawkins turned and stumbled wearily toward the hatch leading down to the Cosmolite.

***

Lance Corporal Natalie Southee – severe wound, abdominal

Cochrane looked across desperately and saw Southee drooped over the HMG, blood dripping from one side of her mouth. She wearily cocked the weapon and brought it back up, firing off another long burst into the enemy positions by the accommodation blocks. Cochrane fired another round in the same direction, and his Combi Rifle clicked empty. He dropped the faithful weapon and unholstered his pistol.

Corporal Sahal Kotal – severe wound, respiratory

"Medic!" A shout came from the south side of the defenses.

Cochrane looked up as the TAG paced over the rough ground to the north, its close combat weapon raised and ready to strike as it finally limped back into the fight. He checked his platoon's weapons inventory. No missiles left. It was over. They were done.

"Zero-One to all units! Cease fire! Cease fire! Alpha-Zero from Three-Alpha-One! Call them off! Tell them we're done! Tell them we're coming out!"

The gunfire from all around him died away quickly, taking a few seconds more before the Yujingyu teams surrounding the defensive circle also stopped firing. Cochrane dashed past tired, wounded soldiers to where Southee was hurriedly reloading her HMG with blood-covered, shaking hands.

"Nat!" Cochrane shouted. "Nat! Cease fire! We're done! Stop!"

The wounded Fusilier looked around groggily at Cochrane and forced a weak smile.

"Coward," she grinned impishly, "you give up... too easily..."

Cochrane wrapped an arm beneath her shoulders and carefully helped her down to a seated position.

"Alright, mate," he forced away a wave of panic as he saw how quickly she was losing blood, "alright. Don't die on me, and I'll write you up for a medal, you bloody idiot."

The TAG stopped in place, one foot on the barricades only meters away from Cochrane's head. The gunfire stopped. The cries of the wounded were all that could be heard beneath the furious, sweltering heat of the midday sun.

"Alpha-Zero," Cochrane called Barker, "I want to send out my wounded for treatment."

There was a momentary pause before the response came.

"They agree. Move your wounded to the Platoon HQ building."

Cochrane holstered his pistol, took off his beret, and removed his ear piece. He looked around at the sea of faces lining the insides of the barricades, grime and blood covered, all staring up at him expectantly.

"Nice one, diggers," he forced a smile, "nice one. Get the wounded across to Platoon HQ."

His shoulders heavy with the burden of failure, Cochrane flashed a smile and a wink to Southee as Mieke dashed across, supporting the wounded soldier and helping her out to limp over toward the Yujingyu firing line at the Platoon HQ. Angelo Garcia was next out. He mustered one last grin and thumbs up to Cochrane as he passed.

"Don't worry about it, Jim," he slurred, "we'll have a ball of a time working out how to escape from the prison camp. It'll be like an old war movie!"

Cochrane patted his friend on the back as he was helped past, and then he sank to lean back against the curved wall of the research hub.

***

Hawkins had taken only a single step down the ladder leading into the Cosmolite itself when he stopped. It was silent outside. The gunfire, the explosions, all had ceased. He brought up his comlog to open his channel with Cochrane, but it was gone. Deleted. He clung to the ladder in the darkness for a long few moments, his breathing echoing off the black, rocky walls around him. In those few moments of dark, peaceful silence, he suddenly thought things through more clearly than he had managed to in as long as he could remember. His calmed mind made more sense of the mayhem. And the lies. Hawkins climbed back up the ladder.

The Hexa operative lay behind a crate at the top end of the corridor, her MULTI Sniper Rifle ready on its bipod and her Combi Rifle lying next to it. The dark-haired woman looked up at him over her shoulder.

"This is your exit strategy?" Hawkins challenged. "The one you said you had all ready?"

The tall woman stood up, her face still devoid of emotion.

"I gave you an option," she said, her subtle accent seeming wrong on her lips, "but you had to choose the hard way."

"Luke's Gospel, chapter twenty-two," Hawkins replied.

The woman folded her arms and stared at him.

"I'm sorry?"

"After Christ was taken away, and Peter ran. Christ said at the Last Supper that Peter would deny him three times. But I'll come back to that. You see, all my life, people have made fun at me for being stupid. Not academically, I'm mediocre at math and science and the like. But common sense? I've got none of that. I'm always the butt of the jokes there."

Silently, coldly, the tall woman continued to stare. One hand moved to her pistol holster.

"But I stopped and thought for once," Hawkins continued regardless, confident in his approach, "about that common sense thing. It occurred to me that you must be lying about something. Either Lisette doesn't exist, as you say, or what you are pretending to be now is the lie. That would make sense because it would force me to run, exactly as you wanted. That's when I thought of Peter and denying Christ three times before rooster crowed."

The woman unholstered her heavy pistol. The threatening action meant nothing to Hawkins.

"So I think this is the lie," the Hospitaller said, pointing at her, "what you pretend to be right now. I think the real you is the one I know. The real you is strong in faith and loves me. So I don't think you could deny Christ, then point that gun at me and pull the trigger. In fact, I'm willing to bet my life on it."

Hawkins walked forward. The woman stared at him, her eyes narrowed and her lips trembling. She holstered the pistol. Tears flowed down her grimy cheeks.

"Why didn't you go?" Beckmann sobbed, wiping the tears out of her eyes. "They've surrendered outside! You've run out of time now! You'll never get clear! Why couldn't you let me do this for you?"

Hawkins smiled and held out his hand.

"I'm not too interested in the odds," he said softly, "so let's forget about those and give these tunnels a go anyway."

***

The last of the wounded disappeared out of view behind the Platoon HQ, each Fusilier helped along by an uninjured soldier. Cochrane was left behind the barricade with half of the defenders. Still, nobody spoke. He looked out over the rough ground at the lines of enemy soldiers – perhaps twenty

Zhanshi and a dozen Terracotta Invincibles lay in prone positions behind their weapons took cover at the edges of buildings or lay on top of their roofs. Cochrane shook his head. Perhaps if they had more ammunition, they could have lasted longer. Perhaps if there was not one last TAG, they might even have won.

Up ahead, Cochrane saw two figures walk out to the edge of the rough ground, along the path from the dining hall that Cochrane had used three times a day, joking with his friends in eager anticipation of good food. Now that path was littered with debris and evidence of fighting. The two men both wore the light armor of Zhanshi, but even from this distance, Cochrane could see their badges of rank now openly worn with the gunfire ceased. Both men stopped just in front of the enemy firing line.

"I guess this is for me," Cochrane smiled to Lance Corporal Reid and then clambered over the barricade.

Dripping with sweat, the high midday sun beating down into his eyes, Cochrane walked tall and proud out toward the enemy soldiers. Thirty guns followed his progress as he walked, reaching up to straighten his beret and wipe dust off the shoulders of his armor. He stopped in front of the two Zhanshi officers. One was a short man of perhaps twenty years of age, with a thin, neat moustache and pale skin. The taller man was a similar age to Cochrane; clean shaven and with short hair, graying at the temples. Both men carried swords at their side.

"My major wishes you to confirm that you have surrendered," the shorter man said.

Cochrane slowly, carefully, reached down to his holster. He took out his pistol, grabbed it by the muzzle, and offered it handle first to the taller officer. The man uttered a few brief words to his lieutenant in a language Cochrane could not understand.

"The major says that you may keep your sidearm," the junior officer translated in good English. "He assures you that after witnessing such a spirited defense, he knows that he is in the presence of a leader possessing courage and integrity."

"Well, your boss here has got me wrong," Cochrane spat bitterly, "so probably best you take this bloody thing off me before I shoot him in his smug, ugly face."

"That would be unadvisable," the lieutenant said without mirth. "This whole unfortunate misunderstanding. It's over now. I cannot blame you for believing the lies your chain of command duped you with. But this site was always ours. PanOceania – you and your soldiers – you are, in your vernacular, the 'bad guys' in all of this. The villains. Please don't compound problems even further by shooting my commanding officer and forcing me to shoot you in turn."

Cochrane bit back a retort, knowing that he was beaten. He obediently holstered his pistol.

"You will order your soldiers to leave their positions now," the lieutenant translated from his major.

Cochrane turned around.

"Diggers!" he called back. "We're done! Weapons down! Assemble out front! No funny ideas!"

Cochrane watched, a bitter ball of pride choking in his throat as the exhausted, disheveled survivors of A Company walked out into the rough ground between the research hub and the Yujingyu firing line. The soldiers formed neatly up into two lines, the front rank bringing up their right arms to check their spacing as if on ceremonial parade. The arms slammed down and each soldier stood rigidly at ease.

"Company HQ, if you please," the lieutenant smiled at Cochrane.

Cochrane eyed the shorter soldier, knowing he should pay the courtesy of saluting the major but deciding against it with great deliberation. He turned about and marched across to his Fusiliers, stopping a few paces short of them.

"Squad! 'Shun!" Cochrane bellowed.

Each soldier brought their right knee up to waist height and then slammed them down, bringing their fists to each side to stand to attention. A cloud of dust wafted up from the slamming of their boots into the dry earth.

"Turning right in twos, right... turn!" Cochrane boomed.

The two ranks turned with well-drilled precision as Cochrane turned to his left to face in the same direction as his soldiers.

"By the right! Quick... march!"

The last soldiers of A Company, 1st Battalion, the 12th Fusilier Regiment, marched smartly off for processing and captivity, their feet crunching into the earth in perfect timing, their backs straight and their heads held high. So many thoughts ran through Cochrane's head as they marched around the shattered base, past debris and destruction, and dead bodies from both sides of the fight. He thought about home and his father. He thought about Priya Shankar. Perhaps a minute later, the earth shook as a series of six explosions erupted spectacularly in quick succession, throwing segments of the research hub high up into the air as dense clouds of acrid, black smoke billowed up from the ruined building and the sunken earth for a dozen yards around it in every direction. Cochrane smiled as he marched.

"Nice one, mate. Nice one."

Epilogue

The main wheels of the bulky, POC-9 Rhincodon touched down at Klugestein aerospace port with a thud, causing the rows of passengers inside the dimly lit cabin to jolt forward against their seat harnesses. As the aircraft lost speed, the nose gradually lowered until the nose wheel also touched down on the runway with a brief squeal, and the groan of the aircraft's massive engines increased in pitch as reverse thrust was applied.

For every last one of the aircraft's thirty-two passengers, even the excitement of the journey's destination had failed to keep them from falling asleep for practically the entire flight. Following the rapid end of hostilities after the assault on Alpha Four-Four, fresh uniforms were flown out to the Pan-Oceanian military prisoners in their detention center, allowing them at least to feel a semblance of humanity in their four-day incarceration.

Sitting at a passenger aircraft's window seat for the first time since his childhood, Cochrane looked out at the runway edge lights as the aircraft continued to slow down. The control tower, terminals, and hangar buildings all swept past in the last light of dusk beneath a gray, overcast sky. Cochrane caught his own reflection in the window, agreeing with a compliment passed to him by one of his Fusiliers only that morning. With his face now clean shaven for the first time in three years, and having had four nights of solid sleep in the admittedly spartan Yujingyu detention facility, Cochrane did look ten years younger. Even if he did not feel it.

The entertainment provided in the detention center was demoralizing, to put it mildly. A single screen for all of the detainees, giving around the clock media updates from Yujingyu StateEmpire-controlled news channels. It was claimed that there was proof of PanOceanian tampering with border posts and that the research site at Alpha Four-Four legally belonged to Yu Jing. Their media claimed that this fully legitimized the Glottenberg Incursion. Cochrane had, at least, had a chance to watch a PanOceanian news update on the flight back to Klugestein.

O-12 decreed Alpha Four-Four to belong to the Yujingyu StateEmpire, but given that O-12 had already stated they would settle the dispute, this made the Glottenberg Incursion illegal. The net result was that both PanOceania and Yu Jing were naughty children and had been placed in O-12's political equivalent of time out. Cochrane grinned as he thought on that final explosion that had decimated the research hub. None of it mattered now. The Yu Jing forces were left with nothing. He hoped Hawkins had escaped.

The lumbering Rhincodon swung smoothly left and taxied off the runway, following the rows of white lights along the taxiway centerline toward a large dispersal area in front of a terminal building. Most of the others were awake now, and a few hushed conversations were struck up along the rows of seats. Cochrane looked around at the other soldiers from A Company. Thirty-two men and women. The other survivors were not yet fit to be repatriated to PanOceania, although in a show of good will, the StateEmpire had agreed to PanOceanian medical staff being granted access to the casualties still recovering in Yujingyu hospitals.

Its nose gently swinging around again, the aircraft's engines powered down to idle as it finally came to a halt. Cochrane yawned and looked along his row of seats. Greg Pine was somehow still asleep. George Trent was already texting on his comlog. Abby Reid looked up at Cochrane.

"What's your plan now, Sarn't?" she asked.

"Dunno," Cochrane grumbled, "find some civvy clothes and go out. Get pissed. How about you?"

"Yeah. Same."

The aircraft's seat harnesses were finally released. Reid nudged Trent to nudge Pine in turn, waking him up so that their row could stand and queue for the forward passenger door along with the other soldiers. Cochrane saw one of the flight crew walk over to the front row of seats and lean over to whisper urgently to Captain Waczek. As the only Fusilier officer to survive the assault without a wound, she was the ranking soldier on the flight of uninjured survivors, leaving Cochrane to assume the conversation was probably related to a senior military officer waiting outside for them on the dispersal area.

Cochrane stood and awkwardly nudged his way along the seats toward the aircraft's gray, utilitarian central aisle. He saw Sergeant Dev Bakshi from Number Two Platoon on the far side of the passenger compartment and exchanged a brief wave. A warm blast of air blew back into the cabin as the aircraft's forward passenger door was opened. Much to Cochrane's genuine surprise, he heard cheering from outside. The Fusiliers exchanged confused and excited looks as they slowly edged along the narrow passageway between the modular rows of seats toward the exit. He was no stranger to coming home from deployment to find a heart-warming welcome prepared by families and friends, but that certainly was not the norm after an intense period of high profile fighting. It tended to be not politically correct and leave certain elements and lobbies unhappy.

Up ahead, Waczek was the first to leave the aircraft and walk down the staircase. The line of passengers edged along slowly, the air becoming warmer as the aircraft cabin's environmental control system lost its fight against the hot, humid air of Paradiso. Cochrane arrived at the door. He looked down and saw perhaps two hundred people waiting behind a barrier on the far side of the dispersal, in front of the four story, U-shaped terminal building.

Wives, husbands, and children waited excitedly to see their loved ones coming home after nearly a week in enemy captivity, the myriad colors of their clothing standing out in stark contrast to the drab hues of the Fusiliers' combat fatigues. Media cameras filmed the soldiers as they walked down the steps, under the close supervision of military media officers who would, no doubt, be ensuring the faces of the Fusiliers were blanked out of any media broadcasts. The excited buzz of conversation rose as each soldier appeared at the aircraft's doorway in turn. Parents squatted down by small children and pointed up at the aircraft. Older children jumped and waved.

Suddenly feeling like he would rather face an entire platoon of Yu-jingyu guns, Cochrane stepped slowly down the metal grate steps of the ladder. His booted feet hit the tarmac, the lights of the terminal and the dispersal edging seeming unnaturally bright against the gray, twilight sky as he followed the line toward the opening ahead in the barrier. Waczek was intercepted by an officer in the uniform of a brigadier and, after an awkwardly staged publicity picture, was quickly led away. Erin Dubois was the next through, where she was excitedly met by her parents and two screaming sisters. Dev Bakshi was nearly knocked to his feet by his son and daughter. The line moved slowly forward.

By the time Cochrane made it through the barrier, the crowd was half broken up into smaller groups as families crowded around their returning loved ones. Cochrane could not help but smile when he saw his father and Danny, his older brother, both waiting for him. Danny paced out and enthusiastically wrapped his arms around his brother, instantly transforming Cochrane from the Indigo Sergeant into the baby of the family he recalled being for his entire childhood.

"Welcome back, dickhead!" Danny beamed. "Even those useless buggers couldn't kill you, hey?"

"They tried!" Cochrane smiled, returning the embrace for a long moment. "Thanks for coming out here!"

Cochrane stepped back and saw his father walk briskly over. His father, like Danny, had chosen to wear civilian clothing despite his rank. Brian's greeting to his younger soon was not as animated or emotional, but Cochrane thought he saw tears in the old man's eyes when he stepped in to warmly shake his hand and clap him on the shoulder with the other.

"Welcome back, James. Are you alright? Were you well treated?"

"I'm alright, Dad," Cochrane shrugged, "I'm alright. They asked us all a few questions and got a bit aggressive, but that was all. They didn't treat us badly. I'm just glad to be back."

Brian took a step back, just as a blue-uniformed member of the ground crew was walking behind him. The older man clattered into the ground handler awkwardly and held up his hands to apologize.

"Watch it, mate!" The ground handler snarled.

Cochrane lunged forward. Weeks of combat, jungle heat, dozens of dead friends and comrades, the uncertainty of capture, all exploded in one moment.

"Oi!" he bellowed from the bottom of his lungs, frantically searching the air force handler for some recognizable rank but seeing only the confusing propeller emblem on his epaulettes. "Propeller man! No! Don't you dare talk to the colonel like that!"

Danny dashed forward to gently but firmly hold Cochrane back as the startled handler blurted out a terrified apology.

"Easy, mate! Easy!" Danny smiled. "C'mon, mate! There's kids here! It's alright!"

Cochrane stared at the retreating handler with venom, taking in a series of deep breaths. Danny led him away from the silent, uncomfortable gazes of surrounding family members of his platoon.

"Come on," Brian pushed his way between his two sons and patted them both on their shoulders, "let's all go get a drink."

Cochrane felt his pulse slowing again as he walked away, screams of delight and cries of joy left behind him as more Fusiliers were reunited with their families. Then Cochrane recognized a face at the back of the crowd. A man he had seen pictures of but never met. The short, rotund man stood high and awkwardly on his tip toes, his panicked, distressed face looking desperately at the soldiers walking down from the Rhincodon's steps. Cochrane stopped.

The man was David, Shankar's fiancé. He would have been told, of course, by now. He knew Priya was dead. Clearly the pale-faced man simply could not accept it. He watched each soldier appear at the doorway of the aircraft, his heart seeming to die a little every time it was not the face he wanted to see. Cochrane knew that of every soldier who served alongside Priya Shankar, it was most appropriate for him to be the one to talk to David. To tell him what an incredible person Shankar was, right to that last, fearless moment. But for the first time in Cochrane's entire adult life, his courage gave way. He turned his back on the shaking man at the back of the crowd and walked away with his father and brother.

***

Hawkins halted his march in front of the aged, dark wood desk and brought himself smartly to attention. The thick, black material of his uniform trousers rubbed abrasively against his still-heavily bruised legs, and his ribcage still felt as though it was throbbing from the cracks he had sustained from what seemed like countless bullet impacts against his heavy armor at Alpha Four-Four. That was nearly a week ago now. Yet, dressed in his black uniform and stood to attention in the very same briefing room he had last met

Father-Officer De Fersen at Kokoda Barracks Officers' Mess, the fighting suddenly seemed a year ago.

Two Hospitaller officers sat waiting for Hawkins' report. Father-Officer Francis Valconi, his immediate superior, waited at his seat behind a long, broad desk no doubt normally used for larger briefings. Valconi was in his early thirties, with thin, receding hair and a hooked nose, but a kindly face that seemed as though it would be better suited to a village priest rather than a fighting man of the church's military orders. Sat almost casually on the sill of a tall, double window was Father-Officer De Fersen. The heavy, red curtains behind him were cracked open, showing the blackness of an overcast, moonless night behind him.

"At ease, Brother," Valconi said, "you may sit."

Hawkins hid a grimace of pain as he lowered himself into his seat, internally cursing the thinner leg plates of ORC heavy armor. Valconi tapped his comlog, opening a shared file between the three assembled Hospitaller officers to record the details of the debrief.

"Quite the first time into action, then, Brother," Valconi offered, his brows raised and his long forehead wrinkled.

"Yes, sir."

"We've read your report regarding the attempted defense of Alpha Four-Four," the Father-Officer continued, "in fact, given the importance of the operation, so has the Grand Master of the Order, and the marshal. Your exploits have gained some attention."

Hawkins sat rigid and upright in his narrow, wooden chair. He looked from Valconi to De Fersen, and then back again.

"That was never my intention, sir," he said quietly.

Valconi flashed a brief smile, but he was cut off when De Fersen spoke from his casual perch, arms folded and sat back on the window sill.

"How did you escape from Alpha Four-Four, Kyle?"

Hawkins looked across at his senior.

"The research hub was surrounded, sir. As I stated in my report. I went inside to transmit as much data as I could from the site before it was destroyed. I then took to the Cosmolite's subterranean tunnels. After two days, I found a way out."

De Fersen hopped down from the window sill and walked across the thick, patterned red carpet. He leaned over the desk, his fists planted on the polished wooden surface.

"But here's the thing," De Fersen continued, "there are some gaps in your report. Some things that don't add up. For example, how you knew that the research hub had been rigged to explode, how you managed to get inside, how you managed to log in to a highly secure MagnaObra data terminal, and how you knew about the tunnels. Nothing really explains all of that, does it?"

Hawkins looked into the piercing stare of the bald-headed Hospitaller. He turned his head and found the open, trusting features of Valconi far more bearable.

"I think it is easy enough to work out how all of that happened," Valconi said quietly.

"I know exactly how it happened!" De Fersen sneered. "I just want to hear him say it!"

"The TAG," Valconi cut in quickly, "your report mentions that you worked alongside a section of Fusiliers whom were instrumental in eliminating a Gūijiǎ type TAG. However, we... let me just check... the post-combat report of Corporal Angelo Garcia, that section's leader, is very explicit in stating that you personally took down that TAG in a close assault, whilst his soldiers merely provided supporting fire where they could. That's quite a discrepancy."

Hawkins cleared his throat and pulled at the collar of his black uniform jacket.

"That is not my recollection, sir," he said, "I remember things rather differently."

De Fersen stood up straight and folded his broad arms again, his piercing stare driving into Hawkins' eyes.

"False modesty does not become us, Kyle, we are soldiers of God. Did you eliminate that TAG? Yes, or no?"

Hawkins looked up into the cool, intimidating eyes of the veteran Father-Officer. He recalled De Fersen's time and support on their last meeting and found himself suddenly resentful of the seemingly unprovoked hostility his mentor now displayed toward him. Hawkins knew De Fersen's wrath was explosive. Hawkins also knew that he himself could take down a TAG with minimal support and so had no real need to fear anybody.

"Yes," he replied, leaning forward in his chair and staring up at De Fersen, "I had some help, but yes, I took the bloody thing down."

De Fersen flashed a brief, aggressive smile.

"Well. Good. Very good for a soldier who graduated from training only a few weeks ago with a final assessment of 'low average.' Battlefield effect, Kyle, that's what we want to see. What we don't want to see is junior officers meddling in the political affairs of the Human Sphere and alien diplomatic relationships. Because, if you had acquired potent political knowledge and had chosen to illegally send that information directly to the Order of the Hospital, well, you'd be in a world of shit right now, wouldn't you?"

Hawkins sank back in his chair. His teeth clenched and his eyes narrowed bitterly. They were seriously going to reprimand him for choosing to send the data to his own Order rather than Strategic Security?

"As I said," De Fersen continued, "good thing that never happened. So we need never speak of it again."

Hawkins opened his mouth to argue his point, to insist that his decision was the correct one, but then thought better of it. Valconi cleared his throat and tapped his wrist, sending a new file across to appear in the upper corner of Hawkins' lens.

"Your overall mission assessment," Valconi said. "I have rated your performance as 'above average.'"

Hawkins leaned forward again. He knew that, to an outsider, those two words heavily implied little more than mediocrity. But within the Order, that simple statement meant far more.

"Three times," De Fersen said, "in all my career, I've only ever heard of an Order soldier being assessed as 'above average' in his first combat engagement on three occasions. If you were a Fusilier, Kyle, you'd probably get a medal. But as you know, we don't really go for that sort of thing. All a bit crass."

Hawkins fidgeted uncomfortably in his rickety chair. His shins itched. His face felt hot and red.

"Thank you, sir," he nodded to Valconi. "Will that be all?"

"No," De Fersen cut in, "no. There is still one other matter. The Form C32 you submitted. Request for Approval for an Interpersonal Relationship."

Hawkins let out a breath. His eyes fell down to the thick, musty carpet at his feet. The cold air of the room's environmental controls suddenly felt stark in contrast against his skin, yet also not nearly enough to keep him cool. That was how they worked out how much he knew about the research hub. De Fersen took a chair and pulled it over to sit next to Valconi, opposite from Hawkins. His eyes moved slowly from side to side as he read lines of text on his own lens.

"Kyle, I'm going to read out something from the Form C32s that have been submitted by Hospitallers this year. I'll list the professions of all the men and women who have been proposed by their prospective partners as suitable romantic matches for consideration for serious relationships with our soldiers. See if you can notice a pattern."

Hawkins clenched his jaw. He knew this day would come but did not realize just how quickly the administration would be processed. He also knew the request would be rejected; that was why he had his answer pre-prepared and rehearsed. What he did not expect was the sarcasm that he would be patronized with.

"Teacher," De Fersen started as he read through the previous forms, "doctor... minister... teacher... student... student... veterinarian... nurse... Special Forces Operative, Strategic Security Division... do any of these stand out to you as, well, the odd one out?"

A silence fell across the room. Hawkins kept his eyes fixed on De Fersen. Was it the transmission from the research hub that was making him so confrontational, or this?

"Naturally, a situation as unique as this was elevated. The Black Friars were kind enough to provide us with all the information they had on the individual. Care to see the file?"

Hawkins shook his head as his comlog alerted him to a file transfer awaiting his approval.

"I don't need to see that, sir."

"Oh, I think you do. Accept the file. Now."

Hawkins obliged. De Fersen began reading.

"Von Beckmann, Lisette Katherine. Captain... selected for unit Garkain straight from military college. Carried out first infiltration mission in an Adriadnan naval base, aged seventeen. First saw combat at eighteen, against the Yujingyu. Pretty much continuous combat operations for ten months... It gets really interesting then. Shot two police officers in a crowded shopping mall. Did you know about that?"

"Yes, I did," Hawkins replied bitterly, "she told me all about that. They fired first. She fired warning shots. They gunned down a civilian bystander in the crossfire. She shot them to protect the crowd. I would have done the same."

"After her conviction, she was sentenced to three life terms in a maximum security prison. She was removed after only six hours and transferred to a psychiatric unit because she killed a prisoner in the dining hall in front of nearly a hundred witnesses. A serial killer twice her size, beaten to death with her bare fists. Brother-Officer, I don't think this is a laughing matter!"

Hawkins quickly surpassed the smirk from his lips.

"Well, sir, if it was a serial killer, then you could argue that she was only doing God's work. And she does have a little bit of a temper. Sir."

"A bit of a temper?" De Fersen exploded.

"Kyle," Valconi cut in quickly, his face cast in a dark, uncharacteristic frown, "when you graduated, I was happy to take you under my command because of your liberal theological views and open-mindedness to non-violent approaches. That makes you a rarity in what we do. Don't change that. Don't become just another pawn. Don't joke about murder, even if you do think the recipient deserved to die. We aren't the judges on such matters. God alone judges."

Hawkins raised his thumb and forefinger to the top of his nose and quickly worked away at the lesser of his itches. The bruises on his legs continued to ache. He thought on Valconi's words. It did feel a lot like he was being judged at that moment, and not by God. Still, he owed them less petulance.

"Sorry, sir," he said with genuine remorse.

"I'll carry on," De Fersen continued, "Beckmann escaped from a psychiatric unit after six months, using her father – a brigadier in intelligence at the time – as a hostage. She largely disappeared for just over a year, where the Black Friars are convinced she worked as a mercenary and assassin in the private sector. For Heaven's sake, Kyle! The Black Friars even think there is a good chance that she was the shooter who assassinated Senator Rose six years ago! The so-called impossible shot that Maya-conspiracy theorists are still arguing about! Tell me, is this honestly the woman you want to take home to meet your mother?"

Hawkins stopped. The file he had accepted waited to be opened, its image flashing in the lower corner of his lens. Part of him thought that he owed it to Beckmann to never open that file, to leave her past in the past until she felt ready to open up to him. That part of him lost the fight. The top sheet of the digital file said everything that De Fersen had read aloud. A single captured image leapt out at Hawkins.

A horrific photograph of a large pit dug into dry earth, filled with perhaps twenty dead bodies covered in blood. Four armed figures stood or crouched at the top of the pit, their hyper modern Combi Rifles and expensive tactical rail attachments marking them out as Special Forces. A censor had blacked out all of their faces. One figure was circled in red. Hawkins recognized her perfect figure and the tattoo of a heraldic eagle on her shoulder.

"The Black Friars," De Fersen spoke again, "describe her as, and I'll quote... 'due to her extensive training and experience, natural ability and disturbingly blunt, violent methodology, Captain von Beckmann stands out as particularly deadly even when compared to other operatives of the Strategic Security Division. It would be fair to assess her as one of the most dangerous covert operatives in the PanOceanian Military Complex, if not the entire Human Sphere.' Again, Kyle, this is the woman you want to meet your parents."

Hawkins deleted the file. He stood up slowly and looked down across the table at his two seniors.

"You just said it wasn't our place to judge. Even the greatest of sinners are entitled to their road to Damascus moment, just as Saint Paul was. Our job as people of faith is to forgive those who ask for forgiveness. Without judgment and unconditionally. Or are the likes of you and I too holy, high and mighty, to sit to dinner with tax collectors?"

Valconi leaned back in his chair, a faint and warm smile playing across his lips. De Fersen's head shook from side to side as if he was mentally debating a series of great questions. Both Father-Officers remained silent. Hawkins lowered himself back onto his chair, content with his use of Biblical references to support his moral stance.

"Your Form C32 request has been approved," Valconi said, "it went all the way up to the Pilier. But he has signed it off, and you are permitted to continue this relationship."

A breath caught in Hawkins' throat. His fingers clutched the thin arms of the rickety chair. He slowly recoiled in shock.

"Pardon, sir?"

"Application approved," De Fersen said, "but be warned, Kyle. A na-ive fool like you probably thinks this is because somebody on high either has a romantic soul or an abundance of forgiveness in their heart. That's not it. This is political. Purely political. I very much doubt whether you or your killing machine girlfriend will see any ramifications from this, but the Order and Stra-tegic Security might very well."

Valconi held up a hand.

"Let's... let's end this on a high, shall we? Brother-Officer, you grad-uated only a few weeks ago as a 'low average' pass. In another time, when our Order's numbers were not so low, that may well have resulted in you failing to graduate altogether. I accepted you into my command taking that risk on. You have now successfully completed your first operational task as 'above average.' That is not only an incredible leap in both ability and the faith this Order has in you, but has also been noted by the Grand Master himself. Broth-er-Officer, you have performed commendably. Well done."

Hawkins let out a long breath. The raw emotions of the cold, clinical debrief of both his performance in combat and his choices in life left his hands shaking slightly. He looked across at Valconi.

"Thank you, sir."

"And," the Father-Officer continued, "you were owed four weeks leave after graduating, which you agreed to give up so that you could take up your assignment on Paradiso. You have now accrued post-op leave. The Pilier has agreed to combine these in recognition of your service. Six weeks, Brother-Officer. The next six weeks are yours and yours alone. Be ready in all respects to hit the ground running for front line combat tasking when you return to us."

That was unexpected. Positive, but unexpected. At least, Hawkins thought as he remained glued to his seat, it should have been positive. His mind was cast back to a moment he had when he pulled back the hatch to the ladder leading down into the Cosmolite. A moment where he had just found out political secrets of the highest level and had his heart ripped out by lies. A moment where dozens of dead bodies lay in bloody heaps only meters from where he crouched, some he personally had shot and cut down. For a brief mo-ment of silence, crouched at the top of that ladder, Hawkins recalled wonder-ing what his school friends back home would be doing at that precise moment.

"What do I do?" he found himself blurting out.

"Sorry?" Valconi asked.

"What do I do, sir?" Hawkins repeated after a pensive pause. "Six weeks leave? Where do I go? I can't go home! I... how do I go back to my family and friends now? How do I go to the bars I used to sneak into as a teen-ager and sit there with my friends, listening to their stories about normality?

Downfall

How do I sit there with a beer and talk to them about their retail jobs and sports results, when I've been here, tearing human beings limb from limb? And all with a cross on my chest! What do I do?"

Valconi looked across at De Fersen. The bald headed veteran soldier's features relaxed in sympathy. He leaned back in his chair.

"The first one is always the worst," De Fersen said. "It's a shock to the system. From here on in, you'll know roughly what to expect. For all the criticism I've just given you, at least you've got a girlfriend who understands this and can help you when you talk to her."

"Go home, Kyle," Valconi added, "put the same trust in your family as this Order has in you. Your family is close. They will be patient and understand that you have been through something traumatic. Six weeks leave is not something that comes around very often. Grab it with both hands. Go home."

***

A chill wind cut through the clear, blue sky above the parade ground. Lined up in ranks of three, some two hundred trainee officers stood at ease in their dress uniforms of dark blue, most wearing the standard light blue berets of the PanOceanian military whilst a handful, sponsored through training by some of the more exotic cadres, wore different headgear. The broad, stone steps in front of the parade ground led up to the long, imposing main building of the Aquila Officers' Academy, where a second set of steps sat before a series of tall, Greco-Roman style marble pillars leading up to a shallow, gabled roof. Highly polished bronze cannons dating back to Earth's Napoleonic era flanked the huge, double doors. The red brick building, built in the style of the officer academies of Earth, spanned out to either side past the parade ground with three floors lit by tall windows set beneath a gothic roof.

The double doors opened.

"Parade! 'Shun!" A single voice yelled out from the front of the assembled officer cadets.

As one, some two hundred men and women lifted up their left foot before slamming it down to stand to attention. The crunch of feet echoed across the parade square as three figures walked out from the tall, double doors. The first was the academy's commandant, a tall light infantry colonel, accompanied by the ceremony's guest of honor and a young captain from the instructional staff. The guest; a short, middle-aged woman in a plain suit, followed the commandant down the second set of steps, well-used to inspecting military establishments.

The assembled officer cadets were organized into platoons, based on their seniority within the college and how close they were to graduation. Those who passed out and graduated would be honored with a commission, becom-

376

ing officers in the PanOceanian army. A lead officer cadet stood front and center before each platoon, a highly polished ceremonial sword held upright in the right hand. In front of all of the cadets, stood facing them in a single line, were the academy's instructional staff, also in dress uniform and carrying swords.

The commandant and the guest of honor – PanOceania's Minister of Defense– made their way to the bottom of the last set of steps, the instructional staff captain in tow. They walked past the instructors and to a single platoon whose men and women stood further forward than the other platoons, also distinguished by carrying Combi Rifles fitted with gleaming, ceremonial bayonets.

"Guard," the sword carrying officer cadet at the head of the platoon shouted, "general salute! Present... arms!"

The officer cadets of the guard platoon brought their right arms smartly across to their rifles, then as one up to a central position in front of them, and down again with a loud slam of the side of the right foot into the left heel. The commandant returned the salute.

"Guard! Slope... arms!"

Rifles were brought smartly up across the left shoulder.

"Guard! Shoulder... arms!"

In another display of precision drill, the twenty soldiers each brought their left hands across to the rifle butt and then swung the weapon around to the right side of the body.

"Guard ready for your inspection, sir!" the sword carrying officer cadet at the front of the platoon announced. "Officer Cadet Bansal reporting!"

"The platoons off on our right are made up of our most senior officer cadets," the colonel said to the short woman in the suit as they followed Bansal around to inspect the front rank. "They'll be graduating in just less than a month. The guard here are traditionally made up of our more junior cadets. They are volunteers taken from our three platoons who have only been here for two weeks."

The suited woman stopped by the first officer cadet; a tall, thin man, perhaps twenty years old.

"Officer Cadet Chuke, ma'am," the captain following the commandant and the minister announced.

"Good morning," the minister smiled up at the towering man, nearly twice her height.

"Good morning, ma'am," the young officer aspirant replied formally, his eyes fixed on an arbitrary point ahead, well above the minister's head.

"Two weeks in the army and you're already doing this," the minister said. "Must be quite a lot to learn."

"Yes, ma'am," the trainee soldier replied monotonously.

"What corps will you be joining?"

"Fusiliers, ma'am."

"The Fusiliers take up the bulk of our training spaces for officers," the commandant explained as the minister walked to the next soldier in line. "Understandably, given the pace of operations."

"Officer Cadet Lavigne, ma'am," the captain announced.

"Hello," the minister smiled again, "I notice your beret badge is different. What will you be doing after graduating?"

"Engineers, ma'am," Lavigne replied.

"Enjoying your training so far?"

"Yes, ma'am," Lavigne lied.

The commandant, minister, captain, and officer of the guard all moved down to the third soldier on the front rank. A barrel-chested man of thirty, his grim face was square jawed and almost clumsy looking in its proportions, the older officer cadet wore a long row of medals on his chest and the darker beret of Indigo Special Ops.

"Officer Cadet Cochrane, ma'am."

"Cochrane has come up through the ranks, Minister," the commandant explained, "about five percent of our officer cadets do. Cochrane has served in Indigo Special Forces and was very recently in command of a platoon during the defense of Alpha Four-Four at the Glottenberg Incursion."

The minister looked up at the veteran soldier.

"You're here to train to be an officer? After all you've done, have you got anything left to learn from this academy?"

"Well, they're teaching me how to hold a knife and fork properly, Minister," Cochrane drawled.

Sniggering immediately rippled through the lines of men and women stood to attention with their rifles and shining bayonets.

"Guard! Steady!" the captain growled. "Steady there!"

The captain stepped up and stared into Cochrane's eyes, his face twisted in fury.

"Officer Cadet Cochrane! Your beret badge is filthy!"

The minister looked up at the soldier, suppressing a smile from his previous comment.

"It is rather dirty, Officer Cadet. The rest of you is immaculate. Why the dirty beret badge?"

The cocky soldier's face darkened. He fell silent for a few moments before replying.

"The badge belonged to my platoon commander, ma'am. She changed her will and left it to me. She was killed in action the next day. She was wearing this badge at the time. Officers badges are different to NCOs, you see, ma'am. She left it to me to tell me I should come to this place, where she graduated from. So here I am. And I'm not taking her badge off, or cleaning it. She was an excellent soldier, and an even better friend."

The minister looked up at the stony-faced soldier.

"Thank you for your service, Officer Cadet," she finally managed before taking a step to the right to inspect the next soldier.

"Captain, ensure this man cleans *every* aspect of his damn uniform, and is appropriately reminded of the need to do so," the commandant whispered angrily to his subordinate.

The minister of defense span on her heel and glared up at the senior officer.

"You'll do no such thing!" she snapped forcefully. "This is my train set, Colonel, and I'll decide what values are taught here! It shouldn't take a damn politician of all people to lecture a soldier on the values of friendship and loyalty! Certainly more important than pomp and ceremony! Clear?"

The commandant swallowed and nodded.

"Crystal clear, Minister."

The short politician exchanged a brief smile with the former sergeant and moved on with her inspection.

***

Checking quickly over one shoulder, Beckmann increased her speed to a full sprint in an attempt to evade her pursuers. She planted a hand on the see-saw and vaulted nimbly over it, ducked deftly beneath a vibrantly colored slide, and then pretended not to notice the tiny climbing wall ahead before clattering into it and falling over onto her back on the grassy verge. Within moments, the two small girls chasing her piled on top of her with gleeful laughs, forcing hysterical laughter from her as they set about pinning her down and tickling her.

"Maria! Shannon!" a voice barked out.

Maria, the older of the two girls at the age of six, immediately obeyed the shouted command and jumped back off Beckmann, rushing quickly across the crowded playground toward her father. Shannon stopped tickling Beckmann but sat on her leg, staring down at the prone woman.

"You're pretty," the little girl declared.

"So are you," Beckmann smiled up at her as the sun appeared around the edge of a thin cloud.

"We should be best friends," Shannon said.

"Shannon!" The tall man at the edge of the playground repeated.

"I gotta go," the girl said sullenly, clambering off Beckmann and stomping sulkily away.

"Hey!" Beckmann called back as she jumped to her feet.

The girl looked around at her.

"Best friends," Beckmann smiled.

Shannon beamed and ran back over to her father. Recovering her faux black leather jacket from where she left it on the park bench, Beckmann pulled it on over her tied black shirt and looked through the outdoor play area toward the far side. The animal enclosures of the zoo – both the real and the virtual – extended down the gentle slopes of the hills as far as the eye could see. Sprawling pens allowed lions to roam free through long grass, separated by only a thin wall from the part-furred, dangerous basilisk lizards of Neoterra. A huge bowl even allowed zoo patrons to look down to see a pair of long dead Tyrannosaurus Rexes from Earth's prehistoric times, recreated painstakingly, pixel by pixel, to the point that the human eye could no longer tell reality apart from the creations of modern technology.

Beckmann saw Hawkins stood alone by a tall oak tree, a little way from the bulk of the stream of visitors moving slowly and methodically around the concrete path weaving between the many animal exhibits. A playful smirk on her lips, Beckmann sneaked stealthily from tree to tree, silently stalking her prey until she leapt out and onto his back, wrapping her arms around his neck.

"Hey!" Hawkins laughed. "You seem in a good mood!"

"I made friends!" Beckmann beamed, jumping down to stand next to him. "I think your nieces like me. I'm not so sure about your brother, though."

Beckmann looked over to where Maria and Shannon walked along with Nathan, their father. The tall man looked across at his younger brother and Beckmann, his face impassive. Beckmann shrugged. She had definitely bagged the better looking brother.

"He's just... protective," Hawkins explained. "When I left home to join the Order, my girlfriend left me. Said it wasn't worth working through the distance. I'd only just hit eighteen, so I didn't take it very well. Nathan just likes to look out for me. We're pretty close. He's a good guy, he'll warm to you."

"This girl," Beckmann narrowed her eyes, "the one who hurt you. What's her name? Where does she live?"

Hawkins smiled uncomfortably and held out his hands.

"Look, it was a long time ago..."

"I'm joking!" Beckmann beamed. "It's just a joke! Well, partially. If we ever bump into her, I'll kick the living shit out of her. Anyway, I'm going to the gift shop to buy some cuddly toys."

Hawkins winced and reached out to hold her hand.

"I dunno, Lisette. Nathan's kind of particular about not spoiling the girls with too many gifts."

"I meant for us!" Beckmann grinned.

"For us?" Hawkins repeated. "Are you... I can't tell if you're joking,

Beckmann walked alongside him toward the main route through the zoo, holding his hand tightly.

"I've proved the whole hard woman of war thing enough," she shrugged, "this is my time now, and I actually like being able to do some of these things I never had a chance to do. I like being able to be soft and sentimental."

Her time. What a rarity. Of course she knew her every move was being tracked. That had nothing to do with the terms of her pardon, it was merely a standard precaution for the few Garkain operatives still alive. But she did, at least, have that time. Her second day back in office after escaping from the Cosmolite had been greeted with news of her promotion.

"You've been confirmed in the rank of Major. Substantive. Congratulations. Don't smoke in my office."

"Fuck you, I'll smoke where I want to. And you can congratulate me properly by giving me six weeks leave."

"Six weeks? Don't take the piss, Razor."

"Six weeks. I'm owed far more than that. My boyfriend just got six weeks leave, so I'm sure you can do the same for me."

"I'll give you two weeks. You know I can't spare you for six."

"Find a way, or you'll see me lose my shit again."

Promotion to major actually meant very little. In the Fusiliers, it equated to command of an entire company; as a Hexa operative, is was little more than an acknowledgement of capability and achievement, and being entrusted with higher profile tasking. At least there were less assholes she had to salute, Beckmann thought; that was probably the best part of the whole thing.

Happy, relaxed, and delighted with the notion of another five weeks away from her duties, Beckmann continued the slow walk through the crowded zoo. She glanced back and saw Hawkins' brother catching up, dragged along by his two grinning daughters.

"I think kids are amazing," Beckmann said quietly, "so fun to be around. So full of life. They're just... awesome."

Hawkins stopped dead in his tracks.

"You've said some pretty terrifying stuff to me in the past few weeks," he swallowed, "but I think that beats all of it."

"No! Not now! But sometime. One day, I really hope. I don't know."

A few paces ahead, a small child accidentally dropped his ice cream. The mother and father instinctively squatted down to the blond boy's eye level and instantly bombarded him with sympathy and promises of a replacement. It was to no avail. The toddler stared straight ahead and let out a high-pitched,

381

ear-piercing wail of sorrow. Just to his left, a trio of red and blue birds leapt out of the bushes and darted up into the air away from the noise. An instant later, perhaps two or three dozen of the same breed of graceful birds flew up after the first three to form a colorful exodus in the sky.

Two figures burst out of the trees ahead and sprinted away. They wore old-fashioned, jungle print camouflage and carried dated, 5.56mm rifles. Beckmann fired two short bursts from her Combi Rifle into their backs, killing both of the cartel guards. The bark of her weapon echoed around the jungle. Two or three dozen red and blue birds leapt up out of the trees and swarmed away from the noise to form a colorful exodus in the sky...

Beckmann stopped, confused. Her chest felt tight and the air was suddenly close and stifling. The boy's screaming faded away until she could no longer hear it, even though she could clearly see him crying and wailing.

To her left, Beckmann saw Roth dart forward, his belt-fed machine gun blazing from the hip. A long, continuous stream of fire cut through the two guards on the edge of the jungle clearing. Two or three dozen red and blue birds leapt up out of the trees and swarmed away from the noise to form a colorful exodus in the sky...

Did Beckmann fire first or was it Roth? She remembered the birds more than anything, but not who fired first. Did it matter? It was so long ago now. She heard her name being called. It was Hawkins. His voice was muffled even though he stood right next to her, still holding her hand.

"Lisette? Are you alright?"

The pain in her chest was worse. It was off-center, spreading to the left and across her ribs. Her breath was short. Suddenly she was no longer hot but felt freezing cold. Who fired first? Was it even that Op?

Beckmann paced straight across the dimly lit bar, her eyes fixed on her target. Renauld was one of the cartel's top lieutenants. He sat with three other men in a corner booth, laughing and joking loudly. Beckmann recognized all three of the other men from the compound. All viable targets. As she approached, the three men look her up and down with salacious smiles. Not Renauld. His smile faded instantly. He knew what was coming. Beckmann brought her submachine gun up in one hand and emptied the entire magazine into all four cartel men. Screams echoed across the bar. The corner booth was covered in blood. The air stank of propellant from the smoking submachine gun.

Beckmann turned to walk away but instantly let out a cry of pain and fell to one knee, raising her hand to her side. She brought her hand up to her face and saw blood. Confused, with no recollection of being shot, she staggered and limped out of the bar after the crowds of screaming patrons. Trailing blood she struggled out of the main entrance and into the open where a car waited for her on the street outside.

"Get in! Quickly!"

Her breathing uneven, she stumbled over to the white car and in through the open back door. She looked up at the sky above her and saw a flock of red and blue birds moving serenely through the blue in the long lines of an extended, asymmetrical V...

Pain shot up her left arm. Beckmann collapsed to her knees. She could see Hawkins knelt in front of her, calling to her, but she could not hear his words. She could not breathe. Hawkins was looking up desperately, shouting for help, but Beckmann could hear nothing but a high-pitched whining. No, it was not the hit on Renauld. That was not where she saw those birds. The hit on Renauld was when she was on loan to O-12. Those bastards were just as dirty as the rest of the Human Sphere, despite their pretenses of playing the virtuous peacekeeping force. The Renauld hit was only three years ago. No, it was in the jungle, further back than that. Was that for O-12, too? Who fired first? Did it matter?

Beckmann pulled the trigger, her Combi Rifle's underslung grenade launcher fired with a hollow thunk, the whole weapon kicking back into her hip. The grenade flew into the wooden hut and exploded spectacularly. Whatever was inside the long hut burst into flames. Fire licked up out of the doorway and open windows. She heard agonized screams inside. Cartel men in jungle print camouflage ran out of the doorway, on fire. Beckmann paced forward, executing the guards with ease. She had emptied her magazine before she was even inside the burning building. She quickly reloaded and headed inside, her Combi Rifle raised to her shoulder. It was over in seconds.

"Eagle One, Marker Emil clear..."

"Adler Eins, Marker Emil klar..."

She was on her back, gazing up at the sky and around at the animal enclosures, the playground and the crowds of people staring at her. Nathan desperately tried to urge people to move back to give them space and privacy. Hawkins knelt over her. He was checking her airway. A woman in a green uniform was sprinting over with a medical box. Shit, was it that bad? Pain wracked the left side of her chest. It hurt so much to breathe that it seemed easier to just stop. Lines of patrons stood and watched her. In their midst was a teenaged girl with a shaved head, her gray military uniform sprinkled with bloody bullet holes. Beckmann could smell burning.

"Eagle Three, Marker Gustav clear," Schrader reported over the team comm channel.

The entire site was burning. The processing plant, the warehouse, the guard hut, and the bodies between them all.

"Eagle Four, I've got a live one here."

Beckmann's eyes narrowed as she loaded another magazine into her Combi Rifle.

"Four from One, you know our orders!" she snapped irritably. "We're here to wipe this aberration off the map! No prisoners!"

"Lieutenant, he's just a kid."

"Don't be such a fucking coward!" Roth growled across the communication channel. "Waste him!"

Beckmann paced forward between the buildings of the blazing narcotics processing plant. She saw Schrader to her right, the flickering blue fire of his flamethrower's ignition head still hissing away and ready. The pale soldier regarded her without emotion but moved down to meet her and walk alongside her. Beckmann checked her tactical map for Eagle Four's location.

"Fuck off, Roth!" Martin snapped. "He's just a kid! I'm not executing some dumb kid!"

"No!" Roth growled. "These guys are drug smugglers! Animals! Pieces of shit! Do you know what this stuff does to people? Ordinary people we're supposed to be protecting?"

Beckmann found Martin and his prisoner at the water's edge, next to the burning jetty. Martin held the cartel guard by the scruff of the neck. He was, as Martin had said, barely an adult. Sixteen at least, possibly a young looking nineteen or twenty. The same age as Beckmann and Schrader. Beckmann was younger than the guard was when she first saw combat. At that age, she knew what top end narcotics could do to a person. She knew right from wrong then. She did now. The young, terrified looking cartel guard stared at her as she walked over with Schrader, practically whimpering as he pleaded for mercy.

"Lieutenant!" Martin urged as he stepped out to meet her. "Come on! The guy is…"

Beckmann unholstered her pistol, pressed it against the guard's forehead, and pulled the trigger. That was the moment the red and blue birds flew up into the clear sky.

Beckmann took another long breath from the oxygen mask secured to her face. A young, female paramedic with eyes too old for her soft face leaned over her, checking the results on a holographic monitor next to her. Beckmann looked around her cramped surroundings, quickly recognizing the interior of an ambulance. She sat upright on a collapsible ambulance stretcher, a thick blanket draped over her shoulders. The doors to the ambulance remained open, giving a clear view to a peaceful pond and fountains she remembered were not far from the zoo playground. The chest pains were gone. Hawkins sat next to her, holding her hand. Panic kicked in.

"What did I do?" Beckmann gasped, tearing the clear oxygen mask off her face. "Who have I hurt? Did I hurt anybody?"

"Put the mask back on and take slow, deep breaths," the paramedic ordered, politely but assertively.

"It's alright, Lisette," Hawkins smiled sadly, giving her hand a gentle squeeze. "You haven't hurt anybody. You didn't do anything. Everything's alright."

Beckmann leaned across to rest her head on his shoulder. He wrapped an arm around her as she obediently concentrated on taking slow, deep breaths through the mask. The paramedic checked the read outs on the flickering holographic screen again. Beckmann focused on the paramedic. The woman was perhaps the same age as her, and with that same dullness in the eyes that Beckmann sometimes caught in her own reflection. The deadened, unfocused look of a person who has seen too much trauma. The difference was that this woman braved that trauma to help others. Beckmann was the one who inflicted the violence in the first place.

"You're fine," the auburn-haired woman said, "physically, you're in the best shape I think I've ever seen. But your heart rate has been through the roof. Have you had mental health issues or episodes before?"

Beckmann slowly removed the mask and nodded.

"Are you currently receiving any support?"

Beckmann shook her head.

"We'll get help sorted," Hawkins promised quietly from her side.

The paramedic pressed a few symbols on the holographic screen. Her face twisted in confusion.

"I'm being denied access to your medical records."

"I'm military," Beckmann said weakly. "I... I do a job which keeps my records locked away."

The woman looked down at Beckmann.

"You've had a panic attack," the young paramedic said, her face sympathetic, "a severe one. Have you ever suffered from one of these before?"

"No," Beckmann answered truthfully.

A second paramedic appeared at the back of the ambulance.

"All alright?" he called up with a broad smile.

"Yeah, she's fine," the auburn-haired woman said, "physically, you're absolutely fine. But this does need follow up. We'll stick around and monitor you for another hour. Look, why don't you do get some fresh air? Stretch your legs?"

Beckmann walked slowly away from the parked ambulance, over toward the scenic, picturesque pond. Long, gold fish the size of her arm threaded their way peacefully through the clear water by her feet. Hawkins stood quietly by her side. Above them, some miles away, a starship blasted up toward the upper atmosphere with a gentle rumble. Beckmann looked down at the water again. She remembered the burning jetty in the jungle from six years before. She remembered pulling the trigger and seeing the insides of the young guard's head dropping down into the water in pieces before his lifeless body slipped down into the river. Her hand clung desperately to Hawkins.

"I've done awful things," she whispered, her shoulders shaking, "really terrible things."

"It's alright," Hawkins smiled sympathetically, gently placing an arm around her shoulders, "we'll find a way ahead, together. Everything will be alright."

Find out more about Infinity and Corvus Belli at:
https://www.corvusbelli.com/

CORVUS BELLI
iNFiNiTY

Downfall

Look for more books from Winged Hussar Publishing, LLC – E-books, paperbacks and Limited-Edition hardcovers. The best in history, science fiction and fantasy at:

https://www.whpsupplyroom.com

https://www. wingedhussarpublishing.com

or follow us on Facebook at:

Winged Hussar Publishing LLC

Or on twitter at:

WingHusPubLLC

For information and upcoming publications

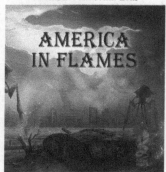

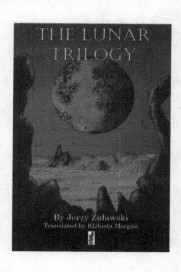